THE GOAT IN THE BEDROOM

THE COCKY KINGMANS
BOOK SIX

AMY AWARD

THE GOAT IN THE BEDROOM

When your love life stinks and you're clearly the worst at choosing someone who won't break your heart, why not ask your best friend to find you a date?

Unless of course...you're in love with her.

I've been friends with Artemis since high school, when we bonded over crushing on the same guy. Six years later, we're roommates in our shiny new post college lives—she's training for the Olympics while I start my pro football career. We've both recently had bad break-ups and she says if she's going to get back out there, she needs dating lessons. Naturally, she asks me—her completely platonic roommate—to teach her.

We practice eye contact. Hand holding. Cuddling during movies. Because that's what best friends do, right? Practice intimacy? For science?

She thinks I'm being helpful. I think I'm losing my mind.

Meanwhile, I'm out here sabotaging her dates, getting jealous of my own teammates, and having heart-to-hearts with our pet goats about my feelings while she's literally in the next room.

But we're definitely just friends.

The evidence we might be idiots:

• The documentary crew filming my rookie season knows.

• Our pet goats know.

• Everyone knows. EVERYONE.

• The only people who don't know? Us.

This sports romance features two bisexual dating disasters who are Olympic-level idiots for each other —a football player who falls first and pines HARD, and a curvy rugby goddess who's oblivious because she's convinced she's "too much,"— matchmaking goats with excellent taste in humans, that Bridgertons-meets-American-Football family that's about to stage an intervention unless someone snaps and locks them in a closet together first, a documentary crew catching every slip and you've got a love story everyone can see coming ... except them.

This is a book of fluff.

We need fluff; it's the insulation from the harsh world around us. There's no shame in needing a break from reality. Especially when reality sucks.

It's important to me to have representation of marginalized communities in the media, and I do that by showing fat women getting happy ever afters without ever having to lose weight.

But fluff and representation doesn't mean there isn't any conflict. The hero and the heroine and some of their friends and family in this story do face a world that has made them feel like there's something wrong with them, and that includes some external fatphobia and homophobia.

There is also talk about loss of a parent and a spouse, in the past. Our Cocky Kingmans were raised by a single father, and life without their wonderful mother is a fact of their existence and has shaped their lives.

I've worked very hard to create an emotionally

nuanced story in the kind of world I want to live in, that includes diversity, equity, inclusion, and accessibility for all kinds of people. I've had help from diversity readers with carefully crafting this story for you to escape into, kick your feet, and feel good. But if you feel I've misrepresented or caused harm, please let me know so that I can do what I need to learn, fix, and be better.

What I can promise you is that my books will always hold a space that is free of physical violence against women including sexual assault. That just doesn't exist in the world I create in my mind.

And finally, I love to write about funny animals and pets. No pets will ever be harmed or die in any of my books.

I like to cry when baby animals are rescued and at touching Super Bowl commercials, not in my romances.

wink

For all the readers who played sports or wanted to, and got made fun of for what your body looked like instead of what it could do.

You're strong, you're beautiful.

You deserve to be seen, and you deserve to take up space.

You deserve to play.

Sport does amazing things and for a girl who didn't understand why her body looked the way it did. Sport gave me an outlet, showed me how capable I can be.

— ILONA MAHER, 2025 ESPY AWARDS
ACCEPTANCE SPEECH

GOAT INTERVENTION

GRYFF

Three weeks before finals and my best friend was buried alive under a mountain of practice tests like the academic apocalypse was nigh. I'd seen Artemis get tackled by an entire women's rugby team, then carry half of them down the field on her back to score without breaking a sweat. But watching her lose a fight to a pile of accounting textbooks? That was where I drew the line.

That was my cue to be the guy who stages an intervention. I was going with the nuclear option, weaponized cuteness involving baby animals.

It was time to remind her that some things were more important than accounting finals, like not losing her damn mind. Most guys would let their friends stress-spiral in peace, but I'd never been accused of being that fucking boring. Especially when Artie was involved.

If we weren't having fun together, we were probably dead.

I took the stairs to her dorm three at a time and

rapped on her door. I wasn't that surprised I got no response. But I knew she was here by the sound of her binaural beats techno flow study music worming its way into the hall.

The fact that I had to use my emergency key to get into her room told me everything I needed to know about how far gone she was. I was intervening not a moment too soon.

"Jesus donkey, Artie," I said, surveying the disaster zone that used to be her dorm room. "It looks like your textbooks staged a revolt in here."

She was buried so deep in papers and books that I could barely see her brown braid poking out from behind the fortress of studying doom. The only sign of life was the swishy sound of a highlighter on paper and the occasional muttered curse.

"How did you get in here?" she asked without looking up. "I locked that door for a reason."

"Emergency key. You gave it to me for exactly this kind of situation."

"This isn't an emergency, Gryff. This is responsible adult behavior."

I picked up one of the practice tests scattered around her like academic confetti. "Artie, you've already taken this same practice test three times. I can see your scores written on all of them."

"Perfect practice makes perfect."

"You got a ninety-eight the first time. There's nowhere left to go except completely insane."

She finally looked up at me, and I bit back a wince. Dark circles under her eyes, hair that hadn't seen a brush in days, and the kind of manic exhaustion that came from too much caffeine and not enough sleep and sunshine.

This is what happened when the rugby season was over. Every damn year. But the added momentum of finals and graduation made it worse this time.

And maybe it was worse for me too, because watching her hurt always made something twist in my chest in a way that went beyond friendship. Not that I'd ever let myself think about that too long. We'd both always been with other people anyway, and some things were too important to risk.

"I need to be ready," she said, gesturing at the chaos around her. "Finals are mere moments away, and I don't want to let my mom down by flunking out of college in my last semester. No one knows if I'll make the Olympic team, and I can't just coast on rugby skills and thick thighs forever."

"First of all, you absolutely could crush skulls with those thighs and make a living doing that if you wanted to. Second, you're one of the best rugby players in the entire world, so the team is going to be lucky to have you. Also, finals are three weeks away, you already have straight A's, your mom is proud of you no matter what, and she called me asking when you had last left your study cave."

Her mom hadn't called me, but that was irrelevant.

Artie looked around like she was genuinely trying to remember what century it was much less if she'd been outside, which was answer enough.

"That's it," I motioned with my hand for her to get up. "You're coming with me, right the fuck now."

"I can't. I have four more practice tests to review, and I want to go through the tax section again because I'm still not confident about—"

"Artie." I used my captain voice, the one that made three-hundred-pound linebackers shut up and listen. "You're starting to resemble that creepy ghost girl who crawls out of the TV, and I'd be afraid, except you've got a cheesy poof in your hair."

I threw open the blackout curtains, letting the sunshine in, and she hissed at me zombie-style.

"That's what I thought. Come on." I started gathering up her shoes from where they'd been abandoned by the door. "We're going outside and getting your blood pumping."

She stuck out her tongue at me.

"Professor Martinez moved class outside today because it's beautiful out and she wants us to connect with nature or some shit like that." The lie rolled off my tongue smooth as butter. I'd been planning this for two weeks, since the end of the rugby season and the beginning of Artie's villain origin story or whatever the fuck was happening here.

"I don't have time for connecting with nature. I have to connect with accounting principles."

"The accounting principles will still be there when you get back. Your sanity might not be."

She looked at me for a long moment, and I watched the internal battle playing out on her face. The responsible part of her that wanted to keep studying versus the part that knew I was right.

"Fine," she said finally. "But only because you're going

to keep bothering me until I say yes, and that'll be more distracting than just going."

"Correct."

She threw a highlighter at my head, which I dodged easily. Good reflexes were useful both on and off the football field.

"Give me five minutes to make myself look like a human being," she said, already heading toward the bathroom.

I had this planned down to the second. By the time we walked across campus to the quad, the animal sanctuary van would be there with a dozen baby goats, class would be set up with yoga mats, and Artie would get the surprise of her life.

Ten minutes later, we were crossing the quad and she still looked tired and stressed, yet somehow was absolutely beautiful, which was not a thought I was supposed to be having about my best friend.

But then she saw the goats.

Her face transformed from resignation to confusion to absolute wonder in the span of about three seconds. Her mouth dropped open, and she just stood there, staring at the pen full of tiny goats like she'd discovered buried treasure.

And fuck if that expression of pure joy didn't make me fall a little bit in love with her, which was a problem I definitely couldn't think about right now.

"Gryff," she said slowly, walking toward me without taking her eyes off the animals. "Please tell me those are real."

"What? I don't see anything," I teased. "You're probably hallucinating from all the vitamin D."

"Are those..." she started, pointing at the portable pen full of baby goats that had been set up on the grass.

"Oh, those? Yeah. Baby goats," I confirmed, trying not to look too smug about her reaction. "For baby goat yoga. Apparently it's a thing."

"You did this?" Her voice had gone soft in that way that made something warm settle in my chest. She was pure joy, uncomplicated and bright. "This is... this is incredible."

"Tempest and Trixie helped me arrange it with that sanctuary they volunteer at. But don't thank me yet. There's a distinct possibility one could pee on you. Or worse."

"Oh my god," Artie breathed beside me. "They're so *smol.*"

"Don't get any ideas," I warned, knowing that look. "You cannot adopt a goat."

"I'm not going to adopt a goat."

"You're thinking about adopting a goat."

"I'm thinking about how cute they'd look in tiny rugby jerseys."

"Artemis."

She was already walking toward the pen like she was in a trance, drawn by the irresistible pull of small, fuzzy creatures. The goats started bleating in greeting, like they knew they'd found their person.

"Look at their little faces," she said, crouching down next to the pen. "Oh my god, look at this one."

She was pointing at a brown and white spotted goat

who was pressed against the fence, trying to get as close to her as possible. The little guy was practically vibrating with excitement, making soft bleating sounds that seemed designed specifically to melt hearts.

"I think he likes you," I said.

"I think I love him," she replied without hesitation. "Look at those spots. He's like a tiny dalmatian but with hooves."

Other students were starting to gather around, phones coming out to document what was clearly about to become the most InstaSnap-worthy yoga class in Denver State U history.

"Alright, everyone," Professor Martinez called out, clapping her hands to get our attention. "Welcome to our outdoor yoga session. Today we're going to be practicing mindfulness and presence with some very special guests."

She gestured to the goat pen. "These beautiful babies are here to remind us that joy can be found in unexpected places, and that sometimes the best way to find peace is to embrace a little chaos."

"That's very philosophical," Artie said, settling onto her yoga mat.

"Just wait until they actually let the goats out," I said, taking the spot next to her.

"They're letting them out?"

"That's kind of the whole point. They wander around during the poses. Sometimes they climb on you."

Her eyes went wide. "They climb on you?"

"Artie," I said seriously, "you're about to have tiny goats using you as a jungle gym. If this doesn't cure your stress-induced study psychosis, nothing will."

And I was right. The moment the woman from the sanctuary opened the pen and the goats came tumbling out, Artie transformed. Gone was the anxious, overwhelmed student who'd been buried under textbooks. In her place was someone completely present, laughing as baby goats explored the yoga mats and climbing over anyone who stayed still long enough.

The spotted goat who'd been trying to get her attention made a beeline straight for her mat, like he'd been planning this moment his whole life.

"You've been chosen," I said, settling into child's pose as Professor Martinez guided us through the warm-up.

"Best decision ever," Artie replied, adjusting her downward dog to accommodate the goat who was now perched on her back like he owned the place.

As we moved through the sequence, more goats explored. They sought out the people who were most delighted by their presence, which meant Artie quickly became their favorite jungle gym. By the time we were attempting warrior three, she had two goats perched on her back and a third trying to eat her braids.

"I think they've adopted you," I said, managing to hold my pose despite the goat that had decided my shoulder was the perfect spot for a nap.

"I'm adopting them," she replied, reaching back to scratch behind the ear of the goat on her shoulders. "Look at this little face. How could anyone not want to take him home?"

"Pretty sure your dorm has a no-pets policy."

"Details," she said airily. "I could smuggle him in. He's small. I bet he'd fit in my backpack."

"No."

"I'm just saying, Tempest hid a whole-ass donkey in her sorority house. How hard could it be to have a teensy baby goat in the dorm?"

The joy on her face was infectious. Around us, other students were laughing and taking pictures as the goats explored their temporary playground. This was exactly what I'd been hoping for, Artie forgetting about finals and the future, just being present and happy.

And if I happened to notice the way her eyes lit up when she laughed, or how graceful she looked even with baby goats using her as a climbing structure, well, that was just me appreciating how good it was to see my best friend smile again.

"Okay, everyone, let's move into our final pose," Professor Martinez called out. "Tree pose. And remember to stay grounded even if your branches have visitors."

I shifted into the pose, finding my balance just as the goat on my shoulder decided to relocate to my outstretched arms. Beside me, Artie was perfectly steady despite having what looked like the entire goat population draped across various parts of her body.

"Show-off," I muttered, which made her laugh again.

"It's all about core strength," she said seriously. "Rugby training. Very applicable to goat management."

"Goat management is definitely going on your resume."

"Right under accounting degree." This mention of her major didn't have that frantic edge of study insanity to it.

I was congratulating myself on a plan well executed when I heard the collective gasp from the other students.

"Oh shit," I said. The spotted goat was a good twelve feet off the ground, sitting on the bronze statue shoulders of DSU's winningest football coach of all time, a.k.a. my father, Bridger Kingman. His triumphant bleating echoed across the quad, like he'd just conquered Everest.

"Language, Gryff," Professor Martinez called out, but she was staring up at the statue with the same mixture of amazement and horror as everyone else.

I looked up at the statue, mentally calculating approaches. The bronze was smooth and offered limited handholds, but it wasn't impossible. Dad's statue was positioned mid-stride, one arm extended like he was calling a play, which could provide leverage if you knew what you were doing. Flynn and I had climbed it as kids more than once.

"Someone should call campus security," a worried voice from the gathering crowd suggested.

"Or the fire department," someone else added.

But Artie was already standing up, brushing off her yoga pants and moving toward the statue.

"I can get him," she said, and something about the certainty in her voice made me believe her completely. "Plus, he came to me first, so he trusts me."

As if to prove her point, the goat looked down at her and bleated what sounded distinctly like a plea for help.

"See? He's asking for backup."

I looked at the statue again, then at Artie, then back at the goat who was now looking significantly less triumphant and more scared as he realized his predicament.

"Bring those football muscles over here." Artie said,

already assessing the situation. "If you boost me up on your shoulders, I can reach his shoulders from there."

"I was thinking the same thing," I said, moving onto the big stone base of the statue. No discussion needed, no argument about who should go or how we should do it. We'd been working as a team for so long that this felt as natural as breathing.

"I'm ready," I said, moving to the base of the statue.

"You sure about this?" Professor Martinez asked, wringing her hands. "Maybe we should wait for professionals."

"The goat's scared," Artie said simply. "And the longer he stays up there, the more panicked he's going to get."

She was right. I could see the little guy's confidence fading as he looked down at the crowd gathering below. What had seemed like a great adventure was starting to feel like a very bad idea.

"Okay," I said, holding out my hands ready to boost her up. "Let's go save a goat."

The trust between us was absolute. Artie stepped into my hands without hesitation, and I grabbed her waist, lifting her up to land her ass right on my shoulder.

"How's the view?" I called up.

"Your dad's got excellent posture," she replied, testing her balance. "Very heroic. Good bone structure."

"I'll be sure to pass along the compliment."

The crowd around us had grown to at least fifty people, all of them recording what was definitely going to be viral by tonight. But I was focused entirely on Artie as she prepared for the next part of our impromptu rescue mission.

"Ready for phase two?" I asked, positioning myself directly beneath the goat.

"Ready," she said, reaching toward the goat with infinite patience. "Hey there, little guy. Ready to come down from your big adventure?"

Her voice had taken on that gentle tone she used with all animals, soft and reassuring. The goat looked at her, then at the crowd below, then back at her, clearly weighing his options.

"That's it," she murmured. "You're okay. I've got you."

And then, with a soft bleat that sounded almost like relief, the goat stepped forward into her waiting arms.

The crowd around us on the quad erupted. Phones were flashing everywhere, capturing the moment from every angle.

"Victory," Artie called down, grinning as she cradled the goat against her chest.

"Hell yeah," I replied, carefully helping her down from my shoulders.

The moment her feet touched the ground, we were surrounded by cheering students. The goat, meanwhile, seemed completely unbothered by his adventure and was already trying to eat Artie's hair.

"That was incredible," a girl from our class said, still recording. "You guys are, like, perfect together."

"Seriously," Tyler added, shaking his head in amazement. "That coordination was epic. You two must be insane in bed."

And there it was. The assumption that made both of us freeze for just a second too long before we started talking over each other.

"We're just friends," Artie said quickly.

"Yep, just friends," I added, maybe a little too forcefully.

"Right. Good friends. Nothing romantic."

"Exactly. Just teamwork. Friend teamwork. Friendwork."

Too many faces in the crowd around us exchanged those knowing looks that said they weren't buying our denials for a second. Which was ridiculous, because we were friends. Best friends. That's all we'd ever been.

"We should get this little escape artist back to his class," Artie said, obviously eager to change the subject.

"Good idea," I agreed, grateful for the distraction.

"I'm keeping him," Artie announced as we approached the sanctuary's truck where the volunteers were trying to corral the rest of the baby goats back into their transport home.

"You can't keep a goat in your dorm room."

"I'll figure something out. Look how calm he is with me." She held up the goat, who was indeed perfectly content, though that might have had more to do with the fact that he was currently chewing on her hair tie than any special bond.

"Your roommate is allergic to everything that moves, breathes, or has fur."

"Details," she said dismissively, but she handed the goat over to the sanctuary volunteer with obvious reluctance. "Don't be surprised if you find a baby goat in a temporary pen of textbooks eating my notes later."

"Don't let finals swallow you whole this time or next

time I'm bringing in the big guns." I wagged a finger at her.

Artie rolled her eyes and rocked her shoulders with hands raised as she sing-songed, "Ooh, oh no. What are you gonna do, bring tea-cup piglets to class next time?"

My phone buzzed with a text.

X

Library. Twenty minutes?

"Nope. I'll call your dad and have him give you the work-smarter-not-harder speech. Again." He gave it to us both before our first semester at DSU in his once-a-semester phone call to her from his oh-so-fancy coaching job in Scotland.

Artie slugged me in the arm. Hard. "Don't you dare."

"I'm hitting the library. Wanna come so I don't have to extract you from accounting practice test hell again?" I already knew she'd say no. Artie might be an amazing team player, but she had an I-can-do-it-myself, independent-woman streak that was gold medal worthy.

The stink eye she gave me called me on my bullshit. "You're not going to the library to study."

Shit. Artie knew me too well. But there was something careful about the way she said it, not quite as teasing as I expected from her.

I might hit the library a lot, but it was never to study. I'd figured out my freshman year that the long dark rows of the school's little used top floor were better used for other more fun activities than studying.

"Hey, I have finals too." That were all going to be a piece of cake.

My phone buzzed with another text.

X

Third floor stacks. Usual spot. Don't let anyone see you.

Right. I hated this secretive hook-up shit. And all I really wanted to do was talk through whatever this not-a-relationship was with Artie or Flynn. But my definitely-not-a-study buddy was complicated, hot as fuck, and great with his mouth.

He also didn't know what the fuck he wanted, except for me. So this was me finding some joy in an unexpected place.

Even if I was better at being the chaos than embracing it.

HUMMERS UNDER THE HEMINGWAY

ARTEMIS

My body and brain were buzzing with some renewed energy while I walked back to the dorms. Only Gryff would think up something wackadoodle enough to pull me from my self-imposed study psychosis. I really had needed that.

I was ready for my finals. I already knew it. I just wanted to pull off this one last semester with straight As so my mom didn't have to worry that I wouldn't be able to get a job when I headed off to LA to train with my new rugby club and the USA Olympic Elite. Or if I got injured and couldn't play.

Like my dad had.

Before I could even contemplate hitting the books again, Olivia's name lit up the screen like a warning I should have seen coming. I'd been putting off returning her calls for two days, telling myself she was just busy with end-of-semester stuff. But the tight knot in my stomach suggested I already knew what this conversation was going to be about.

"Hey," I said, dropping onto my bed among the scattered practice tests. "Sorry I missed your calls yesterday. Finals prep has been—"

"Artie." The way she said my name cut me off mid-sentence. She sounded both excited and like there was something wrong. Like she'd been rehearsing something she wanted to tell me but knew I wasn't going to like it. "We need to talk."

And there it was. Four words that had preceded every major upheaval in my life. We need to talk. Dad had said it before telling us he was taking a coaching position in Scotland. Mom had said it before announcing we were moving to Colorado without him. Now Olivia was saying it, and I already knew how this story ended.

"Okay," I said carefully, settling back against my pillows. "What's going on?"

"I got it." The squeal in her voice was obviously too hard to contain.

And I already knew what was coming.

"I got the call." Her voice had that barely contained excitement that people tried to hide when they were delivering bad news disguised as good news. "Rugby Australia wants me for their development program."

"Olivia, that's incredible." And it was. She'd been dreaming about playing for Australia since before I'd met her a couple of months ago. I'd fully admit I'd fallen for the accent. Wouldn't be the first time, probably wouldn't be the last. "I knew you'd get it."

"But..." She trailed off, and I stared up at the ceiling, just breathing through the all too familiar feelings. "I know we talked about maybe spending the summer together, but this opportunity... Artie, this could change everything for me."

Change everything for her. Not for us. The distinction wasn't lost on me.

"It's an amazing opportunity. You'd be crazy not to head out the second you graduate." I heard myself saying the words, my voice sounding weirdly calm considering the way my chest was tightening. The ache would go away soon enough. "Australia's lucky to have you."

The weight settled in my chest, that hollow recognition that even though I wasn't about to be the one doing the leaving for once, I'd be letting go of another relationship. I'd gotten good at this over the years. All those childhood moves had taught me how to read the signs, how to start pulling back before the official goodbye came.

"You mean that? Even though we might end up playing against each other in the Olympics in a couple years?"

"Absolutely." The words came easily, practiced from years of being the one who had to give the "I'm moving" speech, trying to make things as easy as possible. "I'm so proud of you."

"God, I was so worried about how to tell you. I've been agonizing over this call for days."

Days. She'd known for days and hadn't said anything. Had probably already started planning her new life on the other side of the world. Just like I'd learned to do when Dad got a new contract. Start the mental packing before anyone else knew we were leaving.

"Thank you for understanding. I was so afraid you'd be upset."

Upset. Like that covered the complex mix of emotions

currently churning in my chest. This was the part I'd always been good at, being understanding, being supportive, making the transition easier for everyone involved. I'd had plenty of practice.

Saying goodbye was a skill I'd perfected.

"I should probably let you go," she said. "I'm sure you have studying to do, and I have a million things to figure out before I leave."

I should have seen this coming. The end of college meant everyone moving on. Maybe that's why I'd been holding back a little with Olivia, even if I did really like her.

My life had always been full of temporary relationships. What was one more?

I was better at saying goodbye than I was at building anything worth staying for.

The last six years were an anomaly in my life. Being in one place for that long, having the same friends for more than a year or two at a time wasn't how my life worked, and I'd stupidly gotten used to it.

And I had only myself to blame. Well... and Gryffen Kingman. He was the one who'd charmed me into being his friend when he noticed we were checking out the same guy in class, and then later when we were checking out the same girl. Who he'd asked out... for me.

We'd been practically connected at the hip since that day.

So really, all this mess of being comfortable for the first time in my life was his fault.

Twenty minutes later, I was climbing the stairs to the third floor of the library. Up here it was always quiet, with row after row of dusty stacks housing books that hadn't been checked out since before I was born, old storage rooms that held mysteries untold, and the occasional hidden alcove perfect for private conversations.

Or other much more fun activities.

I heard voices before I saw anything, low and hushed coming from somewhere deeper in the stacks. Following the sound, I turned a corner and stopped.

Gryff was pressed against the end of a bookshelf, his eyes closed and his hands tangled in the dark hair of someone kneeling in front of him.

Oops.

I definitely should look away.

I was going to. In three...two...what the fuck?

It took my brain a moment to process who the other person was. Xander Rosemount, looking nothing like his cocky teammate who'd just been drafted to the Miami Sharks.

I wasn't shocked Gryff was getting his rocks off with Xan. They'd been pretty good at sneaking around to the casual observer. But I knew Gryff better than anyone at this point, besides his twin brother Flynn.

I saw the way Xander's eyes had followed Gryff, the way one of them would disappear at a party, then the other, only to see Xan return with some beard burn and Gryff with a lazy, satisfied grin on his face. What surprised me was I thought they'd broken it off during spring break.

He'd been a wreck that week and only his trip to LA had distracted him from the depths of breakup despair.

Guess I was wrong.

My first instinct was to back away quietly and pretend I'd never been here. This was clearly private, and something Gryff hadn't shared with me yet, and I should respect that and leave them alone.

But I couldn't seem to look away.

I already knew Gryff was a hottie with a body. Football players and those butts in tight pants were half of what continued to confirm to me that I was well and truly bi. Even if most of my attempts to date men were duds.

But seeing my bestie with his pants open, slung low around his hips, Xan's hand pushing his shirt up to caress abs that didn't quit, all while Gryff had his dick pumping in and out of Xan's mouth in a way that had them both groaning... well, damn if that didn't give me tingles in all the right places.

Until Gryff dragged his eyes open and looked right at me down the row of bookshelves.

Then he winked at me, bit his bottom lip, closed his eyes tight, and let out a muffled groan that clearly indicated he was coming.

My brain finally caught up with my body, or vice versa, because I spun around the corner and clasped the far edge of the end cap. What the hell was wrong with me? I would never, ever put my friendship with Gryff in jeopardy by even considering dirty thoughts about him. Now I was going to have the image of him coming seared into my brain.

Nope. No. Not acceptable. I'd need to cram my head full of numbers, math, accounting, statistics, anything else. Where was *Principles of Managerial Accounting* when you needed it?

I was about to make the world's fastest sprint back to my dorm to take a cold shower and scrub out my eyes and brain, but then I heard footsteps on the stairs, voices getting closer, and my protective best friend call of duty kicked in.

If someone found them like this, college was a monster for gossip and Xander wasn't out, as far as I knew. And while Gryff had never hidden his sexuality, this was still his teammate.

Without thinking, I positioned myself to stand with my back at the entrance to the row they were in, keeping watch for anyone who might wander into this section and blocking the view. I grabbed a dusty book from the shelf and flipped it open just to look like I actually belonged there. I could hear hushed voices, movement, the sound of someone being pressed against a bookshelf.

"Someone's coming," I whispered urgently as I heard footsteps approaching.

The sounds behind me went silent immediately. A few seconds later, a group of freshman-looking girls rounded the corner, chattering about their psychology final. I smiled and nodded as they passed, waiting until their voices faded before giving the all-clear.

"Coast is clear," I said quietly and stepped back out of the aisle.

A moment later, Gryff appeared around the corner of the stacks, his hair disheveled and his face flushed. Behind him, Xander looked like he'd rather disappear into the floor, his expression a mix of panic and embarrassment.

"Shit," Xander muttered, running his hands through his hair. "This is exactly what I was worried about."

"No one saw anything," I assured him. "But you might want to go a bit beyond the first row of shelves next time."

"There isn't going to be a next time." Xander's voice came out flat.

Something in his tone made my stomach drop. I glanced at Gryff, who was looking at Xander with an expression I recognized, the carefully neutral face he made when he was trying not to let his emotions show.

"Xan," Gryff said quietly.

"I can't do this, man." Xander's voice was strained, but there was something almost cold about it, like he was delivering a business decision. "This was a mistake."

"Because someone almost caught us?"

"Because someone did." Xander looked at me, and I could see the panic at his disco.

"No one else will know until you're ready," Gryff said. "We can avoid—"

"Can we? Really?" Xander's laugh had an edge to it. "You're Gryffen goddamn Kingman. People pay attention to everything you do. Your family's practically royalty around here. And I can't afford to be part of your... ball bunny club."

Gryff flinched at that. "What the hell, Rosemount?"

Xander was straightening his shirt now, his whole demeanor shifting to something more distant. "Look, this was fun. But let's not pretend it was ever going anywhere."

The casual cruelty in his voice made my hands clench into fists. I could see exactly what he was doing. Trying to hurt Gryff enough that he wouldn't fight the breakup, wouldn't try to change his mind.

"So this was what?" Gryff waved a finger between the

two of them, his voice carefully controlled. "Just a way to scratch an itch?"

"Pretty much." Xander shrugged like they were discussing the weather. "I need to think about my career, my image. I can't be associated with... complications."

"Right," Gryff said, and I could see him rebuilding his walls in real time, his expression going carefully blank.

"Glad you understand."

Xander was already moving toward the exit, like this conversation was just an inconvenience he needed to get through. He paused at the end of the stacks, not quite looking back.

"Oh, and Fraser?" He glanced over his shoulder but didn't actually meet my eyes. "Keep this between us, huh? Gryff's reputation can probably handle some... rumors, but I've got a lot more to lose."

The dismissive way he said it, like Gryff's feelings were completely irrelevant, made my blood boil. But before I could say anything, Xan was gone, his footsteps echoing down the stairs.

We stood there in silence for a long moment, listening to the sound fade. When it was completely quiet, Gryff slumped against the bookshelf and closed his eyes, rubbing his fingers between his eyes.

"Well." He sighed. "That was.... fun."

Yeah, if fun was a bloody true crime documentary and this was the crime scene. "Want to get out of here?"

Gryff opened his eyes and looked at me, really looked at me, then grabbed me into a tight one-armed hug.

"Yeah," he said. "Let's go."

We didn't talk until we were outside, walking across

campus in the general direction of the quad. The late afternoon sun was still warm on our faces, but the earlier magic of baby goat yoga felt like it had happened in another lifetime.

"So," Gryff said eventually. "That happened."

"Yep."

"You're not going to ask me about it?"

I considered this. "Do you want me to ask about it?"

"Not really."

"Then I won't."

We walked toward the Dragon's Brew campus coffee shop in comfortable silence. We'd been friends long enough that we knew both when to push and when to just be present.

When we got inside and up to the counter, I automatically ordered our usual. "I'll have the medium iced strawberry matcha, and he'll have a medium hot honeycomb latte with extra vanilla sweet foam."

I grabbed our drinks when they called my name and handed Gryff his. "Here's your gross sweetened hot bean water."

"At least my bean water tastes good. You had to add strawberries to your chewed up grass drink to make it taste less like pure unadulterated chlorophyll."

We grabbed a table outside. "But I lurrrve strawberries."

Gryff chuckled which was a good sign. "You're a strawberry."

"Your face is a strawberry."

He settled down next to me with a long sigh. "Can I ask you something?"

"About whether I knew about you and Captain Closeted?" I nodded and took a long sip of my drink.

"Was I that obvious?"

"To me? Yeah. But I know you better than most people."

He was quiet for a moment, running his fingers through his beard in that way he did when he was thinking deep thoughts. "When did I give it away?"

I nudged his shoulder. "The hockey house party before spring break. The two of you conveniently disappeared. And Xan's not great at hiding beard burn."

"Shit." He leaned back and looked up at the sky. "That was right after we hooked up. He pulled me into a dark corner and kissed the shit out of me. But then freaked the fuck out and said to forget it ever happened."

"That's what had you in a funk over spring break?"

"Yeah, this isn't the first time we've broken up." Gryff sighed and scrubbed a hand over his face. "I wish he didn't feel like he had to hide it at all."

Uh-oh. Had Gryff caught feelings for that asshat? "It's not stupid to want a real relationship."

"It is when the other person has made it crystal clear they think you're just an experiment." The bitterness in his voice made my chest ache. "Listening to him talk about my 'reputation being able to handle rumors' like I'm some kind of fuck boy who doesn't take anything seriously."

I studied his profile, noting the tension in his jaw, the way he was gripping the edge of the step. "For what it's worth, Xander can go eat a bag of dicks as far as I'm concerned."

This was probably the first time either of us had been single at the same time in... well, ever. Since I'd known Gryff, one of us had always been dating someone, even if it was just casual.

"Well, your misery can enjoy mine as company. Olivia just dumped me too."

Gryff twisted in his seat and scowled like I'd made him eat stinky cheese. "What? When?"

"About an hour ago. Phone call." I kicked at a loose piece of concrete on the pavement. "She got accepted to the development program in Australia. Leaves right after graduation."

"Fuck. I'm sorry."

"It's fine. I mean, it's not fine, but it's not unexpected either." I shrugged because what else was I supposed to do? "It's okay. Long-term relationships probably aren't for me. I'm used to it."

"You shouldn't have to be."

"Yeah, well. Story of my life. People leave. Opportunities come up. Life moves on." Being friends with Gryff was the longest relationship I'd ever had.

He grabbed my braid and gave it a tug, pulling my head down to his shoulder, then wrapped his arm around me. "I'm not going anywhere, my strawberry girl. I mean... I am going to LA, but you'll be there too. And even if you weren't, you can't shake me. You're stuck with me for life. Like a bad toenail fungus."

"Great. Just what I need. Athlete's foot with benefits."

"I am a fun guy." He snort-laughed. I refused to acknowledge his really bad dad joke. "Get it. Fun guy, like fungi, you know mushrooms are fung—"

"You're the worst." But also he was the best.

"Wanna get drunk and play some FortFite?"

This was the next step in the usual distraction when either of us went through a breakup. Pints of ice cream instead of tequila when either of us were in training, but tequila when we weren't. This was definitely a tequila and violent video games night.

"Strawberry margaritas?"

"You know it."

Step two was to swear off dating. I was starting that part early. "Okay. But I'm getting the new *Too Fox Too Furious* movie skin. Because I'm officially swearing off dating and Fox Daws is forever my only man."

"Deal. Then I'm officially swearing off dating, at least until graduation anyway. You can help me pick out a new sexy skin." He stood and pulled me up with him.

I already missed that comforting arm around me and his solid chest under my head. If ever I was going to trust a promise that someone wouldn't let me go, it would be from this man. And for once in my life I was going to try my best never to fuck up this friendship.

"Like you're ever going to change out of the Kelsey Best Lady Bananaconda snake outfit and forever make me do the Real Reputation emote with you every twenty seconds."

"Why would I? She's a badass and I'm undefeated."

Who needed a love life when you had a best friend like mine?

GRADUATIONPALOOZA

GRYFF

I almost skipped my actual graduation ceremony. Watching six-hundred people I didn't know get their name called and handed a fake diploma that said we'd get the real deal in the mail once the school confirmed our fees were all paid up was not my idea of fun on a Saturday morning.

But Dad insisted everyone in the family go to my ceremony, then Flynn's. He was a stickler for tradition. He even insisted on going with me to Artie's ceremony too.

I think he secretly knew she was disappointed her dad couldn't make it over from Scotland for the day. This wasn't the first time he'd stepped into a dad role for a Kingman kid's friend.

And then we had to wait another two weeks before Jules's graduation ceremony.

How in the world my little sister, youngest of the Kingmans, was old enough to be graduating from high school was a mystery of the universe. I was pretty sure she was still eight years old. Not eighteen.

We were definitely the loudest, rowdiest cheer squad when she walked across the stage and got her diploma. You'd have thought she'd just won the Big Bowl and Miss Universe while curing cancer, solving climate change, and declaring world peace by the time she turned and waved to us in the stands of the Thornminster High gymnasium.

Not that she couldn't do all of those things. Knowing the powerhouse that was the Kingman princess, she probably would.

I pulled into the driveway of the family house and immediately laughed my ass off. Palm trees. Enormous fake palm trees lined the walkway to our front door, complete with tiny string lights and a banner reading "California Dreamin'" fluttering in the Colorado breeze. The Beach Boys blasted from the backyard.

"What the hell?" Flynn muttered, shaking his head and laughing as he climbed out of his truck behind me and circled around to open the door for Tempest.

"Maybe she's just excited for you?" Artie asked as she jumped out of the passenger side of my truck. Jules was exactly the type to throw a themed party with an agenda. This had to be her campaign to come spend the summer with us in LA. All she had to do was ask. Little weirdo.

"Like really, really excited." Tempest laughed as we walked up to the porch.

The front door burst open before we could knock, and Chris's wife, Trixie, practically bounced down the steps in a flowing sundress and oversized white sunglasses.

"The grads are here," she announced, wrapping us in hugs that smelled like her vanilla perfume. Behind her,

Willa appeared with a t-shirt in each hand clearly meant for each of us.

"I'm under strict orders not to let you in until you put these on." Willa grinned a little too excitedly. Oh geez. I was afraid to see what was on the shirt now.

Flynn and I each held up the shirts, glanced at each other, and swapped without saying a word, while the girls saved their shirts to change into later.

Mine said "I hope this BS pays off", while Flynn proudly wore "It's official, I'm too cool for school".

We made our way through the house, which had been transformed into some kind of beach paradise. Tiki torches flanked the sliding glass doors to the backyard, and someone had hung fishing nets with plastic starfish from the ceiling. The dining room table groaned under the weight of what appeared to be every California-themed food known to man including fish tacos, avocado toast, California rolls, and a fruit salad that looked suspiciously like it was arranged to spell out "LAX".

I loved that Jules was excited for our move to California, but we were here to celebrate her graduation too. Where was the red and silver of THS, or perhaps the purple and gold of DSU where we were graduating from and where she was going in the fall?

"Boys." My dad's parents, Nana and Coach, were in the family room chatting with my Aunt Kik and her partner Pat. "Don't you look handsome? Ready for your big Hollywood adventure?"

"We're not going to Hollywood, Nana," I said, accepting her kiss on the cheek. "We're going to play football."

"In Los Angeles," she said with a knowing wink. "Surely there can be some Hollywood adventures to be had. Movie stars to date."

Flynn held up his hands. "Not for me, Nana. Tempest is the only star I see."

"Of course," she said smiling warmly at Tempest. "Jules and I read all your books last summer when she visited. I can't wait to chat about them with you." She took Flynn's arm but eyed me like she was waiting to say something about my relationship status.

"I promise to date someone famous just for you, Nan." That was the right answer, because she gave me an eyebrow waggle and put her other arm through mine, escorting us to the backyard. Coach and Artie followed behind us discussing the eternal battle, rugby vs. football.

The backyard was packed with family and friends, all wearing various degrees of California-themed outfits. Dad had somehow been convinced to wear a Hawaiian shirt, while Grandpa De La Reine looked distinctly uncomfortable in sunglasses that said "California Dreamin'" across the frames.

"There are my baby brothers," Chris called out from a colorful lawn chair where he was sitting with my cousin Levi and his girlfriend Olive. "Ready to follow in the family footsteps?"

"Ready to make our own footsteps," Flynn corrected.

Before I could add anything, a blur of motion tackled me from behind. I spun around to find Jules hanging off my back like a koala, her graduation cap somehow still perfectly positioned despite the acrobatic greeting.

"My fellow graduates are finally here," she announced.

"Look at them, all grown up and ready to start a whole new life in California."

Something twisted in my chest, and I didn't like it. I was looking forward to playing football for the Bandits, and moving to LA was going to be a blast. Probably.

I gave Jules a boost up and spun around. "Nah, you'll be too busy with your freshman year at DSU to miss us."

More like we were the ones who were going to miss her.

Jules's grin turned positively wicked. "Oh, I don't know about that."

Dad appeared beside us, and I caught something in his expression, pride mixed with what looked like anticipation. Like he was waiting for something. Very suspicious.

"Jules Jacob Jingleheimer Kingman." Dad was amused by making up crazy middle names for her since she'd forbidden anyone in the family from letting her real name slip in front of mixed company. "Are you ready?"

Ready for what? Flynn and I exchanged confused glances.

"Yeppers," Jules said, sliding down from my back and straightening her cap. She looked around the backyard, taking in all the expectant faces, and I realized half the family was watching her like they were waiting for a show.

"Okay, what is everyone not telling us?" Flynn demanded

"Let's go girls," Jules called and she clasped her hands behind her back, suddenly looking every inch like she was about to deliver a valedictorian speech. But she'd already done that earlier today. Trixie, Kelsey, Pen, and Willa gathered around her like queens in court. When had this family gotten so many ladies?

"You're about to tell us you're ditching college and going backpacking across Europe or Australia or something, aren't you?" It would be just like the Julinator to buck the system and do something crazy like that. College was the expected path for all of us. Jules was eternally the unexpected.

I glanced at Flynn and our twin telepathy was zinging.

"You are going to college, aren't you? You got into DSU," Flynn said carefully. "Academic scholarship and all. We celebrated."

"DSU is a great school," Jules agreed. "For football players. But I'm not a football player."

The words hung in the air, electrified. Around us, I noticed that Dad, Nana, and the aunts were all wearing identical expressions of barely contained excitement.

"Jules," I said slowly, "what are you trying to tell us?"

She threw her arms wide like she was presenting a game show prize. "Haven't you guessed? I threw a whole-ass themed party to celebrate. I'm going to UCLA, boys. I'm headed to Cali with you weirdos." Blue and gold confetti rained down upon her courtesy of two confetti poppers that Kelsey and Willa had seemingly pulled out of thin air.

The explosion of voices from every brother was immediate.

"What?"

"Since when?"

"How long have you known?"

"UCLA? In Los Angeles?"

But underneath the chaos, I caught Dad's voice, "That's my girl."

Jules stood in the center of the commotion, grinning like she'd just scored the winning touchdown. Finally, she raised her hands for quiet.

"I applied to UCLA back in the fall. It's where Mom went to school."

Oh. My sweet baby sister.

"But why didn't you tell us?" Isak asked, looking a little butt hurt.

Jules slugged him in the arm, but with a gentle smile. Being the two youngest, they were pretty close. "Because you never asked, numbnuts."

Isak pouted but pulled her into a big hug. "Didn't think I had to. You know all my secrets."

"You all just assumed DSU," Jules said, but gently. "When's the last time anyone asked me what I wanted to do instead of telling me what I should do?"

Umm... never. No one told Jules what to do.

"I'm proud of you," I said, meaning it. "Really proud."

"Even if it means I'm cramping your bachelor-pad style?" she asked.

"Especially then," Flynn grinned. "Someone has to keep us in line."

The conversation shifted to logistics and congratulations, but I took a step back from the celebration for just a minute. Jules in Los Angeles. My baby sister, following her dreams just like the rest of us. Having another Kingman around was going to be great. Now if I could talk the rest of the family into moving to California too, everything would be perfect.

"Your sister never fails to surprise, does she?" Artie's voice made me turn. She'd appeared beside me with two fruity drinks decked out with umbrellas and all. She had on her Jules designed graduate shirt too. Only hers read "Now I'm Even Hotter By One Degree".

Not wrong, Jules, not wrong.

"No kidding." I accepted the drink and sucked about half of it down. "I guess Flynn and I are gonna have to look for a three-bedroom condo or something. You had any luck finding a place yet?"

"I've been chatting with a couple other girls who are moving out to train with the Olympic Elite team too." She kind of waved it off like moving halfway across the country was no big deal. But, of course, she'd moved halfway around the world before. Several times. I'd never lived anywhere but here. "Hopefully I can room up with some of them. I'm so not ready to pack though. I can't believe how much crap I've accumulated in the last six years."

"Ugh. Do not talk to me about packing. Can't I just buy new stuff when we get there?"

"I guess that all depends on how much your damn signing bonus is."

Right. "The second we win our first Big Bowl ring, I'll buy you all new stuff too."

"You mean when we win the gold medal at the Olympics and I get some badass endorsements that will put yours to shame."

I nodded sagely or risked getting slugged. "Yep, you're right. That is exactly what I meant."

As the excitement died down, the family naturally

rearranged itself into smaller groups. I noticed how the women—Nana Kingman, Grandma De La Reine, Mom's sisters, Sara Jayne Jerry, Mrs. Moore, and Aunt Kik, all formed a protective circle around Jules, celebrating her choice and offering practical advice about living in LA.

"I've already got all my girls ready to look out for you, or show you the best places to shop," Sara Jayne was saying, "I'm always looking for an excuse to hit Rodeo Drive."

"And I know people in the psychology department," Trixie's mom, who'd been our neighbor for years, added. "Have you picked a major yet?"

Jules's eyes lit up. "I'm going undeclared, but psychology sounds cool."

I drifted closer, drawn by the easy way these women stepped in to support Jules's dreams. This was what I'd always loved about our extended family, the way they filled in the gaps, never trying to replace our mom but always letting us know we were supported.

Flynn appeared at my elbow. "They've got it handled," he said quietly.

"Yeah," I agreed, but I couldn't quite make myself move away. There was something comforting about watching Jules surrounded by all these mother figures.

"Plus, she'll have her brothers," Aunt June pointed out, noticing our hovering. "Two strapping young men who can intimidate any boys who come sniffing around."

"We'll be very intimidating," I promised, which made everyone laugh.

"You two are about as intimidating as golden retrievers," Jules said fondly.

"Golden retrievers can be fierce when protecting their families," Flynn protested.

"Exactly," she said. "Fiercely loyal and completely hopeless at actual intimidation."

"The world doesn't need more intimidating men," Aunt May said warmly. "It needs more men like you two. The kind who show up and care."

The conversation continued around me, but my attention was drifting. This easy support network, this automatic safety net and it was exactly what I was going to miss most about home. In LA, we'd have to build this from scratch.

I didn't even know if I knew how to do that.

I caught Artie watching me from across the patio, that same thoughtful expression on her face. When our eyes met, she didn't look away or offer a reassuring smile. Instead, she just nodded slightly, like she understood exactly what I was thinking.

Maybe she did.

The sun started to set, and the core family gathered around the fire pit. Chris cleared his throat, immediately commanding attention.

"Before we call it a night," he said, "I have something for Flynn and Gryff."

"Please tell me it's not another lecture about fiscal responsibility with our signing bonuses," Flynn said.

"Actually, it's the opposite," Chris grinned, pulling out his phone. "Trixie?"

Trixie opened her laptop with a flourish. "Boys, you know how Chris likes to buy houses."

"His hobby that makes the rest of us feel financially inadequate?" I said. "Yeah, we're familiar."

"Well, when you got drafted to LA, he may have gotten a little excited about investment opportunities."

Chris looked slightly embarrassed. "I may have bought a couple of houses."

Flynn and I exchanged glances. "That's... nice?"

"For you," Chris clarified. "As your congratulations gifts."

The silence was so complete I could hear the fire crackling. Finally, Flynn found his voice.

"You bought us houses?"

"As gifts?"

Chris nodded, looking increasingly pleased with himself. "Great neighborhood, close to the training facility, big backyards."

I stared at him, trying to process. "Chris, you can't just buy people houses."

"Why not? I bought Hayes a house. And Declan. And Everett. It's what I do."

"Wait, what?" I looked at my other brothers. "I thought he just talked you into buying those with your signing bonuses when you started with the Mustangs."

"To be fair, I won mine in a bet," Everett said.

"Shut up," Chris groaned. "I was gonna give it to you anyway. I like making sure we can all be together."

"But we're moving to LA." Did Chris not want us to go?

"I guess we can use them in the off-season," Flynn suggested.

"I bought you houses in LA, stupids. They're across the street from each other. Just like all our houses here."

The thoughtfulness hit me unexpectedly hard. Chris had anticipated something I hadn't even admitted to myself. That the idea of being completely alone was terrifying.

"Show them the pictures," Trixie urged pushing the laptop toward him.

The houses were really fucking nice, modern but warm, with big windows and porches that reminded me of home. They looked like places where you could build a life.

"This one's yours, Flynn," Chris said, pointing to the screen. "And this one's Gryff's."

"I don't know what to say," I admitted.

"Thank you usually works," Dad said dryly.

"Thank you," Flynn and I said in unison.

"There's one more thing," Chris added. "They're fully furnished. You can literally just show up with your suitcases."

"Chris," Jules said, awed, "that's incredibly thoughtful. Now what did you get me?"

"Twenty-four-seven security guards. Former Secret Service. You'll never know they're there, but no one touches you without a deep background check."

Jules rolled her eyes and then kissed our oldest brother on the top of his head like he was a little puppy. "Good try. I'll take the necklace of the Flatirons I know you've got in your pocket, thank you very much."

As everyone oohed and ahhed over Jules's new jewelry, Trixie handed over her laptop and I flipped through the photos, studying the images carefully. Three bedrooms. Two-and-a-half baths. A big kitchen perfect for having the whole crew there eating spaghetti meals together like the good old days.

For one person.

I'd never eaten a meal alone, never watched a movie by myself, never gone to sleep without the sound of at least one other Kingman somewhere in the house.

"The houses really are perfect," I said, meaning it. "Chris, seriously, this is incredible."

"Glad you like it." Chris grinned. "Keep one of those rooms for us to stay in when we come visit."

I glanced around at my family, at Dad telling stories about his playing days, at my brothers arguing about whose team would have the better season, at Jules glowing with excitement about her own adventure. This easy chaos, this automatic support system. In a few weeks, Flynn and I would be three states away from all of it.

My eyes found Artie across the fire pit. She was listening to something Tempest was saying, but I caught her looking at me with that same thoughtful expression she'd worn all evening, those knowing blue eyes, like she could see right through my carefully maintained optimism.

Maybe she could.

"You know what?" I said suddenly, loud enough to get everyone's attention. "Tomorrow night can't come fast enough."

"Tomorrow night?" Jules asked.

"Final Kingman family game night," I grinned. "One

last chance to destroy you all before Flynn and I become Los Angeles residents."

"Oh, you're going down, little brother," Declan said immediately.

Hayes pointed my way. "I've been practicing my trash talk."

"I get the lucky pillow," Everett said and literally held the green throw pillow over his head like he'd been planning this all day.

"Cheater," the rest of us all declared in unison.

As my family dissolved into the familiar chaos of competitive planning and good-natured insults, I felt some of the tightness in my chest ease. Tomorrow night, we'd have one more evening of this. One more game night with the lucky pillow and ridiculous arguments and everyone trying to cheat at board games.

One more night to tuck into my heart before we left our home behind.

THE LAST HUDDLE

ARTEMIS

The chaos of Kingman family game night was just as fun as the first scrum of a game, and it hit me before I even made it through the door of the Cool Beans coffee shop. Through the windows, the Kingman brothers were already deep in heated debate about something, hands waving dramatically while Jules stood on a chair orchestrating whatever insanity was about to unfold.

Liam and George, Willa's guncles who owned the coffee shop, were bustling around setting up tables and looking absolutely delighted to be hosting what they'd dubbed "The Last Huddle."

The Kingman family operated at a volume that would have given my mother a migraine. She liked order and stability. My dad would have fit in better. He had that touch of chaos about his life. As demonstrated by the way he'd called me at two in the morning his time while I'd been on my way to game night.

"With this new job coaching the lads," my dad said,

"you and I just might get to meet up at the next Olympics, hen. Wouldna that be a lark?"

The Scottish men's rugby team was lucky to have my dad as a new coach this year. Just the prestige of having him on staff would draw in the kind of players they wanted.

"Yep. It's the best kind of excuse to get together." I hadn't seen him since I graduated from high school, and even then it was just for a few days.

"You sure you don't want to come play for good ole Caledonia? I'd love to have you back home now that you're out on your own. You could just squeak in under the three-year rule in time for the next games."

Scotland hadn't been my home in a long time. But moving thirteen times in thirteen years had taught me well that teams, friends, and even family were fleeting.

"You coming in, or are you planning to stand out there all night like a creeper?" Gryff's voice made me jump. He stuck his head out the door to catch me lurking outside while I finished up my call.

I covered the phone and faux glared at him. "You're the creeper."

He snorted and said, "Your face is a creeper."

"I've got to run, da. I'll think about Scotland, okay? Love you, bye."

"Haste ye back, love."

The moment we walked through the door, the chaos enveloped us like a bear hug. Chris and Declan were arguing about board game superiority while Everett set up what looked like a complex scoring system. Hayes was stress-eating cookies, and Isak was filming everything on his phone.

"The boys are restless tonight," Willa observed, appearing at my elbow with a fancy tea latte. "Apparently the stakes are higher because it's the last game night before you guys abandon us for California."

"We're not abandoning anyone," Flynn said, emerging with an armload of board games. "We're just... expanding our territory."

My usual spot was between Gryff and whoever he was getting too competitive with, which was usually Flynn. Tonight I was surrounded by half a room of Kingman Queens. And any last vestiges of tension and stress I'd been carrying just kind of melted away.

It was the same way I felt when I was on the rugby pitch with my girls. There weren't a whole lot of places in the world where I didn't have to think about how my body was going to fit.

I spent quite a few Sunday evenings just like this, and I liked feeling it was where I belonged, even if it was only for the night.

Bridger let out one of those sharp two-finger whistles which had everyone shutting up and sitting down real fast. His coach voice cutting through the remaining chatter immediately. "Before we commence with the traditional family bonding through competitive gaming, I want to tell you kids a few things because we don't know the next time we might all be in the same room together like this."

Gryff grabbed my hand underneath the table. His family meant everything to him and this had to be hard on him. I squeezed his hand back and for the first time it hit me that this move to LA was going to upend his world. A whole lot more than it would mine.

Bridger continued, "This is our last game night as a complete family unit. After tonight, we're scattered across the country for the first time since... well, ever."

The room went quiet in that way that only happened when Gryff's father shifted into Coach Dad Mode. I'd witnessed this phenomenon dozens of times, but it never failed to amaze me how quickly eight incredibly strong-willed people plus a few of their partners and tonight, even their aunts and grandparents, could turn into attentive team players when Bridger Kingman got serious.

"So tonight," Bridger continued, "we're going to play games, we're going to argue about the rules, someone's going to accuse someone else of cheating, and we're going to remember why we love each other even when we want to throw Monopoly money at each other's heads."

"Dibs on being the banker," Isak called out immediately.

"Absolutely not," Jules shot back. "You can't be trusted with other people's money."

"I'll remind you I turned that twenty bucks you gave me into two thousand, brat."

"Yeah, but you spent it on your... new toy." She definitely caught herself before she revealed whatever that new toy had been.

Isak narrowed his eyes at Jules, but grinned. "I did. But I gave you the twenty bucks back, didn't I?"

And just like that, the cozy, comfortable chaos resumed. I smiled to myself over the family devolving into their traditional pregame arguments. No matter how heated the arguments got, everyone would still be family at the end of the night.

"You're thinking too hard about something," Gryff said, nudging my shoulder.

He studied my face with that particular brand of Gryff attention that made me feel like he could see right through my carefully constructed walls.

He wasn't wrong.

In a few weeks, we'd be moving across the country to start our adult lives. It was life. Old friends were left behind and new friends would be made. This was how it worked.

For the first time in forever, I couldn't imagine starting over somewhere else again. "Just thinking about how much I'm going to miss this."

"It's not like you're losing this, or us even." Gryff frowned like I was on a ridiculous amount of crack. "Distance doesn't change family."

It had changed mine.

Jules had created an elaborate tournament bracket, and the games began in earnest. The night didn't really begin until there was at least one threat to flip the table. Usually from Declan.

It was a hoot to watch how all the couples navigated the competition together. They supported and cheered for the other, even while trying to destroy each other at board games.

Two hours later, Jules was maintaining her lead with her Aunt June through what appeared to be strategic brilliance and psychological manipulation.

"Final game," Jules announced as we cleared the table. "Winner takes all."

She pulled out the lucky pillow from behind her back and lifted it over her head. All the boys gasped, and there were definitely a couple boos and jeers of her being a cheater.

"When the hell did you sneak that out from under my butt?" Penny stood up and looked at her chair in shock.

"When Everett distracted you with cookies and really sloppy and disgusting kisses."

Penny turned to him and glared like he'd done it on purpose. But he lifted his hands, declaring his innocence. "She tricked me by saying you looked like you needed a treat. How was I supposed to not kiss you when I delivered said treat?"

The green embroidered throw pillow that said "In this house, we bleed green" in their mother April's careful stitching had been dubbed the lucky pillow long before I ever played a game with them. It was worn and loved and had so much love and family history attached to it.

"That's a fair and square pillow snatch," Nana Evie declared. No one was going to argue with her.

The final game was a deceptively simple card game called Bluff. Perfect for the sneakiest of Kingmans, which was every single one of them. It was the usual destruction of family relationships through strategic cheating, and more fun than any card game should ever be. Jules won decisively, claiming power of the lucky pillow and bragging rights for life.

"Before we pack it up," Bridger said, "I've got a present for my kids."

The room went quiet again, that particular quiet that meant something important was happening.

"This family," Bridger continued, his voice carrying that slight roughness that meant he was fighting emotion, "has been through a lot together. We've celebrated victories and weathered losses. We've supported each other through everything from broken bones to broken hearts. And through it all, we've had each other."

I felt my throat tighten. I'd watched this family support each other through everything, showing up for each other in ways that my own family had never quite managed.

"Now you're all heading out into the world to build your own lives," Bridger continued. "And I think your mother would want you to take a piece of that love with you wherever you go."

Bridger signaled to the women who all walked over to where Liam and George were hovering behind the counter, clearly having been let in on whatever was about to happen. George handed a box out to Aunts May, June, and Kik. Then two each to Nana Evie and Grandma De le Reine.

"Your grandmothers and aunts," Bridger said, "have been very busy."

He nodded to Grandma Helene, who set a box in front of Chris. The eldest Kingman brother lifted the lid off the box and pulled out an embroidered throw pillow. It looked exactly like the lucky pillow, with the same careful stitching and loving detail, except this one said "Christopher" in elegant script at the bottom.

"In this house, we bleed green," Chris read aloud. Then his face went through about six different emotions before settling on something that looked suspiciously like tears.

One by one, each brother pulled out pillows. Each one carried the same message, the same love, the same connection to their mother and their family. By the time he got to Hayes, there were tears streaming down several faces, and I was fighting to keep my own emotions in check.

This was what family looked like. This was the kind of love that followed you wherever you went. This was what I'd been searching for my entire life without knowing it.

Finally, Bridger took the last box from his sister, Aunt Kik, and handed it to Jules.

She lifted the lid off a box one last time and pulled out the final pillow. But this one was different. Instead of the usual green pillow, it was white, but with the same words embroidered across it. "In this house, we bleed," but it had a blank space where the word "green" should be.

"And for Jules," Bridger said, his voice thick with emotion now, "who's about to go out into the world and decide for herself what she believes in, what she fights for, what matters to her, this blank space is yours to fill in however you choose."

Jules was full-on crying now, holding out the pillow with trembling hands. "Dad," she whispered.

"Your mother would be so proud of the woman you're becoming," Bridger said, pulling his daughter into a hug. "All of you. She'd be so proud of who you've become and the people you've chosen to share your lives with."

The mention of chosen people made my chest tighten with emotion. This family had welcomed me in and made me part of their traditions, had included me in their chaos and their love without asking for anything in return.

"I love you all," Bridger said, and somehow his words seemed to include everyone at the table, even the honorary members like me.

As people started gathering their things, Liam appeared at our table with George right behind him.

"Before you two head off to California," Liam said, "we've got some friends out there we want you to meet."

"Sean and Ren," George added. "They're good people. Been together a few years, know the LA scene inside and out."

"We may have already told them to keep an eye out for a couple of honorary nephews who might need some guidance navigating the queer community out there," Liam said with a grin.

"That's really thoughtful," Gryff said. "It'll be nice to have some connections."

"They'll make sure you actually get out and meet people instead of turning into hermits," George said, giving me a pointed look.

People started gathering their things quietly, but Gryff didn't move for a long time. His knees bounced and squeezed the edges of his pillow, rubbing his thumbs over the soft green fibers at the corners.

When almost everyone was gone, he blurted out. "Can I talk to you for a minute?"

"Sure." I couldn't ever remember seeing him like this before.

Was he about to back out of moving to LA? I think I might have after all of that. To feel that rooted, that much like this was home, that unconditional love was a compelling reason to stay put.

I wouldn't blame him one bit.

"Let's go outside." He nodded toward a small patio area beside the building, strung with lights and furnished with a couple of tables and chairs. It was quiet there, away from the noise of the family saying their goodbyes.

"That was beautiful," I said, settling into one of the chairs. "The pillow ceremony. Your dad is amazing."

"Yeah," Gryff agreed, but he seemed distracted, looking anywhere but at me. "Artie, I need to ask you something."

"Okay," I said carefully. This wasn't my sunshiny best friend asking. The nervousness in his voice was making my chest clench.

"I've been thinking about LA," he started, then stopped and ran his hands through his hair. "Actually, I've been kind of freaking out about LA."

"Freaking out how?" I wanted to be careful. Not seem too biased about what he wanted to say. I wasn't the one he'd give that all up for.

"I've never lived alone," he said in a rush. "I know that sounds ridiculous for a twenty-two-year-old man, but I've literally never been in a house by myself. There's always been family around, always been noise and chaos and people. And Chris bought me this amazing house, and it's perfect, but it's also huge and empty and I'm terrified I'm going to hate it."

He took a deep breath like he'd been holding his breath and not holding this admission in.

Okay. Wow. At least he wasn't telling me he wasn't

going to move at all. He was just anxious about it. That was fair.

I studied his face, seeing real fear there. Gryff was sunshine personified most of the time, but underneath all that confidence was a vulnerability he rarely let anyone see.

"I'm sure it won't be that bad," I said gently. "You'll be busy with training and team stuff. And Flynn will be right across the street."

"I know, I know." He nodded at first, but it somehow turned into him shaking his head. "And I'm not asking you to solve my problems or anything. It's just... would you move in with me? Be my roommate?"

The question hit me like a tackle, not because it was unexpected but because of how much I immediately wanted to say yes. And that wanting had my heart working overtime.

"Gryff—"

"I know it's a lot to ask," he blurted out. "And I know you're planning to get your own place with some of the other rugby girls and figure things out on your own. But I just thought, hoped... maybe we could figure it out together?"

I knew better than to rely on anyone else for stability or security. I'd gotten good at being self-sufficient because depending on other people led to disappointment when I inevitably left or someone you relied on decided they didn't need you anymore.

We'd moved around so much before my parents divorced and that meant I was real used to relying on me, myself, and I when it came time to start over. No one else helped me figure out my place in new schools, on new teams, or who were going to be friends and who weren't.

Except Gryff had done pretty much every single one of those things that first day at Thornminster High six years ago.

Living with Gryff would mean depending on him, trusting that he wouldn't change his mind or decide he needed space or find someone more interesting to share his life with. It would mean putting down roots in a way I'd never had the opportunity to or even allowed myself to do.

He pulled at every single individual whisker in his beard while he waited for my answer, and my heart shifted in my chest with a simple flippy-flop.

This was Gryff.

My Gryff.

My best friend in the whole world.

The person who understood when we crushed on the same guy or girl in class. The person who listened to me complain about my parents' complicated relationship without trying to fix it. The person who'd staged an intervention with baby goats when I'd been stress-spiraling about finals.

"Artie?" he said quietly.

I'd been silent for too long. "I've never had someone to move somewhere new with before besides my mom."

His eyes flickered, hope raising his eyebrows. "So...?"

"So yes." Yeah. That was the right decision. I knew that the second the words fell out of my mouth. "Yes, I will be your roommate. In the fancy-pants house your brother just freaking gave you for graduation."

That decision was a hell of a lot easier than thinking about playing for Scotland.

The smile that spread across his face was blinding. "Hells to the yeah. Really?"

"I'm warning you now, I'm going to want to adopt every stray animal we encounter, and I have strong opinions about couch cushions."

"Done," he said immediately. "We'll rescue all the animals, and you can have as many fluffy, furry, adorkably cute pillows on the couch as you can possibly order."

"I'm making you watch rugby on that enormous TV I saw in the picture of the living room."

"Of course."

"And sometimes I get weird about having to do everything myself, even when I don't have to."

"Artie," he said gently, "You're not talking me out of this by telling me how weird you are. I already know. I want you there because you'll make it feel like home. Even when you try to sneak home a baby goat. It wouldn't be you if you didn't."

He did already know me well enough to predict my future questionable decisions. He was the only one who did.

"Okay," I said, and felt everything settle in my chest that had been restless for as long as I could remember. "Let's do this."

We sat there for a moment, grinning at each other like we'd just solved some major life puzzle. Which, I supposed, maybe we had.

"Thank you," he said quietly. "For saying yes."

"Thank you for asking," I replied. "For wanting me there."

I felt lighter than I had in months.

"There they are," Jules called out when she spotted us. She, Bridger, Flynn, and Tempest were the last ones left. "We were about to send a rescue mission."

"Just getting some air," Gryff said easily, but I caught Flynn looking between us with a speculative expression.

"Everything okay?" Flynn asked.

"Everything's good," Gryff replied, and the contentment in his voice made me smile.

We gathered our things and prepared to leave Cool Beans, and I took one last look around the space where I'd witnessed something more beautiful than I'd ever known family could be like. They'd given me a glimpse of what it meant to belong somewhere, to be chosen and valued and included without having to earn it.

And now I was choosing to build something with Gryff, choosing to trust that some people did stick around, that some relationships were worth the risk of putting down roots.

Somewhere that, just maybe, I could grow too.

I wonder if that big back yard had room for two... or three... or twenty-three baby goats.

ROOKIES RISING

GRYFF

$\mathcal{I}$ woke up to silence.

Not the comfortable quiet of sleeping in after a game day, but the kind of absolute silence that made me question whether I'd gone deaf overnight. No Everett practicing guitar at six a.m., no Flynn arguing with someone on the phone about protein powder, no Jules singing off-key in the shower. Just... nothing.

Okay, maybe not nothing. The house Chris had bought me was fan-fucking-tastic and in a great location with a big backyard just like at home. But the birds here chirped an unfamiliar song, the sound of the cars outside wasn't the same, and even the ocean breeze sounded different than the mountain winds.

I had floor-to-ceiling windows, but without the mountains to the west, I had no idea which way I was facing anyway.

The smell of coffee drifted up from downstairs, and the tightness in my chest loosened. Artie was up.

I found her in the kitchen wearing one of my old

Denver State shirts, which had me pausing in the doorway a minute and staring. She was reading something on her tablet while a piece of toast hung half out of her mouth. Her hair was pulled back in a messy bun, and she had that focused look she got when she was deep in thought about something.

"Your coffee's ready," she said without looking up. "Made extra strong because you're about to get your ass handed to you by actual League players today."

"You know it." I poured myself a mug and settled into the chair across from her. "I'm counting on it. Nothing says welcome to the pros like getting pancaked by a three-hundred-pound defensive tackle."

"Pictures or it didn't happen."

"I'm sure there will be plenty of highlight reels of rookies getting squashed into the grass on all the sports channels later." I'm sure Isak would find every single clip of me and Flynn making fools out of ourselves today and put out a viral highlights reel. That's what he was good at. "What are you studying? It better not have anything to do with accounting. We graduated, remember?"

She finally looked up and grinned. "I may have impulse-bought a dozen throw pillows online because this place is too fancy and needs more personality, and I warned you that I was going to."

The kitchen already looked more lived-in than it had yesterday. Artie's reusable water bottles lined up by the sink with mine, her vitamins scattered across the counter, a stack of books on the island. Little signs that someone actually lived here.

"What kind of throw pillows?" My brand new game

night pillow did look a little lonely all by itself on the enormous couch in the living room.

"You'll see when they arrive. But I'm warning you now, they're aggressively cute."

Asking her to move in with me had been the best decision I'd made in months. Not just because the house felt less like a museum with her stuff scattered around, but because she made everything feel normal. Like we were just two people starting a new adventure instead of me freaking out about every little thing.

"You nervous about your first day?" she asked, studying my face.

"About getting destroyed by guys who've been doing this professionally for years?" I shrugged. "Nah. I mean, that's literally the point of rookie camp, right? Wipe the floor with the newbies until they either quit or figure out how to play at this level. I'm planning to be in the figure it out category, but I expect plenty of floor-wiping between now and then."

"You do belong here," she said firmly. "The Bandits drafted you because they saw something special. That doesn't just disappear because you changed time zones."

Yep. I knew I had the goods to be here, but it was going to be a whole new experience. My whole life I'd been a big fish, regardless of the size of the football shaped pond. But today there was going to be hooks, and fisherman, and nets, and probably some of those craze-balls guys who reach into the water and grabbed fish out of their little fishy caves.

Plus, it was all going to be filmed. Mac Jerry had set this up weeks ago, part of his strategy to build our brand during our rookie season. FlixNChill's *Rookie Rising* series had been following incoming League players for three seasons, and the Kingman twins were supposed to be a big draw for this year.

It meant a shit ton of exposure, which would mean other sponsorships and endorsements would be coming down the pipe. It also meant every move, good or bad, would be on film for the world to see.

"I got you something for your first day." From the other side of the kitchen island, she pulled out a football bedecked birthday style bag with ribbons and tissue paper sticking out the top.

"I think you might have a shopping addiction. No more one-clicking for you." I pulled the tissue out of the top of the bag and threw it at her head.

"You can take my one-click shopping from my cold dead hands." She grasped her tablet like I was going to take it from her. "Now open your present, butt face."

"Is this... did you buy me a LA Bandits lunchbox?" I held the tin vintage lunch box up and twirled it around.

"It'll be good luck." She smiled. "And a conversation starter you can use to make new friends at school today."

God, she was so fucking adorable.

An hour later, I was walking into the training facility with Flynn, both of us putting a little extra swagger into our step so everyone else knew we belonged there.

We'd seen the facilities when we came out for a visit with the team before we'd been drafted and again for mini-camp, but neither of those times had it been filled with players who were ready and willing to smash our asses into the grass.

"We're not in Colorado anymore, Dorothy," Flynn muttered under his breath as we walked into the locker room.

"Linemen, and tight ends, and B-backs, oh my," I said automatically, which made him snort.

First up was our first official meeting with the FlixN-Chill documentary crew. They were already set up in one of the meeting rooms when Flynn and I arrived. Professional cameras, boom mics, the works. At the center of it all was a woman who looked to be in her mid-twenties with perfectly styled blonde hair and the kind of energy that made everyone around her feel important.

"Gryffen and Flynn Kingman," she said, standing up to shake our hands with a warm, professional smile. "I'm Sloane Mitchell, producer for *Rookie Rising*. We are so excited to have you both as part of this season."

She had the kind of enthusiasm that made the project feel genuinely exciting, and I could see why she'd gotten this job. Professional but approachable, with what seemed like real passion for following rookie stories.

"You don't have to worry about us too much today. We'll mostly just be filming. I may pop in to ask you a question or two if we see a great moment." She grinned. "We'll get you both a schedule for our planned filming sessions and home interviews. Nothing too intrusive. And just give us a heads-up when you have events or nights out planned so we can capture some of that authentic LA lifestyle content. Just try to forget we're there and be yourselves."

Flynn and I nodded.

"Perfect. Harry here will get you mic'd up and then you're good to join the rest of the rookies."

The rookie orientation was a blur of paperwork, facility tours, and meetings with coaches who looked at us like they were trying to decide if we were worth their time. Hayes had warned us that the first few weeks would be about proving ourselves all over again but hearing it and living it were two different things.

We didn't get to suit up until that afternoon. Finally something I knew how to do. Which I did not say out loud.

I followed the other offensive linemen onto the field, immediately recognizing the hierarchy. Veterans clustered together, talking in low voices and barely acknowledging the rookies. Second- and third-year players formed their own group, trying to look like they belonged with the vets. And then there were the rookies, all of us trying to figure out where we fit.

"Hey, Kingman," a voice said beside me. I turned to find a good-looking guy about my height with dark skin that made his hazel eyes really pop. Tyson and I had been at mini-camp together last month, which felt like preschool compared to today.

"Freeman, good to see you, man." I shook his hand, grateful for the friendly face. Maybe I should show him my lunchbox later. Because I was that dork.

"Yeah, you too. This is some intimidating shit." Tyson looked around the field, taking in the same scene of upcoming death and destruction we knew was coming our way.

Before I could respond, the offensive line coach blew his whistle and the real work began.

The first drill was simple. Snap the ball, execute the play, don't screw up. I'd done this thousands of times in college. But the moment I took my position and looked across the line at the Bandits' starting defensive tackle, a six-foot-six monster named DeMarcus Clay who'd been to three Pro Bowls, I realized I wasn't in college anymore.

I thought I'd be practicing across from other rookies. Looked like Coach was testing me already.

The snap count felt different. The speed was different. Everything was faster, harder, more precise than anything I'd experienced. DeMarcus ate me alive on the first play, spinning around me like I was standing still and sacking our quarterback before I'd even processed what was happening.

"Again," Coach called out.

Again, DeMarcus destroyed me. But this time I saw it coming a split second earlier.

"Again."

By the time practice ended two hours later, I was exhausted in the best possible way. DeMarcus had thoroughly schooled me for two straight hours, but each rep I'd gotten a little bit better at reading his moves. This was exactly the kind of challenge I'd been hoping for. The chance to learn from guys who'd been perfecting their craft for years.

Tyson looked just as beat up as I felt, but he was grinning.

"Well," he said as we trudged toward the locker room, "that was fucking incredible."

"Right? I mean, I got destroyed, but holy shit, did you see some of those plays?" I was already replaying the best moments, the ones where I'd actually managed to slow DeMarcus down for half a second.

Flynn appeared at my elbow, looking energized despite being covered in grass stains. "How'd the offense go?"

"It was beautiful. Painful, but beautiful. You?"

"Same. These guys are on a completely different level. I can't wait to get back out there tomorrow."

We showered and changed, both of us still buzzing with adrenaline from the intensity of practice. This wasn't like college, where our talent and family name had carried us. This was the real deal, and every rep was going to make us better.

The drive home felt shorter than it should have, my mind racing with everything I'd learned. I kept thinking about the way DeMarcus had read my footwork, how I could adjust my stance to give myself better leverage. There was so much to work on, so much room to improve.

The documentary crew had been pretty unobtrusive too. Sloane seemed to know what she was doing, professional but not pushy. Maybe this whole filming thing wouldn't be as weird as I'd worried about.

When I walked into the house and found Artie on the couch with takeout containers spread across the coffee table, I was still riding the high from practice.

The sight of her curled up there, completely at home in our space, made something warm settle in my chest. She was still wearing one of my old Denver State shirts, and something about seeing her in my clothes sent a flutter through me that I wasn't quite ready to examine too closely. Not when we were both still adjusting to everything, new city, new careers, new living situation. Better to focus on getting settled first before worrying about anything else.

"Thai food," she announced without looking up from her tablet. "Because you look like you just went fifteen rounds with a heavyweight boxer, and I figured you'd want to celebrate surviving your first day with actual League players."

I collapsed onto the couch beside her, accepting the container she handed me. "Best decision ever. I'm starving."

"So? How was it? Did you do anything embarrassing for the cameras? Are you besties with DeMarcus Clay now?"

"Only if letting DeMarcus squash me like a pancake a hundred times in a row counts for both," I said, digging into the pad thai. "That guy is an artist. A terrifying, three-hundred-pound artist who just taught me every-thing I don't know about protecting my quarterback."

She looked up from her tablet, studying my face. "You're grinning."

"Am I?" I reached up to touch my face. "Artie, it was incredible. I mean, I got absolutely destroyed for two hours straight, but I learned more today than I did in my entire senior season. These guys are on a level I didn't even know existed."

"And I'll get to watch it all on repeat when *Rookie Rising* hits FlixNChill," she said, settling back against the cushions. "You know, most people would be traumatized by getting pancaked by a Pro Bowl defensive tackle. You're treating it like Christmas morning."

I tried not to think about how much I liked the way she said "I'll get to watch" like she was genuinely excited to see me succeed. Like she was proud of me in a way that went beyond friendship. But that was dangerous territory, and we had enough to figure out without me making things weird between us.

THE ROOMMATE SITUATION

ARTEMIS

'd never felt more alive.

"Fraser, that was textbook," Coach Maher called out as I rolled to my feet after the tackle drill. "Show them again how to use your momentum instead of fighting it."

I jogged back to the line, ignoring the ache in my side. This was what I lived for. The moment when everything clicked, when my body did exactly what I trained it to do, when I felt like the athlete I'd worked my whole life to become.

The LA Elite Rugby Center was nothing like the makeshift fields and borrowed facilities I'd trained on in college. Everything here was designed for excellence, the pristine pitches, the state-of-the-art recovery equipment, the coaching staff who'd played at the highest levels internationally. Being here meant I was serious about my Olympic dreams, and everyone around me was equally committed.

"Again," Coach called. "This time, Katrina, I want you coming in harder. Fraser's not going to break."

Katrina grinned at me from across the drill setup. She was built like a brick house with arms that could probably bench press a small car, and she'd been eyeing me since I joined the team like she was trying to figure out if I could keep up.

"You sure about that, Coach?" Katrina called back. "She looks pretty delicate to me."

I snorted. "Try me."

What followed was two minutes of the most beautiful violence I'd ever been part of. Katrina came at me like a freight train, but I read her approach perfectly, redirected her momentum, and took her down clean while securing the ball. We both hit the ground hard, but I popped up first with the ball tucked safely against my ribs.

"Again," I said, offering Katrina a hand up.

This time she really brought it. So did I. By the end of the drill, we were both grass-stained and grinning, and I had a new bruise forming on my shoulder that I'd wear like a badge of honor.

"Nice work, Fraser," Katrina said, slapping my back hard enough to rattle my teeth. "You might actually survive training camp."

"Might?" I raised an eyebrow.

"Ask me again in six months."

This was what I'd missed during the college off-season, training with people who understood that rugby wasn't just a sport, it was a way of being in the world. Here, my size wasn't something to apologize for or try to minimize. It was an advantage. My strength wasn't intimidating, it was exactly what the team needed. My body, which had spent so many years feeling too big, too much, too intense for civilian life, fit perfectly into this world of elite athletes.

"Team meeting," Coach Maher called out. "Recovery and strategy session."

We gathered in the team room, twenty women who'd earned their spots through years of dedication and natural talent. I was still getting used to being surrounded by athletes who matched my intensity, women who understood the particular kind of hunger that came with Olympic dreams.

"Alright, ladies," Coach began, pulling up footage on the wall screen. "World Cup highlights. I want you to study how these teams move the ball, how they support each other, how they make decisions under pressure."

For the next hour, we analyzed game footage with the kind of detail that made my accounting brain happy. Rugby was chess played at full speed, and I loved the strategic element as much as the physical challenge.

"Fraser," Coach said as we were wrapping up, "stay after. I want to talk about your role."

The rest of the team filed out, and I settled back in my chair, suddenly nervous. Individual attention could mean anything from praise to criticism to being cut from the squad.

"You've been a center for a long time, right?" Coach asked.

"Yes, ma'am."

"I've been watching your interactions with the other girls on the team, and I'd like to see you take on more of a leadership position. Think like a number eight in fifteens. Your tactical awareness is excellent, and you've got the size and speed to be very effective."

My heart jumped. Number eight was a leadership position, one of the most important spots on the field. "I'd love the opportunity to take on a role like that."

"Good. We'll start working on it next week. And Fraser? You're settling in well with the team. Keep it up."

I practically floated out to the parking lot. Leadership position. That meant serious Olympic potential. This was everything I'd worked for.

My phone buzzed with a text from Gryff as I was loading my gear into the car.

GRYFF

How was practice? Still have all your limbs?

All limbs accounted for. Plus some awesome new bruises to show off.

Can't wait to see the damage. BBQ for dinner?

Perfect. I'm starving.

The drive home through LA traffic should have been annoying, but I was still riding the high from practice. Everything was falling into place. The training, the team dynamics, the possibility of making the Olympic roster. For the first time since graduation, I felt like I knew exactly where I was heading.

Gryff's truck was already in the driveway when I pulled up, which meant he'd beaten me home from his own training. The house looked different than it had this morning. There were boxes stacked by the front door and the sound of music drifting from inside.

I found him in the living room, surrounded by packing materials and what appeared to be half the contents of a store.

"Please tell me you didn't buy more furniture," I said, dropping my gear bag by the door.

"I didn't buy more furniture." He held up his hands innocently. "I bought decorative accessories."

"Gryff."

"And maybe one chair. But look at this stuff, it's all from that list you made."

He was right. Scattered across the coffee table were the throw pillows I'd ordered, a set of ceramic bowls in colors that actually matched, and several picture frames that didn't look like they'd come from a hotel liquidation sale.

"You went shopping," I said, impressed despite myself. "Voluntary shopping. For home decor."

"I may have gotten excited. I wanted our place to feel like home."

Our place. The casual way he said it made something warm settle in my chest. I'd never had an "our place" before, never had someone who wanted to make a space feel like home with me.

"Well, let's see what we're working with."

For the next hour, we unpacked and arranged, arguing good-naturedly about pillow placement and whether the ceramic bowls belonged in the kitchen or on the dining room table as a centerpiece.

"These are perfect," Gryff said, holding up a throw pillow shaped like a sleeping sloth wearing a tiny knitted hat. "Completely ridiculous but perfect."

"I told you they were aggressively cute."

"Where did you even find this stuff?"

"The internet is a magical place full of adorable animal-themed home goods." I was arranging the picture frames on the mantel, trying to figure out the best configuration. "Speaking of animals..."

"Oh no."

"Look at this backyard," I continued, gesturing toward the sliding glass doors. "It's huge. It's practically begging for a dog. Or two dogs. Or maybe a llama?"

"We are not getting a llama."

"But look how much space we have. And the neighbors can't even see into the backyard because of that fence. It's like the previous owners designed it specifically for pet ownership. And don't you think Burrito Petito needs a friend?"

Gryff sank onto the couch and buried his face in his hands. "Artie, we just moved in. We're both starting new careers. The last thing we need is to add pet ownership to the chaos."

"Or," I countered, settling beside him with my laptop, "the first thing we need is something to make this feel like home. Something that depends on us and gives us a reason to come back here every day."

"We already have reasons to come back here. Like food and sleep and not being homeless."

I opened my laptop and navigated to the website I'd

been browsing during lunch breaks. "But look at these faces."

The screen filled with photos of dogs and cats available for adoption from local rescues. I'd been doing research, and LA had an amazing network of animal rescue organizations.

"Artie, that's not fair. You can't just show me pictures of sad animals."

"I'm not showing you sad animals. I'm showing you animals who need homes. Like this little guy." I clicked on a photo of a golden retriever mix with the most soulful brown eyes. "His name is Buster, and he loves playing fetch."

"Buster," Gryff repeated, leaning closer despite himself.

"And look at this sweet girl." I scrolled to a photo of a border collie mix with one blue eye and one brown eye. "Her name is Ziggy Stardust, and she's great with other dogs."

"Ziggy Stardust," he said, and I could hear him weakening.

"Right? And this rescue has a great program where they do home visits to make sure it's a good fit. Very thorough, very responsible."

"We'd still need to puppy-proof the house."

"Only if we're bad dog parents. Which we wouldn't be, because I've already researched proper puppy care and training."

"Of course you have."

I scrolled through more photos, pointing out various adorable animals who definitely needed our love and attention. A three-legged dog named Tripod. A beagle named Sherlock Holmes. A hedgehog named Sir Reginald Pricklebottom.

"You've been planning this," Gryff said accusingly.

"I've been preparing. There's a difference."

"Artie, I love that you want to save every animal in Los Angeles, but we need to be practical. We're both traveling for games and training. Who's going to take care of pets when we're not here?"

"Flynn and Tempest, duh. They'll be excellent pet-sitters. Very responsible, very loving."

"You've thought of everything, haven't you?"

"I've considered the various scenarios, yes."

Gryff was quiet for a moment, studying the photos on my laptop screen. I could see him weakening, the way he always did when presented with something that needed caring for.

"We are not getting a dog right now," he said finally.

"Yet."

"We need to be responsible adults first."

"But you're not saying no to a dog permanently."

"I'm not saying anything definitive about a dog."

"So that's a maybe on the dog."

"That's a 'let's survive our first couple of months in LA before we add any living creatures to the household' on the dog."

"I can work with that timeline." I bookmarked the rescue website and closed the laptop. "But I'm keeping Buster and Ziggy in mind. Just in case."

Gryff's phone buzzed with a notification, interrupting my mental planning of our future fluffy-butt family.

"Oh, that's the documentary crew," he said, checking the message. "They want to do some filming here tomorrow afternoon. Something about 'settling into domestic life in LA.'"

"Right, you mentioned they'd send us a schedule." I didn't love the idea of being on camera, but this was important to Gryff.

The next evening, Sloane and her cameraman Harry arrived exactly on time, armed with professional equipment and what appeared to be a very detailed shot list.

"This place looks amazing," Sloane said, immediately moving through the living room like she was cataloging every detail. "Very... authentic. Lived-in."

"We've been unpacking," I said, suddenly self-conscious about the throw pillows and picture frames we'd arranged so carefully.

"Perfect. That's exactly the vibe we want, real life, not staged. Harry, let's start with some establishing shots of the space, then we'll do the interview on the couch."

For the next hour, they filmed us doing mundane domestic tasks like making coffee, discussing whose turn it was to do dishes, arguing about what to watch on the enormous TV Chris had insisted on including with the house.

"This is great," Sloane said, reviewing footage on her camera. "You two have such natural chemistry as roommates. It really comes through on film."

Something about the way she said "roommates" made me glance at Gryff. He gave me a shrug. This was a dance we'd done so many times before.

"Yep. Friends and roommates. It works really well for us."

"Now let's do some individual interviews," Sloane continued. "Gryff, we'll start with you. Artie, if you don't mind giving us some space?"

I retreated to the kitchen, ostensibly to start dinner but actually to give them privacy. Through the open doorway, I could hear Sloane asking questions about Gryff's adjustment to LA, his goals for the season, his thoughts on living with a friend.

"And how's the roommate situation working out?" Sloane asked. "It must be nice to have someone you're so comfortable with."

"Yeah, it's been great," Gryff replied. "Artie makes everything feel more like home."

"You two seem very close. How long have you been friends?"

"Since high school. She's... she's important to me."

Something in his tone made me look up from the vegetables I was chopping, but I couldn't see his face from this angle.

"Any challenges with the living arrangement? Conflicts over space, different schedules, dating lives?"

There was a pause before Gryff answered. "No major conflicts. We're both pretty focused on our careers right now."

"Right, of course. And Artie's pursuing Olympic dreams while you're starting your professional football career. That must create some interesting dynamics."

"We support each other. That's what friends do."

When it was my turn for the individual interview, Sloane's questions felt more personal than I'd expected.

"You're training for the Olympics while living with one of the most eligible bachelors in professional football," she said with a smile that didn't quite reach her eyes. "That must be... distracting."

"Not really," I said, confused by the question. "Gryff's my best friend. We're both athletes, so we understand each other's schedules and priorities."

"Of course. And you're both openly bisexual, which must create a unique understanding between you."

"I guess? I mean, we've never really talked about it in those terms."

"No? You don't discuss your dating lives, your attractions, what you're looking for in relationships?"

The questions were making me uncomfortable in a way I couldn't pinpoint. "We talk about everything, but we're just friends."

"Just friends," Sloane repeated, making a note on her tablet. "And you're not dating anyone currently?"

"No, I'm focused on training right now."

"What about Gryff? Is he seeing anyone?"

"You'd have to ask him." I did not like where this was going.

"I'm asking you. As his roommate and closest friend, you must have insight into his romantic life."

"I don't really think about Gryff's romantic life," I said, which wasn't true. We talked about it, commiserating when it went wrong and how to make it better. "We're roommates, not... I don't know, whatever you're implying."

"I'm not implying anything. Just trying to understand the dynamic between you."

She was doing something all right.

After they left, I felt oddly unsettled. Sloane's questions stuck with me.

"Was that weird to you?" I asked as we cleaned up from filming.

"What part?"

"The way she was asking about our relationship. Like she was fishing for something."

Gryff shrugged but also nodded. "Reality TV producers always want drama. She's probably hoping we'll have some massive roommate conflict she can film."

"Yeah, probably." I hope that's all it was.

My phone rang, interrupting the conversation. Dad's name flashed on the screen, and I felt the familiar mix of excitement and anxiety that came with his calls. I usually only talked to him a few times a year. This was the second phone call this summer already.

"Hey, Da," I said, settling onto the couch.

"Artemis, love. How's the training going?"

"Really well. I'm working with an amazing team, and Coach thinks I might be ready for the number eight position."

"That's fantastic. Leadership on the field, just like when you were little." His pride came through clearly, even across the ocean. "I've been thinking about our conversation from graduation."

Here it was. The conversation I'd been avoiding thinking about.

"About Team GB?"

"Aye. The opportunity is still there, you know. The team would be lucky to have you. Gotta get something out of that dual citizenship."

I know it was supposed to be a little joke, but I think that was really a way for him to feel more connected to me. "I know, Da."

"It's just... it's been so long since we've lived in the same country. Since we've been able to see each other regularly. If you played for Great Britain, we could spend more time together. I could watch you compete, help with training, be part of your rugby life again."

The longing in his voice made my chest tight. "I'm committed to Team USA, Dad. I've been training with them for two years."

"I know, I know. And I'm proud of you regardless. But the transfer rules... you'd need three years between your last match for the US and playing for GB. If you're serious about considering it, you'd need to make that decision soon. Can't wait too long."

Three years. That sounded like forever and no time at all, but also like a very concrete deadline. "I'll keep that in mind."

"That's all I ask. Love you, hen."

"Love you too, Da."

After we hung up, I sat staring at my phone for a long moment. Gryff had finished cleaning and was now researching something on his laptop, probably football related.

Gryff flopped down on the couch across from me. "What's up with Poppa Fraser? You've been talking to him more lately."

"He wants me to consider playing for Great Britain instead of the US." It would mean another big change in life, which was nothing new. I could do it. My mom wouldn't like it though.

Gryff looked at me like he was trying to see inside my brain. "That's a big decision."

"Yeah. He keeps bringing it up, and I know he misses me. We haven't lived in the same country since I was sixteen."

"Do you want to play for Great Britain?"

I thought about it. "I don't know. Part of me does, because it would mean spending more time with him. But the US team feels like home now."

When had anyone or anything ever felt like home? I don't even know why I said that. Except that the one person in my life who would understand that concept was Gryff.

His gaze moved over my face, then down to the floor like he was thinking of how to fix this for me, and I appreciated that more than he could ever know. I was always the one who had to just take care of myself. It was exhausting. "You don't have to decide anything right now, right?"

"Sort of soon, though. If I wanted to transfer, I'd need three years between playing for the US and being eligible for GB. So the clock is ticking if I'm going to consider it seriously."

Gryff moved closer on the couch. "You gotta do whatever feels right for you. Not what makes your dad… or your mom happy or what seems logical, but what actually feels right in your heart."

I leaned back against the couch cushions, grateful for his steady presence. He listened and trusted me to figure things out.

"I need a little time to think on it. Besides moving to LA, this is really the first time I'm the one who has to make the decision to uproot my life or not. And to be honest, there's something to be said for the stability my mom wanted so badly."

He looked like he wanted to say something else but didn't. Weird, because he knew he could say anything to me.

I picked my phone back up. "You know who else needs stability?" I found the cutest picture I could find and shoved the adorableness right up in his face. "Buster, that's who."

Gryff groaned and buried his face in the couch cushions. "Artie, no."

"Buster is still available. And he's got a friend who is a chocolate lab named Murphy."

"We are not getting a dog."

"Yet."

"Ever."

But he was smiling when he said it, and I was already bookmarking the rescue website.

RAINBOWS AND UNICORNS

GRYFF

Great Fucking Britain.

Ugh. I didn't think anything was great about it at all.

Two days after her conversation with her dad and I was still processing the gut-punch realization that she might move to another continent. Not might... could. Would, if she decided her father and Team GB were more important than everything she'd built here.

Including me.

Training camp had officially started, which meant longer days, more intense practices, and the kind of physical exhaustion that should have wiped out any capacity for overthinking personal problems. Instead, I spent way too much time replaying her words during every drill break, every water timeout, every moment when my mind wasn't completely occupied with not getting pancaked by three-hundred-pound defensive tackles.

Three years. The clock was ticking like a damn time

bomb. She could stop playing for Team USA right now, move back to Scotland or England or wherever her dad was coaching the men's team so they could spend time getting to know each other again, as adults. She'd get to see her father regularly, be part of his rugby world again, rebuild the relationship that distance had complicated.

And in three years she'd be eligible to represent Great Britain in the Olympics. It made perfect sense. It was probably what she should do.

And the thought of it made me want to throw up.

"Kingman," Coach's voice cut through my spiral. "You planning to join us, or are you just here for the scenery?"

I snapped back to attention, realizing I'd been standing in the wrong formation while the rest of the offensive line had moved to the next drill. DeMarcus Clay was looking at me with the kind of patient amusement reserved for rookies who were clearly having personal crises on company time.

"Sorry, Coach," I called back, jogging to my position.

"Get your head in the game, rook," DeMarcus said quietly as I took my stance across from him. "Whatever's eating you, deal with it after practice."

He was right. I was being unprofessional and unfocused, exactly the kind of rookie mistake that got you benched or cut. But knowing that didn't make it easier to stop thinking about Artie packing up her life and moving six thousand miles away.

The rest of practice was a disaster. I missed assignments, jumped offsides twice, and generally played like someone who'd never seen a football before. By the time

Coach blew the final whistle, I was covered in grass stains and humiliation.

I wasn't going to be a starter with this kind of performance. Shit.

Flynn appeared at my elbow as we trudged toward the locker room. "You want to tell me what the hell that was about?"

"Bad day." Which of course was all caught on camera. Harry was a nice guy, but I wanted to dropkick his camera today.

"That wasn't a bad day. That was you being somewhere else entirely." He grabbed my arm, stopping me before we reached the locker room, before we had to face cameras again. "Seriously, what's going on?"

I stared at my twin brother, identical in almost every way except for his ability to stay focused when his personal life was imploding. Flynn had fallen hard for Tempest earlier this year, and being in love had only made his game stronger. Then again, Flynn had never had to worry about his girlfriend moving to another continent.

I glanced around quickly to make sure Harry and his camera, or worse, Sloane and her questions, weren't going to overhear this conversation. Then I turned off my mic and nodded to Flynn to do the same. He pointed to the little power box and showed that he already had.

"Artie might transfer to Team GB," I said finally.

Flynn's eyebrows shot up. "What?"

"Her dad wants her to play for Great Britain instead of the US. I think his way of trying to connect to her now that she's not under her mom's thumb. She'd have to stop playing for Team USA now and wait three years, but it's possible."

"And this affects you how?"

The question was simple, but the answer was complicated in ways I wasn't ready to examine too closely. And Flynn fucking knew it.

"She's my best friend. If she moves back to Scotland or England or wherever, I'll barely see her."

"Right," Flynn said slowly. "Your best friend."

There was something in his tone that made me look at him more carefully. "What's that supposed to mean?"

"You've been weird about Artie since graduation. Even more so since we moved here."

"I haven't been weird, you're weird."

"You have. You get this look on your face whenever she talks like she's made of rainbows and unicorn farts, and you practically vibrate with anxiety whenever she's not around."

What the hell did he know anyway. Maybe Artie was made of rainbows and unicorns. "I'm just adjusting to the roommate thing. Jules is the only girl I've ever lived with before."

"Right. And it has nothing to do with the fact that you're clearly crazy about her."

Flynn studied my face with the kind of twin intuition that made it impossible to lie to him. "Gryff. Do you have feelings for her?"

"She's my best friend."

"That's not what I asked."

I opened my mouth to deny it, to give him the same

explanation I'd been giving everyone for years about how Artie and I were just friends, how we'd never crossed that line, how our friendship was too important to complicate with romance.

Instead, what came out was, "I think I'm falling in love with her."

Flynn's expression shifted from suspicious to concerned. "How long?"

"I don't know. Maybe always? But definitely since we moved in together." I scrubbed my hands over my face. "And now she might move to another country, and I realized that the thought of losing her makes me want to set the entirety of the United Kingdom on fire."

But not the Commonwealth. Canadians were too nice, except when it came to hockey.

"Have you told her?"

The center of my chest went hollow from the inside out. "Are you insane? No, I haven't told her."

"Why not?"

Because I can't risk destroying the most important relationship in my life with my need to hold her, and pet her, and call her my squishy little strawberry. Which is not what came out of my mouth. "Because she's dealing with huge career decisions and family pressure, and the last thing she needs is her longtime friend and roommate complicating everything by declaring his undying love."

Flynn rolled his eyes and looked like he wanted to smack me upside the head. "Is this what I was like before I let Tempest into my heart? Good god. Or maybe the last thing Artie needs is to make a life-changing decision without knowing how you feel about her."

Before I could respond to that terrifying suggestion, my phone buzzed with a text.

SEAN

Hope you guys are settling in well. Ren and I are planning a proper LA night out this weekend. You in?

Saved by the perfect distraction bell. I stared at the message, remembering what Liam and George had told us about their cruise besties Sean and Ren who'd help us navigate LA's queer scene.

Definitely. Mind if we invite a couple friends? Parker and Freddie are new to LA too.

The more the merrier. Saturday night, Abbey Cat in West Hollywood. 9 p.m.

Flynn read the messages over my shoulder. "Good. You need to get out and explore the city. Make some friends. Kiss your roommate. See where it goes."

I wasn't really paying attention to him. I was thinking about how excited Artie would be that we'd go out like she'd been telling me we needed to do. "Liam and George mentioned Sean... wait, what? Fuck you. Good try."

And now I was thinking about kissing Artie. Fuck me.

We both turned our mics back on and headed into the locker room. Sloane was right there, staring at us like she'd heard everything. Or was mad that she hadn't. Crap.

I was probably supposed to invite the camera crew to the night out. Next time. I'd invite them to the next thing.

When I got home that evening, I found Artie in the

kitchen making what appeared to be enough stir-fry to feed a small army. She looked up when I walked in, and the smile she gave me made my very core go tight and warm.

"Rough practice?" she asked, taking in my grass-stained appearance.

"You could say that."

"Well, I made comfort food. And I may have gotten slightly carried away with the portion sizes."

"This is definitely why I asked you to move in with me," I said, accepting the plate she handed me. "Your ability to anticipate my emotional needs through food."

"That and my sparkling personality."

"Sparkling like a rainbow unicorn fart."

We settled at the kitchen island, and I watched her talk about her day, practice highlights, team dynamics, a funny story about one of her teammates trying to teach the others how to balance a rugby ball on their noses. She was animated and happy, completely settled into her LA life.

Which made the thought of her leaving even worse. This ability she had to uproot her whole life and then fit in anywhere so easily was astonishing and I hated myself for wishing it wasn't so.

Maybe if I showed her how great life here could be, she wouldn't leave me.

"Remember when Liam and George said they had friends out here to show us around?"

She shoved a giant bite of veggies and noodles into her mouth and nodded.

"Sean texted me today about going out Saturday night. You in, right?"

"Absolutely." She gave a little double handed raise the roof dance move. "I could use a night that doesn't involve protein shakes and ice baths."

"We could invite Parker and Freddie too. You know, bring the whole Colorado rainbow mafia with us."

"Perfect. I haven't seen Parker since graduation, and Freddie texted me yesterday about wanting to explore the queer scene here."

The casual way she said it, like this was just friends hanging out, like there wasn't any undercurrent of anything more complicated, reminded me that whatever I was feeling, she was completely oblivious to it. And that she didn't have the same feelings even a little bit.

I wasn't going to fuck up our friendship.

"Great. I'll set it up."

We finished dinner together, and I cataloged all her cute and adorable idiosyncrasies that I usually took for granted. The way she laughed at her own jokes. How she absently reached over to steal bites from my plate even though she had her own. The perfectly comfortable silence when conversation lapsed.

If she moved to Great Britain, I'd lose all of this. The daily domesticity, the shared meals, the easy companionship that had become the best part of my day.

And I'd lose it without ever telling her how I felt about her.

Saturday we headed out to Abbey Cat, a converted church in West Hollywood that had been transformed into one of the most welcoming queer spaces in LA. The building still looked vaguely religious from the outside, but the rainbow flags and the sound of music spilling onto the street made it clear this was a very different kind of worship.

Sean and Ren were waiting by the entrance, both dressed in the kind of effortlessly cool outfits that made me feel like I'd never understood fashion.

Sean had the sophisticated style of someone who knew exactly what worked for his plus-size frame in a perfectly fitted suit vest with a crisp shirt over dark jeans that made him look like a sophisticated but casual academic, until you noticed the tiny superheroes on his tie. He wore his confidence like an accessory, the kind of self-assurance that came from being completely comfortable in his own skin.

Ren was taller, with really striking Asian features, and wore a vintage jacket that probably cost more than my truck.

"There they are," Sean called out, pulling me into a hug like we were old friends instead of people Liam and George had connected through their network of honorary family. "Ready for some fun?"

"As ready as we'll ever be," Artie replied.

Parker arrived moments later, her purple hair catching the light from the street lamps. She looked exactly the same as she had at graduation, confident, slightly mischievous, with the kind of energy that suggested she was always planning something interesting.

"This place is amazing," she said, looking up at the building. "Very Gothic chic meets pride parade."

"Wait until you see the inside," Ren said with a grin.

Freddie was the last to arrive, looking slightly overwhelmed but excited. They'd cut their hair since I'd last seen them at a Kingman family gathering, and the shorter style made them look older, more settled into their identity.

"Thanks for waiting for me," they said. "Getting here from campus was... weird."

"No problem," Artie said, giving them a hug. "How's the soccer team looking?"

"Intimidating but amazing. I think I'm going to love playing here."

We all made our way inside, and I felt some of the tension start to ease out of me. This was exactly what I'd needed. Friends, music, the kind of social connection that reminded me there was more to life than football and complicated feelings about roommates.

The interior of Abbey Cat was even more impressive than the outside suggested. High ceilings, stained-glass windows that had been repurposed with rainbow lighting, and a dance floor that was already packed with people of every age, gender, and style imaginable.

"Drinks first," Sean announced, leading us toward the roped off VIP area where they had a table reserved. Fancy pants. "Then I want to hear everything about how you're all settling into LA life."

The next few hours flew by in the best possible way. Our table was in a quieter corner where we could actually talk, and the conversation ranged from career updates to LA apartment hunting to stories from our respective teams and schools.

Parker regaled us with tales from her new job at Flix-NChill. "Being besties with the author of the books they're making into the most anticipated show next year has it's benefits. One other girl in IT cried a little when I got Tempest to sign a book for her."

Freddie talked about the adjustment to UCLA, the competitive dynamics of the soccer team, and their excitement about training with coaches who actually understood their Olympic aspirations. "Everyone here is serious about their sport. No one thinks it's weird that I'm planning my life around soccer."

"Same with rugby," Artie agreed. "It's nice to be around people with the same kind of goals."

Sean and Ren shared stories about LA life, the best neighborhoods for young professionals, and the city's surprisingly robust community of transplants from smaller places.

"The thing about LA," Ren said, "is that almost everyone here is from somewhere else. I was worried when I came over from... Asia. But there's this under-standing that everyone's trying to figure it out as they go."

"Except the people who were born here," Sean added. "They're a whole different species."

This felt like what Artie and I'd been missing, a genuine connection with people who understood the particular challenges of being young, queer, and trying to build a life in a new city.

I tried not to but I watched Artie more carefully than I should have. The way she laughed at Sean's stories, how she and Parker fell into easy conversation about college days, the comfortable way she interacted with everyone so easily.

This was Artie in her element, social, confident, completely herself. And seeing her like this made me realize how much I wanted to be part of her world, as something more.

"You're staring," Freddie said quietly, appearing at my elbow while the others were distracted by one of Sean's more animated stories.

"What?"

"At Artie. You're staring at her like she's about to disappear."

I looked down at my drink, suddenly self-conscious. "I'm just... making sure she's having a good time."

"Uh-huh." Freddie's tone suggested they weren't buying my explanation. "You know, Jules mentioned that you two have been living together."

"We're roommates."

They narrowed their eyes at me. I was getting tired of people doing that. "Right. Roommates who look at each other like that."

I sighed. Yep. I was going to go through this dance again, because when you know all the names of the streets in hell, why move? "Like what?"

Before they could respond, the group's attention turned back to our conversation.

"What are you two plotting over there?" Parker asked.

"Just discussing the dating scene here," Freddie said smoothly.

The evening wound down around midnight, with everyone exchanging numbers and making plans for future hangouts. As we gathered our things to leave, Sean pulled me aside.

"This was fun," he said. "You guys should definitely

come to our place for brunch next weekend. I love to put on a spread and introduce old friends to new ones."

No wonder George and Liam had become fast friends with Sean and Ren. "That sounds great."

Then Sean gave a subtle nod toward Artie who was saying goodbye to Parker and Freddie. "And remember, some chances don't come around twice."

I didn't need to ask what he meant. Our car pulled up and we headed home with Sean's warning ringing in my head the whole way.

When we got home, I followed Artie to the front door. I had this crazy energy still flowing through me from the evening and I didn't know what to do with it.

Artie leaned against the front door, waiting for me to get the keys out. "I forgot how much I missed having queer friends who actually get it."

"I know, right?" She was the one who got me. She always had.

"I get so tired of the weird assumptions people make. The way some people act like you have to pick a side." She stretched and yawned. "It's nice to just be yourself without having to explain anything."

I fumbled with the keys, hyperaware of how close she was standing. "That's exactly what I needed too. People who don't care about football or family names, who just... like us for us."

"See? I told you making new friends in LA wouldn't be as scary as you thought."

"You were right. As usual."

I turned to face her, and suddenly we were standing much closer. Close enough that I could see the flecks of silver in her blue eyes, could count the freckles scattered across her nose. I could smell her strawberry shampoo, could feel the warmth radiating from her body in the cool night air.

She looked up at me, and something shifted in her expression. The easy friendliness was still there, but underneath it was something I refused to acknowledge. Not yet.

"Gryff," she said quietly.

"Yeah?"

For a moment, I thought she was going to say something that would change everything. Something that would make this conversation about more than just friendship and mutual support.

Instead, she reached around me to unlock the door, her arm brushing against my chest as she did. The brief contact sent electricity through me, and I had to resist the urge to pull her closer.

But neither of us moved to actually go inside. We stood there in the doorway, looking at each other, both of us aware that something had almost happened but neither willing to acknowledge what it was.

Finally, she stepped back slightly and smiled. "Goodnight, Gryff."

"Goodnight."

But we still didn't move, both of us lingering in that charged moment until finally, reluctantly, we stepped inside together.

I stood in our living room for a long moment after we'd said our final goodnights and headed upstairs, staring at the ridiculous and cute throw pillows Artie had insisted on buying and trying to process what had almost happened.

Sean's words echoed in my head. *Some chances don't come around twice.*

He was right. And if Artie was seriously considering moving to Great Britain, my chances were running out fast.

KINGMAN MEN PLAY BETTER

ARTEMIS

Gryff had another rough day at practice.

I could tell from the way he slumped into the kitchen when he got home in that particular shade of frustration that came from knowing you'd underperformed. Again.

"Let me guess," I said, looking up from my laptop where I'd been reviewing game footage from my own training. "DeMarcus ate you alive?"

"Clay, Mahelona, and pretty much everyone else on the defensive line." He grabbed a protein shake from the fridge and downed half of it in one go. "Tyson pretended not to know who I was after practice. He was kidding around, but I'm playing like shit."

This was becoming a pattern. For every good practice day Gryff had, there seemed to be two or three where he came home looking like he'd been put through a blender. It wasn't that he was bad, or that he wasn't cut out to play in the pros. He was clearly talented enough to be there, but he wasn't playing at the level that had made him a Heisman winner.

And in the League, talent wasn't enough. You had to be consistent. You had to prove yourself every single day.

"You're still adjusting," I said, though we both knew that excuse was wearing thin. They'd been in training camp for weeks now.

"Flynn's adjusting fine. Flynn's playing like he belongs there."

That was true. From what I'd observed, Flynn seemed to be settling into professional football with the same steady competence he'd brought to everything else in his life. But then again, Flynn had Tempest. Flynn was happy and settled and in love.

I knew what I had to do.

The running joke that wasn't really a joke about how Kingman men played better when they were getting laid was absolutely true. It was practically a legend at DSU by the time we'd been freshmen. There were more than enough warm and willing partners to keep both Flynn and Gryff playing at the top of their games.

The pattern was undeniable, even if people laughed it off as coincidence.

But what if it wasn't about sex at all? What if it was about happiness, about having something stable and wonderful in their personal lives that freed them up to excel professionally?

Gryff was clearly not happy. He was stressed about proving himself, worried about fitting in, probably still processing the huge life change of moving halfway across the country, away from his family for the first time. And all of that anxiety was showing up in his performance on the field.

"You know what you need?" I said, closing my laptop and giving him my full attention.

"Better reflexes? Faster footwork? A time machine so I can go back to college where I actually knew what I was doing?"

"You need to get laid."

He choked on his protein shake. "Excuse me?"

"It's a proven fact. Kingman men play better when they're getting action. Everyone knows it."

"They do not."

"They absolutely do. Your brothers dominated the field last season and won the Big Bowl game like it was just for funsies. It's like a family superpower or something."

Gryff stared at me like I'd suggested he take up interpretive dance. "That's... that's not how athletic performance works."

"Isn't it? Think about it. When you're happy and relaxed in your personal life, you play better. When you're stressed and lonely and spending all your free time worrying about whether you belong on the team, you play like shit."

"I'm not lonely. I have you."

The simple way he said it made something flutter in my chest, but I pushed the feeling aside. It was sweet of him, but I wasn't the one who was going to sleep with him. This wasn't about me. This was about helping my best friend succeed.

And I knew the surest way to make that happen. Mr.

Fix It would be more than willing to go along if he thought he was going to be fixing my love life too.

"Bestie support is not the same thing as romantic fulfillment, and you know it."

He was quiet for a moment, considering. "Even if that were true, which I'm not admitting it is, what exactly are you suggesting? That I download a dating app and start swiping my way to better football performance?"

"I'm suggesting we both get back out there. We've been hiding in this house like hermits ever since we swore off dating after our respective disasters."

"We haven't been hiding. Unless of course you mean you've been hiding from making a decision about moving to the other side of the world."

Damn, he could see through me like a clear mountain morning. Which I had been counting on. Come into my web said the spider to... the other spider. "Shush your face. That's not what this is about."

"Mmm-hmm."

"Look, everyone else in our friend group is either coupled up or actively dating. Parker's been meeting people, Freddie's connecting with classmates, Sean and Ren are obviously settled. We're the only ones who aren't pursuing anything romantic."

"And?"

"And maybe it's time. We've had enough time to get over our breakups. We're both settled in here for the most part. Plus, you asked me to move in with you partly because you were nervous about meeting new people in a new city, right?"

He nodded reluctantly.

"Well, we've met people now. Good people. But neither of us is going to meet potential romantic partners if we keep spending all our free time meal prepping and watching game film."

Gryff was starting to look interested despite himself. "So what are you suggesting?"

Gotcha. "I'm suggesting we help each other. We're both clearly terrible at picking partners for ourselves, hence the spectacular breakups, but we know each other better than anyone. Who would you trust more to find someone compatible with me than my best friend?"

"That's..." he paused, considering. "Actually not the worst logic you've ever used."

"Thanks for the ringing endorsement. And since we don't know a ton of people in LA yet, we could ask Sean and Ren to help. They seem like they'd be great at matchmaking."

"They do seem like the type who'd enjoy that."

I could see him warming to the idea, which was exactly what I'd hoped for. If I could get him focused on finding me someone great, he'd be distracted from his own anxiety about dating and might actually agree to let Sean set him up too.

He was quiet for a moment, and I could practically see the wheels turning. Gryff loved solving problems, especially when those problems involved taking care of other people.

"There's just one issue," he said finally. "Sloane."

"What about her?"

His expression shifted, becoming more serious. "I got a call from her today about Abbey Cat. She saw Freddie's

InstaSnap posts and wanted to know why we didn't bring the documentary crew along."

Oh, crappola. "How upset was she?"

"She wasn't upset, exactly. More like... disappointed. In that way that's somehow worse than being yelled at." He rubbed his forehead. "She was very sweet about it, but also very clear that we have a contract and obligations. Apparently 'authentic LA lifestyle content' means they need to actually document our social activities."

"Ooph. I'm slightly regretting signing that release now."

"Sorry. We don't have to. I can just like... I don't know, get her to film me babysitting Burrito Petito while Flynn and Tempest go out. I'm sure Sloane would be happy to make me out to be the loneliest rookie in the League this season."

Nope. Make an immediate U-turn, you have missed your exit. "No way. If Sloane's going to want to document every second of your life we need to get back on her good side first. Because I'm not going to the premier with a loo-hoo-zerrrr."

Gryff grinned for the first time in the whole conversation. "You're the loser."

"Your face is a loser." I settled onto the couch next to him, stealing a handful of the almonds he was snacking on. "What if we invited everyone to something that would actually be good for filming? Like that yoga in the park thing I keep seeing flyers for?"

"You want them to film us doing yoga in public?"

"Why not? It's outdoors, it's very LA lifestyle, and Sean and Ren would probably love it. Plus we could actually have a proper conversation without worrying about loud music. And remember how fun goat yoga was?"

"You did not find a goat yoga class, did you?"

"This is just regular yoga."

"We are not adopting goats just to take to this class."

"Spoilsport."

I grabbed my phone and pulled up Sean's contact. "I'm texting Sean and Ren now. You text Sloane and make nice with her."

> Want to try yoga in the park this week? Very LA of us. Fair warning: documentary crew will probably want to film.

SEAN

OMG YES. Ren and I have been meaning to try that. And we're going to be on FlixNChill?? This is so exciting.

> Thursday? There's a session at Griffith Park at 4 p.m.

Perfect. Can't wait.

"Sean's in," I announced. "He seems thrilled about the filming part."

"Of course he is. He's got that personality that was made for cameras."

On Thursday the documentary crew arrived early to set up, and Sloane seemed genuinely pleased with the setting.

"This is exactly the kind of content we need," she said, adjusting her sunglasses. "Very authentic, very aspirational lifestyle."

Sean arrived with perfectly coordinated athletic wear

and the kind of yoga mat that probably cost more than my monthly coffee budget. His enthusiasm was infectious as he waved at the camera crew like they were old friends.

"This is so cool," he said, setting up his mat next to mine. "I've always wanted to be on a reality show."

Ren appeared moments later, looking significantly less excited about the filming aspect. He'd positioned himself carefully at the edge of our group, far enough from the main camera angle that he'd be barely visible in most shots.

"You're not camera shy, are you?" I asked him quietly as we settled into our starting positions.

"I've spent plenty of time in front of them," he said, but there was something guarded in his expression. "But I don't want to make this about me."

How interesting and strange.

The yoga instructor, a woman named Dharma who had the kind of serene energy that made you immediately trust her even if she did tell us to put our worries in a bubble and blow them away, guided us through a flow that was challenging enough to be engaging but not so difficult that we couldn't maintain conversation during the easier poses.

"So," Sean said during a particularly long warrior pose hold, "how's the roommate situation working out? Living with your best friend in a new city?"

Sean's tone was casual, but I caught him glancing toward the camera crew. Why did I have the feeling Sloane had planted that question?

"It's great," Gryff said, though there was something slightly strained in his voice. "Very... comfortable."

"Comfortable," Sean repeated, like the word held some hidden meaning. "That's important."

We transitioned into downward dog, and I found myself thinking about that word choice. Comfortable. It was accurate, but it also felt insufficient somehow. Living with Gryff was comfortable, but it was also energizing and grounding and a dozen other things that were harder to articulate.

"It is, and that's maybe part of the problem," I said during the brief rest period between flows. "A problem I think you two might be able to help us with."

"Do tell." Sean said it in that gimme-the-tea kind of way.

"Everyone in our friend group is either coupled up or actively dating. Gryff and I are the only ones who aren't... pursuing anything romantic."

"And how do you feel about that?" Sloane called out from behind the cameras, clearly intrigued by this conversational direction.

"Maybe it's time to start thinking about dating."

Gryff's warrior pose wobbled slightly. "Is it?"

"Why not? We've been in LA for a while now. We're both doing well with our training. We've had enough time to get over our respective breakup disasters."

"What breakup disasters?" Sean asked, immediately invested.

"We both swore off dating after some particularly spectacular relationship implosions," I explained. "I gave up women, he gave up men. But maybe it's time to get back out there."

"Ah, yes. This is a problem that Sean will be thrilled to

help you with," Ren said, speaking up for the first time since we'd started.

Now that it was on camera, Gryff would have to go along with it. But just for a little extra oomph I poked where I knew he needed it. "Sweet. Clearly we're both terrible at picking partners for ourselves. I was thinking maybe we could pick for each other. There's no one I trust more than my very best friend in the whole wide world to help me find the right person who will treat me like a queen."

"This is fascinating," Sloane said, clearly delighted with the direction our conversation was taking. "So you'd essentially be each other's matchmakers?"

Sean was abuzz with excitement, his eyes lighting up. "Oh, this is brilliant. We know tons of people in the city."

Ren made a noncommittal sound that could have been agreement or mild panic.

"You'd really be up for that?" I asked Sean. "Playing matchmaker for us?"

"Are you kidding? I live for this kind of thing. Finding the perfect person for someone is like... it's an art form."

"What kind of people are you looking for?" Sloane asked, and I could practically see her mentally planning future episodes around our dating adventures.

I thought about it seriously. "Someone who can handle that I'm an athlete, who isn't intimidated by my size or strength. Someone who sees my ambition as attractive, not threatening."

"And you, Gryff?"

Gryff was quiet for a long moment, and when he spoke, his voice was carefully measured. "Someone who's interested in me as a person, not as a football player or a celebrity."

"Those seem like very reasonable requirements," Sean said. "Definitely workable."

"So we're really doing this?" I asked, looking around our little circle. "The mutual matchmaking project?"

"If you're serious about it," Sean replied. "I think it could be fun. And very good for the show," he added with a grin toward the camera crew. Sloane had definitely coached him.

Gryff nodded, though there was something in his expression I couldn't quite read. Something that looked almost... reluctant. "Yeah. Let's do it."

After class Gryff waited until the camera crew packed up and we'd said goodbye to Sean and Ren before he swatted me with his rolled up yoga mat. "I know what you're doing, Artemis Ingvar Fraser."

Uh-oh. "Who me?"

"You can't fool me. This is the perfect distraction from avoiding the decision about Team GB, isn't it?"

The question caught me off guard, and I felt heat rise in my cheeks. "You're a distraction."

"Nice try. You've been talking about everything except your dad's offer lately. And now you want to focus on finding relationships in LA. It seems like maybe you're looking for reasons to stay."

I opened my mouth to deny it, then closed it again. Because he wasn't wrong. The thought of making that decision, choosing between my father and the life I was building here, felt overwhelming in a way I wasn't ready to deal with.

"Maybe a little," I admitted. "Is that terrible?"

"It's not terrible. It's human. But you should know that's what you're doing."

"Maybe focusing on building a life here will help me figure out if it's worth staying for."

"And if I find you someone amazing, that would make the decision easier?"

"Potentially." I shouldered my yoga mat and looked at him seriously. "Same for you, right? If Sean finds you someone perfect, you'll have more reasons to love LA."

"Right," he said, but something in his tone suggested that wasn't quite what he wanted to hear. "More reasons to love LA."

As we walked back to the parking area, I felt satisfied with our plan. It was logical, systematic, and had the potential to solve multiple problems at once. We'd integrate better into LA's social scene, we'd have the support of friends who understood the queer dating landscape, and we'd approach relationships with more intention than either of us had managed in the past.

The fact that it also gave me an excuse to postpone the biggest decision of my life was just a bonus.

And most importantly, if the Kingman family legend was true, getting Gryff happily settled with someone would improve his performance on the field. His rookie season would be successful, he'd make the team, and I'd have helped my best friend achieve his dreams.

"So," Sloane said, catching up with us as we reached our car, "when do we start filming the dates?"

"Let us actually find some people first," I said with a laugh.

"Fair enough. But I want to document the whole process. The matchmaking, the preparation, the actual dates. This could be a really compelling storyline for the season."

Great.

While I wasn't that excited to see my potentially disastrous dates on TV, it was still a good plan.

The only thing I couldn't figure out was why Gryff seemed so unenthusiastic about a plan that was clearly going to benefit both of us.

DOUBLE BLIND TEST

GRYFF

"That's the fifth one, Gryff. The one, two, three, four, five... count them, fifth perfectly nice guy you've rejected." Sean's exasperated face filled my phone screen as I sprawled on the couch, trying to look casual about systematically destroying every dating option for Artie.

"The sommelier was pretentious," I said, scrolling through my tablet like I wasn't fully invested in this conversation.

"This is California. He knows about wine."

I gave him a no-duh nod. "Exactly. Pretentious."

Sean rubbed his temples. "Okay, what about Kylie? The pediatric nurse?"

"Too tall."

"She was five-eleven."

Yeah, but so was Artie. "That's basically six feet."

"That's basically not how math works." Sean looked ready to throw something at me through the phone. "Manuela, the personal trainer?"

"Too into CrossFit."

I think Sean growled. Maybe it was just gas. "You're a professional athlete."

"Exactly. I know the type."

"Oh my sainted grandmother." Sean disappeared from frame for a second, and I heard him muttering to Ren in the background. "Your weird twin friend is being impossible... No, the other twin... Yes, the one who's in love with his roommate..."

"I can hear you," I called out.

Sean reappeared, his expression shifting to something craftier. "Okay, last chance. If you reject this one, I'm telling Artie you're sabotaging her love life."

My stomach dropped. "That's not—I'm not—"

"Sure you're not." Sean's phone shifted, and suddenly he was showing me a photo. "Rob Kramer. Five four, stunt coordinator, rock climber, teaches kids' martial arts on weekends, volunteers at the aquarium, and literally everyone who meets him falls a little bit in love with him. Literally."

I stared at the photo. Rob was... annoyingly attractive. Compact, muscled in that functional way that came from actually using your body rather than just sculpting it. Confident stance, genuine smile, surrounded by kids in tiny gis in what was clearly a charity event.

"How do we know he's not a serial killer?" I tried weakly.

"Because I've known him for three years, and the most violent thing he's ever done is choreograph fight scenes where no one actually gets hurt." Sean pulled the phone back to his face. "Also, he fosters senior cats. Serial killers don't foster senior cats, Gryff."

Fuck. I couldn't find a single legitimate reason to reject him.

"He seems..." I swallowed hard. "Fine."

"Fine? He's perfect. He's confident, funny, emotionally intelligent, and completely unfazed by tall, muscled, athletic women. He dated a six-foot blonde goddess of a volleyball player for two years."

Each word felt like a nail in the coffin of my stupid, hopeless feelings for Artie.

"Great," I managed. "Set it up."

"Done. Tomorrow night, seven o'clock, Constellation in West Hollywood." Sean looked entirely too pleased with himself. "You're welcome."

"Yeah. Thanks." I ended the call and immediately wanted to throw my phone across the room.

Why had I agreed to this mutual dating setup thing? Oh right, because Artie had asked for my help. Because she'd looked at me with those blue eyes and said she trusted me to find her someone good. Because I was apparently a masochist who enjoyed watching the woman I was falling for date other people.

My phone buzzed with a text from Artie.

ARTIE

> Your date is all set. You're going to LOVE him. Meeting at Constellation at 7. Ren says he's perfect for you!!!!

That was entirely too many exclamation marks. She

was clearly joyfully excited about her plan. I wasn't going to be the one to rain on her dating parade.

You didn't send me a picture or anything

It's more fun as a surprise. Trust me, he's exactly what you need.

Great. I was so looking forward to a double blind date. To watch Artie with Rob the Perfect while some stranger tried to make conversation with me. This was going to be the longest night of my life.

I arrived at Constellation ten minutes early, wearing the dark jeans and button-down Artie had insisted made me look "approachable but still hot." Not that it mattered what I looked like when I'd be spending the evening watching her with someone else.

The restaurant was one of those trendy LA places where they cared more about how the food photographed than whether humans could actually sit comfortably. Every surface was either marble, exposed brick, or Edison bulbs. The hostess looked like she weighed less than my left earlobe.

"Reservation for Kingman," I said.

Her eyes widened in recognition. "Oh, yes, Mr. Kingman. Your party is already here. Right this way."

I followed her through the maze of tiny tables and decorative chairs that looked like they belonged in a dollhouse, and there was Artie, standing by a table, looking absolutely stunning in a dark blue dress that made her eyes pop. Her hair was down in waves, and she'd done that thing with her makeup that made her look like she was glowing from within.

And right behind her was Harry the cameraman and, joy of joys, Sloane. She gave me a little finger wave and I tight-lipped smiled. She'd been very insistent on recording every second of this date. Had even made me and Artie send contact info for our dates in advance so they could sign the filming releases before the date.

"Gryff," Sloane waved me over. "You look great. Your date's running a few minutes late, but he texted that he's almost here. I'm anxious to see if it's love at first sight. He's adorable and apparently doesn't follow sports at all, so he won't care that you're famous."

I glanced over at Artie who shrugged and smiled. "I think you'll like him. Ren assured me he isn't a serial killer."

Before I could respond, someone cleared their throat behind me. I turned to find myself looking down, way down, at a man who barely came up to my chest. He stepped around me and held his hand out to Artie.

"You must be Artemis." Rob's voice was warm and confident, completely unfazed by the fact that he had to tilt his head back to make eye contact. "Wow, Sean completely undersold how beautiful you are."

Artie's face went through about six different expressions as she looked down at him, her body automatically bending at an awkward angle like she was trying to figure out the logistics of... existing near him. She extended her hand for a shake, then seemed to second-guess it, pulled back, started to lean down for a hug, aborted that mission, and ended up doing an odd curtsy-bow hybrid that made Rob grin.

"I'm... yes. Hi. You're... compact," she blurted out, then immediately turned red. "I mean, Sean mentioned you were... I just meant..."

"That I'm short?" Rob laughed, easy and genuine. "Five four on a good day. Five six if I spike my hair, which my ex said made me look like an anime character, so I stopped doing that."

Fuck. Sean was right. Rob was sweet, funny, confident, and good-looking, and Artie was going to fall in love with him tonight.

Before Artie could respond, a tall whirlwind of energy bounded up to our group.

"Oh my god, you're even taller than me. This is uh-mazing."

I looked over to find possibly the most willowy adult man I'd ever seen beaming at me. He couldn't have been bigger around than my pinky, with platinum blond hair in a short spiky cut that matched his personality perfectly.

"I'm Puck." He actually bounced on his toes. "This is so cool. I've never dated someone I could actually climb like a tree."

The hostess, who'd been watching our group with increasing concern, cleared her throat. "Right this way to your table."

She led us to a booth that was clearly designed by someone who'd never actually eaten food before. The table was fixed in place, at a height that would hit both Artie and me somewhere around our sternums if we managed to squeeze into the seats.

"Here you are," the hostess chirped.

We all stared at the booth. Rob tilted his head, assessing it like a stunt he was planning. Puck was probably the only one who could fit at the table at all. Artie was doing that thing where she tried to make herself smaller, shoulders hunching in.

"Actually," the hostess said, apparently realizing the geometric impossibility of fitting us into the space, "let me show you to our bar seating. Much, uh, better lighting for your camera crew."

The bar seating turned out to be backless stools that looked like they were made from repurposed bicycle seats, positioned at a counter that would have both Rob swinging his legs like a child, and have me and Artie dying about three minutes in from having the sides of the metal seats digging into our larger-than-those-seats asses. I couldn't subject her to that.

"Those are a Larry, Curly, and Mo style accident waiting to happen," I said, louder than necessary. Several nearby diners looked over. "Look, I'm six four and built like a truck. Those things are going to snap the second I sit down, and then you'll have a viral video of League Player Destroys Pretentious Restaurant on your hands."

The manager materialized instantly, probably sensing the bad publicity.

Rob stepped forward smoothly. "We're going to need your VIP booth, the one you keep for celebrities who actually want to eat their food."

"I... we don't..."

"The one in the back corner," Rob continued pleasantly. "With the adjustable table and real chairs. The one you gave to that action star Fox Daws last week. It looked great in his InstaSnap post."

The manager's face went through a journey. "Right this way."

The VIP booth was like finding an oasis in a desert of aesthetic discomfort. Real chairs with backs and cushions. A table at actual table height. Space to exist as humans with bones and muscles and the need for back support.

"Thank god," Artie breathed, then caught herself. "I mean, this is lovely."

We settled in, and immediately the careful choreography of a first date began. Artie reached for the wine list at the exact moment Rob did. They had a brief tug-of-war that ended with the list tearing slightly down the middle.

"I'll order for us," Artie announced, at the same time Rob said, "What does everyone like?"

They stared at each other. Rob gently extracted the torn wine list from Artie's grip.

"How about," he said easily, "we each pick something? Make it more fun?"

"Fun. Yes. I love fun." Artie grabbed the appetizer menu with both hands while trying not to look directly into the cameras quietly documenting this bizarre mating ritual. "I'll order some starters for us."

She proceeded to order what appeared to be one of everything she thought sounded sophisticated, including something called "deconstructed Caesar salad" that turned out to be a whole head of romaine lettuce with a raw egg on top.

Meanwhile, I was trying to pay attention to Puck, who was telling me about his work as a yoga instructor, but my eyes kept drifting to Artie as she attempted to pull out Rob's chair for him while he was already halfway to sitting, causing him to have to stand back up awkwardly.

"So you live with Artemis?" Puck asked, following my gaze.

"Yeah, she's..." I watched Artie try to pour wine for Rob but overfill his glass so it nearly overflowed. "She's perfect. I mean, it's perfect. The living situation. Very... situated."

Puck studied me with surprising intensity for someone who looked like a real-life fairy. "Oh honey," he said softly. "You've got it bad."

"What? No, we're just—"

"Roommates who stare at each other with cartoon heart eyes? Sure." He patted my hand sympathetically. "How long have you been in love with her?"

I choked on my water.

Across the table, Artie was announcing, "I love escargot. They're almost my favorite food."

Rob brightened. "Interesting. I've never actually had them. This should be an adventure."

"I'm basically a snail-eating expert," Artie said with confidence that absolutely did not match the panic in her eyes as the server placed a dozen brown swirly snails in some kind of butter sauce in the center of the table.

I watched in slow-motion horror as Artie picked up a pair of tong-looking instruments, clearly having no idea what to do with it. Rob was saying something about loosening it from the shell first, but Artie had already shoved a tiny fork into the shell.

In the perfect Julia Roberts *Pretty Woman* moment, the

snail shot out of the shell like a slimy missile, arced grace-fully through the air, and landed with a wet splat directly on Rob's shirt.

"Ten points for perfect aim," Rob laughed, reaching for his napkin.

"Oh god, I'm so sorry." Artie lunged forward with her own napkin, knocking over Rob's overfilled wine glass in the process.

Red wine cascaded across the table. Rob jumped back, shoving his chair directly into a passing server.

The tray went flying and a chocolate soufflé landed directly on a woman at the next table who looked like she'd stepped out of *Real Housewives of Beverly Hills*. Her scream could have shattered crystal.

"Ooh, look," someone nearby held up their phone. "Is that Gryff Kingman, football player, or wait, is it Flynn? I can't tell the difference between them."

More phones appeared. The manager looked like he might faint. The Real Housewife was now shrieking about her Hermès bag. Rob was covered in wine and oyster juice. Puck was wide-eyed and frozen like a telephone pole about to be plowed down. Artie looked like she wanted the earth to open up and swallow her.

"I have to go to the bathroom," Artie gasped and fled.

I stood there for a second, then announced, "I should... check on her," and followed, leaving Rob and Puck to deal with the manager and the still-shrieking bag owner. I looked at Sloane whose face had gone full shocked Pikachu as she stared, her crew now filming the people filming us. "You stay here."

I followed Artie into the unisex bathroom, and found her with her back against the wall, eyes closed.

"Hey," I said softly.

She opened one eye. "Did I actually just assault my date with shellfish and cause a comedy of errors?"

"Technically, it was the snail that did the assaulting. Is a snail even a fish? They live on land."

"They are a mollusk." Artie says sadly.

I wrapped her in a hug and kissed the top of her head. "He laughed. It was funny. No one will even remember a year… or twenty from now."

"Gryff, I'm acting like I was raised by caffeinated wolves." She muttered against my chest.

"You're not—"

"I tried to pour his wine and nearly flooded the table. I ordered a salad that was just… lettuce and sadness."

"The egg was also sad," I offered.

She let out a laugh that was half sob. "This is a disaster. He's so nice and confident and completely unfazed by me being a giant next to him, and I'm ruining everything."

"You're perfect." I swallowed hard. "I mean, you're doing perfect. You're fine. You're doing perfectly fine."

"Puck seems nice," she said weakly.

"All I can think every time I look at him is that he's like a cute little meerkat. This is insane. We're both terrible at this."

"The worst," she agreed, looking up at me.

My eyes dropped to her lips. I leaned in slightly...

Someone banged on the bathroom door from inside. "Other people need to pee. Stop having your crisis in the bathroom."

"We should..." Artie gestured vaguely toward the dining room.

"Yeah."

We walked back to find Rob and Puck deep in conversation, completely oblivious to our return. Rob was showing Puck something on his phone, both of them leaning in close.

"You've done base jumping in New Zealand?" Rob was enthralled with Puck.

"Six times. Have you done the Nevis Bungy?"

"Next month, I'm going for my birthday."

"Oh my god, I'll be there next month for a yoga retreat. We should totally jump together."

Rob suddenly noticed we were back. "Oh. Hey... so this is awkward but..."

Puck bounced in his seat. "Could we maybe switch? Rob's literally my dream man. He teaches aerial stunts."

"And he does aerial yoga," Rob added. "We're already planning to go skydiving tomorrow."

"We could do a tandem jump," Puck suggested, batting his eyes at him.

"Or side by side. I have my own rig."

"That's so hot," Puck sighed.

Artie and I looked at each other, then said in perfect unison, "Check, please."

Twenty minutes later, after I paid the check, we were walking to our cars. Rob and Puck were a few feet behind us, making actual concrete plans to throw themselves out of a perfectly good airplane together.

"Did our dates just... date each other?" Artie asked.

"I think we're so bad at this, we created a rom-com for other people."

"You're right. I think I saw this in an old movie once."

Rob and Puck exchanged knowing looks, then gave us a wave and climbed into Rob's Jeep together, already discussing which skydiving location had the best views. Sloane and her camera crew headed out as well after deeming the evening 'a thing that definitely happened' and she muttered something under her breath about saving what she could.

Artie and I stood in the parking lot, alone finally, the weight of the evening's disaster settling over us.

"You know what?" Artie said suddenly. "Flynn and Tempest are expecting a full report. We might as well go commiserate with people who actually like us."

"Strawberry margaritas?"

"And that non-dairy ice cream Tempest hides from Flynn."

"He knows about it. He just pretends he doesn't because he thinks it's cute that she thinks she's being sneaky."

"Of course he does." Artie shook her head. "Those two are disgustingly perfect for each other."

Ten minutes later, we were walking up to Flynn and Tempest's front door. They lived directly across the street from us—Chris's real estate empire at work—in an almost identical house except for Tempest's collection of potted plants that had taken over the front porch.

Flynn opened the door before we could knock, already grinning. "How bad was it?"

"Our dates are currently planning to jump out of a plane together," I said.

"Wait, what?" Tempest appeared behind Flynn, wearing pajama pants covered in tiny donkeys.

"Come in," Flynn said, stepping aside. "This sounds like a multiple margarita story."

Their living room was cozy chaos with manuscripts scattered on the coffee table, Flynn's playbook balanced on the arm of the couch, and Burrito Petito's toys everywhere. The donkey himself was currently asleep in his custom bed in the corner, occasionally twitching his ears.

"Okay," Tempest said, already pulling out the blender. "Tell us everything while I make drinks."

"They're soulmates," Artie said. "Adrenaline-junkie soulmates who are probably going to have beautiful, death-defying babies."

"So you successfully set each other up," Flynn said slowly, "just not with yourselves."

"We're so bad at dating, we're contagious," Artie moaned, flopping back on their couch.

We spent the next hour rehashing every mortifying detail of the evening, with Flynn and Tempest alternating between sympathy and laughter. By the time we'd finished the pitcher of margaritas and demolished a pint of Tempest's "secret" cashew milk ice cream, my face hurt from laughing.

"You know what the worst part is?" Artie said, now lying with her feet in my lap while I absently rubbed her ankle. "Rob was actually perfect. Like, objectively perfect. Confident, funny, didn't care that I'm bigger than him, loves animals..."

"Teaches children's martial arts," I added glumly.

"Fosters senior cats," she continued.

"Called you beautiful within ten seconds of meeting you."

"And I ruined it with shellfish violence."

"Assault with a deadly mollusk."

"You didn't ruin anything," Tempest said gently. "You just weren't compatible. There's a difference."

"I don't know," Artie said, sitting up slightly. "I think there's something fundamentally wrong with how I interact with men. I turn into this weird, awkward, catastrophe person."

"You're not a catastrophe," I said. "You're just... enthusiastic."

"I tried to pour his wine and created a flood, Gryff. That's not enthusiasm, that's a natural disaster."

"Maybe," Flynn said, looking directly at me with twin telepathy activated, "you just need practice being comfortable with someone you actually trust."

Artie was quiet for a moment, then looked at me. "That's actually not a bad idea."

My stomach dropped. I was in so much trouble.

TRUST IN ME

ARTEMIS

Tempest, ever the romance author looking for story fodder, leaned forward with that expression she got when she was analyzing relationship dynamics for her next book. "That gives me an idea."

"Uh-oh. I think I know where this is heading."

Gryff's words hung in the air while I tried to figure out what exactly he thought he knew, because I had no idea where anything was heading. My dating life was a disaster, I'd just weaponized seafood against a perfectly nice man, and I was three strawberry margaritas deep into what was shaping up to be an existential crisis about my inability to function like a normal human around men.

"Where what's heading?" I asked, looking up at him from my spot on Flynn and Tempest's couch.

"Nothing," he said quickly, but Flynn made a choking sound that suggested otherwise.

Tempest gave them both a death stare and then turned back to me with the softest, sweetest smile on her face. "Artie, can I ask you something?"

"Sure?" She was basically the relationship expert since she wrote about happy ever afters every day.

"What exactly makes you so uncomfortable with people you're dating?" The question didn't come out as judgy or accusatory or anything. She was sincere and clearly wanted to help me.

I took another sip of my margarita, considering. "I don't know. I just... freeze up. Or worse, I turn into this awkward person who's nothing like me."

"Is it anyone you date or specific to men or women?"

"Anyone I'm dating. Or trying to date. Or thinking about maybe dating." I groaned and flopped back against the cushions. "Basically any human being who might potentially see me naked."

"Interesting," Tempest said in that way that meant she was filing information away. "What kind of person do you feel most comfortable with?"

"Well, with... Gryff, but that's different—"

Tempest and Flynn exchanged a look that I figured was another assumption about our friendship being more, but they knew better, so that must just be the strawberry margaritas talking.

"Why is it different?" Tempest asked innocently.

"Because he's my best friend. There's no pressure. I don't have to perform or be something I'm not." I gestured vaguely at Gryff, who seemed to be having some kind of silent twin telepathy conversation with his brother. Sometimes I wondered if they really could talk in each other's heads. "He's seen me at my absolute worst and he's still here."

"So you trust him," Tempest said.

"Completely."

"You know," she said, settling back in her chair with the air of someone about to dispense wisdom, "in my books, when characters have intimacy issues, I have them, let's say, practice. With someone safe."

I sat up slightly. "Like therapy?"

"Not quite, more like... trust exercises. Getting experience doing the thing they think they can't do, but with someone who won't judge them. Someone they're completely comfortable with."

Flynn started coughing violently. Tempest passed him his water without looking at him.

"Trust exercises," I repeated, the margaritas making the idea seem less insane than it probably was. "That's... actually not a terrible idea."

"Terrible," Flynn wheezed.

"No, it's brilliant," Tempest corrected, shooting him a look. "Think about it. You need to learn to be comfortable with male attention without the pressure of it being a real date. What better way than practicing with someone you trust?"

I looked at Gryff, who had gone very still. "But who would—" The answer was obvious. "Oh."

"It doesn't have to be weird," Tempest continued, her voice taking on that encouraging tone she used when she was trying to convince someone of something. "Simple things. Eye contact exercises. Learning to be present in your body. Practicing asking for what you need. The key," she added, "is picking someone you completely trust.

Completely. Someone you know won't cross boundaries or make things complicated."

One of the boys made another strangled sound.

I turned to Gryff, suddenly nervous. "Wait, but only if... I mean, we're good, right? Like, you don't see me... that way?"

His face did something complicated before settling into what looked like resignation. "What way?"

"You know. Romantically. Sexually." I waved my hand between us. "We've been friends for six years and nothing's ever been weird between us."

"Right," he said, his voice sounding strange. "Never. Nothing weird."

"And I mean, we're both bi, so if something was going to happen, it would have by now, right?" I laughed, but it came out more nervous than I intended. "Not that we've ever been single at the same time before but neither of us has ever made a move or admitted feelings or anything crazy like that."

Flynn looked like he was about to spontaneously combust. Gryff seemed to be having trouble breathing. What in the world were they saying to each other in their twin brains? Weirdos.

"Exactly," Tempest said smoothly. "Which is why this could work. No complications, no mixed signals, just two friends helping each other get better at relationships."

"You want to help me get better at relationships?" I asked Gryff.

He closed his eyes for a moment, then opened them and looked directly at me. "Whatever you need."

"Really? You'd do that for me?"

"Of course."

"And it won't be weird? You promise? Because I can't lose you as a friend, Gryff. You're too important to me."

Something flickered across his face, but he managed a smile. "It won't be weird. We're helping each other, right? I could use some practice asking for what I want in a relationship too. You know that."

"I certainly know it," Flynn said with a raise of his hand.

"Trust exercises," Tempest said brightly. "Start small. Eye contact or staring into each other's eyes. Hand holding and cuddling. Learning to communicate what you need. Building up from there gradually. Communicating what you feel."

"We could try it," I said, the idea taking shape in my margarita-soft brain. "Just practice. Safe practice with my safe person."

"I'm your safe person?" Gryff asked quietly.

"The safest," I confirmed, reaching over to squeeze his hand. "I trust you more than anyone."

Flynn stood up abruptly. "I need more ice. For the... drinks. That we're drinking." He practically fled to the kitchen.

Tempest watched him go with amusement. "He's being weird tonight."

"When isn't he weird?" Gryff said, but his eyes were still on where my hand touched his.

"So we're really doing this?" I was asking but just wanted to really make sure he wasn't just people pleasing at the moment. I just had to make sure.

"Yes," he said, the word came out slightly strangled,

and I realized he was nervous. And it was sweet. He wanted to do a good job, for me.

"Thank you." The tension that had been in my shoulders, my spine, and my core all night finally released and I relaxed back into my chair. "I know it's a lot to ask, but I really need help. And you're the only person I trust enough to be this vulnerable with."

Tempest smiled in a way that seemed oddly satisfied. "I think this is going to be exactly what you both need."

Twenty minutes later, Gryff and I were making the short walk across the street to our house. The night air was warm and slightly humid, and I was just tipsy enough that everything felt soft around the edges.

"Thank you again," I said, probably for the fifth time. "I know it's weird to ask your best friend to teach you how to be comfortable with sex, but—"

"It's not weird," Gryff said quickly. "We're helping each other."

"Right. Helping each other." I stumbled slightly on a crack in the sidewalk, and he automatically steadied me with a hand on my lower back. The touch was warm and comforting and exactly the kind of thing I needed to learn to accept from men I was dating.

"See?" I said. "You do stuff like that without even thinking about it. That's what I need to learn to be okay with."

"Stuff like what?"

"Taking care of me. Little touches. Being... gentle." We reached our front door, and I fumbled with my keys. "Most guys I've dated weren't gentle or didn't want me to be."

Gryff took the keys from me and unlocked the door in one smooth motion. Another caretaking gesture I didn't even think he was aware of.

Inside I immediately collapsed on the couch, grabbing my favorite throw pillow, one with a baby goat wearing a flower crown that I'd bought our first week here. Gryff disappeared into the kitchen and returned with two glasses of water, handing me one before sitting on the opposite end of the couch.

"Drink," he said.

"See? You're doing it again."

"Doing what?"

"Taking care of me without me having to ask." I pulled my legs up under me, getting comfortable. The margaritas were making me more honest than usual. "That's what I need to learn to accept. Or ask for. Or... something."

"You have trouble asking for what you need? I don't think so. Maybe when we were in high school, but..."

I laughed, but it came out bitter. "But the entire rest of my life. Just not with you."

"But why? You can have anything or anyone you want, babe."

Maybe it was the alcohol, or maybe it was the safety of being here with Gryff in our house, but suddenly I wanted to tell him everything.

"I've been thinking about it, and I have an idea," I said. "I don't blame my parents, and I wouldn't change a thing about the way I grew up, except for maybe the way my dad got hurt."

I really didn't blame them. It was just the way life worked out. But that also didn't mean it didn't shape the way I thought about myself and the world around me. "But thirteen different cities, eight different schools, a whole new life every year is part of it. Every time I'd finally settle in, make friends, find a favorite spot to read or a teacher I connected with, Dad would get a better deal at another team, and off we'd go again."

Gryff shifted closer on the couch, not saying anything, just listening.

"I learned pretty quick that it didn't matter what I wanted in this situation because it wasn't just about me. It was what was best for the family." Although, in the end, it was what my mother blamed for the breakup.

"It didn't matter if I begged to stay, or promised to be perfect, or cried until I made myself sick. We were moving regardless." I picked at a thread on the throw pillow. "So I stopped asking. Stopped wanting things to stay the same. Stopped expecting my needs to matter."

"Artie..."

"And I guess that carried over into... other things." I took a deep breath. This was the hard part. The part I'd never told anyone. "Things I... feel some shame and embarrassment about."

"You can tell me anything, but you don't have to. Just, you know, I will always be your safe person, just like you said."

I sighed. "I'm... not good at, well, anything in the bedroom. Guys have told me I'm bad. In bed."

The silence stretched between us. I couldn't look at him.

"Who told you that?" His voice was surprisingly angry.

I forced myself to continue. "The people I've slept

with. They all wanted me to be the dominant one. In charge. I think it's because I'm tall and strong and athletic, so obviously I must want to throw them around and take control, right?"

"I get it, babe. Guys I've been with have always expected me to be the dominant one as well. It's just automatically assumed that I am going to be the one topping, I never get a chance to try anything else." He gave a little shrug that I instantly understood. "But that's not always what I want."

"That's totally not what I want." The words came out in a rush. "In the rest of my life, I have to be the strong, independent woman. But that's exhausting, honestly. Sometimes I want to be taken care of. I want someone to be gentle with me. I want to be able to be soft and vulnerable and have someone notice what I need without me having to be in charge of everything."

I finally looked at him. He was staring at me with an expression I couldn't read.

"That's what I need to learn," I said quietly. "How to be present in my body when I'm with someone. How to trust someone to take care of me. How to ask for what I want without feeling selfish or needy or... embarrassed about it."

"You're not selfish for wanting that."

"Aren't I though? I've been told by three different guys and two women that I'm basically a dead fish in bed. And honestly, it's made me question my own sexuality. But... like, guys are hot, women are hot, it's not like it's a choice I made to be bi. I just... am."

"They were wrong." His voice was firm, almost angry. "They were completely wrong."

"Were they? Because the evidence suggests otherwise."

He moved closer, close enough that I could feel the warmth radiating from him. "Artie, wanting to be taken care of doesn't make you bad at intimacy. It makes you human. And it sounds like some of the people you were with just fetishized you."

"But I don't know how to communicate any of that. I open my mouth to say anything and freeze up. I don't know how to be vulnerable like that with someone I'm dating." I met his eyes. "That's why I need your help. You already take care of me without me having to ask. You got me water. You steadied me when I stumbled. You unlocked the door. You do these things naturally."

"Because I—" He stopped abruptly.

"Because you're my best friend," I finished for him. "Which is why you're perfect for this. You already know how to take care of me. And you have no idea how much I appreciate that. But I have to learn how to ask for it. How to be present for it instead of freezing up or performing what I think someone wants. Just like rugby, I need to practice the skills until they feel natural."

He was quiet for a long moment. When he finally spoke, his voice was rough. "What exactly do you want me to do?"

"I don't know. Start small, like Tempest said? Eye contact. Hand holding. Maybe work up to... other things. Kissing. Touching." I felt my face heat. "Just so I can practice being present and asking for what I need without the pressure of it being a real romantic situation."

"Right. Practice."

"We could start with something small," I said suddenly, sitting up. "To see if we can even do this."

"Now?" His voice cracked slightly.

"Tempest said to start with eye contact, right? That's pretty basic. We look at each other all the time."

"We do?"

"Well, yeah. But she probably meant... sustained eye contact. Intentional." I shifted to face him properly, tucking one leg under me. "Let's try it."

"Artie, you're tipsy—"

"I'm relaxed. There's a difference." I reached out and took both his hands in mine. "Please? Just for, like, thirty seconds. If it's too weird, we stop and never speak of it again."

He stared at our joined hands for a moment, then looked up at me. "Okay."

"Okay." I took a breath. "So we just... look at each other. Really look. No talking, no looking away."

"For thirty seconds."

I popped up the stopwatch timer on my phone. "Starting... now."

Our eyes met, and immediately I understood why Tempest had suggested this. Looking at Gryff, really looking at him, was different from the casual eye contact of everyday conversation. His eyes were blue but with flecks of green I'd never noticed before, darkening to almost forest green around the edges.

Ten seconds in, and my heart was beating faster. There was something intense about being seen like this, about seeing him. Without words to fill the space, without the ability to look away, it felt like he could see straight through all my defenses.

Fifteen seconds. His pupils had dilated, making his eyes look darker. His thumbs were brushing over my knuckles, probably unconsciously. I could feel the warmth of his hands, slightly rough from football, but gentle in how they held mine.

Twenty seconds. The air between us felt charged, like the moment before lightning strikes. I was hyperaware of everything, the sound of our breathing, the way his chest rose and fell, the fact that we'd moved closer without meaning to.

Twenty-five seconds. His gaze dropped to my lips for just a fraction of a second before returning to my eyes. My breath caught. The room felt too warm. This was supposed to be practice, but it felt like—

Thirty seconds and the chimes played on my phone.

Neither of us looked away.

We sat there, frozen, still holding hands, still maintaining that intense eye contact. The space between us had shrunk to almost nothing. I could feel his breath on my face. When had we gotten so close?

"Artie," he said, his voice rough.

"Yeah?"

"The thirty seconds are up."

"Oh." But I didn't move back. Neither did he. "That was…"

"Intense."

"Very intense." My voice came out breathier than intended. "Is it supposed to feel like that?"

"I don't know." His eyes dropped to my lips again, lingered this time. "How did it feel?"

"Like..." I struggled to find words. "Like being plugged into an electrical socket. But in a good way?"

He laughed softly, and I felt it more than heard it. "I was going to say something about lightning."

"My heart's racing." Without thinking, I took one of his hands and placed it over my heart. "See?"

His hand was warm through the thin fabric of my shirt, and his expression shifted to something I couldn't read. "Mine too," he said quietly.

"Really?" I moved my free hand to his chest, feeling the rapid thump of his heartbeat under my palm. "Oh."

We stayed like that, hands on each other's hearts, eyes locked, and I suddenly understood why people wrote poetry about moments like this. The air between us was alive with possibility, with something unnamed but undeniable.

He leaned in slightly, maybe unconsciously, and I found myself mirroring the movement. His eyes were so dark, bottomless, this close, and his lips were right there, and all I had to do was...

The chimes on my phone got louder, crescendoing.

"That was—" I started.

"Good practice," he said quickly, but his voice was still rough. "Really good... practice."

"Right. Practice." I tucked my hair behind my ear, trying to calm my racing heart. "I think this is going to work."

"Yeah." He cleared his throat. "It's going to work."

I shifted on the couch, not sure whether to move

closer or farther away. The moment had passed, but the tension was still there, humming under my skin like an itch I couldn't scratch.

We sat there in awkward silence for a moment, not moving, waiting for the other to do the next thing.

"Gryff?"

"Yeah?"

"I'm really glad you're my best friend."

He wrapped an arm around me and tucked my head against his shoulder in the soft, comforting snuggle I needed. "Me too."

I couldn't stop thinking about the way he'd looked at me, the way his heartbeat had raced under my hand, the way we'd almost...

No. It was just the intensity of the exercise. The vulnerability of the moment. The margaritas.

It didn't mean anything. It couldn't. Because I needed my best friend to be exactly that. Lovers would come and go, but Gryff... he was home in a way I never thought was possible.

I must have fallen asleep in his arms on the couch, because I woke up there with a blanket over me. I felt surprisingly good for someone who'd spent the evening drinking margaritas and making questionable life decisions.

Actually, I felt great. No headache, no nausea, no regret-induced stomach churning that usually accompanied my morning-after experiences. I lay there for a moment, trying to figure out why I felt so clear-headed when I distinctly remembered at least three drinks.

Then it hit me.

Flynn didn't drink. And both twins were in the middle of serious preparation for their rookie seasons. There was no way Tempest would have served us actual alcohol when her fiancé was maintaining strict training discipline.

Those margaritas had been mocktails.

Which meant I hadn't been tipsy at all last night.

ACCIDENTALLY IN LOVE

GRYFF

The morning sun streaming through our kitchen windows was perfect, golden and warm, the kind of light that made everything look like a movie. Artie was sitting at the island in that one Dragons t-shirts of mine that she'd stolen and soft pajama pants, her hair in a messy bun, completely unaware of how the light was making her glow like some kind of breakfast angel.

"Hey." She smiled at me and handed over a cup of coffee. "How do you feel this morning?"

About being this close to kissing her last night?

She popped the top off the fancy honeycomb creamer I liked and poured just the right amount into my cup. "I don't have even the slightest hangover. Do you?"

Oh, right. She meant after all those strawberry margaritas we'd had. "Nope. I think Tempest accidentally on purpose forgot to add the tequila."

"So... that means everything I told you, everything we, well, we were a hundred percent sober." She set her head down, forehead to the marble. "It wasn't the tequila talking, just me admitting all the things wrong with my sex life."

She'd had the guts to admit that out loud, why couldn't I say what was in my heart?

Because what if it fucked up everything? I really fucking needed to figure out a plan. What worried me was what if that plan had to be how to live my life without her in it when I told her exactly how I felt and she didn't feel the same.

I already knew she didn't. She'd said as much last night.

"Artie, babe," I stroked her hair. "I don't regret anything we talked about or did last night. You shouldn't ever be embarrassed to tell me anything."

She kept her head down and shook it. "Why are you so good to me?"

"You're my girl." That was a movie quote, and I'd been trying to lighten the mood a little, but it came out totally sincere. Probably because it was.

She finally sat back up, smiling. "Just like peas and carrots."

I held up my mug to cheers, and she clinked her coffee to mine. After a few minutes she peered over the top of the mug at me. "Should we, do you want to, you know, maybe, try the eye contact thing again?"

My heart did that stupid stuttering thing it had been doing ever since last night.

"Sure," I said, setting down my mug. "Practice makes perfect, right?"

"Exactly." She shifted on her stool to face me properly.

"Maybe it won't feel so intense this time? That's the point, right?"

Right. Friends aren't supposed to want to lean in and kiss their friends. Because that's what we were. Friends who stared into each other's eyes and practiced intimacy and definitely didn't almost kiss every single time.

"Ready?" she asked.

"Ready."

Our eyes met, and immediately I knew this was going to be worse than yesterday. The morning light was turning her blue eyes almost silver, and she'd been biting her lip while reading something on her phone, so it was slightly swollen and pink and...

One breath in and her breathing had already changed. I could see her pulse jumping in her throat. Her hands were wrapped around her coffee mug, knuckles white from gripping it too hard.

A few seconds more and she leaned in slightly, probably unconsciously. I found myself matching the movement, drawn to her like gravity was personally invested in my torture.

Time slowed, and we might have been there for ten seconds or ten minutes or ten hours or ten years.

Her lips parted slightly. Her eyes darkened. The kitchen island between us felt like both a blessing and a curse, keeping us apart but not far enough to break this magnetic pull.

"Gryff," she whispered, and the way she said my name made every nerve in my body light up.

Neither of us looked away. Again.

We sat there, frozen, breathing the same air, the

moment stretching between us like taffy. I was about to do something monumentally stupid, like confess everything or kiss her senseless, when my phone buzzed on the counter feeling like a goddamned earthquake.

We jumped apart so fast Artie nearly fell off her stool.

"Nana" flashed on my screen with a photo of her holding a foam finger at one of my college games.

"Hey, Nana," I answered, trying not to sound like I'd just been eye-fucking my roommate.

"We just landed, sweetheart. On our way to the luggage claim. Ready for pickup whenever you can get here."

My brain short-circuited. "You're... at LAX? Now?"

"Yes, dear. For your big game on Sunday. Remember?" I completely forgot my own grandparents were headed into town for a few weeks to visit at my father's request.

He wanted to come himself but he was recovering from knee surgery brought on after years of the wear and tear of being an athlete. He had tried to make an escape and come anyway on the family jet but my Aunt Kik was now playing warden and making him stick to his rehab routine.

"Fuck." I pulled the phone away from my ear. "Sorry, Nana. I mean... shoot. I just didn't realize what day it was. Sorry."

Artie was already laughing, her hand over her mouth. "You forgot your grandparents were coming?"

"We'll get a car if you're busy—" Nana started.

"No, no, I'm coming. Forty-five minutes-ish. Don't move."

I hung up and looked at Artie, who was now fully cackling.

"You forgot your grandparents."

"I've been distracted." I gestured vaguely between us.

"Oh my god, they're staying here. In our guest room, aren't they?" Her eyes went wide. "The guest room that currently has my rugby gear all over it."

"Shit."

We both bolted from the kitchen.

The drive to LAX gave me too much time to think. Specifically, about yesterday's conversation with Artie where she'd made it crystal clear that she didn't see me romantically. Six years of friendship without anything happening was her proof that we weren't meant to be anything more.

But these exercises... they were my chance. If I couldn't tell her how I felt, and I couldn't, not without risking everything, maybe I could show her. Every practice moment was an opportunity to demonstrate how good we could be together. How natural. How right.

She just needed to see it.

By the time I got to arrivals, I had a plan. The new play, Show Artie We're Perfect Together, was officially in motion.

Nana and Coach were waiting at pickup, looking exactly the same as always. Nana in one of her signature tracksuits that she claimed was athletic wear despite not playing competitively or coaching in a thousand years, and Coach in his uniform of a plaid flannel shirt with jeans and suspenders.

Nana squeezed me tight, then pulled back to study my face. "You look good. Happy. California agrees with you."

"It's been good," I admitted.

"And how's Artemis? Still putting up with you?"

"She's great. She's at the house, setting up your room." I grabbed their bags. "Fair warning, she might have stress-cleaned everything. She was worried about making a good impression."

"That sweet girl," Nana said, exchanging a look with Coach that I couldn't quite read. "As if we haven't already adopted her."

The drive home was filled with updates about family, Isak's new quarterback position this semester at Denver State, Jules's adjustment to UCLA, Everett and Penelope's wedding we got the save the date for in the mail.

When we got home, Artie had indeed stress-cleaned. The house looked like a magazine spread, she'd put fresh flowers in the guest room, and she was wearing actual clothes instead of my stolen t-shirts, jeans and a soft v-neck t-shirt that made her look touchable in the most dangerous way.

"Nana, Coach." She hugged them both like they were her own grandparents. "I'm so glad you're here. How was the flight?"

And just like that, she was in full hostess mode, getting them drinks, asking about their plans, showing them where everything was in the guest room. I watched her move through our house—our house—like she belonged there, because she did. She knew where we kept the extra towels, which coffee mugs were for guests, how to work the complicated TV remote that had taken me three weeks to figure out.

"Look at you two," Nana said, settling into our couch with her iced tea. "So domestic."

"Turns out we're really good roommates," Artie said quickly.

"Mmm-hmm." Nana's tone was perfectly neutral, but I'd heard that particular "mmm-hmm" my whole life. It meant she saw everything and would be commenting on it later. "And Artie, Flynn tells us you're working for one of those sports companies?"

"PerformanceFirst," Artie nodded, settling next to me on the loveseat without thinking about it. Our thighs touched. I tried not to react. "I work in their accounting department, helping with payroll and stuff. It's only three days a week, so I can keep up with rugby training."

"That's wonderful," Coach said. "Using that accounting degree. Your mother must be proud."

"She is." Artie's smile was genuine. "It's actually perfect. I get to use my business skills while staying connected to sports."

"Smart girl," Nana said, then looked at me. "You could learn something about planning ahead."

"I have a plan," I protested. "Play football. Win the Big Bowl. Retire."

"That's not a plan, that's a wish list," Coach said, but he was smiling.

That evening, we headed to Flynn and Tempest's for dinner. AbuelaNovela and AbueLeo had arrived that afternoon, and Tempest warned us she was "in full dramatic mode."

We weren't prepared.

AbuelaNovela took one look at Artie and me walking in together, not even touching, just walking side by side, and pressed her hand to her heart with a gasp that would've won her an Emmy.

"¡Ay, el amor no correspondido! ¡El anhelo! ¡La tragedia!"

Tempest quickly intervened. "She says she's so happy to see everyone."

But I knew enough from Flynn's smirk that's not what she said.

"Abuela, please," Tempest hissed.

AbuelaNovela waved her off and grabbed Artie's hands. "You are so beautiful, mija. Such power and grace. You could carry a man to safety."

"Um, thank you?" Artie looked delighted and confused.

"O llevar su corazón roto," AbuelaNovela added, looking directly at me.

"She's just trying to say you're very athletic," Tempest translated with forced brightness.

Dinner was organized chaos. Grandma and Grandpa De Le Reine drove over from their vacation house and we had three sets of grandparents sharing stories, comparing photos on phones, arguing about whether Denver or LA had better weather. Artie and I fell into our natural rhythm. She knew I hated brussels sprouts so she took them off my plate, I passed her the hot sauce before she asked for it, we shared the garlic bread without discussing it.

"You two have such wonderful chemistry," Abuela-

Novela announced. "Like dancers who know each other's every move."

"We've been friends for a long time," Artie explained, completely missing the implication.

"Friends." AbuelaNovela said it like she was tasting something bitter. "What a waste of passion."

"Abuela," Tempest looked mortified.

"What? I'm old. I can say what I want."

Flynn was trying so hard not to laugh he was turning red. Nana and Coach were watching everything with interest. And Artie? Artie was helping herself to more enchiladas.

A couple days later, we took the grandparents to Santa Monica Pier. It was touristy and cheesy and exactly what they wanted, street performers, overpriced snacks, the works.

Nana and Coach walked ahead, stopping to watch a guy juggling flaming batons. Artie and I hung back, and I saw my opportunity.

"Hey," I said, taking her hand. "Perfect practice opportunity."

She looked down at our joined hands, then up at me. "Here? But your grandparents—"

"Won't even notice. Look, they're completely absorbed in that mime." I interlaced our fingers properly, the way couples did. "Hand holding in public. Very couple-like. This is exactly the kind of practice you need."

"Right. Practice." But her cheeks were pink, and she didn't pull away.

We walked the pier like that, hand in hand. I rubbed my thumb over her knuckles the way I'd wanted to for months. When we passed a cotton candy vendor, I bought her one without asking—pink, because I knew she liked strawberry everything. At the ring toss, I won her a stuffed goat that made her laugh so hard she snorted.

"You're really good at this," she said, squeezing my hand.

"At ring toss?"

"At the boyfriend stuff. The hand holding, the cotton candy, winning me prizes. Some girl is going to be really lucky."

The words were a knife between my ribs, but I kept smiling. "Maybe I'm just good with you."

She laughed like I'd made a joke. "Well, yeah. You know me better than anyone."

I caught Nana glancing back at us, saw her note our joined hands, the way Artie was pressed against my side. She didn't say anything, just smiled and turned back to watch Coach argue with the mime about proper juggling technique.

Thursday evening was Artie's rugby scrimmage. She'd mentioned it casually at breakfast, but Nana had immediately demanded to come watch.

"Your grandparents want to come watch? Really?" Artie seemed genuinely delighted.

"They've adopted you," I said. "Resistance is futile."

At the facility, I barely had time to warn Artie before my grandparents became THOSE grandparents.

The second Artie made her first tackle, Coach was on his feet like a human megaphone. "THAT'S OUR ARTIE! SHOW THEM HOW IT'S DONE!"

"GET HER!" Nana bellowed when Artie was running with the ball. "RUN THROUGH THEM!"

Other spectators were turning to stare. Some of the other players' families looked genuinely alarmed by the two seventy-something-year-olds screaming like they were at WrestleMania.

Artie scored a try, and both my grandparents lost their minds.

"THAT'S HOW YOU DO IT!" Coach roared. "DID YOU SEE THAT FOOTWORK?"

"NOBODY CAN STOP OUR GIRL!" Nana added.

Artie was laughing so hard she could barely run back to position. Her face was red, but she was glowing. After a particularly brutal tackle that sent her opponent flying, she immediately looked to the sideline.

I gave her a huge grin and double thumbs up, my chest tight with pride. God, I loved watching her play. She was magnificent, powerful and graceful and completely in her element.

But what got me most was the way she kept looking for my grandparents' reaction, the way she lit up when they cheered for her. Like she'd been waiting her whole life for grandparents who'd embarrass her with their enthusiasm.

"She's something special," Coach said, sitting down next to me during a break.

"Yeah, she is."

"The way you look at her, sweetheart..." Nana said softly.

"We're practicing. Trust exercises. For her dating confidence."

Nana's expression said she wasn't buying a word of it, but she just patted my knee and went back to screaming encouragement when play resumed.

That night, after my grandparents had gone to bed, Artie and I were cleaning up the kitchen.

"Your grandparents are wonderful," she said, drying dishes while I washed. "I can't believe how loud they were at the scrimmage."

"They love you." The words slipped out before I could stop them. I almost added "I love you too," but caught myself just in time.

"I love them too. I never had grandparents like that. Mine were all very... proper. Quiet." She stretched, rolling her shoulders. "God, that scrimmage was rough though. I'm gonna have a huge bruise on my ass tomorrow."

"You were incredible out there."

She smiled at me, soft and pleased. "You always say that."

"Because it's always true."

There was a moment, standing in our kitchen, dishes half-done, her looking at me with something I couldn't quite read in her eyes. The air felt charged, like the moment before our eye contact exercises, but without the excuse of practice.

"Do you think we should move on to more, umm, intimate exercises? I didn't feel too off-kilter or awkward with anything this week. Although you surprised me with that hand holding thing." she said finally.

"Yeah," I agreed, dying inside that this was still just practice to her. "Whatever you need."

I watched her walk away, heading to bed, and once

again felt like I'd missed the perfect opportunity to tell her what was in my heart.

I went to bed too, but I couldn't sleep and went to the kitchen for water and found Nana sitting at the island with a cup of tea.

"Couldn't sleep either?" I asked.

"Old habits." She patted the stool next to her. "Sit with me."

I sat, and we were quiet for a moment before she spoke.

"That girl doesn't know you're in love with her."

"Nana—"

"I see how you're trying to show her. The hand holding, the cotton candy, the way you watch her play like she hung the moon." She sipped her tea. "But, sweetheart, sometimes you have to use words."

"She doesn't see me that way."

"Doesn't she? Or have you just not given her the chance?" She stood, pressing a kiss to my forehead. "Don't wait too long, Gryffen. The things we don't say have a way of becoming the things we regret."

She left me sitting in the dark kitchen, thinking about all the moments from this week. How natural it felt holding Artie's hand at the pier. How she'd looked for me after that tackle. How she fit perfectly in my life, my home, my family.

Tomorrow was our first preseason game. Artie would be there watching me play professionally for the first time. Maybe if she saw me in my element, doing what I was born to do, maybe she'd finally see ME.

Or maybe I'd just keep torturing myself with trust

exercises and stolen moments, pretending to teach her how to be with other men while dying to show her she should be with me.

I stood in my dark kitchen, in the house I shared with the woman I loved, with my grandparents asleep down the hall, and wondered how much longer I could keep this up.

The answer, I knew, was as long as she needed me to.

Even if it killed me.

BLACK & BLUE AND HARD ALL OVER

ARTEMIS

The bruise on my ass was the size of a dinner plate and roughly the color of a ripening eggplant.

I twisted around in front of the mirror in my bathroom, trying to get a better look at the damage from the scrimmage. The bruise extended from just below my butt cheek down to mid-thigh, a spectacular purple Rorschach that hurt like hell. But it had totally been worth it.

What I needed was a good long soak in a hot bath. What I had was a shower stall that definitely wasn't designed for therapeutic soaking.

But Gryff's master bathroom? That had a tub that could probably fit three people comfortably, with jets and everything.

He was at practice for another hour and his grandparents were off visiting Jules for the day. I had the perfect amount of time for an Epsom salt and bubble bath. He wouldn't mind.

Three minutes later, I was settled into the most luxurious bath of my life, my headphones in and music turned up loud enough to drown out any thoughts of tub theft. The hot water was already working magic on my sore muscles and bruises, and I was singing along to my favorite Kelsey Best playlist.

In the middle of belting out the poppiest of pop songs, I did a mermaid bathtub twirl and caught a glance at the bathroom door... open.

And Gryff, leaning against the door jamb with his arms folded, biceps bulging, watching me with a grin on his face.

I screeched and sank down into the tub so fast I nearly sloshed all the water and bubbles out. I needed those to cover my very naked, wet body.

Gryff only smiled wider. He was standing there wearing nothing but a white towel wrapped around his waist, clearly getting ready for his own shower. Rays of sunshine from the row of tiny windows across the top of the room highlighted his chest and shoulders, like angels were about to sing songs to his muscles. And for a second I completely forgot how to form words.

"I—" I yanked my headphones out, my ears burning hot. "You're supposed to be at practice."

"I was. Now I'm home." His eyes were doing this thing where I was sure he had x-ray vision and was trying to see right through the bubbles covering up my girlie bits. "Why are you in my bathroom?"

"Your tub has jets," I said weakly, gesturing at the fancy controls. "Mine's just a shower. I have this massive bruise and I thought maybe—"

"Is it bad?" His expression immediately shifted from

humorous come-hither to concern. "Are you okay? Do we need to get you to the doctor?"

Aww, I loved this caretaker, protective side of him. So adorable. "It's fine. I've definitely had worse." I shifted slightly, trying to show him the damage while keeping everything important underwater. "It's pretty spectacular, actually. Want to see?"

The moment the words left my mouth, I realized what I'd just offered. And apparently so did he, because his eyes went wide and something very interesting happened to the front of his towel. Something...massive.

Oh.

OH.

Was that...? Did he just...?

"I don't think that's—" he started, his voice rougher than usual. "I mean, I should probably—"

But he wasn't moving. He was just standing there, staring at me in his bathtub, and the terry cloth tent situation was becoming increasingly obvious.

"Gryff?" I said softly.

"Yeah?"

"You're, um." I gestured vaguely in the direction of his towel.

He glanced down, and he raised one eyebrow. Like he was silently giving his dick a stern talking to in his head. "Shit. Sorry. I should—" He backed toward the door, one hand clutching his towel. "I'll just give you some privacy to finish."

He paused in the doorway, and for a second something passed between us that felt charged with possibility. Then he cleared his throat and looked away.

"Take your time." He moved to leave, then turned back. "Is the bruise really that bad?"

"Want photographic evidence?"

His towel tent got... tentier. "I'll take your word for it."

The door closed behind him with a soft click, leaving me alone in the suddenly too quiet bathroom. I sank deeper into the water, my mind racing around like a teeny tiny speedboat.

That had definitely been an immediate physical reaction to seeing me naked in his bathtub. There was no way to misinterpret the tent physics.

Then there was the way he looked at me. The way his eyes had lingered before he remembered to look away. The way his voice had gone rough when he'd asked if I was hurt.

Holy shit.

All of that had nothing to do with friendship and everything to do with... nope, no. Not going there. Gryff and I were friends.

Just.

Friends.

And I was being ridiculous. He'd confirmed he didn't think of me like that. I never, ever would have asked him to help me with this whole dating and intimacy thing if there was even a chance he had feelings for me.

It was just biology. Men got erections from everything, morning wood, random boners during the day, a strong breeze. Seeing any naked woman would cause that reaction. It didn't mean anything specific about me.

After I'd escaped the bathroom and retreated to my room to process... whatever that was... I found a box on my bed. It was wrapped in tissue paper like something precious, with a little bow on top.

Inside was a jersey. Not just any jersey, a Bandits jersey with G. KINGMAN across the back and his number, 62, below it. There was a note in his handwriting:

Can't wait to see you wearing this in the stands. - G

Of course he'd get me a jersey. That's what friends did. Flynn probably got Tempest one too. Not that they were just friends. Whatever.

I pulled it on over my towel and looked at myself in the mirror. It was extra roomy on me, which I appreciated. It looked like it could actually fit Gryff, but somehow that made it better. Cozier. Like being wrapped in a Gryff hug.

Not that I was thinking about Gryff hugs. Or Gryff's towel situation. Or Gryff's abs with water droplets running down them.

Nope. Definitely not thinking about any of that.

The next morning, Gryff was up and out of the house before I was even awake, but the house became ground zero for the Kingman family convoy headed to the twins' first preseason game.

To make sure the boys felt well-loved, it took several cars to move four aunts, three sets of grandparents, two girlfriends, one sister, and partridge in a pear tree.

I wasn't the only one repping Gryff with my jersey, the whole group was pretty even with the twin love. But

AbuelaNovela had gone fancy, which was her natural state. Her sequined jersey with rhinestone number one featuring her own moniker caught the sun like a disco ball, temporarily blinding anyone who looked directly at it. "The one and only AbuelaNovela, darling."

Nobody was going to tell her the Bandits' quarterback Jalen Heals was also number one.

Jules wore her custom jersey that had both the twins' numbers across the back and the name FLYFF. "I called them that when I was little, Flynn plus Gryff equals Flyff. It stuck."

"Smart," AbueLeo said, then looked at my jersey. "And you wear Gryffen's number. Very supportive... friend."

"Exactly. Friend. That's what I am. His friend who lives with him and supports his career. Platonically."

Is verbal diarrhea a thing? Do they make pills for it?

Mac Jerry was handing out our tickets. Instead of being squirreled away in box seats we were going to be right in the thick of it with amazing fifty-yard line views. His wife, Sara Jayne, pulled me into a one-armed hug.

"Ah, my fellow tall girl who understands the struggle of shower heads and jeans shopping, you can sit next to me."

She was gorgeous, as tall as me, with the kind of confidence that came from being a supermodel who'd made it in an industry obsessed with size zeros.

"Oh my god, yes," I said, immediately bonding. "And don't get me started on people asking how the weather is up here and short men who want to go mountain climbing."

"Ooh, I see we need drinks and a whole evening to discuss that and how you are liking LA LA land."

Once we were in our seats, I found myself in between Sara Jayne and Tempest. While everyone else was distracted with food orders and getting settled, I took advantage of the moment to pick Tempest's brain.

"Can I ask you something about... a hypothetical situation?" I asked Tempest as quietly as possible. She was the only one who knew about these exercises Gryff and I were doing. Hopefully she'd help me figure out if his reaction in the bathroom had been a sign that I was totally wrong about, well, everything.

"Ooh." She glanced around to see if anyone else was listening. "About what might happen when one stares deeply into the eyes of very trusted, sweet, muscle-bound, caretaking certain football player?"

"Well, hypothetically, say after several days of practicing things like that, let's say, again hypothetically, someone saw someone else naked in the bathtub and... an involuntary physical reaction happened."

"This is a little too hypothetical. You're going to have to actually tell me what happened."

Crappola.

"Gryff saw me naked in his bathtub and he got... you know...." I wave my hand around.

Sara Jayne's head whipped around. "Excuse me, what now?"

"It's hypothetical," I protested.

"Girl," Sara Jayne scooted closer, "spill everything."

So I told them, hypothetically, about the bathtub incident. Sara Jayne's eyebrows climbed higher with every detail. At some point AbuelaNovela began listening in as well while consuming a hot dog almost as big as she was.

"And these trust exercises you mentioned earlier?" she asked when I finished.

"They're just... we're helping each other with dating confidence. Eye contact. Hand holding. Basic stuff."

"Basic stuff." Sara Jayne's smile was knowing. "Honey, what you're describing? That's foreplay."

"No, no, it's completely platonic. We have boundaries. Rules. It's basically therapeutic. Like physical therapy but for dating. Very clinical. Nothing romantic at all."

"Tontos enamorados. No es mi tropo favorito," AbuelaNovela muttered.

Tempest glared at her grandmother, "She said it definitely sounds more than friendly."

"We. Are. Just. Friends," I said slowly, like the speed might make it truthier.

"The lady doth protest too much, methinks," Tempest said, glancing at me sideways.

"Don't quote Hamlet at me."

"It's actually from—"

"I don't care. The point is, you're all reading too much into a completely normal biological response to unexpected stimuli."

Sara Jayne snorted. "Unexpected stimuli. Is that what we're calling your—"

I slapped my hand over her mouth.

I didn't have time to try and convince anyone, not that I could because Sloane appeared with her camera crew, looking polished and ready for game day action in a Bandits jersey that was definitely tailored.

Great.

"Artemis. So good to see you." Her smile was very white. "That double date disaster is going to make for some great TV. Did you hear Rob and Puck are actually engaged now? They're getting married in Vegas next month after a couples skydiving trip."

"That's... fast."

"When you know, you know." She studied me with calculating eyes. "So what did you and Gryff do after your dates left together?"

"We went to Flynn and Tempest's. Had margaritas. Normal friend activities."

"Interesting that you both picked such wrong people for each other." She tilted her head. "Almost like you were sabotaging each other's love lives."

"We're just bad at matchmaking." I waved her off and laughed too loud. "Very normal friend incompetence."

"Some might say that suggests hidden feelings." I suddenly noticed the camera pointed right at me along with everyone's eyes. "Not wanting the other to date anyone else?"

"Some would be wrong. We're friends. Furr-endzz. Amigos," I said smiling at AbuelaNovela, who rolled her eyes.

She made a note on her tablet. "Right. Friends who live together and set each other up on terrible dates." She made another note, and something about her expression made my skin crawl. Thankfully, the teams ran onto the field before she could probe further.

The game was incredible. I'd watched Gryff play football since high school, knew all his moves, his rhythms, the way he commanded his position. But this was different. This was professional football, faster and harder than college, and he was magnificent.

He made a massive block in the second quarter that sprang a touchdown. The stadium erupted, but before celebrating with his teammates, his head turned toward our section. Found me in the crowd. Grinned right at me.

"Did you see that?" Tempest asked. "He found you immediately."

"He's looking for his family."

"Mija, he looked right at you," AbuelaNovela said.

"Every good play, he looks for you," Sara Jayne added. "That's not friend behavior."

"It's absolutely friend behavior. Very supportive friend behavior."

Nana leaned over from behind me. "He's not looking at all of us, dear."

"He's acknowledging his support system. Very healthy."

Jules studied the field while handing out trays of nachos. "He's playing like he's been getting laid. Have you two been—"

"No!"

"Huh. Could've fooled me." She stared at me pointedly. "That kind of energy usually comes from somewhere."

"Maybe he's just excited about his first professional game?"

"Is that what you kids are calling it today? Excited?" Et tu, Grandma De le Reine? Really?

Jules raised an eyebrow. "Sure. That's definitely it."

Flynn made an incredible tackle, and Tempest jumped

up screaming. I jumped up too when Gryff made another key block, and I realized I was cheering louder for him than anyone.

"Just roommates though?" Tempest asked with a smirk.

"Best friends can be enthusiastic supporters."

"The lady doth—"

"I will throw these nachos at you."

In the third quarter, a massive defensive tackle from San Diego, built like a mountain, broke through the line and hit Gryff hard. He went down and didn't immediately get up.

I was on my feet before I realized it, my hands pressed to my heart, a sound escaping that might have been his name.

He rolled over, pushed himself up, and immediately looked toward our section. Found my face. Gave me a thumbs up and that grin that meant he was fine.

I sat down, shaking.

AbuelaNovela leaned over and patted my hand. "¡Solo bésalo ya!"

"She is happy he is okay," Tempest explained.

"Sí," I agreed.

After the game, families were allowed down on the field. The moment Gryff saw us approaching, he bypassed his grandparents, his agent, even Flynn, and came straight for me.

He was sweaty and glowing from the win, his hair stuck to his forehead, and he looked so happy I couldn't help but smile back.

"Did you see that block in the third?" He was practically vibrating with excitement.

"You scared me when that mountain of a man hit you."

His expression softened. "Were you worried about me?"

"Of course I was worried. You're my—"

Before I could finish, he picked me up in a hug, spinning me around. I shrieked, laughing, my hands automatically going to his shoulders, which were very broad and solid under his pads.

When he set me down, he didn't immediately let go, his hands staying on my waist. "The jersey looks perfect on you."

"It's a little big."

"It's perfect," he repeated, and something in his voice made my stomach flip.

Sloane was definitely filming this. Everyone was watching with knowing looks. But for a moment, I forgot about all of them, caught in whatever was happening in the space between us.

Then Flynn cleared his throat loudly. "Are we interrupting something?"

"Nope," I stepped back quickly. "Just celebrating. With my friend. Platonically."

"Right," Flynn said, exchanging a look with Tempest. "Platonically."

Gryff didn't seem phased by any of this. "DeMarcus Clay has some trendy bar called The Beach reserved for a celebration. Who wants to take the grands home and who wants to partay?"

"I nominate Jules for grandparent duty." She'd been far too nosy all night, and she was overly perceptive.

"Ah, man." Jules whined.

"Come, mija. We will take you to get the best tacos in LA and we will tell you how our families were fated to be united."

"Okay, that sounds like the tea. I'm in." She flipped the four of us off. "See you suckers later. I'm getting tacos and hot gossip."

When we got to the bar, we were some of the first to arrive, so we were able to get a table. Tempest gave Flynn a kiss on the cheek and then a shove. "Go find us some drinks, boys."

"Temperino." A gorgeous Latina woman waved. "What did you think of your first game?"

"Everyone, this is Artie," Tempest introduced me. "She's—"

"Gryff's girlfriend." The woman, Martinez's wife, according to her jersey, pulled me into a hug. "We've been dying to meet you. I'm Vanessa, this is Jade and Priya, the unofficial welcome committee to the PALs club. We need to get you involved."

"Oh, I'm not... we're just roommates. Friends. Platonic cohabiters."

The stunning, sophisticated Black woman gave me a wave. "I'm Jade. You're the roommate? My fiancé says Gryff doesn't shut up about you."

"He talks about me?" Something fluttered in my chest that I squashed immediately.

"According to DeMarcus, constantly," Jade said. "He

says your name comes up more than plays in the locker room."

"My husband says the same," added Priya. "It's actually kind of adorable."

"We're just very close friends. We've been friends for a real long time. If something was going to happen, it would have happened. We're basically siblings. Well, not siblings, that's weird. But like... cousins? No, that's worse. Just very, very platonic friends who happen to live together. Platonically."

The women all exchanged looks like they were looking at an animal gnawing its own leg off in a trap. I was saved from any further verbal explosions from the boys bringing back drinks.

"Strawberry margarita," Gryff said, handing it to me with that grin that made my stomach do things I was ignoring.

The night became a blur of congratulations, teammates introducing themselves, more PALs making knowing comments about Gryff and me. Every time I turned around, someone was assuming we were together, and my denials were getting weaker.

"Just friends," I said for the hundredth time when DeMarcus Clay asked how long we'd been dating.

"Sure," DeMarcus said, clearly not believing me. "The way he looks at you is very... friendly."

Three margaritas in, actual alcoholic ones this time, surrounded by people who kept insisting Gryff was in love with me, something shifted in my slightly tipsy brain.

What if they were right?

What if everyone, Tempest, Sara Jayne, the PALs, his

grandparents, his teammates, what if they all saw something I was missing?

The bathtub incident flashed through my mind. The way he looked for me after every good play. How he'd bypassed everyone to hug me first.

Gryff had been pulled away, and I glanced over at him across the bar, laughing with Flynn and some other players. He must have felt my stare because he looked up, caught my eye, and smiled that soft smile that was just for me.

My heart did something complicated.

"Hypothetically," I said to Tempest, who'd appeared at my elbow, "if I wanted to test whether someone had feelings for me..."

"Oh my god, are you finally—"

"Hypo. Thetic. Ally."

Tempest studied my face. "Hypothetically, you could try something that would give you a definitive answer. Something that friends wouldn't do."

"Like what?"

She raised an eyebrow. "You know what."

I did know what. The idea was insane. Completely ridiculous. It would change everything.

Everyone kept insisting he was in love with me, and I needed to know. I needed to prove once and for all that we were just friends, that everyone was wrong, that the towel incident was just biology and nothing more.

I picked up the remainder of my strawberry margarita and drained it in one gulp. Then I turned toward the bar and found myself staring right into his eyes.

FML

GRYFF

I was standing at the bar talking to some of my guys from the O-line when I looked back to check on Artie and my heart stopped. Tyson Freeman, all six foot three of him, looking like a Swoosh ad in his perfectly fitted henley, was talking to Artie.

My Artie.

Who was wearing my fucking jersey, her hair down and wavy, cheeks flushed from margaritas and laughter. She looked fucking gorgeous, and Tyson was staring at her like he'd just discovered pumpkin spice lattes.

Fuck a truck.

I could have let them figure it out themselves. Could have turned away, grabbed another beer, pretended I didn't see what was about to happen. But that wasn't who I was. I was the guy who fixed things, who helped, who made sure everyone else got what they needed.

Even when it murdered my heart like a true crime documentary played over and over.

With a sigh that came from somewhere deep in my chest, I walked over to where Artie stood frozen, still staring at Tyson.

"Hey," I said, touching her elbow gently. "So you met my man Tyson."

"What? I wasn't... I was just..."

"Tyson's on the offensive line with me." I pushed through the words like ripping off a Band-Aid. "Tyson, this is my roommate, Artemis Fraser."

"The rugby player?" Tyson's face lit up. "Gryff talks about you constantly."

And there it was... the blush. The real one, not the embarrassed flush she got when people assumed we were together, but the attracted, interested, possibility-filled blush of meeting someone new.

"He does?" she asked, glancing at me quickly before looking back at Tyson.

"All the time. He mentioned you're trying for the Olympic team?" Tyson extended his hand, and when she took it, he held on just a beat too long. "That's incredible."

"It's a long shot, but yeah." She tucked her hair behind her ear, her nervous tell. "You were amazing out there today. That block in the fourth quarter?"

"You noticed that?" He looked genuinely pleased.

They were still holding hands.

"I'm gonna grab another beer," I said to no one in particular, because they'd already forgotten I existed.

I made it about three steps before Tyson called out, "Yo, Kingman, hold up."

He jogged over, leaving Artie at the bar looking

slightly dazed. "Just to be clear, man, you two are really just friends? Because I don't want to step on any toes here. Bros before... you know."

The ethical thing. The right thing. The thing a good friend would do.

"Yeah, just friends." The words tasted like ash. "She's single."

"You sure? Because the way you look at her—"

"I'm sure." I forced myself to meet his eyes. "Actually, you're kind of perfect for her."

"Yeah?"

God help me, I kept talking. "You're both athletes, so you get the lifestyle. Both new to LA, figuring things out. You're from a sports family, so you understand the pressure." I paused, then added the thing that hurt most because it was true. "Plus you won't be intimidated by her size or strength. Most guys can't handle that she could probably bench press them."

Tyson grinned. "Intimidated? Dude, she's fucking perfect. Those arms? That confidence? And she's beautiful."

Each word was a nail in my coffin, but I made myself nod. "She is."

"Think she'd give me her number?"

No. Tell him no. Tell him she's yours even if she isn't, even if she never will be.

"You should ask her. She'd probably like that."

Tyson clapped me on the shoulder. "Thanks, man. You're the best."

The worst part was that he meant it. Tyson was

genuinely grateful, genuinely excited, genuinely one of the good guys. If I had to watch Artie fall for someone else, at least it was someone who would treat her right.

I watched him walk back to her, watched her face light up when he returned, watched her snort-laugh at something he said. The rest of the bar, our celebration, everything else faded into background noise.

"You look like you need this."

Sloane appeared at my elbow with two drinks. Whiskey, neat. The good stuff.

"I don't—"

"Just take it." She pressed the glass into my hand, keeping one for herself. "To being a good friend."

The way she said it made it clear she knew exactly what had just happened. I looked over and sure enough, her camera guy was positioned perfectly to have captured everything. Artie's approach, her stopping for Tyson, my introduction, all of it.

"Turn the camera off," I said quietly.

"It's for the show. Human interest. The rookie who helps everyone else find love." She sipped her whiskey. "Very noble."

"Sloane—"

"Must be difficult," she continued, moving closer. "Being such a good friend. Watching her with him."

"I don't know what you mean."

"Sure you don't." She was standing too close now, her perfume overwhelming, something expensive and trying too hard. "You know, I understand what it's like. Wanting something you can't have."

Her hand touched my arm, fingernails trailing down to my wrist. Everything about it felt wrong, calculated, performative, like she was playing a role she'd seen in a movie.

"I should find my brother," I said, stepping back.

"He's busy." She nodded toward where Flynn and Tempest were deep in conversation with Mac and Sara Jayne. "Everyone's busy. Except us."

Before I could respond, a familiar voice cut through the bar noise.

"Gryff, there you are." Sean materialized like a guardian angel, Ren right behind him. "We've been looking everywhere for you. We're planning a brunch to celebrate your first pro game at our place."

"Cool. When?" I grabbed onto the subject change like a lifeline.

"Tomorrow?" Ren asked, his eyes flicking between me and Sloane with an expression that said he knew exactly what he was interrupting.

"We have practice. Mondays are brutal now that preseason's started. No more weekends off. But we could do Tuesday."

"Perfect, Tuesday it is." Sean had somehow positioned himself between me and Sloane without being obvious about it. "Bring everyone, Flynn, Tempest, Artie." He paused, glancing toward the bar. "And her new friend, if she wants."

"Tyson," I supplied, trying not to let it sound as bitter as it felt.

"Right. Tyson." Sean's expression was sympathetic.

"Bring swimsuits. Ren's got something ridiculous planned."

"Not ridiculous," Ren protested. "Memorable."

"Memorably ridiculous," Sean corrected.

Artie's laugh rang out across the bar. She and Tyson were doing shots with some of the other rookies, and she looked happy. Really happy. He was teaching her some complicated handshake, and she was laughing so hard she could barely follow along.

They looked good together. Natural. Easy.

Everything we weren't.

Everything in me screamed to leave, go home, leave her to flirt her ass off.

Great. Now I was thinking about her ass. Which immediately led to thinking about her in my bathtub.

Three fucking days later, and I was still replaying every second of walking into my bathroom to find Artie naked and singing in my tub. The way the water had made her skin glow. The way she'd looked at me when I'd stood there like an idiot in nothing but a towel. The way my body had reacted so immediately, so obviously, that there was no pretending it was anything other than what it was.

I was hot for my best friend. Hot like lava. Like the temperature of the sun.

And fuck if I wasn't on the verge of getting hard in the middle of the bar thinking about seeing the bruise on her ass. Not because I wanted to see her hurt. But imagining her standing up out of the water like Venus, water dripping down her body, turning so I could see every inch of her thick thighs that I wanted to crush my skull while she rode my beard.

Fuck. Fuckity, fuck, fucking fuck.

I wasn't going anywhere tonight. Not if that meant leaving her at the bar with some strange guy she'd just met. Not that Tyson was strange.

"I should go check on Artie," I said, even though it was the last thing I wanted to do.

"That's very masochistic of you," Sean observed.

We made our way back through the crowd to where Artie and Tyson were with Flynn, Tempest, and some other players. The moment Artie saw me, her whole posture relaxed.

"Gryff. Where'd you go?" She grabbed my arm, pulling me into their circle. "Did you know Tyson's dad played for Chicago and now his older brother does? It's so Kingman of them."

And just like that, I was part of the conversation. More importantly, Artie was completely at ease, chatting and laughing, her hand occasionally touching my arm when she made a point, using me as her anchor while she flirted with Tyson.

She had no idea she was doing it.

"You two have known each other a long time," Tyson observed, watching our dynamic.

"Six years," Artie said proudly. "Since junior year of high school. Gryff taught me how to watch football, and I taught him how to appreciate rugby."

"She means she yelled at the TV until I learned the rules," I clarified.

"You love rugby now," she protested.

"I love watching you play rugby. There's a difference."

The words came out more honest than I'd intended. Artie just laughed and squeezed my arm, but Tyson's eyes narrowed slightly, like he was recalculating something.

The rest of the night, she stayed close to me while talking to Tyson. Using me as her security blanket while she tested out this new attraction. She'd lean into me when she laughed at Tyson's jokes, grab my hand when she got excited about something, check my reaction when Tyson said anything significant.

Tyson noticed. I could see him trying to figure out our dynamic, why she needed me there to be comfortable with him.

But Artie? Artie was oblivious. She thought she was doing great, being natural and flirty and confident.

She had no idea it was only because I was right there, making her feel safe.

Which meant if they went on an actual date, just the two of them, without me as her emotional support blanket...

Well. That was going to be interesting.

Tuesday morning came too fast. I'd barely slept, replaying Sunday night over and over. The way they'd fit together so easily.

Sean and Ren's beach house was insanely cool. Cars were already lining the driveway including a camera van that made my stomach sink.

"Ooh, this place is amazing," Tempest said as Sean led us to the drinks bar, manned by someone making bespoke fresh squeezed juices. "Are you guys movie producers or something?"

"Oh, no, I'm a librarian for LAPL." Sean shook his head and smiled like he had an inside joke.

But Ren came up and gave Sean a kiss on the shoulder. "Which is why we have an excellent home library."

Sean grinned and gave me a wink. "This is actually Ren's place, and he is not a librarian."

"Babe, this is our place and has been since you moved in." That was all he said. Nothing about what he did to have the money to own a beach house like this. Hmm. I'd been around enough celebrities in sports to know when someone didn't want to be recognized for their fame.

Our hosts left us to get our drinks, all non-alcoholic and weirdly healthy, while they moved around the group with the kind of easy efficiency that came from years of hosting things together.

Sean dinged the side of a glass to get everyone's attention. "Drink and hydrate yourselves friends, because we are headed down to the beach for the fun activity of the day, after which brunch will be served. And if you need to change into your swimsuits, there are cabanas right down there."

Sean pointed toward the beach, where there were indeed some striped cabanas, but there was also a row of surfboards and something I absolutely did not expect to see.

Goats. Surfing goats.

Artie squealed and sprinted down the stairs, followed closely behind by the rest of the girls.

"Oh god. Why do I have a feeling I'm going to end up with a pet goat by the end of the day?"

The rest of us got down to the beach and damn if Tyson wasn't already by Artie's side.

"This is the most California thing I've ever seen," Artie said, immediately crouching down to pet a brown and white spotted goat wearing what appeared to be a custom wetsuit. "I can't wait to tell everyone back home that I went goat surfing."

"How did you find out about this?" Tempest asked, watching as Flynn attempted to introduce himself to a black goat who seemed more interested in investigating his flip-flops.

"Sean has connections everywhere," Ren said. "He's like the social coordinator you never knew you needed."

The camera crew was set up right at the water. Ren gave them a glare, but Sloane mouthed *public beach* and shrugged. "This is great, guys. We'll just be over here capturing this authentic LA lifestyle content."

"Welcome, everyone, to Floats With Goats," the volunteer explained with a grin. "Why have a cow when you can float with a goat?"

"Of course," Tempest said. "This place is amazing. Do you rescue all kinds of animals?"

"We do. Goats, pigs, chickens, horses, even donkeys. We've got about two hundred animals here. The surfing program is our main fundraiser and outreach. People come for the novelty, but they leave understanding how incredible these animals are."

"Ooh, I can't wait to get Burrito Petito out on the water. This gives me an idea for a meet-cute," Tempest said and whipped out her phone and rapidly typed.

Artie was drawn to a bulletin board set up at the

cabana. The board was covered with photos and information about animals available for adoption.

"Gryffen," Artie called out from over by the adoption board. "Come look. This is clearly fate."

I walked over to find her staring at photos of baby goats, chubby little piglets, and a rooster that was far too reminiscent of Luke Skycocker.

"Look at these faces," she said, pointing to a photo of two particularly adorable baby goats that were brother and sister. "How does anyone resist adopting them all?"

"Easily," I said, but I was studying the photos too. "We live in a house, not a farm."

"A house with a big backyard," she pointed out.

"Not big enough."

"Oh my god, Gryff." Her voice was the most adorable whine and pointed to one of the photos "This little guy only has one ear. He needs us. We are meant to adopt him."

"We are not adopting a goat." There was no way I was getting out of adopting a goat.

"Yet," she said with a grin that made my heart bust out its best dance moves.

Before I could argue further, Tyson appeared beside us. "Checking out the adoption board?"

"Yeah, that's Artie. She would adopt a feral raccoon and its squirrel army if I'd let her." I forced myself to sound casual. "She's got a weakness for animals that need homes."

Tyson made a weird bleating sound that I think was supposed to be a goat. I was definitely making fun of him for that later. But then he says in that weird goat voice, "I need a home."

They were laughing together, easy and natural, while I stood there looking at photos of baby goats pretending not to think about how she'd said we were "meant to adopt them" like we were a couple making decisions together.

"Alright, everyone," one of the surf instructors called out. "Let's get you on some boards. We'll start with some basic instruction on the beach before we get the goats involved."

What followed was an hour of the most surreal experience of my life. We started with basic surfing instruction on the sand, which was challenging enough. But then the instructors brought out the goats.

"Meet your surf partners," the head instructor announced as goats in custom life vests and harnesses were led over to our group. "These guys have been doing this for years, so just follow their lead."

What should have been a disaster was actually incredible. The goats seemed to understand surfing in a way that defied all logic. They balanced perfectly, knew how to turn the boards, and appeared to genuinely enjoy riding waves.

"This is insane," Artie called out as MoonGoattie guided their board toward shore. "My goat is better at this than I am."

Through it all, I watched her instead of focusing on my own goat. The way Artie laughed, the obvious joy on her face as she experienced something completely ridiculous and wonderful.

And I wasn't the only one watching. Tyson kept finding excuses to surf near her, offering tips and encouragement.

After an hour of goat-assisted surfing, we gathered on the beach while the animals were toweled off and given treats. Sean and Ren had drinks and sandwiches brought down, and the group settled into the kind of lazy conversation that happened after sun and saltwater and shared absurdity.

"So, Artie," Tyson said, settling on the sand next to her while one of the goats munched on a special goat treat. "What's your favorite thing about LA so far?"

"Besides the goat surfing?" She scratched behind the goat's ears. "Probably the fact that I can do things like goat surfing. I mean, where else in the world is this just a normal Saturday activity?"

Flynn grabbed my arm and steered me away from the group. "WTF, man?" he said quietly.

"What are you flipping out about?"

"About the fact that you're in love with Artie and you're sitting here like a sad puppy who lost his last brain cell watching her with Tyson."

I nearly choked on my water and looked around to make sure the cameras weren't on us. "What?"

"Don't what me. I'm your twin. I know you better than anyone, and you've been pining over her since you moved in together and now she's letting another guy make goo-goo eyes at her, and you aren't doing shit."

Before I could respond, Tempest appeared at Flynn's elbow with a look that meant I was about to get a lecture.

"Please tell me you're talking sense into him," she said.

"I'm trying, but he's a stubborn ass."

"Of course he is. They always are in these situations." Tempest fixed me with the kind of stare that probably helped her write believable relationship conflicts. "Gryff, cariño, you're being an idiot."

"Thanks, but that's super not helpful."

"I'm serious." Flynn poked me right in the heart. "And before you give me some speech about not wanting to ruin your friendship, let me point out that you're already ruining it by pretending you don't have feelings for her."

Before I could defend myself, I heard Artie laugh at something Tyson had said. The sound made me look over automatically, just in time to see him lean closer to her.

"Artie," Tyson was saying, "I know this might be fast, but want to get coffee sometime? Maybe explore some more of LA together?"

My stomach dropped to my flip-flops and buried itself in the sand.

"Oh… uh, yeah, I'd love that," Artie said with a smile. "I've been meaning to find a good coffee shop in the neighborhood."

"Perfect. How about tomorrow afternoon?" Tyson was grinning and I wanted to slap it off his face. "I found a place in Venice Beach that has great coffee and an amazing view."

"It's a date."

"You okay?" Flynn asked quietly.

"I'm fine."

"You're not fine."

"I'm fine enough."

He followed my gaze to where Tyson was making her laugh. "You could tell her."

"Tell her what? That I'm in love with her? That I think about her every second? That watching her with him makes me want to punch something?" I shook my head. "She's happy. That's what matters."

"You matter too, dumbass."

I might be dumb, and I was definitely an ass because I was not going to just stand by and watch the love of my life fall for another guy.

ALPHA WEIRDO

ARTEMIS

I was excited about my coffee date with Tyson. I was also terrified.

Not because Tyson wasn't great. He absolutely was. Sweet, funny, athletic, the kind of guy who remembered details about conversations and asked thoughtful follow-up questions. Exactly the type of person I should be thrilled to go out with.

Which was exactly the problem.

At the beach on Tuesday, everything had been perfect. Natural. Easy. I'd been confident and flirty and completely myself. But that was with everyone around, with Gryff right there beside me, his familiar presence making everything feel safe.

Now it was just going to be Tyson and me. No buffer. No safety net. No Gryff.

"You're going to be fine," Gryff said from the couch, not looking up from his tablet. "Just do what we've been practicing."

"The trust exercises?"

"Yeah. Eye contact, being present, asking for what you need. All that stuff." He finally looked up, and something flickered across his face too quickly for me to read. "Tyson seems like the kind of guy who'd appreciate that direct approach."

"You think so?"

"Definitely. In fact..." He set down his tablet and sat up straighter. "You should definitely do the eye contact thing. Guys love that. Shows confidence."

"The thirty-second stare?"

"Exactly. And remember to maintain it. Don't look away first. It's about dominance, I mean, connection. Deep connection."

Something about his tone seemed off, but I was too nervous to analyze it. "What if it gets weird?"

"It won't. Trust me. You two had great chemistry at the beach. This is just building on that." He stood up, stretching. "Oh, and Tyson loves sweet coffee drinks. Like, really sweet. Extra pumps of everything."

"Really? He seems more like a black coffee guy." I didn't remember him eating sweets at brunch.

"Nope. Total secret sweet tooth. He mentioned it at practice." Gryff headed toward the kitchen. "Actually, you should order for him. Shows you were paying attention to details about him."

"That seems kind of presumptuous..."

"It's confident. Guys like confidence, right?" He was rummaging in the fridge now, his back to me. "Just trust me. I know Tyson. This is what he responds to."

I nodded, filing away his advice. Gryff knew Tyson better than I did, had been practicing with him all summer. If anyone would know what worked, it would be him.

"Text me if you need anything," he added, still facing the fridge. "I'll just be here. Working out. Definitely not thinking about your date at all."

"Thanks," I said, grabbing my purse. "You're the best friend ever."

He made a sound that might have been agreement or might have been choking. Hard to tell.

The coffee shop in Venice Beach was cute—all exposed brick and Edison bulbs, the kind of place that photographed better than it actually functioned. Tyson was already there when I arrived, looking unfairly good in jeans and a tank that showed off exactly how built he was.

"Hey," he said, standing to greet me. "You look great."

"Thanks. You too." I could do this. I'd been practicing. I knew exactly what to do.

We got in line, making small talk about traffic and the weather, and I kept thinking about what Gryff had said. Be confident. Order for him. Show that I'd been paying attention.

"What can I get you?" the barista asked when we reached the counter.

"I'll have a large strawberry matcha," I said, then turned to Tyson with what I hoped was a confident smile. "And he'll have a large hot honeycomb latte with extra vanilla sweet cream foam, oh and add a couple extra pumps of vanilla."

Tyson's eyebrows shot up. "I... what?"

Oh. My. God. I'd just ordered Gryff's drink. For my date. Who was not Gryff.

Panic mode one hundred percent activated. "Gryff mentioned you like sweet drinks."

"Gryff said that?" He looked genuinely confused, then a slow grin spread across his face. "Did he now? That's interesting, considering I've been drinking black coffee in front of him every morning for weeks."

"Oh." My face went hot. "I can change it—"

"No, it's fine. I'll try it." He was clearly fighting back laughter. "This should be educational."

Strike one.

We found a table by the window, and I tried to recover. Maybe the eye contact thing would help. That had been working so well with Gryff, creating this intense, intimate connection. Surely it would work with Tyson too.

"So," I said, once we were settled with our drinks, "want to try something?"

"Sure?"

"Let's just... look at each other, like into each other's eyes. For thirty seconds. No talking." I leaned forward, fixing my gaze on his. "It's about connection."

"Is this a staring contest?" He looked more amused than uncomfortable.

"No, it's about being present. Intimate. Trust me."

I set the timer on my phone and then locked eyes with him, trying to recreate that electric feeling from my exercises with Gryff. But instead of intensity, there was just... awkwardness. Tyson's eyes were crinkling at the corners like he was trying very hard not to laugh.

Ten seconds felt like ten minutes.

"This is weird," he said at fifteen seconds, but he was smiling.

"Just a little longer," I insisted, leaning in more.

"Artemis, you look like you're trying to download my thoughts directly into your brain."

"I'm not, it's supposed to be intimate."

"It's intense, I'll give you that." He finally broke, laughing. "Is this something from a magazine? 'Ten ways to hypnotize your date'?"

I broke eye contact, mortified. "Sorry. I was just trying to... connect."

"Maybe we could just talk?" he suggested, taking a large gulp of his too sweet coffee and immediately making a face. "Whew, this is like drinking candy."

My phone buzzed.

GRYFF

How's it going? Use the eye contact yet?

It didn't go well. He said I looked like I was trying to download his thoughts.

You probably weren't doing it right. Try again. But this time, touch his hand while you do it.

That seems like a lot

Trust me. Physical contact enhances the connection.

I looked up at Tyson, who was stirring his drink, presumably to make it tolerable.

"Sorry about the coffee thing," I said. "I thought—"

"It's fine. Just unexpected." He pushed the drink aside. "So tell me about your rugby training. How's it going?"

This was better. Normal conversation. I could do this.

"It's good. Intense. I actually have been working on being more present in my body, more aware of what I need."

He gave me a once over, and that sparkle in his eye told me he liked what he saw. "That's... good?"

"Yeah, like right now, I need..." What did I need? What had Gryff taught me to ask for? "I need someone who notices when I need water without me having to ask."

Tyson looked at the water glasses on our table, then back at me. "There's literally water right there."

"No, I mean, metaphorically. Or actually both." Why was this so hard? With Gryff, expressing needs felt natural. "I need someone who anticipates my needs."

He tipped his head to the side, thinking. "Like a psychic?"

"No, like... forget it."

My phone buzzed again.

GRYFF

How's it going now?

I'm dying. This is awful.

Try the vulnerability thing. Tell him something real.

Like what?

Like how you've been told you're bad in bed.

WHAT? No!

Trust me. Vulnerability is attractive.

I looked at Tyson, who was now scrolling through his phone probably because I'd been on mine. This was going so badly already. Maybe radical honesty would help?

"I've been told I'm bad in bed," I blurted out.

Tyson nearly choked on his sugar-coffee. "I'm sorry, what?"

"I'm being vulnerable. Sharing something real." Oh god, why had I listened to Gryff? "Multiple people have said I'm not good at... intimacy."

"And you're telling me this because...?"

"Vulnerability is attractive?"

He stared at me for a moment, then burst out laughing. "Artemis, you're trying so hard right now. Like, SO hard. It's actually kind of adorable."

"It is?"

"In a train wreck sort of way." He was grinning now. "Let me guess, you read some dating advice article? Or wait, did Gryff—?"

"No. Maybe. Sort of."

"This is like watching someone follow IKEA instructions for a first date. Step one: order for him. Step two: intense eye contact. Step three: overshare dramatically."

Despite my mortification, I found myself laughing too. "It's that obvious?"

"Honey, you just announced you're bad in bed as a conversation starter. Yeah, it's obvious." But his tone was warm, not mean. "Look, you were completely natural at the beach. Funny, confident, yourself. This..." he gestured vaguely, "this is like you're playing a character in a bad rom-com."

My phone buzzed again.

GRYFF

Maybe you should kiss him. Reset the energy.

Now???

Quick kiss. Shows confidence.

I was desperate enough to try anything. I leaned across the table quickly, aiming for Tyson's lips.

Except he was reaching for his water at the exact same moment.

Our faces collided with a crack that made people at nearby tables turn to look. His nose hit my cheek, my chin knocked into his jaw, and we both jerked back with matching expressions of pain and surprise.

"Ow. What the...?" He touched his nose, checking for blood.

Oh my gawd. I was going to murder my best friend later. They'd make a documentary about us, I was sure of it. "I was trying to kiss you."

Tyson touched his nose, clearly looking for the break. "Why?"

"To reset the energy."

"What energy?"

This was an absolute disaster. Everything I'd practiced, everything that worked with Gryff, was failing spectacularly.

My phone was buzzing nonstop now.

> **GRYFF**
>
> What's happening?
>
> Are you okay?
>
> I'm coming.

Tyson moved like he was going to leave, probably to go call 9-1-1 to report that his date had assaulted him and he needed medical assistance.

"Wait—"

But then, like he'd been summoned by the sheer force of my humiliation, Gryff appeared in the coffee shop, protein shake in hand, looking like he'd just happened to be in the neighborhood.

"Freeman. Fraser." He approached our table with fake surprise that wouldn't fool a toddler. "Crazy running into you guys here."

"This is your coffee shop," Tyson said, clearly amused. "You told me about it. You said you come here every day after training."

"Do I? Huh." Gryff's eyes darted between us, taking in our body language. "Everything okay?"

"We're having an adventure," Tyson said, grinning. "Your roommate just tried to romance me using what I can only assume is advice from a 1950s dating manual."

"That's... specific," Gryff said carefully.

"She ordered me a drink that could rot my teeth, stared into my soul for thirty seconds, announced she's bad in bed, and then tried to face-plant into a kiss." Tyson was openly laughing now.

Gryff's eyes went wide. "She did all that?"

"The trust exercises were supposed to work," I protested.

"Trust exercises?" Tyson looked between us with interest. "Is that what's been going on? You two have been—"

"Nothing," we both said too quickly.

"Right." Tyson stood up, still looking thoroughly entertained. "I'm gonna go. Artemis, you're awesome, but maybe next time just be yourself? You were great at the beach. Natural. Easy." He paused. "Of course, you had your emotional support roommate there, so maybe that helped."

He clapped Gryff on the shoulder. "See you at practice."

After he left, Gryff and I stood there in the middle of the coffee shop.

"That went well," Gryff said weakly.

"He thinks I'm insane."

"He thinks you're trying too hard. There's a difference."

"The trust exercises didn't work at all." I slumped into a chair. "Everything we've been practicing just made things worse."

"Maybe they're not meant to work with everyone," he said quietly.

"What's that supposed to mean?"

"Nothing. Come on, let's go home."

Back at the house, I sat on the couch replaying the disaster while Gryff made apology brownies in the kitchen. Well, reheated store-bought brownies, but it was the thought that counted.

"I don't understand what went wrong," I said for the fifth time. "The eye contact thing works perfectly when we do it."

"Maybe it's different with different people," he offered, bringing me a brownie.

"But it shouldn't be. It's just a technique. A skill. Like... like a rugby play. It should work the same no matter who I'm doing it with."

"Rugby plays work because your whole team knows them. Maybe intimacy is the same. It requires the right partner."

I looked at him, something clicking in my brain. "I couldn't kiss him."

"You tried. You just missed."

"No, I mean... even if I hadn't collided with his face, it would have been wrong. There was no... spark. No antici-pation. Nothing like..."

"Like what?"

"Like when we almost kissed during our exercises."

The words hung between us. We'd never actually talked about those moments, the times when our practice had gotten so intense we'd nearly crossed that line.

"We've never actually kissed," he said carefully.

"No."

"Maybe that's the problem." I knew what we needed to do. "Maybe I need to practice actual kissing. Not just the lead-up."

My heart started racing. "It's the only thing we haven't covered in our trust exercises."

"That's true." My mouth was suddenly dry. "So you think we should... practice?"

Gryff took a deep breath and I couldn't tell what it meant. Was he about to tell me to fuck off? He scooted a little closer. "It would be the logical next step."

"Right. Logical." I turned to face him fully. "But what if you don't want to? What if it makes things weird?"

"Artie—"

"Because I know we're just friends and this is just practice but kissing seems like a big line to cross and what if—"

He grabbed my face with both hands and kissed me.

It wasn't gentle or tentative or practice-like. It was immediate and overwhelming and absolutely perfect. His lips were soft but insistent, one hand sliding into my hair while the other cupped my jaw. I made a sound, surprise or relief or both, and he deepened the kiss, pulling me closer until I was practically in his lap.

Every kiss I'd ever had paled in comparison. This wasn't awkward or forced or performative. It was like coming home. Like finding something I didn't know I'd been looking for. My whole body lit up, every nerve ending singing, and I kissed him back with everything I had.

When we finally broke apart, we were both breathing hard.

"Oh," I said brilliantly.

"Yeah," he agreed, his hands still in my hair.

"That was..." Not very practice-like. Better do it again to make sure. "Kiss me again."

"Thank god," he breathed, and pulled me back in.

This time was slower, deeper. His hands were everywhere, my hair, my back, pulling me closer, and I let myself melt into him completely.

When we broke apart again, I was fully in his lap, my arms around his neck, his forehead pressed against mine.

"So," I said, trying to catch my breath, "I think I know how to kiss now."

Well, I knew how to kiss Gryff. My best friend. My roommate. And I think I just changed everything.

PRACTICE MAKES HELL

GRYFF

Artie was still in my lap, her lips swollen from kissing, her hands tangled in my hair, and I was having the kind of out-of-body experience usually reserved for near-death situations or really good drugs.

We'd just kissed. Really kissed. Not accidentally, not almost, but full-on, tongue-involved, hands-everywhere kissed. And it had been perfect. So perfect that my brain was short-circuiting trying to process how kissing my best friend had felt more right than anything I'd ever done in my life.

"We should do that again," Artie said, her voice breathy. She looked at me, her eyes flicking back and forth between mine as if she was studying me, waiting for me to say or do something.

"Yeah, we should." What else could I possibly say. Yes, please?

For a half a millisecond, I thought I saw disappointment flash through her eyes.

"For practice."

Right. Practice. The word was like ice water on my internal celebration. Shit. That's why she was disappointed. She thought I was telling her she needed more practice. Fuck.

She shifted slightly in my lap, and I had to bite back a groan. "I think I'm getting the hang of it. The kissing thing. You're a really good teacher."

Teacher. Friend. Practice partner. Not boyfriend, not the love of her life, not the person she actually wanted to be kissing.

But then she was kissing me again, and I couldn't make myself care about the logic. Her mouth was soft and demanding, and she made these little sounds that were going to haunt my dreams forever. I pulled her closer, one hand sliding up her back, the other cradling her face like she was something precious.

When we broke apart this time, we were both breathing hard.

"Maybe I should try this with Tyson too?" she asked, and the words hit like a physical blow. "Now that I know what good kissing feels like."

I was dying. Actually dying. My heart was being ripped out of my chest and tap-danced on, and I had to sit here and smile about it.

"That's... that's great," I said, proud that my voice didn't crack. "He'll definitely appreciate your... technique."

"You think so?" She climbed off my lap, and the loss of contact felt like losing a limb. "I mean, that wasn't too much, was it? The kissing? I don't want to seem too eager."

"It was perfect." The words came out too honest, too

raw. I cleared my throat. "I mean, you did perfect. Any guy would be lucky to be kissed like that."

She beamed at me, and I wanted to scream. How could she not see it? How could she not feel what I was feeling? That kiss had been everything, intimate and desperate and real. But to her, it was just practice for another man.

The next week was torture. Pure, exquisite torture.

We kept having "practice sessions" that were slowly killing me. Each one got more intense. More hands, more touching, more of those little sounds she made that were definitely going to send me to an early grave. And every single time, just when I thought maybe she was feeling it too, she'd pull back and say something about how this was really helping her confidence with Tyson.

I was literally teaching the woman I loved how to seduce another man. There had to be a special circle of hell reserved for this exact situation.

"His abs are ridiculous," I found myself telling Flynn on Wednesday while we were getting ready for practice. "Have you seen them? They're like... architecturally impossible."

Flynn looked up from his playbook. "Whose abs?"

"Tyson's." I pulled on my practice jersey with more force than necessary. "They're perfect. He's perfect. He volunteers at animal shelters."

"Okay?"

"He speaks three languages, Flynn. Three. I can barely handle English some days." I sat down to put on my cleats. "And his laugh. Have you heard his laugh? It's like... musical."

Flynn was staring at me with an expression I couldn't read. "Are you having a breakdown?"

"He builds homes for Habitat for Humanity. In his spare time. For fun." I stood up, pacing now. "His parents are still married. He has a great relationship with his sister. He can cook actual food that doesn't come from a box."

"Gryff—"

"Oh god." I stopped pacing, a horrible realization washing over me. "Am I in love with Tyson too?"

Flynn made a choking sound. "What?"

"Think about it. I can't stop talking about him. I notice everything about him. I think about him constantly." I sank onto the bench. "Oh fuck, I'm in love with Tyson Freeman."

"You're not in love with Tyson," Flynn said slowly, like he was talking to a child or a confused animal.

"But he's perfect."

"You don't want to date him, you idiot. You want to BE him. Or better, you want him to disappear so Artie will notice you exist."

"She notices I exist. I'm her practice dummy." I grabbed my helmet. "Her kissing crash test dummy."

"You made out with her for an hour three days ago."

"For practice," I shouted, then looked around to make sure no one heard. "She's very committed to proper technique."

Flynn muttered something that sounded like "idiots in love" but before I could respond, Tyson walked by.

"Hey, Kingmans," he said with that perfect smile that probably never had spinach in it. "Ready for practice?"

"Always," Flynn said, and I swear he gave Tyson some kind of look. Like they were sharing a secret.

Great. Even my brother was Team Tyson now.

Saturday arrived too fast. Flynn and I had generally agreed we didn't need a big thing for our birthday, but Sean and Ren had insisted on throwing us a party. "You only turn twenty-three once," Sean had said, "and it's your first birthday in LA. We're celebrating."

So our house was full of people, teammates, their partners, Sean and Ren's friends, even family who'd flown in. Nana and Coach were holding court in the living room, Grandpa Hunter was already chatting with some players, while Grandma Helene was definitely checking out their butts. Jules was directing food placement like a tiny general, and AbuelaNovela was telling anyone who'd listen about the telenovela plot this all reminded her of.

"Dos hermanos, dos destinos, pero solo uno conoce el amor verdadero," she said dramatically.

"She's saying happy birthday," Tempest translated unconvincingly.

Sloane and her camera crew were everywhere, documenting every moment. She'd been particularly interested in what she called "the roommate dynamic" all week.

I was in the kitchen stress-eating cheesy poofs when Tyson arrived.

He looked perfect, because of course he did. A tight t-shirt that showed off those ridiculous abs, jeans that looked professionally tailored, and he was carrying not one but two gift bags.

"Birthday boys," he called out, then caught Flynn's eye and... winked?

What the fuck? Why was he winking at my brother?

Flynn grinned back and gave him a thumbs up.

"Hey, Artie," Tyson said, producing a bouquet of gerbera daisies from behind his back. "These are for you. I remembered you mentioned they were your favorites."

When had she mentioned that? I didn't even know those were her favorites.

"Aww," Artie's face lit up. "Tyson, that's so thoughtful."

"Just wanted to brighten your day," he said, and was that a flex? Did he just unconsciously flex while handing her flowers?

Then, and I swear this was not an accident, he knocked over his water bottle all over his shirt.

"Oh man," he said, pulling at the wet fabric. "This is soaked through. Mind if I..." And then he was pulling his shirt off in my kitchen, revealing those absolutely ridiculous abs that looked like they were carved by angels who majored in architecture.

"Oh my," Nana said from the doorway. "That's a very fit young man."

"Abuela approves," AbuelaNovela added with an appreciative whistle.

Flynn was turned away, but I could see his shoulders shaking. Was he laughing?

"I'll get you a towel," Artie said, but she wasn't moving. She was staring at Tyson's chest like it held the secrets of the universe.

"I've got an extra shirt in my car," Tyson said. "But first, want me to help move that couch? Looks heavy."

He then proceeded to help rearrange our living room furniture, shirtless, flexing with every lift, while Artie watched and I died inside. Flynn and Tyson kept making eye contact, and at one point I swear Flynn mouthed "nice" when Tyson did a particularly unnecessary muscle flex while moving an ottoman that weighed maybe ten pounds.

"Your roommate is very strong," Coach observed, settling into his newly positioned chair.

"He's not my roommate," I said. "He's just a teammate."

"I meant Artemis," Coach said, pointing to where Artie was now helping Tyson move the coffee table. "Look at those arms."

Right. Artie. My actual roommate. Who was currently admiring my shirtless teammate's abs from very close range.

"Gryff," Artie called out, and I was instantly at her side because I had no self-control. "Come outside with me for a second?"

She led me to the front porch where a pet carrier was complete with a bow on top.

"Happy birthday," she said, suddenly shy. "I know we said no big gifts, but I couldn't resist."

She opened the carrier and out walked the most perfect baby goat I'd ever seen. Black and white spotted, with one ear that flopped sideways and eyes that looked like they held wisdom beyond his weeks.

"This is Vincent Van Goat," she said, picking him up and placing him in my arms. "He's ten weeks old, he was born without one ear, and he absolutely needs a home with someone who'll love him exactly as he is."

Vincent looked up at me and bleated softly, then immediately tried to eat my shirt.

"Artie," I breathed, falling completely in love with this little creature. "He's perfect. I have something to give you too."

"But it's your birthday. I don't understand." she replied as I tucked Vincent under my arm like a football and took her hand to lead her around the house into our fenced in backyard.

"Wait," she said, looking around.. "Is that... did you build a goat pen?"

I grinned, walking over to where I'd set up a professional-grade goat pen, complete with a wooden shelter that looked like a tiny barn. "I may have known about your surprise. The rescue called to confirm the home visit."

"Gryff, you ruined my surprise."

"No, I enhanced it. Because..." I opened the door to the little barn, and out trotted Holly Goatlightly, smaller than Vincent, a tawny brown with a white spot that resembled a heart on her forehead. "Meet Holly Goatlightly. She's Vincent's best friend from the rescue. They're bonded, can't be separated."

"You got me a goat?" Artie's voice cracked. "You actually got me a goat?"

"I know how much you wanted one. And when I found out about Vincent, the rescue mentioned he had a bonded friend, so..." I picked up Holly, who immediately started investigating my collar. "Happy just-because-I-wanted-to day."

"We both got each other goats," Artie said, starting to laugh through her tears. "We're those people who get each other goats."

"Technically, I got you a goat because I knew you wanted one. You got me a goat for my birthday. Totally different."

"Shut up." She was holding Vincent and crying and laughing at the same time. "This is the best gift anyone's ever given me."

"A goat?"

"Someone knowing me well enough to know I needed a goat." She looked at the pen, where I'd hung a hand-painted sign that read "Vincent & Holly's House" with little hearts around it. "You even made them a house."

"They're our goats. We're co-parenting." I set Holly down, and she immediately ran to inspect Vincent, who was still in Artie's arms.

She launched herself at me, careful not to squish Vincent between us, wrapping her free arm around my neck. "This is the best gift anyone's ever given me," she whispered against my neck. "You're the best friend anyone could ever have."

Friend. Right. That's what I was.

"Dios Mio," AbuelaNovela's voice carried across the yard. "El amor! The yearning! Someone kiss someone already!"

We jumped apart to find half the party had migrated to the back door to watch us.

"We were just—" Artie started.

"Hugging," I finished. "Platonically. About goats."

"Right," Sean said, not even trying to hide his smirk. "Platonic goat hugs."

Vincent chose that moment to walk over to where Tyson was standing and headbutt him directly in the shin.

"Yowch." Tyson stepped back, but Vincent followed, bleating aggressively.

Holly joined in, grabbing Tyson's shoelace in her teeth and pulling.

"I don't think they like you," Jules observed with obvious delight.

"Animals usually love me," Tyson said, trying to gently shake Holly off his shoe while Vincent continued his shin assault.

Flynn was definitely laughing now, not even trying to hide it. He caught Tyson's eye and they shared some kind of look that I couldn't interpret.

"Maybe they're just excited," Artie said, trying to call Holly back. But Holly had successfully untied Tyson's shoe and was now trying to steal it entirely.

"Or maybe they're excellent judges of character," Nana suggested innocently.

"Vincent, no," I said, scooping up my new son before he could do actual damage to Tyson's shins. Vincent immediately settled in my arms, looking angelic.

The party moved back inside, but the goats had to stay in their pen after they kept forming a protective barrier between Artie and Tyson every time he got close to her. It would have been funny if it wasn't so clearly what I wanted to be doing myself.

As the night went on, Tyson turned his charm up to eleven. He told stories about building schools in Guatemala, mentioned his volunteer work teaching kids to read, and casually dropped that he'd been accepted to Harvard but turned it down to play football.

"Of course he did," I muttered to Flynn. "He probably also saves puppies on weekends."

"Actually, kittens," Flynn said with a completely straight face. "He fosters orphaned kittens."

"I'm going to throw myself into the ocean."

"The ocean's, like, an hour away with traffic."

"Then I'll throw myself into the pool."

"We don't have a pool."

"I'll dig one and then throw myself into it."

Flynn patted my shoulder. "You're handling this well."

Then, because the universe hated me, Tyson chose that moment to make his move. He waited until everyone was gathered in the living room, until I was definitely within earshot, and then turned to Artie with that perfect smile.

"So," he said, loud enough for everyone to hear, "there's this new action movie coming out next week. The one with that actor you mentioned you liked? Fox Daws. Want to go see it with me?"

How did he know she wanted to see that? I'd been planning to ask her to that exact movie.

Artie glanced at me quickly, and for a second I thought maybe she was looking for a reason to say no. But I kept my face carefully neutral, supportive even, because that's what good friends did.

"Sure," she said, and my heart cracked a little more. "That sounds fun."

Flynn and Tyson did some kind of quick fist bump that they probably thought I didn't see. Great. My brother was literally celebrating my romantic demise.

"Perfect," Tyson said. "It's a date."

A date. Not hanging out, not catching a movie as friends. A date.

"I'm gonna check on the goats," I announced to no one in particular, needing to escape before I did something stupid like cry or challenge Tyson to single combat.

The backyard was quiet, peaceful. Vincent and Holly were curled up together in their little barn, and they both looked up when I approached.

"Hey guys," I said, sitting down next to their pen. "At least you two tried."

Vincent bleated softly and stuck his head through the fence for scritches.

"She's going on a date with him," I told the goats. "A real date. To the movie I wanted to take her to."

Holly made a sound that seemed sympathetic.

"The practice sessions worked. She's confident now. Ready to date someone perfect like Tyson." I rubbed Vincent's one floppy ear. "Mission accomplished, right?"

"Talking to the goats?"

I turned to find Artie standing behind me, backlit by the house lights.

"They're good listeners," I said.

She sat down next to me, close enough that our shoulders touched. "Today was perfect. Thank you for the goats. I can't believe you did all this for me."

"I'd do anything for you." The words slipped out before I could stop them.

"Gryff?" She sounded hesitant. "About the movie with Tyson..."

My heart stopped. Was she going to cancel? Tell me she'd rather go with me?

"Yeah?"

"Do you think I'm ready? The practice kissing helped, but what if I freeze up again?"

Right. She wanted advice. Friend advice. Practice partner advice.

"You'll be great," I said, dying inside. "The practice sessions really helped your confidence. You're like a totally different person now."

"Because of you," she said softly. "I couldn't have done any of this without you."

"That's what friends are for."

Friends?

The word friends hung between us like a wall. She opened her mouth like she wanted to say something else, then closed it again.

"We should probably get back inside," she said finally. "It's your party."

"Yeah."

But neither of us moved. We sat there in the dark with our goats, shoulders touching, both waiting for something that neither of us seemed able to say.

Finally, Artie stood up. "I'm really glad you're my best friend, Gryff."

"Me too," I lied, because being her friend while being in love with her was actually killing me.

After she went inside, I stayed with the goats a while longer. When I finally made my way back to the house, I found Flynn and Tyson in the kitchen, sharing a beer and talking quietly.

"The movie date should do it," I heard Tyson say.

"You think so?" Flynn asked. "Maybe you should turn

it up even more."

"Trust me, he's about to crack."

My stomach sank. They were talking about Artie. About how she was finally ready to open up to someone, to be vulnerable with Tyson on their date. Flynn was literally coaching Tyson on how to win her over.

"Hey," I said, and they both turned to look at me with expressions I couldn't read.

"Hey, birthday boy," Tyson said, raising his beer. "Great party."

"Yeah," I managed. "Great."

Flynn was studying my face. "You okay?"

"Perfect. I'm gonna go check on Nana and Coach."

I left them to their conspiracy, my chest tight with the realization that everyone, even my own twin, could see that Tyson was perfect for Artie.

Everyone except the goats.

But what did they know? They were goats.

WHAT HAPPENS IN VEGAS

ARTEMIS

I stood in front of my closet, holding up different tops and trying to decide which one said "casual movie date but maybe we'll kiss after." I held them out to Holly who was curled up at the foot of my bed. "Which one do you like better?"

She said, "Meheheh."

"I agree. They are kind of meh."

My phone buzzed which made Holly jump about three feet in the air. When she landed she tried to eat it. I barely grabbed it from her in time. Through the goat slobber I couldn't see who it was from. I was going to have to invest in wet wipes. For now my duvet cover would have to suffice.

TYSON

Hey, I'm so sorry but I have to cancel tonight. My sister's cat's groomer's cousin's mom just flew in and she's lost somewhere on Rodeo Drive and I'm apparently her only hope. Rain check?

I stared at the text, waiting for disappointment to hit. Instead, all I felt was... relief? Which was weird because Tyson was perfect. Handsome, sweet, built like a god, good with animals, except apparently our new goats, and actually interested in me.

> Of course. Go be Obi Wan and save the resistance. Let me know if you need any back up.

> Thanks for understanding. We'll definitely reschedule.

I tossed my phone on the bed and sat down, giving Holly some head scritches. Why was I relieved? This was supposed to be our second date, the one where maybe things would actually click. Where I'd feel that spark everyone talked about.

"You're overthinking again."

I looked up to find Gryff leaning against my doorframe, Vincent tucked under one arm like a football.

"How do you know I'm overthinking?"

"You have that little crease between your eyebrows." He walked over and sat next to me on the bed, Vincent immediately tried to eat one of the shirts in my hands. "What's wrong?"

"Tyson canceled."

His face flashed with what looked like pure joy before settling into sympathetic concern. "Oh no. That's... terrible."

"His sister asked him to go save someone from death by Rodeo Drive."

"That's awful," Gryff said, not sounding like he thought it was awful at all. "So terrible. Very bad. Poor Tyson."

"You're literally smiling."

"I'm not." He was. "I'm just... Vincent and Holly are just so dang cute."

The two of them were eating my comforter.

Before I could call him out on his obvious lie, the front door burst open with a bang that made both of us jump.

"Road trip." Flynn's voice boomed through the house.

We headed out to the living room where Flynn and Tempest were both wearing Mustangs jerseys and grinning like kids on Christmas morning.

"Pack a bag," Tempest announced. "We're going to Vegas."

"Vegas?" I'd never been to Vegas. My mom thought Vegas was where good decisions went to die and people lost their college funds at blackjack tables.

"The Mustangs are playing Thursday night football," Flynn explained. "Everett called and said he got us tickets. We can drive out, watch the game, maybe stay the night, drive back tomorrow. Oh and pack something fancy. He said something about going out after the game."

Jules appeared in the doorway with a backpack and a grin. "Get in, losers, we're going to Vegas. I call shotgun."

"You picked up Jules before even telling us about this?" Gryff looked offended.

"She responds faster." Flynn shrugged. "Also, she threatened to disown me if I ever went to Vegas without her."

"It's true," Jules confirmed. "I have it in writing. Notarized."

Gryff glanced over at me. "What about the goats?"

"Oh, don' t worry," Tempest said. "Sean and Ren have volunteered to goat and donkey sit. They seem very excited about it. Maybe too excited."

Thirty minutes later, we were piled into Flynn's SUV, snacks scattered across the middle console and Jules's road trip playlist blasting through the speakers. She'd claimed DJ rights with the authority of someone who'd been preparing for this moment her whole life.

"Okay, ground rules," Jules announced from the passenger seat where she'd claimed "navigation duties" despite us all having phones with GPS. "Everyone has to sing along to at least three songs. No exceptions. Yes, Flynn, even you."

"I don't sing," Flynn protested.

"You do now." Tempest patted his shoulder. "It's Vegas, baby. Different rules."

The three of us were in the backseat, but about three minutes into the drive, Tempest suddenly remembered she had a deadline. "I'm just gonna pop the third row seat, put my noise-canceling headphones on, and see if I can finish these edits before we get to Vegas. That way I can have fun tonight and not worry about how my football player and his lady love have to stay at the inn with only one bed."

Did she just wink at me?

That left Gryff and me alone in the back, the middle seat between us feeling both too small and too large at the same time.

"I spy with my little eye," Jules started, "two people in love with each other."

"Jules," Gryff and I said in unison.

"What? I spy is a classic road trip game."

"That's not how you play," I protested.

"It is now."

We stopped at a truck stop halfway through the drive, everyone piling out to stretch legs and stock up on road trip essentials. Gryff disappeared while I was browsing the chip aisle, then reappeared with his arms full of my favorites, strawberry Twizzlers, the cheesy poofs we're both obsessed with, and an enormous neon red slushie.

"How did you know I wanted a slushie?"

"You always want a slushie on road trips," he said, like this was common knowledge despite us never having been on a road trip.

"We've never been on a road trip together before."

"No, but you told me about how your mom would only stop at 'approved' rest stops and how you'd always beg for a slushie but she'd say they were just sugar and food coloring."

He remembered that? I'd mentioned it maybe once, years ago, like in high school.

"So I figured you should have one now," he continued, handing it to me. "Vegas rules, right?"

"Right," I said, taking a sip and immediately getting brain freeze. "Vegas rules."

The rest of the drive was a blur of Jules forcing us all to sing along to everything from Taylor Swift and Kelsey Best to Hamilton. Gryff's thigh pressed against mine in a way that should not have been as distracting as it was.

"You've really never been to Vegas?" Gryff asked

quietly while the others were debating the best Elvis song for a theoretical wedding.

"Never. Mom thought it was irresponsible. Too much risk, too much temptation, too much... everything."

"And what do you think?"

I looked out the window at the desert flying by, the sun starting to set and painting everything gold. "I think maybe a little too much everything is exactly what I need."

His hand was resting on the middle seat, and without thinking, I let my pinky finger brush against his. He didn't move away.

"Then we'll make sure you get the full Vegas experience," he said softly.

"What happens in Vegas stays in Vegas?" I tried to make it sound like a joke.

"Something like that."

We arrived at the stadium just as the sun was setting, the lights of Vegas starting to twinkle to life in the distance. The Kingman suite was already packed with family. Mr. Kingman was there with Isak, along with Trixie, Kelsey, Penelope, and Willa. Even the aunts and grandparents had made the trip, and I was excited to see Coach and Nana again so soon. The house seemed empty without them.

"Artemis." Trixie pulled me into a hug immediately. "I'm so glad you came. The boys are going to be so excited you're all here."

The first half of the game was intense, with the Mustangs up by just three points. During halftime, the guys went to get more food, and I suddenly found myself surrounded by Kingman women.

"So," Kelsey said without preamble, "what's happening with you and Gryff?"

"What? Nothing. We're just friends." The line I'd said a billion and two times in the past few years just sort of fell out of my mouth.

"Friends who live together," Willa added.

"And raise goats together," Trixie chimed in.

"And stare at each other with cartoon heart eyes," Penelope finished.

"We don't—" I started, then stopped. Because we kind of did. "It's complicated."

"Honey," Kelsey said gently, "complicated is my middle name. Well, actually it's Noelle, but you get the point. Talk to us."

I looked around at these women who'd welcomed me into their family without question, who cheered for me at rugby matches and sent care packages during finals week, and something in me broke.

"We kissed," I admitted. "A lot. Like, a LOT a lot."

"Finally," Willa exclaimed.

"For practice," I added quickly. "He was helping me with... trust exercises. To get better at dating."

The women exchanged looks that suggested they thought I was insane.

"Practice," Trixie repeated flatly. "Why does that sound familiar?"

"Yes. To help me be more comfortable with physical intimacy. Because I'm bad at it. Especially with men, but also I guess, in general."

"And Gryff volunteered to help you practice... physical

intimacy?" Kelsey's tone suggested she was trying very hard not to laugh.

"It was my idea. Well, Tempest's idea. But I asked him."

"And how did these practice sessions go?" Trixie asked but as if she already knew the answer.

My face went hot. "They were... educational."

"I bet they were," Willa muttered.

"But now I don't know what to do," I continued, the words spilling out. "Because the kissing was amazing. Like, earth-shattering, life-changing kissing. But he hasn't said anything about it meaning anything more than practice, and we just pretend it didn't happen, and now I'm supposed to be going on another date with Tyson but all I can think about is—"

"You're in love with Gryff," Trixie said simply.

"I... maybe? Yes? I don't know." I buried my face in my hands. "What if I tell him and it ruins everything? What if he doesn't feel the same way? What if I lose my best friend because I couldn't keep my feelings in check?"

"Oh, honey," Kelsey said softly. "Have you seen the way that boy looks at you?"

"Like I'm his friend. His buddy. His roommate who needed help with kissing practice."

The women exchanged another round of those looks.

"Artemis," Trixie said firmly, "I've known those boys most of their lives. I've seen them through crushes and girlfriends and boyfriends and everything in between. The way Gryff looks at you? That's not friendship. That's a man completely gone for someone."

"Then why hasn't he said anything?" I basically begged

him to say it was something more after the first kiss, hadn't I? Oh god.

"Because Kingman men are idiots," Willa said. "Loveable, wonderful, absolutely dense idiots who need things spelled out for them in neon signs."

"Sometimes literally," Kelsey added. "I once serenaded Declan from a stadium jumbotron."

"And I'm not totally sure Hayes realized just how much I was in love with him until I married him," Willa added.

"The point is," Trixie said, "sometimes you have to be the one to make the first move. Or the second. Or the seventeenth. I will admit that as someone who didn't realize they were in love with their best friend either."

Before I could respond, the guys returned with arms full of nachos and drinks, and the second half started. But I couldn't focus on the game. All I could think about was Gryff sitting next to me, his arm casually draped over the back of my chair, his thumb occasionally brushing my shoulder.

The Mustangs won by ten points, and the suite erupted in celebration. Everett appeared moments after the game ended, still in his uniform and grinning like he'd won the lottery.

"Everybody get changed. We're doing a thing," he announced. "You're all coming. No arguments."

"What thing?" Flynn asked suspiciously.

"You'll see." Penelope said holding Everett's hand. "Just trust us. See you in an hour. There will be cars outside." Then she disappeared along with Kelsey and Declan.

Everybody got dressed and when we stepped outside,

a caravan of limos was waiting outside the stadium, champagne already chilling inside.

"This seems excessive for a victory celebration," I said as we all piled in.

"Vegas gonna Vegas," Gryff said, but he looked as confused as I felt.

Twenty minutes later, we pulled up to a building with a neon sign featuring a Lobster Elvis in a light-up jump-suit declaring it the High C Wedding chapel.

"Did we just crash someone's wedding?" I whispered to Gryff.

"Not crashing if you're invited," Penelope called out, and that's when I noticed the bouquet in her hands and the beautiful white dress she was wearing. Everett stood proudly next to her in a tux.

"Oh my god," Jules squealed. "Are you—"

"Yup, we are. Just us and the people who mean the most to us." he said with a meaningful look in Penny's eyes.

What followed was the most chaotic, joyful, ridiculous hour of my life. Elvis was Chinese and did an incredible impression while wearing a bedazzled white jumpsuit and carrying a Triton. Declan gave a best man speech that made everyone cry. Kelsey, the matron of honor, sang an acoustic version of "Can't Help Falling in Love" that had me sobbing.

During the actual vows, the couple looked at each other like there was no one else in the universe but each other. I felt Gryff's hand find mine. Our fingers inter-laced, and he squeezed gently.

I didn't let go.

Not during the kiss, not during the ridiculous Elvis hip thrust dance, not during the champagne toast with sparkling cider for the very pregnant Penny. His hand in mine felt like coming home.

By two a.m., we were all exhausted and definitely too tipsy to drive home.

"Good news," Flynn announced, looking at his phone. "I got us rooms at the hotel next door."

"Bad news," he continued, not looking sorry at all, "they only had honeymoon suites left. Two of them. So Jules is staying with the aunts, and Tempest and I can share one..."

Gryff and I looked at each other in panic.

"We'll take the other one," Gryff said, his voice carefully neutral.

The honeymoon suite was... a lot. Heart-shaped bed. Red velvet everything. A mirror on the ceiling that I was definitely not looking at. Rose petals scattered on every surface. A champagne bucket with a note that said "Congratulations Mr. and Mrs. Goatlightly" because apparently that was the alias Flynn had used.

"This is so excessive," I said, staring at the bed that seemed to be the only piece of furniture in the room besides a chair shaped like a giant high heel.

"Vegas gonna Vegas," Gryff repeated, but his voice was strained.

We stood there awkwardly, both a little drunk on champagne and wedding feelings, neither knowing what to do next.

"That was beautiful," I said finally, sitting on the edge of the heart bed. "The wedding. Even with Elvis."

"Especially with Elvis," Gryff corrected, sitting next to me.

"They looked at each other like..."

"Like she was his whole world," Gryff finished softly.

"Yeah." I pulled my legs up under me, turning to face him. "I want someone to look at me like that someday."

"Someone will," he said, and the way he was looking at me right then made my heart skip.

"I'd be terrified though," I admitted, the champagne making me brave. "Of the wedding night, I mean."

"Why?"

I took a breath. We'd already crossed so many lines with our trust exercises. What was one more confession?

"I've never... I mean, I can't..." I started over. "I've never had an orgasm with a partner. Only by myself. I can't let go with someone else there. I freeze up or perform or just... disconnect."

Gryff was quiet for a moment, and I immediately regretted saying anything.

"Sorry, that was too much information—"

"No," he said quickly. "I'm just... processing. So you've never...?"

"Never. I've tried, I swear, and it's not like I want to fake it. But my brain won't shut off. I get too in my head about what I should be doing or feeling, and how I need to get my partner off. Then I'm basically just watching myself from outside my body, and it's..." I shrugged. "It's why they all said I was bad in bed."

"They were idiots," Gryff said firmly. "You're not bad at anything. You just need to learn to let someone else take care of you."

"That's the problem. I don't know how."

He turned to face me fully, and there was that look again, the one that made me feel like I was falling and flying at the same time.

"This is just another trust exercise," he said slowly. "Like the eye contact, like the kissing practice."

"Gryff, this is... different."

"Only if we make it different." His hand found mine. "What if we just approach it the same way? No pressure, no expectations. Just you learning to trust someone else with your pleasure."

"You'd do that for me?" My voice came out smaller than intended.

"I'd do anything for you," he said, and the weight of those words hung between us.

"What if I can't?"

"Then we'll figure out why. We'll go as slow as you need. Or we stop. Whatever you need."

I looked at him, my best friend, the person who knew me better than anyone, who'd already taught me so much about trusting someone else. "Okay."

"Okay?"

"Okay."

Well okay then. Here we go.

STAYS IN VEGAS

GRYFF

"*O*kay."

The word hung between us in the ridiculous Vegas honeymoon suite, and I felt the weight of it settle into my bones. She was trusting me with this. Trusting me with her vulnerability, her insecurities, her body.

This was the only time I'd ever get to show her how she should be loved.

I took a breath, trying to center myself. This wasn't about me. This couldn't be about me or the fact that I was so in love with her it felt like drowning. This was about Artie learning she deserved to be cherished.

"We go at your pace," I said, shifting to face her fully on the heart-shaped bed. "You're in control here."

"But I don't know what I'm doing," she said, that little crease appearing between her eyebrows.

"That's the point. You don't have to know. You just have to feel. I've got you, sweet strawberry girl." I reached out slowly, telegraphing my movement. "Can I touch your face?"

She nodded, and I cupped her cheek gently, thumb stroking over her cheekbone.

"You tell me if anything doesn't feel good. Even if you think you should like it, even if you think I want you to like it," I said, keeping my voice soft and steady even though my heart was trying to break out of my chest. "You tell me."

My number one rule had and would always be about having enthusiastic consent from my partner. Anything else and I didn't want it.

She bit her bottom lip for just a minute, like she was thinking about whether she was going to agree to my rules. No, that wasn't quite it. She was trying to talk herself into being strong enough to actually express what she wanted tonight. "Okay."

"That's my good girl. We can stop anytime. Just say the word. No questions, no disappointment, we just stop."

"What if I can't... what if I freeze up again?"

God, I wanted to bury every other person she'd ever been with under a whole-ass field of columbines for not realizing they hadn't taken care of her when she so clearly needed someone to. "Then we stop. We talk. We figure out what you need." I moved my thumb to trace her bottom lip. "This isn't about performing or doing anything right, Artie. This is about you feeling safe and good. That's all I want."

Liar. You want so much more than that.

"Can I kiss you?" I asked.

"We've been kissing for weeks," she said with a nervous laugh.

"Not like this," I said. "This is different. This is... can I kiss you?"

"Yes."

I leaned in slowly, giving her time to change her mind, and pressed my lips to hers. Soft, gentle, nothing like the desperate practice sessions we'd been having. This was reverent. This was worship.

She sighed into the kiss, her hand coming up to rest against my chest, and I had to fight not to deepen it, not to take more than she was offering.

"Still good?" I asked against her lips.

"Still good."

I swept her hair back and gently wove my fingers into her waves and deepened the kiss. I teased her with my tongue, savoring every moment that she responded with her own. We lay back together, still fully clothed, just kissing. I kept one hand on her face, the other resting carefully on her waist, not moving, not pushing. Just being present with her.

When I felt her start to tense up, overthinking, I pulled back.

"Where'd you go?" I asked. "You left me for a second there."

She blinked a few times and looked down, hiding from me. But then I felt her muscles relax and she took a fortifying breath, like she remembered she'd said she would tell me when things got uncomfortable. "I'm trying to figure out what I should be doing."

"Nothing. You should be doing absolutely nothing

except feeling." I traced my fingers along her jaw. "Tell me what you're feeling right now. Not what you think you should feel. What you actually feel."

"Nervous. But also safe. Warm." She paused. "Tingly."

Was it the same electricity that was coursing through my…every cell in my body? "Good tingly or bad tingly?"

"Good. Very good."

"Then we're on the right track." I pressed a kiss to her forehead. "Can I tell you something?"

"Yeah."

She was doing such a good job of being honest with me, I was going to do the same. "You're so beautiful it hurts to look at you sometimes."

She laughed, but it was self-deprecating. "You don't have to—"

"No." I cut her off firmly. "You're perfect. You're strong. You're powerful." I ran my hand down her arm, feeling the muscle there. "These arms that can tackle anyone on the rugby pitch. Do you know what it does to me watching you play?"

Her breath hitched. "What?"

"Drives me fucking crazy. The way you move, all that controlled power." I shifted, hovering over her slightly so I could look directly into her eyes. "These beautiful, strong shoulders." I traced my fingers across her collarbones. "This body that does so many incredible things."

"Gryff…"

"Can I see you? All of you?" I asked. "Will you let me?" Of course I knew what she looked like, but I'd had to leave it up to my very, very fucking vivid imagination to fantasize the color of her nipples, or the way her ass would fit into my hands.

She tensed immediately. "I—"

"We don't have to. We can stay just like this."

"No, I want to, I just..." She bit her lip. "I'm sure I'm not going to look like the other women you've been with. There's never been anything delicate about me. Or—"

"Thank fucking god," I said with such vehemence that she laughed. "Artie, you could crush a man between these thighs and he'd die happy."

She smiled for the first time. "That's a weird compliment."

"But accurate." I ran my hand down to her hip, squeezing gently. "Can I?"

She nodded, and I slowly, carefully, helped her out of her shirt. The bra underneath was simple, black, and I had to take a breath because she was so fucking perfect it hurt.

"Jesus Christ, Artie. Look at you." I was so awestruck by getting to see even this much of her, I could barely get the words out.

"Stop." A soft pink rose up her throat and cheeks. "I don't need to be flattered."

"I'm not being nice. I'm being honest." I traced my finger along the edge of her bra. "You're like a fucking goddess. All powerful curves and soft skin."

Don't say you want her thighs wrapped around your head. That's too much. Don't scare her.

"Can it be your turn, now?" she asked quietly. "I... want to see you too."

I pulled my shirt off without hesitation, and her hands immediately came up to touch my chest, exploring. When her fingers traced over my abs, I had to bite back a groan.

She was a hundred percent with me, then her eyes went to the side and I could practically see the fear gears trying to tell her to stop. "Touch me like you were, if you want to."

I wasn't beneath begging, but we were on a precarious edge here and one push too far, and I might lose this one chance with her.

"I do want to." Her hand hovered inches from my chest.

"Hey." I caught her hand, brought it to my lips. "Stay with me, baby. Tell me what you're thinking."

"That I should be better at this. That I should know what to do."

"There's no should here. There's just us." I kissed each of her fingertips. "Remember freshman year when we went to that terrible party at the baseball house?"

She laughed. "The one where someone tried to make jungle juice in a kiddie pool?"

"That's the one. You wore that blue dress and spent the whole night teaching me rugby rules using beer cans as players."

She smirked at me in such a cute way. The way she did when we truly were just friends, being friends. "Why are you bringing that up now?"

"Because that's when I first noticed your thighs," I admitted. "You were demonstrating a scrum and your dress rode up and I completely forgot how to speak for like five minutes."

"You did not." She chuckled and rolled her eyes at me.

"I absolutely did." I think I'd been in love with her even back then. "Flynn had to elbow me because I was staring."

She was full out laughing now, relaxed, present. Perfect.

"There's my girl. Can I touch you?" I asked. "Really touch you?"

"Yes." Her eyes, already dark with arousal, sparkled for me. Just for me, as she whispered the word.

I started slow, hands skimming over her sides, her soft stomach, the silvery stretch marks I wanted to come all over. I mapped every inch of exposed skin, committing it all to memory for the inevitable lonely nights I had ahead of me. When I unclasped her bra, asking permission with my eyes, she nodded.

"Fuck," I breathed, taking her in. Her nipples were the softest pink, hard, and calling to me to lick and suck them. "You're perfect. Every inch of you is perfect."

"I'm not—"

"You are. These curves, this strength." I ran my hands over her breasts, watching her face for any sign of where she liked to be touched. "Do you know how many times I've thought about this?"

Shit. Too honest.

But she just arched into my touch, making a soft sound that went straight through me.

"Still good?"

"Don't stop."

I took my time, worshipping every inch of her with my hands and mouth. Her breasts filled my hands perfectly and I swear to god above her nipples tasted sweet. The curve of her rib cage and into the dip of her hips would haunt me the rest of my life. When I got to her jeans, I paused.

"We can stop here," I offered.

"No." She didn't hide her smile from me this time. "I trust you."

I love you. I love you so fucking much.

I helped her out of her jeans, taking my time, pressing kisses to each newly exposed bit of skin. Her thighs were thick and strong and perfect, and I couldn't help myself.

"These thighs," I groaned. "Artie, these fucking thighs."

"You're obsessed with my thighs."

"Completely. Utterly. Obsessed." I ran my hands up them. "They're perfect. You're perfect."

When she was down to just her underwear, I could see her starting to overthink again.

"Hey, where'd you go? Look at me."

She met my eyes.

"There you are. Stay with me." I moved back up to kiss her. "We don't have to do anything else. This can be enough."

"I want to. I just... I'm scared."

"Of what, sweetheart?" The endearment slipped out before I could stop it.

"Of being too much. Of not being enough. Of disappointing you." The shudder that went through her eyes had to be the memory of every lover who'd let her think she'd disappointed them.

I'd never been more irritated in my life that I wasn't a serial killer. They all deserved torture at best.

"You could never disappoint me." I cupped her face

with both hands. "You're exactly right. You're exactly perfect. You don't have to be anything but yourself."

"What if I can't... come?"

"Then we try again. Try something different. Whatever you need."

She was quiet for a moment, then her tongue darted out wetting her lips. "I want you to touch me."

"Where?" Why, oh why wasn't I born a supernatural being who could touch her everywhere at once?

She took my hand and guided it between her legs, over her underwear. "Here."

Thank god I still had my jeans on, because I was going to go off like a rocket and she didn't need to see that right now. I gave my cock a stern but quick lecture to regain control. This. Wasn't. About. Me. "Are you sure?"

"Yes. Just... keep talking to me. Keep me here."

"Always."

I started slow, gentle pressure over the fabric, watching her face for every reaction. When her eyes started to flutter closed, I called her back.

"Look at me. Stay with me."

She swallowed hard. "It's intense."

"I know. But you're safe. I've got you."

I kept up the gentle rhythm, talking to her the whole time. Telling her how beautiful she was, how perfect, how strong. When I felt her starting to respond, her hips moving slightly, I asked for the one and only thing I wanted, "Can I use my mouth?"

Her eyes went wide. "What?"

"Can I use my mouth on you? I want to taste you." I

was never going to get more than this, so if she'd let me, I'd fuck her with my mouth and tongue.

"I... umm...I don't know if I'll be able to come like that. Nobody's been able to..."

"Then let me be the first. Let me show you how good it can be."

Let me worship you the way you deserve. Let me love you the only way I can.

"Okay."

I moved down her body slowly, pressing kisses to her stomach, her hips, the inside of her thighs. When I pulled her underwear off, I took a moment just to look at her.

"Fuck," I murmured. "So fucking beautiful."

I should have kissed and licked and teased her, but I just couldn't wait anymore. The first touch of my tongue was straight to her plump little clit and made her gasp. She immediately tried to close her legs and I reveled in her thighs wrapped around my head.

"Too much?"

"No, just... I didn't expect the rub of your beard to feel so... good."

Thank god for the beard. "We can stop."

"No. No, please don't stop."

I took my time, learning what made her gasp, what made her moan, what made her hands tighten in my hair. When I slipped one finger just barely into her, she tensed up, overthinking, I reached up and took her hand.

"Stay with me. Just feel."

"I can't... I don't think I can..."

"You can, you already are. Trust me. Trust yourself." I

squeezed her hand. "Stop thinking about what should happen. Just feel what is happening."

I went back to work, pouring everything I felt for her into this act of worship. Every stroke of my tongue was an I love you. Every kiss to her pussy was a promise I couldn't make out loud. This was my one chance to show her how she should be loved, and I was going to make it count.

Slowly, I slipped my finger back in, and stroked in and out, matching the motion with flicks of my tongue. Her thighs started to tremble, and I looked up at her.

"Look at me," I commanded gently. "I want to see you when you let go."

"Gryff, I can't—"

"Yes you can. I've got you. Let go for me."

I eased a second finger in and curled my fingers, looking for just the right spot to push her over the edge.

She let out a low moan, and for the first time with another person, she let go completely. Her back arched, my name on her lips, her thighs tightening around my head, and fuck if that wasn't the hottest thing I'd ever experienced. I worked her through it, licking and stroking, holding her steady, watching her face as she came apart.

It was the best thing I'd ever witnessed in my life. And the worst, because I'd never get to see it again.

She finally collapsed back, breathing hard, and I moved back up to hold her.

"Oh my god," she gasped. "That was... I didn't know..."

"That's how it should always be," I said, pulling her

against my chest. "Someone who sees you, really sees you, and gives you what you need."

Someone who loves you like I do.

Overwhelmed by the intensity, a couple of soft tears pooled in her lashes, and I held her tighter, stroking her hair the way I knew she liked. "You're okay. You're perfect. That was perfect."

"I didn't know it could be like that," she whispered against my neck.

"That's how it should be. Someone who makes you feel worthy of being cared for."

"Thank you," she said, so quietly I almost missed it.

"For what?"

"For making me feel... needed. Beautiful, worthy. Like I'm enough."

You're everything. You're my everything.

"You're worthy of everything," I said instead. "The right person is going to worship you."

And it was going to kill me that I couldn't be that person for her.

"Like you did?"

"Better," I lied, the word bitter on my tongue. "So much better."

She was getting sleepy now, the emotional and physical intensity catching up with her. As she drifted off in my arms, she murmured, "I don't think anyone could be better than you."

I held her while she slept, memorizing everything. The weight of her against me. The way her hair smelled like strawberries even after a night in Vegas. The little sounds she made in her sleep. The way she'd said my name when she came.

This was it. My one night. Tomorrow we'd go back to being friends. Tomorrow I'd help her with Tyson, watch her fall in love with someone else, pretend this meant nothing more than practice.

But tonight, just tonight, I got to pretend she was mine.

"I love you," I whispered into the darkness, pressing a kiss to her forehead. "I love you so fucking much it's killing me."

She stirred slightly, murmuring something that might have been my name, and I froze. But she just curled closer, still asleep, trusting me to hold her.

So I did. I held her through the night, watching the Vegas lights paint patterns on the ceiling, counting her breaths, storing up every second of this feeling.

Because tomorrow, I'd have to let her go.

But tonight? Tonight she was mine, even if she didn't know it.

Tonight was everything.

ZERO FOX GIVEN

ARTEMIS

I woke up still wrapped in Gryff's arms, my face pressed against his chest, our legs tangled together like we'd been trying to merge into one person while we slept. For a moment, I let myself have this—the warmth of him, the steady beat of his heart under my ear, the way his hand had found its way into my hair even in sleep.

Then reality crashed in.

Vegas. The honeymoon suite. What we'd done. What he'd done. What he'd made me feel.

That's how it should always be. Someone who sees you, really sees you.

His words from last night echoed in my head, and I had to fight the urge to burrow deeper into his chest and pretend the morning hadn't come.

"You awake?" His voice was rough with sleep, and I felt it rumble through his chest.

"Yeah."

Neither of us moved. We lay there, both awake, both

aware, neither willing to be the first to pull away. The weight of what had happened hung between us like a physical thing.

Finally, Gryff cleared his throat. "That was... Artie, I..." He pressed a kiss to the top of my head and held me tighter for just a moment.

"The practice helped, right?"

Practice.

The word hit like cold water. Right. Practice. Trust exercises. Me learning to be comfortable with physical intimacy so I could date other people. That's all this was.

"Right," I managed, finally pulling away. The loss of his warmth felt like losing a limb. "Super helpful practice."

"Good. That's... good."

We got ready in painful silence, both of us being way too careful not to accidentally touch, not to make eye contact for too long, not to acknowledge that something fundamental had shifted between us.

The car ride home was torture. Jules had claimed the front seat again, chattering about the wedding and Elvis and how Everett's face had looked when he saw Penelope. Flynn and Tempest kept exchanging worried looks from the front seat to where Tempest was all the way in the back again. And Gryff and I sat in the middle, each pressed to our own windows, the space between us feeling like the Grand Canyon or the Mariana Trench.

Every time Jules said something about love or romance or feelings, Gryff tensed up. Every time I shifted, he seemed to stop breathing. We were so hyperaware of each other it was like the air between us was charged with painful electricity.

"You two are being weird," Jules announced, turning around to study us. "Weirder than normal."

"We're not being weird," we said in unison, which was definitely weird.

"Right." She narrowed her eyes. "Did something happen in Vegas?"

"No," Gryff said too quickly.

"Nothing," I agreed too forcefully.

"Because you know what they say about Vegas—"

"Jules," Flynn warned from the driver's seat.

"I'm just saying, if something hypothetically happened—"

"Nothing happened," Gryff said, and something about the firmness in his voice made my chest tight.

Right. Nothing happened. Just practice. Just my best friend giving me my first orgasm with another person while looking at me like I hung the stars in the sky. Nothing at all.

When we finally got home, Vincent and Holly were waiting by the door like furry little judgmental parents. Vincent immediately headbutted Gryff's shin while Holly grabbed my shoelace in her teeth and pulled, clearly punishing us for our abandonment.

"I should deal with them," Gryff said, already scooping up Vincent under one arm and Holly under the other.

"Yeah, I should... unpack," I said, even though I barely had anything to unpack.

We fled to opposite ends of the house like we were on fire.

And we stayed like that for a week. Everything between us was awkward and weird and horrible.

I went to practice and work and sucked at both. Gryff went to practice and played so bad in his game on Sunday that he got benched in the first quarter.

The next week went exactly the same.

And the next.

Moving to the UK was starting to look like a good idea.

Mid-week I was rotting in my bed when my phone buzzed.

TYSON

Hey, would love to reschedule for tonight if you're free? That Fox Daws movie's still playing.

I stared at the text. Three weeks ago, I would have been excited. Tyson was perfect, handsome, sweet, genuinely interested in me. But now, after Vegas, after Gryff's hands and mouth and the way he'd made me feel...

Tonight works.

What was wrong with me? Why was I agreeing to this?

Because Gryff had made it very clear in Vegas it was just practice. Because I needed to prove to myself that I could do this. Because maybe if I went out with Tyson, I could stop thinking about my best friend's mouth between my thighs.

I found Gryff in the kitchen, making a protein shake and studiously not looking at me.

"Tyson wants to reschedule that movie date for tonight."

His head whipped around and I prayed he was going to tell me not to go.

Stop me.

"Oh. Right. That's... cool."

"I should probably get ready for my date," I announced, watching his face carefully.

Tell me not to go.

"Cool. Have fun." He didn't even look up from the blender.

Tell me that night meant something.

"I'm going to shower," I said, louder than necessary. "For my date. With Tyson."

Why couldn't I just tell him how I felt? Because it clearly didn't matter.

"Sounds good."

I stood there for another moment, willing him to say something, anything. Willing myself to do the same. But he just kept adding ingredients to his shake like it required his complete concentration, and I just stood there.

"I'm going to wear that blue dress," I tried.

His hand paused for just a second on the protein powder. "The one where you taught me rugby with beer cans?"

"Yeah."

"Cool. You look good in that dress."

Tell me not to wear it for him. Tell me to stay home. Tell me you want me.

But he didn't. He just started the blender, the noise effectively ending the conversation.

An hour later, I stood in front of my mirror, blue dress

on, trying to feel something other than wrong. The dress looked good. I looked good. But all I could think about was Gryff admitting he'd noticed my thighs in this dress years ago.

I walked back to the living room where Gryff was now on the couch, Vincent and Holly in his lap, all three of them looking morose.

"How do I look?"

He looked up, and for a moment, his face was completely unguarded. Raw want flashed in his eyes before he shuttered it away.

"Perfect," he said quietly. "Tyson's a lucky guy."

I don't want Tyson to be lucky. I want you to tell me not to go.

"Thanks."

We stared at each other for a long moment, so many unsaid things hanging in the air between us. Then my phone buzzed.

TYSON

On my way. Be there in a minute.

"He's coming," I said unnecessarily.

"Great."

"Yeah. Great."

Neither of us moved. We just kept looking at each other like we were trying to memorize something we were about to lose.

A car honked outside.

"That's him," I said.

"Have fun," Gryff said, his voice hollow.

"Yeah. Thanks."

I left him sitting there with our goats, all of us looking lost.

Tyson was perfect, as always. He opened my door, complimented my dress, had already bought our tickets online so we wouldn't have to wait. He held my hand as we walked into the theater, and it was warm and nice and completely wrong.

His hand was too big. Too smooth. He didn't rub his thumb over my knuckles the way Gryff did. He didn't interlock our fingers properly.

"You want popcorn?" he asked.

"Sure."

He ordered a large with butter, not knowing I preferred it with that weird cheese powder Gryff always made fun of me for. He got me a Coke, not the cherry one Gryff would have grabbed without asking. He chose seats in the middle of the theater, not the back corner where Gryff and I always sat so we could whisper without bothering people.

Everything was fine. Nice. Polite.

Wrong.

The previews started, and all I could think about was movie nights with Gryff. How he'd make up ridiculous alternate plots for every trailer. How we'd share Twizzlers and argue about whether they counted as real licorice. How his hand would always end up on my knee, not romantically, just naturally, like it belonged there.

Tyson's hand was on the armrest between us, clearly available for holding. I didn't take it.

The movie started, and if anyone could distract me from this disaster it should be, Fox Daws driving fast cars unnecessarily shirtless, and I tried to focus. But Tyson was sitting so properly, watching so intently. Gryff would have been making quiet comments about the plot holes by now. Would have been stealing my popcorn even though he had his own. Would have been existing in my space in that way that felt like breathing.

Then, about twenty minutes in, I heard a familiar snort-laugh from somewhere behind us.

No.

I turned slightly, and there, three rows back, was Jules in the world's worst disguise. Sunglasses indoors, a baseball cap that said "INCONSPICUOUS" (where did she even find that?), and what looked like a fake mustache that was coming unstuck on one side.

Next to her, slouched down like he was trying to disappear into his seat, was Gryff.

Our eyes met across the dark theater, and even in the flickering light from the screen, I could see everything written on his face. Longing. Regret. Something that looked a lot like love.

"Is that Gryff?" Tyson whispered, following my gaze.

"Unfortunately."

"And his sister?"

"Apparently."

Jules chose that moment to throw popcorn at the screen, shouting, "That's not how physics works!"

Several people shushed her. Gryff sank lower in his seat.

"Do you want to... move?" Tyson asked.

"No," I said, because even having Gryff here being

ridiculous was better than him not being here at all. "They'll get bored eventually."

They did not get bored.

Jules provided running commentary through the entire film. During the romantic subplot, when the leads finally kissed, Gryff had a coughing fit that lasted so long someone offered him a lozenge.

"Your friend seems..." Tyson paused, clearly searching for a polite word.

"Yeah," I agreed. "He really does."

But the thing was, even with all the ridiculous sabotage, having Gryff there made everything better. I found myself waiting for his reactions, turning slightly to catch his expression during the good parts. When the hero made a terrible decision, I heard Gryff's frustrated sigh and had to bite back a smile.

This was what was missing with Tyson. This connection. This knowing. This feeling like even watching a stupid action movie was better when Gryff was involved, even if he was three rows back being an absolute disaster.

When the movie ended and the lights came up, Jules and Gryff were already gone. Probably fled the scene of the crime.

I caught Tyson checking his phone with what looked like a small smirk as we walked to the car.

"I had a nice time," he said, though his smile was a bit too knowing. "Despite the... interruptions."

"Tyson, I—"

"You're in love with your roommate," he said simply, not unkindly.

I opened my mouth to deny it, then closed it again.

"Flynn might have mentioned something," he continued, putting his phone away. "About Vegas."

I literally felt the blood drain from my face.

"Flynn's dead," I muttered.

"He's worried about his brother. Apparently Gryff's
been miserable for weeks." Tyson leaned against the car.
"Did you know he texted me fifteen times? Asking about
my intentions, whether I'm good enough for you, sending
me a list of your favorite things."

"He did?"

"Including a note about your weird popcorn prefer-
ences and that you hate when people pick the middle
seats at movies." He grinned. "Then he showed up to sabotage our date anyway."

"With Jules and her fake mustache."

"Which was definitely her idea. She texted me during
the movie that it was part of something called 'Operation
Make My Brother Stop Being an Idiot.'" He shook his
head. "Your whole friend group is... intense."

"They're conspiring."

"Because you two are too stubborn to admit what
everyone else can see." He touched my arm gently. "Look,
I genuinely think you're amazing. In another universe
where you weren't completely gone for Gryff, I'd absolutely want to date you for real. But Artie, you watched
him more than the movie."

"They were distracting."

"You wore that dress for him, not me."

Crap. "I—"

"Even the goats know it. Vincent tried to eat my
shoelaces specifically to keep me away from you."

"Vincent eats everyone's shoelaces."

"While making direct eye contact? That goat has an agenda." He opened the car door for me and we started the drive home. "Talk to him. Or don't, and Flynn will probably orchestrate something even more ridiculous."

The drive home was too short to figure out what I was going to say. My head was spinning with Tyson's words, with the memory of Gryff's face in the theater, with the ghost of Vegas still on my skin.

I found Gryff exactly where I expected, on the couch with both goats now, pretending to watch TV, snuggled up with the goats again.

"How was your date?" he asked, not looking at me.

"You were there, so you tell me."

"I don't know what you're talking about."

"Gryff. Jules had a fake mustache."

"That doesn't sound like Jules."

"It was coming unstuck. During the romantic scene, she tried to stick it back on and got it stuck to her cheek."

He cracked then, a small smile tugging at his lips. "That did happen."

I collapsed onto the couch next to him, exhausted from pretending everything was fine. "It was all wrong."

"What was?" His voice was carefully neutral, but I felt him tense beside me.

"The date. The movie. Everything." Without thinking, I curled into his side, my body naturally finding its place against his. "His hand felt wrong. He got the wrong snacks. He sat in the wrong seats."

Gryff's arm came around me automatically, pulling me closer. "Wrong how?"

Wrong because he wasn't you.

"Just... wrong."

We sat there in silence, watching whatever was on TV without really seeing it. This felt more intimate than Vegas somehow. Vegas had been about physical sensation, about trust and pleasure. This was about the simple intimacy of existing together, of fitting perfectly into each other's spaces.

"Gryff?"

"Yeah?"

"In Vegas..."

His whole body went rigid. "Yeah?"

I lost my nerve. All the words I wanted to say—*it wasn't practice for me, I'm in love with you, please tell me you feel it too*—got stuck in my throat.

"We can't do practice anymore," I said instead.

His voice came out hollow. "I know."

"It's too..."

"I know."

We sat there, still curled together, both afraid to move. Holly climbed into my lap while Vincent stretched across both of us, and we stayed like that, pretending to watch TV, pretending everything was normal, pretending we weren't both dying inside.

Finally, I couldn't take it anymore. I stood up, dislodging Holly who bleated in protest.

"Goodnight," I said.

Gryff caught my hand as I passed, his fingers wrapping around mine. He looked up at me, and for a moment I thought he was going to say something real. Something that mattered.

"Goodnight, Artie," he said instead, letting my hand go.

I made it to my room before the tears came. Holly had followed me, and she climbed onto my bed, curling against my stomach as I cried.

"I'm in love with him," I told her, my voice breaking. "Vegas wasn't practice for me. It was... it was everything. But I'm too much of a dumb butt to tell him."

Through the wall, I could hear Gryff pacing in his room, the floorboards creaking with each step. Back and forth, back and forth, like he was trying to walk off whatever was eating at him.

We were so close. Just a wall between us. But it might as well have been an ocean.

"I think I ruined everything," I whispered to Holly. "I think we broke something we can't fix."

Holly made a soft sound and nuzzled closer, and I held onto her like she could somehow make everything better.

But she was just a goat. And I was just a girl in love with her best friend who would rather sabotage her dates than tell her how he really felt.

And tomorrow, we'd wake up and pretend everything was fine again.

Even though we both knew it never would be.

I TOLD YOU SO: A SIX-YEAR JOURNEY

GRYFF

I sat on my bed, listening to Artie's muffled voice through the wall as she talked to Holly. I couldn't make out the words, but the tone was enough, sad, confused, lost. Just like I felt.

She had curled into me on the couch like she belonged there, and then she'd stood up and walked away. Said we couldn't do practice anymore. And I'd let her go because that's what I did. I let people go. I made things easier for everyone else.

Even if it was killing me.

My phone sat on my nightstand, and before I could overthink it, I grabbed it and called the one person who might understand.

"Son?" Dad's voice was rough with sleep but immediately alert in that way parents get when their kids call in the middle of the night. "It's past midnight here. You okay?"

"No," I admitted, the word cracking. "I'm not okay."

There was a pause, then the sound of covers ruffling, and him sitting up in bed. "This is about Artemis, isn't it? And your feelings for her?"

I almost dropped the phone. "How did you—"

"Flynn called earlier. Said you were spiraling." I heard the click of him turning on the lamp on his bedside table. "Also, Gryff, I have eyes. I've watched you two for six years."

His voice carried that mix of exasperation and fondness that only parents could manage. "Remember when you brought her to Christmas that first year? You looked at her the way I used to look at your mother."

"Everyone knows?" It was meant to be a question, but it came out so flatly, I knew it was the truth. My whole body sank back against my headboard. Everyone could see what I'd been trying so hard to hide.

"Everyone except Artemis, apparently."

My dad was the only person I could say the thing I feared the most out loud to. "Or she knows and doesn't feel the same way."

Dad made a sound that was part sigh, part laugh, with years of parenting experience behind it. "Son, I've been waiting to have this conversation with you for a very long time."

"What?" I thought I was about to get the patented 'pull your head out of your ass' talk.

"Gryff, when did you decide your happiness matters less than everyone else's?"

The question hit me like a slap. "It's not like that—"

"Isn't it?" His voice was gentle but insistent. "You've

been putting yourself last since..." He paused, and I could hear him choosing his words carefully, the way he did when he was about to say something that mattered. "Since your mother died."

The words hit like a physical blow, knocking the air from my lungs. "Dad—"

"I've watched you for seventeen years, son. Seventeen years of you taking care of everyone else." His voice cracked slightly. "You were six years old, Gryff. Six. Your mother had just died, and instead of letting yourself be a grieving child, you looked around at all of us falling apart and decided it was your job to hold us together."

I remembered it. God, I remembered it so clearly. The funeral, everyone crying, Chris trying to be strong at twelve, baby Jules screaming because she didn't understand where Mama went. And me, standing there, thinking *someone has to help them stop crying.*

"Someone had to—"

"No. I had to. I was the adult. I was the father." His voice was thick with old guilt. "But I was drowning in my own grief, and you... you saw that and appointed yourself the family peacemaker. The one who makes everyone laugh when things get too heavy. The one who smooths over fights. The one who fixes things."

"That's not—" But it was. God, it was exactly that.

"Do you remember what you said to me the week after the funeral?" Dad asked quietly.

I didn't want to remember, but the memory was there, clear as day. "I said I'd be good so you wouldn't be sad anymore."

"You were six years old, and you were promising to be good enough to fix my broken heart." I could hear tears in his voice now. "And you've been trying to fix everyone's hearts ever since."

Vincent, who'd been sleeping at the foot of my bed, climbed into my lap and butted his head against my chest, like he could sense the ache there.

"You introduced Chris to Trixie when he was too scared to approach her. You practically threw Flynn at Tempest when he was being an idiot. You helped to orchestrate half the relationships in this family." Dad's voice got firmer. "But when it comes to your own happiness, you always, always step aside. Like you don't deserve the same love you fight for everyone else to have."

"I just... I don't want to be selfish."

"Wanting to be loved isn't selfish, Gryff. It's human." He took a breath. "Do you know what your mother said to me on your third birthday?"

I couldn't speak around the lump in my throat.

"She said, 'This one's going to love so hard it might break him. We have to make sure he knows he deserves to be loved just as hard in return.'" Dad's voice broke completely. "I failed at that. I let you become the caretaker instead of making sure you knew how to be cared for."

"Dad, no."

"Yes. I was so grateful that you kept us all together, kept us laughing, kept us functioning, that I didn't see what it was costing you. You learned that your value was in what you could do for others, not in who you are."

The truth of it hit me like a freight train. Every relationship, every friendship, every interaction, I was always the one giving, fixing, supporting. And with Artie…

"You think you're protecting Artemis by not telling her how you feel," Dad continued, like he could read my thoughts. "But, Gryff, what you're really doing is making her choice for her. You're deciding she's better off without you, that she doesn't get a say in whether she wants you or not."

"I'm trying not to ruin our friendship—"

"You're so busy sacrificing yourself that you won't let her choose you." His voice softened. "Think about it, son. Really think about it. You're pre-rejecting yourself to save her from having to do it. But what if she wants to choose you? What if she's been trying to choose you this whole time and you keep pushing her toward other people?"

I thought about Vegas, about her trust, about the way she'd looked at me. About tonight, curled into my side like she belonged there.

"Your mother would have wanted you to fight for your happiness, Gryff. She would have wanted you to be brave enough to not just love, but to accept being loved. To believe you're worthy of it."

"What if Artie doesn't feel the same?"

"Hmm." That tone meant I was about to get another figurative slap upside the head. "What's happening right now?"

I thought about her on a date with Tyson, about the defeated look on her face when she said we couldn't practice anymore. "She's dating other people."

"So you're already living your worst-case scenario." He let that sink in for a moment. "The only difference is, right now you're choosing it instead of actually finding out the truth. You're so afraid of losing her that you're pushing her away."

"But—"

"No buts. I've watched that girl look at you like you like you're her home for six years. Six years, Gryff. She moved across the country to live with you. She bought you a goat after you—"

"She named the goat Vincent Van Goat."

My dad laughed. "Flynn told me all about you two getting them for each other. She trusts you with her whole heart. Stop being noble and start being honest. Trust her enough to let her decide what she wants."

"What if what she wants isn't me?" The thought of it made my whole chest ache.

"Then at least you'll know. But, son? I'd bet everything I have that she's sitting in her room right now, wishing you'd knock on her door. Wishing you'd stop being her protector and start being her partner."

What if I couldn't do that? Taking care of Artie was a part of me that I didn't want to let go. "I'm so scared that she doesn't want me, and then I won't be able to take care of her anymore."

"You don't have to stop taking care of her. Just... let her take care of you too. Let her love you back. Stop making yourself small so others can be big. You know the message Trixie and the others are trying to spread, right?"

What did their body positivity movement have to do with me?

"You're allowed to take up space too, Gryff. You're

allowed to want things. You're allowed to be someone's first choice, not just their safety net."

Fuck. It wasn't just about loving your body. It was about loving yourself enough to be truly happy from the inside out. How had I never realized that before?

Because I never thought it applied to me.

I was crying now, silent tears rolling down my face as seventeen years of holding myself back, of putting myself last, of being afraid I wasn't enough, all came crashing down.

"I love her so much it terrifies me," I admitted.

"Good," Dad said firmly. "Love should terrify you. It should feel like jumping off a cliff. Your mother terrified me every single day. All that love, all that life, all that possibility. But, Gryff? The jump is worth it. It's always worth it."

"What if I'm not enough for her?"

"Son, you've been enough since the day you were born." His voice was rough, and I thought he was maybe crying too. "You just need to believe it. And you need to give her the chance to show you that you are."

After we hung up, I sat there staring at Vincent. I thought my world had changed the night I'd kissed Artemis for the first time, and while it had, it was nothing like when she'd let me see her, touch her, make her mine for just one night.

But this conversation, the one I'd just had, and the one I was about to was really going to rock my whole goddamned world.

"Am I really going to do this?" I asked Vinnie, glad he

seemed cognizant enough to be an emotional support animal right at this very moment..

He bleated and headbutted my stomach.

"I could lose everything."

Harder headbutt.

"She's my best friend. If this goes wrong—"

Vinnie climbed down and walked to my door, then looked back at me with an expression that clearly said *get your ass up.*

"Since when are you the boss of me?"

He bleated again, more insistently.

"Okay, okay. I'm going."

I stood up, my heart pounding so hard I was sure Artie could hear it through the wall. What was I going to say?

Artie, I'm in love with you. Too abrupt.

Vegas wasn't practice for me. Better, but still not right.

I've been in love with you since... Since when? Since graduation when she said yes to being my roommate? Since the first time I saw her play rugby and those thick thighs began living rent free in my brain? Or since high school when she was the first person I ever came out to?

Maybe since always.

Vinnie was literally pushing me from behind now, his little head shoving against the back of my knees.

"I'm going, I'm going."

I made it to my bedroom door, hand on the knob, heart in my throat. I could do this. I could tell her the truth. I could stop being a coward and finally—

I opened my door and there was Artie standing in hers.

We stood there in the hallway, staring at each other.

Her eyes were red like she'd been crying. Her hair was messy. She was wearing my old Dragons shirt. She was the most beautiful thing I'd ever seen.

"Artie."

"Gryff."

We both spoke at the same time, then stopped.

"I need to tell you something," we said, again in unison.

A nervous laugh escaped both of us.

"You first," I said.

"No, you," she insisted.

Holly appeared behind Artie, and Vincent was still behind me, and suddenly both goats were pushing us forward, literally shoving us together in the hallway.

"The goats want us to—"

"Yeah, they're not subtle," she agreed, stumbling a step closer from Holly's insistent pushing.

We were maybe two feet apart now, both breathing hard, both clearly on the edge of something monumental.

"Vegas wasn't practice for me."

"I wasn't practicing in Vegas."

We both blurted our words out, one barely after the other.

The words hung between us. My heart stopped. Her eyes went wide.

"What?" I breathed.

"You felt it too?" she whispered.

"Felt it? Artie, I…" The words I'd been holding back for months, maybe years, came pouring out. "I'm in love with you. I've been in love with you for so long I don't remember what it feels like not to be."

"Gryff."

"Vegas wasn't practice for me. It was... it was everything. I gave you everything because I thought it was my only chance to show you how you should be loved. How I want to love you. Every day. Forever. If you'd let me."

She was crying now, tears streaming down her face. "I can't date Tyson."

"What?"

"Tonight I couldn't even hold his hand because he wasn't you." She took a shaky breath. "It's only ever been you. Even when I was dating other people, even when I thought I was broken at intimacy, it was because none of them were you."

"Artie..."

"I love you," she said, the words coming out in a rush. "I'm so in love with you it's eating me alive. Vegas wasn't about learning to be intimate. It was about being with you. You're the only person I've ever been able to be completely myself with."

"Why didn't you say anything?"

"Why didn't you?" She laughed through her tears. "And why are we such idiots?"

"Complete idiots," I agreed, moving closer. "I'm sorry I kept saying it was practice."

"I'm sorry I let you."

We were inches apart now. I felt her breath on my face, saw every tear track on her cheeks, felt her heart beating as if it was my own.

"I love you," I said again, because now that I'd said it, I never wanted to stop.

"I love you too," she whispered.

I cupped her face with both hands, thumbs wiping away her tears. "This is real?"

"So real."

When I kissed her, it was different from every kiss we'd shared before. There was no pretense, no practice, no holding back. It was just us, finally being honest, finally letting ourselves have what we'd both wanted for so long.

She made a soft sound against my mouth and pressed closer, her arms coming around my neck. I backed her against the wall, needing to be closer, needing to make up for all the time we'd wasted.

"Wait," she gasped, pulling back slightly. "How long? How long have you been in love with me?"

"I don't know, a long time," I admitted. "But when you said yes to being my roommate, I realized I didn't want to do life without you. You?"

"Probably the same, but the bathtub incident that shall not be named clinched it for me," she said, and I groaned.

"The bathtub?"

"When you got..." She gestured vaguely downward, blushing. "I realized I wanted to affect you that way. That I wanted you to want me. But honestly? Maybe always. Maybe I've always been in love with you and just didn't know it."

Vincent and Holly were sitting in the hallway watching us, their little tiny tails wagging, looking extremely pleased with themselves.

"I think they planned this," I said.

"Definitely. They're probably wondering what took us so long."

My phone started buzzing on my bed. Then Artie's started from her room. We ignored them, too wrapped up in each other to care.

"Flynn's going to be insufferable," she said against my lips.

"Jules probably already has a PowerPoint presentation ready."

"Titled 'I Told You So: A Six-Year Journey.'"

"With graphs."

"So many graphs."

We were laughing and crying and kissing, and it was messy and perfect and everything.

"So what now?" Artie asked, pulling back to look at me.

"Now we stop pretending."

"No more practice?"

"No more practice. This is real. You and me."

"I like the sound of that."

I kissed her again, deeper this time, trying to pour everything I felt into it. Six years of friendship, months of pining, weeks of torture, all culminating in this moment.

"Your room or mine?" I asked against her mouth.

"Yours is closer."

We stumbled backward into my room, still kissing, tripping over Vincent who bleated in protest. We fell onto my bed, laughing, and Holly immediately jumped up to join us.

"We're not having sex with the goats watching," Artie said firmly.

"Agreed." I wasn't going to fuck this up again. "As much as I want to make love to you right now, I also want to do this right. Let me romance you, take you out on a real date. But can we just... lie here for a while? I feel like I'm dreaming, and I want to wake up with you in my arms."

She curled into my side, her head on my chest, and it was the same position we'd been in that morning in Vegas. Except this time, there was no pretending, no panic, no pulling away.

"I love you," she said quietly. "I feel like I need to say it a thousand times to make up for not saying it before."

"I love you too. And you can say it as many times as you want, but I'm going to say it more."

She hit me with a pillow. "Yeah, well, I said it first, so I win."

"Technically Vincent heard it first. I've been telling him for weeks."

She sat up and glanced between me and little Vinnie. "The goat knew before me?"

"He's been very supportive."

Vincent bleated in agreement, then climbed between us, settling in like he belonged there. Holly followed, curling up against Artie's side.

"We're never going to have privacy again, are we?" Artie asked, but she was smiling.

"Probably not. Is that okay?"

"As long as I have you? Everything's okay."

"That was cheesy."

"You're cheesy."

"Your face is cheesy."

"Say it again."

I didn't pretend I didn't know what she meant. I

wanted to say it again, and a million more times. "I love you, Artemis."

"I love you too, Gryffen."

We lay there, finally together, finally honest, finally home. Tomorrow we'd have to face our friends' told-you-so's and figure out what this meant for everything else. But tonight?

Tonight was ours.

And it was perfect.

IDIOTS IN LOVE

ARTEMIS

Gryff and I stayed up almost all night just talking and laughing and kissing. It was the perfect night, even though we didn't do anything more than that. I honestly thought it was so incredibly sweet that he wanted us to date and do all the girlfriend-boyfriend things first.

At some point we must have fallen asleep, and I swear it was mid-deep conversation, because I woke up still wrapped in Gryff's arms. Our legs were tangled together, we were fully clothed and holding each other like we might disappear if we let go. For a moment, I kept my eyes closed, afraid that if I opened them, it would all have been a dream.

My body felt different. Aware in new ways, the slight beard burn on my neck, the tender spot where Gryff had sucked a mark just below my collarbone, the pleasant ache in my lips from hours of kissing.

Six years of careful distance, and now I knew exactly how much pressure Gryff liked when you bit his bottom lip, how he made this tiny gasping sound when you traced your fingers along his ribs, how his hands shook when he was trying to go slow.

"I can feel you overthinking," Gryff's voice rumbled against my hair, and god, I'd heard his morning voice thousands of times but never like this, never with his lips pressed against my temple.

"How do you know I'm awake?"

"Your breathing changed. Plus you're doing that thing where you scrunch your nose when you're thinking too hard."

I opened my eyes to find him watching me with so much affection it made my chest tight. This was Gryff looking at me without having to hide it, without having to mask it as friendship. The difference was devastating.

Vincent and Holly were at the foot of the bed, looking extremely pleased with themselves.

"I think they're taking credit," I said.

"They should. They're smarter than us."

"Everyone's smarter than us. We took six years to figure this out."

"Six years, two months, and twelve days," Gryff corrected, his fingers tracing patterns on my arm. "But who's counting?"

"You were counting?"

"Since the day you walked into gym class." His voice went soft, vulnerable.

My throat went tight. All those years, he'd been counting.

He kissed me then, slow and deep, nothing like our practice kisses. Those had been careful, controlled, with clear boundaries and endpoints. This was Gryff kissing me because he wanted to, because he could, because stopping wasn't required anymore. His hand came up to cradle my jaw, thumb stroking my cheek, and I melted into him completely.

When we finally came up for air, I was half on top of him, my hands in his hair, both of us breathing hard.

"We have to get up." I kissed just the very tip of his nose. "You have practice, and I have work."

He grabbed my hips and held me tight against him. "I'll call in sick. Lovesick."

"I need to thank Tempest," I said, trying to calm my racing heart.

"Please tell me you've been reading her sex scenes and have ideas. Wait, does it involve tying me to the bed?"

I smirked at him, but I was remembering that for later. "For pushing us when we were too scared to push ourselves."

I grabbed my phone, dropped down and pressed myself against Gryff's side, unwilling to put any distance between us. I snapped a quick selfie of us still in bed, Gryff pressing a kiss to my temple, both of us looking completely blissed out and thoroughly kissed. I sent it to Tempest with:

> Thank you for the trust exercises idea. I think they worked.

Her response was immediate.

> TEMPEST
>
> !!!!!!!!!!!!

OMG OMG OMG

JULES NEEDS TO SEE THIS

"Oh no," I said, but I was laughing.

My phone exploded.

The Kingman family group chat, which I'd been added to years ago, suddenly had fifty-hundred notifications. Fifty-hundred and one. Fifty-hundred and two.

JULES

[Photo]

FINALLY! I thought we'd have to lock you two fools in a closet to get you to admit you are in love.

CHRIS

Wait, they weren't already together? Like since high school?

DECLAN

Chris, how are you this dense?

CHRIS

They live together! They have goats!

FLYNN

They were "roommates" 💀

CHRIS

But they've been together at every family thing for six years

JULES

PLATONICALLY

CHRIS

They share clothes

JULES

STILL PLATONICALLY

TEMPEST

I'm a genius. Romance author powers activate. LOVE WINS! Also Flynn is crying.

FLYNN

I AM NOT CRYING.

Okay I'm crying a little.

Shut up.

KELSEY

This is definitely going in my next album

TRIXIE

Book club is going to SCREAM. I've been shipping you two since page one.

JULES

I have a PowerPoint ready. 47 slides. IDIOTS IN LOVE: A six year saga of denial. I was going to base my thesis on it.

CHRIS

SIX YEARS?! And they're just now...? How is that possible?

But they seemed so together. Like a couple

FLYNN

That's because they SHOULD HAVE BEEN

CHRIS

I'm so confused. Trixie, did you know?

TRIXIE

Everyone knew, babe

CHRIS

I didn't know!

JULES

We know, Chris. We know.

"Your family is insane," I said, watching the text continue to fly.

"Our family," Gryff corrected, reading over my shoulder, his chin hooked over my shoulder. "And yes, they're completely insane."

We'd have to deal with all of that eventually, but right now I just wanted to stay in this bubble where Gryff's hands were allowed to wander under my shirt, where I could kiss him whenever I wanted.

"Want to be idiots in the shower?" he asked, his voice low and promising.

"Together?"

"I'm never showering alone again if I can help it."

"Hmm." I crawled out of bed, and headed for the bathroom, dropping my shorts and then my shirt along the way. I was going to have so much fun teasing and flirting with him in every way I possibly could. Just in the doorway to the bathroom, I turned, standing there only in my bra and panties. "I thought you wanted to take things slow, do boyfriend and girlfriend things first."

"Uh... did I say that?" He sat there in bed looking dumb-founded, and also very turned on. "I don't remember saying that. But I also can't remember my own name right now either, so..."

"Don't boyfriends and girlfriends wash each other's backs, or hair, or something?"

He jumped out of the bed and was half naked before I even took another breath. "Yes, they definitely do."

I'd never let myself look at Gryff before. Not really. Now I could catalog every detail. I loved the way water ran down the muscles of his back, how his eyes went dark when I pressed him against the tile wall, the sound he made when I dropped to my knees.

To be fair, it was his turn.

Also, god bless whoever had the foresight to install the tile bench seat and that fancy-ass eight-jet-plus handheld sprayer.

"How," I gasped later as Gryff hung that sprayer back on its hook, after giving me the cleanest pussy on the planet, and two, count them, two more orgasms, "did we do this for months without jumping each other?"

"No idea," he said against my neck, sucking another mark that I'd have to cover for work. "I wanted to do this every single time."

"The practice sessions were torture."

"Torture," he agreed, his hands skimming down my sides, learning every sensitive spot. "Sweet, perfect torture. Do you know how many cold showers I took?"

"Not as many as me."

"Want to bet?"

I traced the muscles of his back, the ones I'd been wanting to touch freely for so long. "We're going to be so late."

"Don't care."

"Flynn's coming to pick you up for practice."

"Really don't care."

But eventually we had to get out, mostly because the hot water ran out and partly because my legs were shaking too much to stand.

We stumbled into the kitchen, me in his robe that smelled like him, Gryff in boxers and nothing else, looking edible.

That's how Flynn found us when he walked in, negotiating bed arrangements, which was headed toward combined mega-bed for us and room for the goats, while Gryff remained plastered to my back like an oversized koala.

"Oh good, you're both alive," Flynn said, taking in our disheveled appearance, the visible marks on my neck, Gryff's refusal to stop touching me. "I was worried you'd died of sexual frustration. Finally."

After they left for practice, I tried to focus on getting ready for work, but everything felt different. The house looked the same but felt transformed. This wasn't just where we lived anymore, it was our home in a new way. Our towels hanging side by side in the bathroom meant something different now. The way Gryff's clothes mixed with mine in the laundry suddenly seemed romantic instead of practical.

At work, I was useless. Completely, utterly useless.

Nichelle from Accounts Receivable appeared at my cubicle. "Spill. Now."

"I don't know what you mean."

"You've been smiling at your computer for an hour. You've checked your phone twelve times. And is that a hickey?"

My hand flew to my neck. "No."

"It absolutely is. Oh my god, did something happen with Hot Roommate?"

"His name is Gryff."

She stole a chair from the next cubicle over and sat down. "Did something happen with Hot Gryff?"

I couldn't help the smile that spread across my face.

At lunch, I stepped outside to call my mom. She needed to hear this from me, not from the Thornminster gossip network.

"Hi, sweetheart," she answered. "How's work? Are you contributing the highest percent of your paycheck to your 401(k)?"

"Yes, Mom. And another ten percent of my paycheck to my rainy day backup savings account. But that's not why I'm calling. I have news."

"Oh god, you're not pregnant, are you?"

"Mom." She always went for the worst-case scenario first. "No."

"Sorry, mother's prerogative to panic. What's the news? Oh, I know, you've impressed your bosses so much with your work ethic they're giving you a promotion. Be sure to get a raise and make them pay you for what you're worth. You're very smart and they're lucky to have you."

"No, that's not it." Here goes. "Gryff and I are together now. Like, together together."

There was a pause, then she let out a hard breath. "I can't say I didn't see this coming, but, honey, he's an athlete. Do you really think that's wise? Consider what that kind of unstable lifestyle did to our family."

"I'm an athlete too."

"Yes, but that's not your career. You were smart and got a degree and work in a field that is stable."

And boring. And not necessarily what I wanted to do with the rest of my life. But I'd definitely never said that to her.

"Gryff got a degree too. He's not a dumb jock. You like him." I couldn't believe I had to defend my best friend to her. She knew Gryff, she loved him. Said more than once that he was a good influence and liked how grounded he was. I even think she had a little crush on Zaddy Kingman.

"He's a lovely young man, but so was your father at twenty-two. But Gryff could get hurt, will likely get traded to one team or another, and you'll just have to pick up and move to wherever he's called to go. What if you end up in someplace like Cincinnati or Timbuktu."

Then I'd adjust exactly like I always did. I was quite literally raised to be adaptable.

But what struck me was that in all of this what she didn't understand was that it didn't matter where Gryff and I lived, or what we did. We could live in little huts in the Indian countryside making goat milk soap and weaving hats out of the fur Holly and Vinnie leave on our pillows every morning, and I would still be happy.

"Mom, I'm going to say this as gently as I can because I love you and know you're just trying to keep me safe. But Gryff is not dad. He prioritizes family above everything else."

"Ouch, sweetheart. But... that's actually helpful. I'm sorry I put my own worries and fears on you. I just want you to be happy."

I knew she was sincere, but that didn't mean I wasn't a bit frustrated with her. "I am happy. Happier than I've ever been."

"Good. That's all that matters."

After I hung up, I stood there for a moment, letting the frustration drain away. But then I smiled, because when I got home from work, I was going to get to tell my boyfriend all about the crazy conversation I had with my mother and he was going to hug me and kiss me and tell me every little thing was gonna be all right.

My phone buzzed with a text and it made my heart sing to see it was him.

GRYFF

Can you take time off work/practice next week?

Why?

Thought you might want to see your dad?

What? I mean, of course I do, but...what?

Bandits are playing in Edinburgh next week. It's one of those weird international games. Wanna come with?

I had to sit down on the bench outside the office building. He was doing it again, taking care of me, thinking of what I needed. After that conversation with my mom, the contrast was overwhelming. Here was Gryff, remembering that I hadn't seen my dad in years, knowing how much I missed him, planning around it.

Are you taking care of me?

Always. But also I selfishly want you there.

I want to see Scotland with you.

And meet your dad as your boyfriend, not your roommate.

Plus I want to see where little Artie learned to be a badass.

I was born a badass.

True. But Scotland made you a rugby badass.

Also I already bought you a ticket and booked a hotel.

Of course you did.

You know me so well.

I love you.

Never going to get tired of hearing that.

I love you too.

Flynn started a tally.

Of?

Times I've said "my girlfriend" or "Artie and I are together".

I'm at twenty-three.

TWENTY-THREE?

Might have announced it in the locker room.

And at the coffee shop.

And to the janitor.

You're ridiculous.

Ridiculously in love with you.

Your face is ridiculously in love with me.

It is, my strawberry girl. It so is.

WHITE HEATHER FOR LUCK

GRYFF

I grinned, settling deeper into my seat on the plane waiting to take off for Edinburgh. Two weeks since that night in my room when she'd finally said she loved me, and I still couldn't quite believe it was real. That Artemis Fraser was mine. That I could call her babe and she'd call me an idiot but in that fond way that meant she loved me.

Artie and Tempest were at the airport in New York getting ready to board their connecting flight. It was going to be a long overnight without her in my arms.

"I gotta go," she said. "Tempest is gesturing wildly about something involving the duty-free shop."

"She's going to buy something ridiculous, isn't she?"

"There's apparently a stuffed Loch Ness monster that she claims Flynn needs."

"He does need that."

"You're both ridiculous."

"You love ridiculous."

"I love you," she said softly, and my chest went tight the way it did every time.

"I love you too. Text me when you land?"

"Obviously. Try not to let Flynn get you both in trouble on the plane."

In a few hours, I'd be in Scotland. Meeting James Fraser not as Artie's roommate or friend, but as her boyfriend. The man she loved.

No pressure or anything.

When we landed, the girls were actually waiting at the hotel for us, having spent the morning having something called cream tea, which looked like little biscuits with blobs of sticky cream and strawberry jelly on them with fancy, fragile-looking teacups.

We had a whole day in Edinburgh to help us adjust to the time change, and Artie had a whole itinerary planned for us. It was going to be a blast. Aside from Sloane and her camera crew following along with us everywhere.

We did our best to ignore them from the castle, a huge hill called Arthur's Seat, and another castle called Holyrood Palace. The only time I let them get close was at the palace's abbey ruins. We did need to give them something.

"Did you guys see that?" I pointed to the entrance to the ruins. "I swear I just saw a unicorn."

The girls giggled and Flynn joined in. "Wait. Didn't you see the dragon following it in? That unicorn better watch out."

Sloane and Harry were loving every minute of this. Which hopefully meant she wouldn't be pissed when we ditched her later for dinner. "No way. The unicorn will poke it in the ass with its magical horn."

"Dragons breathe fire, dude. The unicorn is the one that's toast. Literally."

"But what if they were in love and that's why the dragon is following the unicorn around like a sweet golden retriever of a monster?" Tempest asked, ever the romance novelist.

"Now that would be a romance I'd read," Artie said. "The unicorn is Scotland's national animal."

"Oh, I have one. It's called *Defy Me* and I've read it at least a dozen times. I brought it to read on the plane, but you can borrow it for the flight home."

"Ooh," I stuck my face between them. "Is it dirty, spicy, smutty?"

Flynn flicked his eyebrows up and grinned. "It is. Trust me. I have benefited greatly from Tempest's romance market research."

Sloane looked horrified and the four of us practically fell down laughing.

That evening we were headed to a pub for dinner, and I was nervous. Not about weird things like haggis and warm beer. We were meeting up with Artie's dad. I had met him briefly when he came to Colorado for Artie's high school graduation but there is a difference between meeting your friend's dad and meeting your girlfriend's father who happened to be a sports legend on his own turf. That was a whole different level.

Artie must have changed outfits five times before we left for her hotel.

"It's your dad," I pointed out. "He's seen you covered in mud and blood from rugby."

"That's different. That was rugby Artie. This is please approve of my boyfriend Artie."

"Is that a different person?"

"Yes. She wears nice sweaters and doesn't swear as much."

I pulled her in for a hug. "Hey. It's going to be fine. He's going to be so happy to see you."

"What if he's not? What if he's weird about us? What if…"

Such a worrier. Just like her mom. Not that I'd ever say that to her. "What if he's just happy for us?"

She laid her head on my shoulder. "I know."

"Just… trust me. It's going to be okay."

James Fraser was a tall, broad man with Artie's same sharp blue eyes and stubborn jaw and slightly crooked nose. His size and stern look made him naturally intimidating but when he saw his daughter his whole face softened and a warm smile bloomed there.

"There's my girl," he said, and his voice was rough with emotion.

Artie made a sound somewhere between a laugh and a sob and threw herself into his arms. I stepped back, giving them space, but James looked at me over her head.

"Good to see you again, Gryff," he said.

"You too, sir."

"Bridger has kept me informed of all your successes, congrats."

Artie pulled back, looking between us. "What?"

James smiled, the same crooked smile I'd seen on Artie's face a thousand times. "Did you think I wouldn't keep tabs on you, hen? Bridger Kingman and I have been having monthly calls since I met him at your graduation."

"You... what?"

"Your mother wouldn't ever tell me anything beyond that you were fine, but Bridger understood what it was like for a father to worry." He looked at me again. "He said you were the one who made sure she had a family every holiday. Made sure she wasn't alone."

"Dad..." Artie's voice was small.

"I know I haven't been the father you deserved," James continued. "But I've never stopped worrying about you. And knowing you had the Kingmans, had Gryff..." He extended his hand to me. "Thank you for taking care of my daughter."

I shook his hand, my throat tight. "She takes care of herself, sir. I just... make sure she doesn't have to do it alone."

"Aye, that's what Bridger said you'd say."

"I can't believe... all this time..." Artie looked between us, then at her dad. "Why didn't you tell me?"

"Would you have let them help if you knew I'd asked?"

She was quiet for a moment. "Maybe. It's not like they gave me much of a chance. They kind of make everyone feel like family."

Over dinner, the awkwardness faded. James told stories about Artie as a kid that had her covering her face in embarrassment. He asked about my family, about football, about our life in LA. And when Artie excused herself to the bathroom, he leaned forward.

"She deserves someone who sees her for exactly who

she is. Not too much, not too strong, not too anything. Just... Artemis."

"That's all I've ever seen."

He nodded, satisfied. "Then you'll do."

The next night I was pacing the room Flynn and I had been assigned at the team hotel.

"This is a terrible plan," Flynn muttered as we waited for the signal from Tyson. We were fully dressed in joggers and hoodies like we were about to rob a bank instead of sneak our girlfriends into our room.

"It was literally your idea," I reminded him.

"Past Flynn was an idiot. Present Flynn recognizes that Coach will actually murder us if we get caught. Not to mention penalties from the League."

"We're not going to get caught." I checked my phone. Artie had texted that she and Tempest were in the lobby, waiting for our go. "Tyson's got this."

Right on cue, we heard Tyson's voice in the hallway. "Oh shit, Coach, I think I did something to my hamstring at practice."

"What? When?" That was Coach, immediately concerned.

"I don't know, man, but it's seizing up. You better grab that security guard and help me to the elevator."

Flynn and I pressed our ears to the door, listening as Tyson led Coach away from our room and the stairwell, his fake injury getting more dramatic by the second.

"Now," I whispered to my phone.

Two minutes later, there was the softest knock on our door. I yanked it open to find Artie and Tempest in all black like cat burglars, complete with black beanies.

"Are you wearing tactical gear?" Flynn asked.

"It's called commitment to the bit," Tempest said, pushing past him. "Also, your hotel has terrible security. We just walked right in."

But I wasn't listening because Artie was in my arms, and she smelled like strawberries and home.

"Hi," she whispered against my chest.

"Hi." I pulled back to look at her. Three hours apart shouldn't have felt like three years, but it had. "Missed you."

"Missed you too."

"You guys are gross," Tempest announced, already sprawled on Flynn's bed. "But also, Tyson deserves an Oscar. We could hear him from the elevator talking about muscle spasms and his grandmother's arthritis."

"He's really going for it," Flynn agreed, sitting next to Tempest. "Think he'll actually get checked by medical?"

"Nah, he'll miraculously recover right before—"

A knock on the door made us all freeze.

"Room check," Coach's voice called out.

"Shit, shit, shit," I hissed. "Into Tyson's room, go." Hopefully Ty's roommate was fully dressed.

Thank god we'd gotten the adjoining and made a plan B especially for a situation like this. Which was, of course, all Tempest's idea. She was the brains of this operation. The rest of us were the muscle.

Artie and Tempest dove for the door while Flynn and I tried to look casual, which was impossible because we were both fully dressed, instead of in bed asleep like we were supposed to be.

I opened the door, trying to look sleepy. "Hey, Coach, didn't you already check our room?"

He looked at us suspiciously. "Yes. I did. And now I'm doing it again." He walked right in and even looked in the bathroom and under the beds.

Coach stared at us for a long moment and walked toward the adjoining room door. We were so busted. Then DeMarcus Clay appeared behind him.

"Coach, Tyson's asking for ice. Kid's really worked up about his hamstring."

Coach sighed. "Fine. You two better be asleep in ten minutes. Big game tomorrow."

"Yes, sir," we said in unison.

The door closed, and we waited a full thirty seconds before the door between rooms creaked open.

"Is it safe?" Artie whispered.

"That was way too close," Tempest said, but she was grinning. "Also, Tyson and DeMarcus's bathroom is tiny. Artie elbowed me in the boob."

"You stepped on my foot."

"Ladies, please," Flynn said. "You're both disasters."

They emerged, and something about seeing Artie in my hotel room, in Edinburgh, made everything feel more real. We'd been living together for months, but this was different. This was choosing to be together even when it was complicated, and only for a few hours.

"Come here," I said, pulling her onto my bed.

She curled into my side immediately, fitting against me perfectly. "This is nice."

"Yeah?"

"Yeah. Even if your bed is tiny and probably has athlete germs."

"My athlete germs are exclusive to you now."

Flynn made a gagging noise. "I'm begging you both to stop."

"You're literally spooning Tempest right now," I pointed out.

"That's different. We're cute. You two are nauseating."

Tempest hit him with a pillow. "Be nice. They're in their honeymoon phase."

"Yeah, but they've only been openly disgusting for two weeks," Flynn said. "Trust me, it gets worse before it gets better. Gryff's already said my girlfriend approximately eight thousand times."

"Eight thousand and one," I corrected. "My girlfriend is very patient with my enthusiasm."

Artie hid her face in my chest. "Oh my god."

"My girlfriend gets embarrassed easily."

"I'm going to smother you with this pillow."

"My girlfriend is also violent."

She did try to smother me then, which devolved into a pillow fight that we had to keep quiet, which made everything funnier. By the time we collapsed back onto the beds, breathless and laughing, it was past midnight.

"We should probably go," Artie said reluctantly.

I held her tighter. We'd agreed the girls wouldn't actually spend the night. Nobody needed to see their twin brother canoodling overnight. Ew.

"Five more minutes," I bargained, pulling her closer.

"You have a game tomorrow."

"I'll play better if I get five more minutes."

"It's true." Flynn held Tempest close too. "Everyone knows Kingman's play better when they're in love."

Artie gave me a tiny nip with her teeth on my earlobe and whispered into my ear. "I heard it was when Kingman's get laid."

"Stay, I'll make Flynn sleep in the hall and we can find out."

She gave me another kiss. "Good try. You'll just have to dream about it. I know I will be."

It took another ten minutes of goodbye kisses and promises to be careful sneaking back out before they finally left. Flynn and I stood at the door, watching them creep down the hallway like very giggly ninjas.

"We're idiots," Flynn said.

"Complete idiots," I agreed.

"Worth it though."

"Absolutely worth it."

Game day in Edinburgh was surreal. The stadium wasn't as big as what we were used to, but it was packed with curious Scottish fans who'd come to see what American football was all about. During warm-ups, I kept scanning the stands, looking for Artie.

"Northwest section," Tyson said, appearing beside me. "With the other wives and girlfriends."

"How did you—"

"Dude, you've looked at that section twelve times already." He grinned. "Also, she's wearing your jersey. Kind of hard to miss."

I found her instantly after that. She was sitting with Tempest and the other PALs, and making it look like she was exactly where she belonged. My number on her back, her hair pulled back in a ponytail, laughing at something Jade Clay was saying.

This was big. It was huge. It was Artie claiming her spot as my girlfriend in front of everyone, no more pretense, no more practice.

And I was going to ignore the fact that Sloane had Harry pointing directly at me as I grinned like a fool.

"Freeman," Coach barked. "Your hamstring better be perfect."

"Miraculous recovery, Coach," Tyson called back, then lower to me, "You owe me so big."

"Name your price."

"Introduce me to one of Artie's rugby friends."

"Done."

The game itself was brutal. The Cincinnati Tigers had a shit offense, but their defense were hungry and mean. But we won, 24-17, the crowd loved it, and I had the game of my fucking life. Probably because of the very, very realistic sex dream I had where Artie was a unicorn and I was a dragon and we shape-shifted into human forms and had magical orgasms.

After the game, showered and changed, I finally made it to where the PALs were waiting. Artie launched herself at me, and I caught her easily, spinning her around while she laughed.

"You were amazing," she said.

"I missed you," I said, setting her down but keeping my arms around her.

"It's been four hours."

"Four hours too long."

"You're ridiculous."

"You love ridiculous."

"I love you."

And right there, in front of teammates and PALs and a bunch of Scottish strangers, and yes, even Harry the cameraman, I kissed her. Really kissed her. The kind of kiss that made Flynn yell "Get a room," and DeMarcus whistle.

"Well, well, that was golden. The cameras sure loved the two of you."

Sloane appeared like she'd been waiting for us.

"Mind if I grab you both for a quick chat? Just want to get your thoughts on the international experience while it's fresh."

Artie tensed beside me, but I'd agreed to cooperate with filming, and she had already been in my home life segments. We knew the deal.

"Sure," I said, though everything in me wanted to tell her to fuck off.

WE FOUND ourselves in the hotel bar, Sloane sitting across from us. She started with softball questions like how was the game, how was the city, how were the fans. Normal stuff.

Then she shifted, and so did my protective instincts. I shifted closer to Artie and took her hand.

"You two make such a beautiful couple," she said, smiling in that way that didn't reach her eyes. "It must be such a relief to finally be in a normal relationship after all that experimentation in college."

I felt Artie's hand tighten in mine.

"Experimentation?" Artie asked carefully.

"Well, you know. You've both dated men and women. But now you've found your way to something more traditional. Stable."

Aw, fuck.

"Bisexuality isn't experimentation," I said, trying to keep my voice level. "It's not a phase or a waystation to something else."

"Of course not." Sloane said, all fake understanding. "I just mean it must be easier now. Being in a straight-passing relationship. No one questions you, no one judges. You can just be... normal."

"We've never been trying to be normal," Artie said.

"But you are now, aren't you? I mean, look at you. The football star and his girlfriend. Very all-American. Very traditional." She leaned forward. "Do you think your past relationships with the same sex were just about finding yourselves? Like, you needed to explore that side before you could settle into something real?"

The silence in the room was deafening. I could feel my pulse in my ears, anger building with each word.

"Because that's what it looks like from the outside," Sloane continued, her voice honey-sweet and poisonous. "Two people who went through their bi phase and came out the other side in a nice, heterosexual relationship. It's actually quite sweet. You experimented, you explored, and you found your way back to normal."

She smiled, tilting her head. "So tell me, would you say being bisexual was just something you both needed to get out of your system before finding real love with each other?"

Artie's hand in mine was trembling now, but I couldn't tell if it was from rage or hurt. My own anger was a living thing in my chest, clawing to get out. Sloane's question hung in the air like the challenge it was.

Waiting for us to defend ourselves, our identities, our love.

Waiting for us to give her the drama she so desperately wanted.

She wanted drama? I was going to give her fucking drama.

HERE ME ROAR

ARTEMIS

Gryff was coiling beside me like a spring, ready to explode. His jaw clenched so tight I could hear his teeth grinding, and his free hand had curled into a fist on his thigh. In about two seconds, he was going to say something that would definitely make it into the show, probably edited to make him look unhinged.

I squeezed his hand once and gave him the smallest shake of my head.

"I got this, babe," I said to Gryff, keeping my voice light.

Then I turned to Sloane with my sweetest smile. "Can I ask you a question?"

She blinked, clearly not expecting me to take control of the interview. "Of course."

"If I walked over there right now and kissed you, which I'm not going to do because consent matters, would that make you a lesbian?"

Her face went pink. "What? No, that's not—"

"No?" I tilted my head. "But by your logic, one kiss,

one relationship, one experience defines someone's entire sexuality. So which is it?"

"That's different—"

"Is it? Because last time I checked, me eating a salad doesn't make me a vegetarian. I'm bisexual when I'm with a man, when I'm with a woman, when I'm single, when I'm married. It's not about who I'm with, it's about who I am."

Sloane's mouth opened and closed like a fish.

"And just to be crystal clear," I continued, my voice steady and firm, "Gryff and I aren't together despite our bisexuality or because we've somehow 'moved past it.' We're together because we love each other. All of each other. Including the parts that make people like you uncomfortable."

"I'm not uncomfortable—"

"Really? Because you just spent five minutes trying to erase fundamental parts of our identities to fit some narrative you've created about what 'real' love looks like." I leaned forward. "Our love is real. Our identities are real. And if you can't see that, that's a you problem, not an us problem."

The silence stretched out. Sloane's phone was still recording, but she looked like she wanted to be anywhere else.

"I think we're done here," she said stiffly, grabbing her phone.

"I think we are," I agreed pleasantly.

She stood up so fast she nearly knocked over her chair, muttering something about needing to check footage before hurrying away.

The moment she was gone, I let out a breath I didn't know I'd been holding. My hands were shaking slightly from the adrenaline.

"Holy shit," Gryff said quietly. "That was..."

"I know. I'm amazing."

"You are." He turned to face me fully, his eyes intense. "You protected me."

"That's what we do," I said simply. "We protect each other."

He kissed me then, right there in the hotel bar, deep and thorough and claiming. When we broke apart, both breathless, he rested his forehead against mine.

"I love you," he said. "Every part of you. Including the parts that just verbally destroyed a reality TV producer."

"Especially those parts?"

"Especially those parts."

BACK IN MY HOTEL ROOM, we barely made it through the door before Gryff pressed me against it, his mouth hot and insistent on mine.

"We have the Team GB dinner in an hour," I managed between kisses.

"I know." His hands framed my face, thumbs stroking my cheekbones. "I just... watching you defend us like that. Defend yourself. God, Artie."

"I wasn't going to let her diminish what we have."

"No, you weren't." He kissed me again, softer this time. "You're incredible."

The tension from Sloane's interview finally flittered away like nothing more important than a fall leaf on the wind. The way we felt about each other, protected each other, and loved each other more than someone like Sloane could ever understand was what was important.

I pushed him toward the bed, and he sat down, pulling me between his knees.

"We really do have to get ready for dinner," I said, running my fingers through his hair.

"I know. But after?"

The promise in his voice made my stomach flip. "After."

THE TEAM GB dinner was at a restaurant that screamed Scottish wealth—all dark wood and tartan and pictures of rugby legends on the walls. My dad had undersold it as "just a wee chat about possibilities," but there were five coaches there, all in matching Team GB polo shirts like they'd coordinated.

"Artemis," The head coach, Teddy Riata, stood to greet us. "So wonderful to finally meet you properly. Your father speaks very highly of your abilities."

"Thank you," I said, trying not to feel like I was at a job interview.

"And this must be Gryffen," he continued, shaking Gryff's hand. "James mentioned you'd be joining us."

My dad had the grace to look slightly guilty. "Thought it would be good for everyone to be on the same page."

What followed was less dinner and more full recruitment presentation. They'd done their homework—they knew my stats, my playing style, my injury history. They had tablets with training facilities, showed me videos of their current squad, talked about coaching philosophy and Olympic preparation.

"The facilities in Edinburgh are world-class," Coach Riata said, swiping through photos. "And with your father on the men's coaching staff, you'd have family support right here."

Family support. I glanced at my dad, who was trying to look neutral but failing. He wanted this. He wanted me home, wanted to make up for lost time, wanted to share rugby with me again like when I was little.

"The timeline is what's crucial," another coach added. "You'd need to step back from Team USA within the next six months to meet the three-year residency requirement for the next Olympics."

"That's... soon," I said.

"It is. But think about what you'd be gaining. A chance to represent your own people, represent your homeland."

Your homeland. Your own people.

I looked around the table at these men who looked like my dad, sounded like my dad, came from the same rugby tradition I'd been raised in. This was my culture, my heritage, my blood.

"You belong here," Coach Riata said, as if reading my thoughts. "This is where you're from. This is your rugby home."

Under the table, Gryff's hand found my knee, just resting there. Not pushing, not pulling, just... present. Reminding me he was there.

"Plus," my dad added quietly, "we could finally have time together. Real time. Not just phone calls and the occasional holiday."

And there it was. The thing that made my chest tight. Three years of getting to know my father again. Three years of Sunday dinners and rugby talk and rebuilding what distance had taken from us.

But three years without Gryff.

I looked at him then, really looked at him. He was listening politely, asking intelligent questions about the program, being perfectly supportive. But I knew him. I could see the tension in his shoulders, the way he kept touching his water glass but not drinking, the careful neutrality of his expression.

He was prepared to let me go if that's what I wanted. He'd smile and support me and slowly die inside because that's who he was, someone who put everyone else first.

But that's not who we were together.

Together, we protected each other. Together, we chose each other.

"The opportunity won't come again," Coach Riata was saying. "This is a once-in-a-lifetime chance."

I thought about all the times in my life I'd had to pack up and leave. Thirteen moves in thirteen years, each time telling myself not to get attached, not to put down roots, not to expect permanence. I'd gotten good at leaving. Expert at it, really.

But Gryff had changed that. The Kingmans had changed that. For the first time in my life, I'd found something worth staying for.

"I need time to think about it," I said diplomatically.

"Of course. But don't take too long. These decisions have a way of making themselves if you wait."

The rest of dinner was less intense, more social. My

dad told embarrassing stories about my youth rugby days. The coaches talked about the Six Nations tournament. Gryff charmed them all by asking about Scottish rugby history.

But through it all, I kept thinking about that word. Home.

AFTER DINNER, we walked through Edinburgh's old town, the castle lit up on the hill above us. My dad had offered to walk with us, but I'd asked for some time alone with Gryff.

"They made a compelling case," Gryff said carefully.

I stopped walking. "Are you doing the thing?"

"What thing?"

"The noble self-sacrificing thing where you pretend you want me to leave even though it's killing you."

He was quiet for a moment. "Maybe."

"Don't."

"Artie, this is your dream. Playing in the Olympics—"

"Is my dream. You're right. But you know what else is my dream?" I turned to face him fully. "You. Us. The life we're building in LA. Vincent and Holly probably destroying our house right now. Sunday dinners with your family. That's my dream too."

"But your dad—"

"Will understand. Because he chose love once too. He chose my mom and rugby and a life that took him all over the world." I took his hands. "I need to tell you something."

"Okay?"

"Three years is too long."

His face fell slightly. "To wait for the Olympics?"

"No. Three years is too long to be away from my home." I squeezed his hands. "And you're my home, Gryff. You've always been my home."

The look on his face, relief and joy and love all mixed together, made my chest ache in the best way.

"Really?" he asked, voice rough.

"Really. I've moved thirteen times in thirteen years. I know what home feels like, and it's not a place or a country or even blood family. It's you. It's where you are. It's where we are together."

He kissed me then, right there on the Royal Mile with tourists streaming around us, deep and desperate and full of promise.

"I love you," he said against my mouth. "I love you so much I can't breathe sometimes."

"I love you too. And I choose you. I choose us."

"Your dad—"

"Will be disappointed but he'll understand. He knows what it's like to choose love." I pulled back to look at him. "I want the Olympics, but I want them with you in the stands. I want Team USA with you waiting for me after practices. I want our life, our home, our future."

"Our goats," he added, and we both laughed.

"Especially our goats."

WHEN WE WERE ONCE AGAIN ALONE in my hotel, the energy was different. This wasn't Vegas with its tentative exploration or LA with its comfortable familiarity. This was Edinburgh, where I'd chosen him over everything else, where we'd defended each other, where we'd claimed our future.

"Are you sure?" he asked as I pulled him into my room.

"I've never been more sure of anything in my life."

We took our time. Slow kisses that built like fire, hands relearning familiar territory with new intent. When he pulled my sweater over my head, his hands were shaking slightly.

"You're nervous," I observed.

"This is different," he said. "This is... this matters."

"The other times mattered too."

"Not like this." He cupped my face in his hands. "This is me making love to the woman I'm going to marry someday. This is the beginning of our real story."

My throat went tight. "You want to marry me?"

"Artie, I've wanted to marry you since you tried to fight Xander for me in the library." He kissed me softly. "But we can talk about that later. Right now, I just want to show you how much I love you."

And he did. Oh, how he did.

It was different from Vegas, from our practice sessions, from every other time I'd been with anyone. This was worship and claiming and promising all at once. This was Gryff showing me with his hands and mouth and body that I was cherished, that I was precious, that I was exactly right exactly as I was.

"You're perfect," he whispered against my skin. "Every inch of you is perfect."

I'd never felt small before, never felt delicate, but in his arms I felt both those things while still feeling powerful. It was magic, the way he looked at me, touched me, loved me.

He kissed his way down my throat, taking his time, mapping every inch like he was memorizing me. His hands skimmed along my sides, tracing the curves there with obvious appreciation.

"God, Artie," he breathed, pulling back to look at me. "Do you have any idea what you do to me? How gorgeous you are?"

I was ready to deflect. It was so much to have his attention so fully on me. I couldn't imagine doing anything like this with anyone else. He stopped me from spiraling back to a place I no longer belonged with a kiss.

"Don't," he said softly. "Don't minimize this. Let me appreciate you, every single inch of you."

His mouth traveled lower, across my collarbones, down to the swell of my breasts, where he licked and sucked one nipple and then the other. His hands continued to explore, down, down, pushing between my legs until his fingers found me already wet and wanting.

"I fucking love how wet you get for me. Next time I'm going to make you ride my fingers while I suck these nipples until you come so hard you can't breathe."

Just hearing him tell me his fantasies like this was already taking my breath away. "Only if you let me do the same to you."

I love knowing he was the one person in the world I could truly let go with. But I wanted to be that for him too. "Let me touch you, explore you too."

He groaned as I pushed my hands into his hair and

gripped it tight. Seemed my Gryff liked a little edge to his pleasure. I was going to remember that.

"Mmm. I promise to let you have your way with me, sweetheart." He withdrew his fingers, bringing his hand between us, and painted my lips with my own arousal. My stomach did flip-flops and a little whimper escaped me.

When he kissed me, he licked my lips and hummed like the taste of me was the best thing in the world. "I fucking love the taste of you."

He slipped those same fingers into my mouth, giving me another taste of myself. My mind and body were soaring from such an intimate act.

No one else had ever made love to me in a way where we shared the act with each other so much.

He dragged his fingers down my throat, between my breasts and then to my stomach. His kisses followed the path to the soft roundness of my belly, his hands gripping my waist, thumbs stroking the stretch marks that decorated my hips like silver ribbons.

"Beautiful," he murmured, tracing one with his tongue, making me gasp. "Every mark, every curve, every inch of your body is full of gorgeous strength."

"Gryff—" I loved the way his voice was husky and so filled with awe. It had me finding my own body sexy too.

"Do you know how long I've wanted this? How many times I've thought about your thighs?" His hands moved to stroke the muscles there, reverent and hungry at once. "The power in them. The way they felt wrapped around me in Vegas. I've been obsessed, Artie. Completely obsessed."

He proved it, kissing along the inside of my thigh,

appreciating every inch of soft skin and firm muscle. When he nipped gently at the sensitive skin there, I nearly came off the bed.

"That's it," he encouraged, his voice rough. "Don't hold back. I want all of you."

"Please, Gryff. Stop teasing me. I need you. I need you inside of me."

"Oh, I will be. I promise," he interrupted firmly. "You're strong and soft and powerful and feminine and I want you to wrap these incredible thighs around me and never let go."

The raw want in his voice made me brave. When he moved back up my body, I did what he asked, wrapping my legs around him, using my strength to pull him closer.

"Fuck," he groaned. "Yes. Just like that. Do you feel how perfect we fit?"

I did. For the first time in my life, I wasn't worried about being too much, too strong, too big. With Gryff, I was exactly enough.

"Tell me," he said, pressing kisses along my jaw. "Tell me what you need."

No one had ever asked me that before. Previous partners hadn't cared enough to check, or expected me to be the one to ask them. For me to be in charge of our pleasure. But not my Gryff. He waited, patient and attentive, until I found my voice.

He wanted to take care of me.

"Just... don't stop looking at me," I said, feeling vulnerable admitting it, but telling him what I would make this better for us both. "I need to see you seeing me."

His expression softened into something so tender it

made my chest ache. "Artie, I couldn't look away if I tried. You're the most beautiful thing I've ever seen."

"Even when I'm—"

"Especially when you're like this," he interrupted, moving to kiss me deeply. "Open and trusting and mine."

"Yours," I agreed against his mouth, and felt him shudder.

We moved together slowly, relearning each other with this new context, this new meaning. Every touch felt weighted with significance. His fingers tangled with mine, holding tight like he was anchoring himself. Or maybe anchoring me. Maybe both.

"Is this okay?" he asked as he settled between my thighs, and the question felt important. Even though he knew I wanted this, wanted all of him, he still took care of me, asking for consent in the sexiest of ways.

"More than okay," I assured him, pulling him down for another kiss. "Perfect."

He laughed softly against my mouth. "You're perfect."

Even now, even in this moment, we were still us. "Your face is perfect," I managed, then gasped as he shifted against me, teasing, close but not close enough.

"Keep your legs around me," he said, his hands gripping my thighs. "I want to feel how strong you are. Want you to hold me like you're never letting go."

When he finally slid inside me, we both gasped. It was coming home and leaving earth at the same time. It was everything.

"I love you," I told him, over and over, like a prayer.

"I love you," he answered, like a promise.

We moved together, slow and deep and intense, eyes

locked, hands clasped, hearts hammering in sync. My thighs tightened around him, and he groaned my name like it was the only word he knew.

"That's it," he encouraged. "Use your strength. Show me what that incredible body can do."

When I got close, he slowed down, drawing it out.

"Gryff, please—"

"I've got you," he promised. "I've always got you."

And when I finally fell apart, he was there to catch me, following me over with my name on his lips like he never wanted to forget this moment.

I certainly never would. Every touch, every sigh, every single second would be painted on my heart, my body, my soul for the rest of our lives.

I KNEW YOU WERE TROUBLE

GRYFF

Coming home from Edinburgh felt like returning to a different universe. One where Vincent and Holly had apparently staged a coup in our absence.

"Oh my god," Artie said, standing in the doorway of our house.

The living room looked like a goat tornado had hit it. Couch cushions were on the floor, one of them thoroughly chewed. Several plants had been knocked over, dirt everywhere. A roll of toilet paper had been dragged from the bathroom and shredded across the entire space. And in the middle of it all, Vincent and Holly sat on our coffee table like tiny dictators surveying their kingdom.

"Vincent Van Goat," I said sternly. "Holly Goatlightly. What did you do?"

Vincent turned his head away from me with such deliberate disdain that Artie burst out laughing.

"They're giving us the cold shoulder," she said. "We abandoned them for Scotland and this is our punishment."

Sean appeared from the kitchen, looking frazzled. "They were angels until about an hour ago. I swear. Then it's like they sensed you were coming home and decided to express their feelings through destruction."

"Where's Ren?" I asked.

"Hiding in your bedroom. Holly ate his shoelaces while they were still on his feet and he needed a timeout." Sean looked at the destruction. "I was going to clean up, but then I thought you should see what your children are capable of."

Holly bleated at him reproachfully.

"Don't you sass me, young lady," Sean told her. "I know you're the one who figured out how to open the bathroom door."

Vincent hopped off the coffee table and walked over to Artie, butting his head against her leg in what looked like forgiveness. But when I reached down to pet him, he dodged my hand and trotted away.

"Seriously?" I asked him. "You're mad at me?"

He bleated once and went to hide behind Artie's legs.

"I think someone's jealous that you were gone," Artie said, scooping Vincent up. He immediately snuggled into her arms, shooting me what I swear was a triumphant look.

"Traitor," I muttered.

Holly, not to be outdone, launched herself at my shins, demanding attention. I picked her up and she immediately started chewing on my shirt collar.

"We missed you too," I told her.

"So," Sean said, grinning, "how was Scotland? Did anything interesting happen?"

Artie and I exchanged a look. Everything had happened. We'd defended ourselves against Sloane's bigotry, Artie had chosen us over Team GB, we'd made love for the first time in a way that actually meant everything.

"It was good," I said.

"Good?" Sean's eyebrows shot up. "You two are practically glowing and you're going with good?"

"Really good," Artie amended.

"Oh my god, you totally banged," Sean exclaimed.

"Sean," Ren called from the bedroom. "Leave them alone."

"I'm not leaving them alone. Look at them. They're all post-coital and glowy."

"We're not glowy," I protested.

"You're extremely glowy," Sean insisted. "It's disgusting. I love it."

After Sean and Ren left, with many promises to goat-sit again despite the destruction, we spent the rest of the day cleaning and trying to win back our goats' affection. By evening, they'd mostly forgiven us, though Vincent still insisted on sitting between us on the couch like a furry chaperone.

Monday meant back to reality. Practice was brutal—Coach was preparing us for the Sharks game on Sunday, and the rivalry meant everything had to be perfect. The Sharks were having a good season and beating them would secure our playoff spot.

"Kingman," DeMarcus called out during a water break. "Your head in the game?"

"Yeah, why?"

"You keep looking at the sidelines. Documentary girl isn't even here today."

He was right. Sloane and her crew were notably absent, which should have been a relief but somehow felt more ominous.

"Just focused," I said.

DeMarcus studied me. "Everything good? You seem tense."

"Everything's fine."

"Uh-huh." He didn't look convinced. "Just remember, rook, we take care of our own here. Whatever's going on, you don't have to handle it alone."

Before I could respond, Coach was calling us back to drills.

THAT EVENING, Artie came home from practice looking troubled. She dropped her gear bag by the door and went straight for the couch, where Holly immediately claimed her lap.

"What's wrong?" I asked, sitting beside her.

"Coach Maher wanted to talk to me privately after practice."

My stomach dropped down to the floor and rolled around. "About Team GB?"

"No. About the documentary." She scratched Holly's ears absently. "Someone from Sloane's team contacted USA Rugby. They were 'fact-checking' stories about my history."

"What?"

"They framed it as background research, but the questions were invasive." Her voice was tight with anger. "They wanted to know if I'd ever dated women on the team, if my bisexuality affected team dynamics."

"That's—"

"Not journalism. I know. Coach Maher shut them down, but she's worried. She said they seemed more interested in gossip than sports." Artie looked at me. "She asked if I was safe."

"Safe?"

"That's what worried me. The way she said it, like she was concerned about more than just invasive questions." Artie shifted to face me fully. "She also said two other players on the team were contacted. Similar questions about their personal lives."

"Sloane's building something," I said.

"Yeah, but what? And why?"

WE DIDN'T HAVE to wait long to find out.

Sunday's game was intense from the start. The Sharks came out aggressive, and Xander was playing like a man possessed, but not in a good way. He was off, making mistakes I'd never seen him make, getting called for penalties that were high school rookie errors.

During a timeout, I caught him looking up at the stadium boxes where the VIPs and press sat. His face was tight with something that looked like fear.

"Rosemount looks like shit," Flynn said beside me.

"Yeah."

"You think he's injured?"

"Maybe," I lied. But I knew that look. It was the same

one he'd had in the library when he'd ended things. The look of someone backed into a corner.

We won, barely. 20-17, with a field goal in the last two minutes. The celebration felt hollow, though. Xander had disappeared before the final whistle, not even staying for the post-game handshakes.

"That was weird, right?" Tyson asked in the locker room. "Rosemount just bouncing like that?"

"Very weird," I agreed.

THAT NIGHT, Artie and I were on the couch watching film from her rugby match when someone knocked on our door. Not rang the doorbell, knocked, quiet and urgent.

Vincent and Holly immediately went into guard-goat mode, which involved a lot of bleating and very little actual guarding.

I opened the door to find Xander standing there, and for a second, I thought I was seeing things. His eyes were red-rimmed, his usually perfect hair was a mess, and his hands were shaking.

"Xan? What—"

"Can I come in? Please?"

"Yeah, of course." I stepped aside, and he practically fell through the doorway.

Artie stood up from the couch, taking in his appearance. "I'll make tea," she said simply, heading to the kitchen.

Xander laughed, but it came out cracked. "Tea. Very British of you."

"Technically Scottish," Artie called back. "But sit down before you fall down."

He collapsed onto our couch, and Holly immediately tried to eat his shoelaces, which at least made him smile weakly.

"Xander, what's going on?" I asked, sitting across from him.

He was quiet for so long I thought he might not answer. "She has video. The kind that's going to ruin my life."

"Who has... wait, Sloane?"

He nodded, his jaw clenched.

Artie returned with three mugs of tea, setting them down carefully. "What does she want?"

"She wants me to come out. On the show. She wants to make it this big dramatic reveal about the closeted football player finding his truth." He laughed bitterly. "She said either I give her the story or she makes me the story."

"That's blackmail," Artie said flatly.

"She calls it 'authentic storytelling.'" Xander's hands were shaking as he picked up his mug. "She has stuff on other people too. Not just me. The other rookies on the show, the linebacker at Seattle. The center on the Beagles."

"All queer players?" I asked, though I already knew the answer.

"Yeah. She's specifically targeting us. She said..." He paused, took a shaky breath. "She said America loves a coming out story. That we're being selfish by hiding who we are. That we owe it to young queer athletes to be visible."

"That's not her call to make," Artie said fiercely.

"I know. But she has the footage. And if it gets out…" Xander looked at me. "She's got something on all of us and… well, fuck, I owe you, Gryff. I'm sure she's got something on you too."

The weight of that settled over us. I was already out and open about it. But those questions she'd been asking about Artie and me being straight now had my blood building up a slow, hot simmer.

What Sloane was doing in the name of good television was a violation of the worst kind. I hated that athletes thought they had to hide themselves, but nobody had the right to make anyone come out before they were ready.

"When?" I asked.

"She wants an answer by Friday. Either I agree to her terms, or she leaks everything."

"We're not letting that happen," Artie said.

Xander looked at her with something like hope. "We?"

"You're family," she said simply. "And nobody threatens our family."

God she was hot when she got all protective.

When Xander walked in here looking like a lost puppy, I thought I was going to have to protect him, try to save him, like I always did with everyone in my life. But Artie had been the one who stood so fiercely by my side, and I didn't have to do anything by myself anymore.

I squeezed Xander's arm. "Listen, I want to bring in some help. This is bigger than us, and I don't think we can do anything without a whole shit ton of support. I won't if you're not ready for anyone else to know. But if you can trust anyone, it's family."

"You… you want me to come out to your family? To Hayes and Willa?" Old fears and hurts flashed through his face. His face went pale. "I can't—they don't even know—"

Artie sat down beside him. "You deserve to have support through this."

"Willa doesn't even know," he whispered. "My own sister doesn't know."

"What about Liam and George?" I asked carefully. "Your uncles?"

Xander's face crumpled. "They would have supported me. They would have understood. But my mom… she said it would ruin my career. Said I couldn't be like them if I wanted to succeed in football. She made me promise never to tell anyone, especially not them."

"Xander," Artie said softly. "Would you consider telling them now? Just the family? They need to know what they're fighting for."

He was quiet for a long moment. "What if they hate me for hiding it? For not trusting them?"

"They won't," I said with certainty. "That's not who the Kingmans are. Or who Liam and George are."

"You're already family," Artie repeated. "This just makes it official."

My own coming out had been easy breezy. I told Flynn, then Jules first. They both acted as if I'd told them I like Cheerios and Fruit Loops instead of coming out as bisexual. No one in my family treated it like a huge deal, or something they needed to think about and process. It was just a part of me that they understood and loved.

But not everyone's family was like mine. "You don't

have to if you can't yet, and we'll work hard to figure out another way."

"No. Shit." He ran his hands through his hair. "I'm really goddamn tired of feeling so alone in this. I think Willa might already know, or at least has a clue. Hard to hide something this big from your twin."

"That it is." I pulled out my phone to start calling the Kingman cavalry, but it started buzzing before I even could. "It's Flynn."

I answered and didn't even get to say hello before he asked, "What's wrong?"

Twin telepathy proving the point. "Sloane has blackmail material on Xander. And me. And others."

There was a pause. "Emergency game night?"

"Yeah. Call everyone. I'll start with Jules, you start with Dad, and we'll work our way to the middle." God, was I grateful for my family. "Flynn—"

"Nobody threatens our family, Gryff. Nobody. I'll call Chris and the others. They can take the jet. Kelsey has her plane too. We can have everyone here in two hours."

Two hours later, our living room was packed. When Flynn said emergency protocol, the Kingmans had mobilized like an army. Dad, Chris, Declan, Everett, Hayes, and Isak had taken the Kingman jet. Kelsey had flown down with Penelope, Trixie, Willa, her father, and her guncles George and Liam on her private plane. Jules just drove on over from UCLA to be here.

Everything felt like another Kingman family gathering, but it got instantly emotional when Xander's father and uncles, Liam and George, who were being towed by his twin sister, Willa, walked in.

"Where is he?" Willa demanded the moment she walked in. "Where's my idiot brother?"

Xander stood up from where he'd been hiding in the corner, and Willa crossed the room in three strides, pulling him into a fierce hug.

"Whatever it is," she said into his shoulder, "we're here. We're all here."

The room settled, everyone finding seats, and Xander stood up. "Before we start, I have something I need to tell everyone."

Xander looked terrified. I moved to stand beside him, Artie on his other side.

"I'm… gay," he said, the words coming out in a rush. "I've always been gay. I've been hiding it my whole life because I thought... because I was told it would ruin everything. And now someone's trying to blackmail me with it."

The silence lasted about three seconds.

Then Liam and George were both on their feet, crossing to their nephew. George pulled him into a hug while Liam stood guard, looking ready to fight anyone who had a problem with it.

"We've got you," George said fiercely. "We've always got you."

"Why didn't you tell us?" Liam asked, but his voice was gentle, not accusatory.

"Mom said—" Xander started, then broke off.

"Ah," Mr. Rosemount said, understanding flooding his face. "Your mother."

He shook his head and grabbed Xander into a huge hug that lasted just as long as it needed to. "I'm just sorry that, once again, you didn't think you could come to me."

"She said it would ruin my career. Said I couldn't be like Liam if I wanted to succeed."

"That bitch," Willa said flatly. "Our mother is a monster, and I'm done pretending otherwise."

"Willa—" Xander started.

"No. She kept you from us. From your uncles who would have helped you, from me, Dad, from everyone who would have supported you." She looked around the room. "From all of this."

"You're here now," my dad said, his coach voice carrying across the room. "That's what matters. You're family, and we protect our own."

"Sir, I'm not really—"

"You're Willa's brother," Dad said. "So let's skip the part where you try to argue about it and get to the part where we destroy whoever's trying to hurt you."

Xander looked overwhelmed. "I don't... I don't know what to say."

"Say you'll let us help," Dad said. "And then tell us everything about this Sloane person."

So he did. He told them about the video, the threats, the other players being targeted. "She wants an answer by Friday," Xander finished.

"She'll get one," Flynn said grimly. "Just not the one she's expecting."

"I've got, let's say a hacker connection, and she's digging into Sloane's background." Tempest said. "We'll get the goods for you."

Penelope, Kelsey, and Trixie exchanged looks. Trixie

nodded and said, "We've all had enough experience with the press that we'll know exactly what to do with anything you dig up."

But our three eldest brothers exchanged similar looks between the three of them, then they glanced over at dad, whose scowl would probably make a grizzly bear run away squealing.

"And if we don't find something that FlixNChill will fire her for, we know what to do."

I wondered briefly what California's state flower was.

"Emergency game night protocol," Flynn announced. "With a twist. Xander, you know how to play Monopoly?"

"Everyone knows how to play Monopoly," Xander said, confused.

"Wrong," Isak said. "You know how to play regular Monopoly. You're about to learn Kingman Monopoly."

"There are only two rules," Chris said, grinning.

"Rule number one," all the Kingman brothers said in unison: "Nobody messes with our family."

"Rule number two," they continued, "always cheat at Monopoly."

Despite everything, Xander laughed. Real, genuine laughter.

"But what about the other players she's blackmailing?" Xander asked.

"We reach out to all of them." I was about to make every queer man in the League my besties and let them all know they had fucking badass allies on their side. No more feeling scared or alone. Not on my watch. "Carefully, quietly. We build a coalition."

"And then?"

"As a family, we finish this."

Xander looked around the room, at Liam and George who'd been denied the chance to support him for years, at Willa who was ready to fight the world for him, at Hayes who'd been his brother-in-law all this time without knowing this crucial piece of him, at all the Kingmans who'd claimed him without hesitation.

"Okay," he said. "Let's do this. Let's take her down."

"That's the spirit," Jules said. "Now, who's going to teach Xander how to properly cheat at Monopoly?"

"I will," George said, putting his arm around his nephew. "After all, I've got years of uncle-nephew bonding to make up for."

As everyone started setting up for the strangest game night ever, part strategy session, part family bonding, part war council, Vincent and Holly wandered through the crowd, accepting pets and treats from everyone.

Holly had claimed Xander's lap, and he was absently petting her while listening to George explain why you should always be the banker.

"Thank you," he said quietly to me. "For this. For getting your family involved. For not hating me."

"I never hated you," I said. "I was hurt but never hated you."

"Still. This is... more than I deserve."

"No," Willa said, overhearing. "This is exactly what you deserve. What you've always deserved. A family who loves you for exactly who you are."

"Even though I hid it?"

"Especially because you hid it," Liam said. "Because

now we get to make up for all the years you felt like you had to."

"This is insane," Xander said, watching it all unfold.

"This is family," I corrected.

"Your family's about to go scorched earth on Sloane Mitchell," Artie said, appearing with a plate of cookies that Holly immediately tried to steal.

And somehow, in the middle of a blackmail crisis, surrounded by chaos and goats and an ever-expanding definition of family, everything made perfect sense.

Sloane Mitchell had no idea what she'd unleashed.

The Kingmans were coming for her, and they were bringing everyone.

KINGMANS GO TO WAR

ARTEMIS

Monday morning in our house looked like a Kingman family explosion.

There were brothers sprawled on every available surface. Chris was asleep on one side of the L-shaped couch with Isak on the other. Declan had claimed the floor with just a pillow and Vinnie curled up on his chest. Everyone else was spread out across the rooms, and thank goodness I'd ordered all those throw pillows. Over at Flynn and Tempest's we had a girls only slumber party. Jules even stayed.

One text from Gryff saying Bridger was making pancakes had us all standing back in my kitchen waiting not so patiently for his fluffy flapjacks of fun.

This must have been what it was like for Gryff growing up.

The beautiful chaos of never being alone. Always having someone to catch you when you fall. Never questioning if you belonged because of course you did. You were family.

"More tea, baby?" Gryff appeared beside me with the pot, looking surprisingly rested for someone who'd slept on the floor of his own bedroom because his brothers had claimed the bed.

"Always." I held out my mug. "Is it always like this?"

"Like what?"

"Your entire family mobilizing like an army when someone needs help?"

He grinned. "Pretty much. You should've seen when the press and paparazzi showed up for Trixie and Chris. I'm pretty sure Dad was ready to commit crimes."

"Speaking of family..." I nodded toward the kitchen table where Xander sat with his father, both nursing coffee in companionable silence that felt new and fragile.

Mr. Rosemount was saying something quietly, and I caught the words "proud" and "brave." Xander's eyes were suspiciously bright.

"I wish you'd trusted me," Mr. Rosemount said, just loud enough for us to hear.

"I wish Mom had let me," Xander replied, and his father's face darkened.

"We're going to have a conversation, your mother and I. A long overdue one."

Willa appeared, dropping into the chair beside her brother. "I call first dibs on that conversation. I have some things to say about keeping siblings apart."

"We were never apart," Xander protested.

"We were," Willa said firmly. "You were hiding a whole piece of yourself. That's a kind of distance just like me running off to Europe and Asia, Xan."

Before he could respond, Liam and George joined them, George's hand landing on Xander's shoulder.

"Flight's at noon," George said. "But we'll be reachable every second until this is handled."

"You don't have to—"

"Kiddo," Liam interrupted. "We have years of guncle-ing to make up for. You're stuck with us now."

Xander's composure finally cracked. He pulled both his uncles into a hug that looked like it might never end.

"I used to watch you both," he admitted, voice muffled. "Like at your wedding. And I'd think 'they're so amazing' and wish I could be like you. But Mom said—"

"Carin said a lot of things," Mr. Rosemount interrupted, his voice hard. "Most of them wrong, all of them designed to control you both."

Willa snorted. "That's the understatement of the century."

"I should have protected you better," Mr. Rosemount continued. "Both of you. When I found out what she'd been doing to Willa, I should have realized she was damaging you too, just differently."

"Dad—" Xander started.

"No. I let you convince me to let you take her with you to Miami. You shouldn't have to be managing her along with your career."

"She's settled in her condo," Xander said weakly. "She's fine."

"You're paying for it with money you earned while being blackmailed," Willa pointed out. "That's not fine."

"She's still our mother."

"Who told you that being like your uncles would ruin

your life," Liam said flatly. "That's not a mother. That's a warden."

The morning became a blur of departures. The Mustangs brothers had to get back for practice. Kelsey's plane would take the Denver contingent home. Xander and his dad were flying back to Miami.

"Remember," Kelsey said, pulling Gryff and Flynn into a hug. "Document everything. Every interaction with Sloane, every threat, every conversation. We're building a case."

"I'm staying a couple more days," Bridger announced. "I've got some calls to make. Coaches who might know these other players, get us contact information."

"I'm staying too," Penelope added, already pulling out her tablet. "Someone needs to coordinate this properly, and no offense, but athletes are better at executing a plan than planning the plan."

"Offensive but accurate," Flynn admitted.

Gryff and Flynn got ready to leave for practice, both tense about having to face Sloane.

"She's going to be there filming like nothing happened," Gryff had said, jaw clenched.

"You have to act normal," I'd reminded him. "We can't tip her off that we're organizing."

"Flynn's going to punch her."

"Flynn's going to be perfect," I said firmly. "Because he knows what's at stake."

By noon, the house felt eerily quiet with just me, Penelope, and Bridger.

My phone buzzed with texts from Gryff throughout the afternoon.

Meanwhile, Bridger was working his coaching network from our dining table, his phone constantly at his ear.

"Tom? Yeah, it's Bridge. Listen, I need a favor. You remember that linebacker you coached at Oregon State that got drafted to the Bruins? I need his number. It's important."

Penelope had transformed our living room into a command center, laptop open, multiple spreadsheets running.

"Okay," she said, "we have seven confirmed players being threatened. Gryff knows three personally. Bridger's got connections to two more. That leaves two we need to reach."

By the time Gryff and Flynn returned from practice, we had contact information for six of the seven players.

"How was it?" I asked.

"Brutal," Flynn said. "She kept trying to get reaction shots. Asked about why our family was in town. I hate that she somehow knew that. We're going to have to be very careful.

Gryff collapsed on the couch. Holly immediately

claimed his lap, still punishing him for leaving her all day. "DeMarcus kept running interference, distracting Sloane whenever she got too close."

"He's a good captain," Flynn said. "Protects his rookies."

"Harry definitely knows something," Gryff added. "He wouldn't look at Sloane, and he kept apologizing to me. Just randomly saying sorry when she wasn't around."

"You think he'd help us?" I asked.

"Maybe. He seems like a decent guy who got caught up in something he didn't sign up for."

Gryff's phone buzzed with another text from one of the threatened players. He'd been fielding messages all day, even during practice.

"Tyler from the Chefs," he said, reading. "He wants to know if we're sure this will work."

"What are you telling them?"

"The truth. That I don't know but doing nothing definitely won't work."

On Monday night, after everyone left, Bridger and Penelope over at Flynn and Tempest's for their well-appointed guest rooms, and the calls were done, the house felt too quiet. Gryff found me in the kitchen, washing dishes from the chaos of the day.

"Hi," he said, wrapping his arms around me from behind.

"Hi yourself."

"Today was..." he trailed off, pressing his face into my neck.

"I know."

We stood there for a moment, him holding me while I

had soapy hands, and it struck me how normal this felt already. How right. Three weeks since Edinburgh and I couldn't imagine not having this.

"I can't stop thinking about Edinburgh," he murmured against my skin.

"Yeah?"

"Yeah. Even with all this chaos, I keep thinking about that hotel room. About you choosing me. About how you felt—"

I turned in his arms, sudsy hands and all. "How I felt?"

"Perfect. You felt perfect."

The kiss was inevitable, deep and claiming. My wet hands fisted in his shirt, his hands sliding under mine to hold me around the waist.

Vincent bleated loudly from the doorway, either offended by the display, or approving. I wasn't quite sure

"Your son is judging us," Gryff said against my mouth.

"He's going to have to get used to it."

Tuesday, I woke up to Gryff pressing kisses along my shoulder, his hand splayed possessively across me, one hand cupping my breast like he was staking claim to it.

"I have to go to practice," I mumbled into the pillow.

"Five more minutes."

"You said that twenty minutes ago."

"And I'll say it again in five minutes."

I turned to face him, and the look in his eyes made my stomach flip. "We're in the middle of a crisis."

"I know. But you're also right here, in my bed, wearing my shirt, and I just..." He traced a finger along my jaw. "I can't believe I get to have this."

"Even with everything falling apart?"

"Especially with everything falling apart. You're what makes it bearable."

I kissed him softly. "You know people think you're going to propose soon."

He went very still. "People? What people?"

"Crazy, right?"

"Completely crazy," he agreed, but something in his eyes made me wonder.

"I really do have to go to practice," I said. "Coach Maher is already worried about the documentary stuff. I can't be late."

"How are you going to explain being this happy when you're supposed to be stressed about Sloane?"

"I'll tell her the truth. That my boyfriend makes everything better, even disasters."

The smile that spread across his face was worth being late.

The coalition building started in earnest after I got back from practice. Gryff spent the morning on video calls with players, each conversation following a similar pattern, disbelief, fear, anger, and finally, relief at not being alone.

"We stand together," he kept saying. "She can't take us all down if we refuse to let her."

I watched him work, this man who'd been the safe harbor for so many scared athletes. He knew exactly what to say because he'd been there.

The first call was with Ray, a defensive back from Seattle. I watched Gryff's face soften as Ray nearly broke down on the other end.

"I can't," Ray was saying, his voice tinny through the

phone speaker. "My grandmother, she's religious, she won't—"

"Hey, breathe," Gryff said gently. "No one's forcing you to come out. We're stopping her from forcing you. There's a difference."

"But if she releases the photos—"

"Then we'll deal with it together. You won't be alone. I promise you that."

"Why do you care? You don't even know me."

"We met at the combine," Gryff reminded him gently. "In the hotel bar afterward. You told me you wished you could be as open as I was."

"I was drunk."

"You were honest. And you asked me how I did it, how I came out and kept playing."

There was silence on the other end, then Ray said, "You told me that courage wasn't the absence of fear, it was playing through it anyway."

"Still true."

"I'm not ready to come out."

"You don't have to be. Ever, if that's your choice. But it should be YOUR choice, not Sloane's."

The next call was with Jamie, the center from the Beagles. I remembered him from Gryff's stories about the All-star game.

"Kingman?" Jamie's East Coast accent was thick with stress. "That really you?"

"Yeah, man. You okay?"

"Fuck no, I'm not okay. This crazy woman has photos from college. My boyfriend... ex-boyfriend... shit, I don't even know what we are anymore."

"Deep breath," Gryff said. "Tell me what happened."

"She showed up at practice. Said she was doing a segment on rookie life around the League, as part of the new season of *Rookie Rising*. Then afterward, she pulled me aside and showed me the photos on her phone. Said she knew about Treyvon, about us, about everything."

"When does she want an answer?"

"Friday. Same as everyone else apparently." Jamie laughed bitterly. "At least I'm not special."

"You're not alone," Gryff corrected. "There's seven of us that we know of. We're handling it."

"How?"

"Together. As a team. Same way we play."

"You're their lifeline," I said between calls.

"I was just someone who understood," he replied. "Sometimes that's all you need."

I got home from rugby practice that evening to find Gryff on the couch with his laptop, still making calls. He looked exhausted.

"How many more?" I asked, dropping my gear bag.

"Two. But Jamie from Philly is melting down. Might call him back."

I curled up next to him, and he immediately pulled me closer, like he needed the contact to stay grounded.

"You're incredible, you know that?" I said. "These guys are lucky to have you."

"I just fucking hate that anyone has to be that scared to be who they are."

"You never worried about that?"

"No. I have you. I have my family. I have everything."

Holly chose that moment to jump on his laptop, ending the video call he was on.

"Holly Goatlightly," Gryff scolded, but he was laughing. "You're a poop."

"She's helping," I said. "Forced break."

"I love you," he said suddenly. "Sorry, I know I keep saying it—"

"Say it again."

"I love you."

"Good. Because I love you too, and I plan on saying it annoyingly often."

We were laughing when his phone rang again, another scared player needing reassurance. But this time, I stayed curled against him while he talked, my hand in his, grounding each other through the storm.

Later that night, Penelope and I worked on coordinating schedules and responses while she grilled me about my relationship.

"So, Edinburgh was pretty romantic, huh?"

"It was... significant."

"Significant enough for a ring?"

"Penelope." Since she'd just gotten married, she was one of those beautifully annoying people who wanted everyone else to get married and have their happy ever afters too.

"What? I'm just saying, you two have been dancing around each other for six years. Now that you're together, why wait?"

Here we go. "We've been officially together for like three weeks."

"After six years of foreplay," she pointed out.

"That's not—"

"Isn't it though?" She tilted her head. "The trust exercises? Living together? Raising goats? That's all relationship building. You just finally added the physical component."

She wasn't wrong, which was delightfully annoying.

"When did you know?" I asked her. "With Everett?"

"Honestly? About five minutes after meeting him. But it took us a while to get there too. The knowing and the doing are different things." She studied me while rubbing her belly absentmindedly. "You've known for a while, haven't you?"

"I... maybe. I don't know. It's all mixed up with friendship and not wanting to ruin things and thinking I was too much for anyone—"

"Too much?" Penelope interrupted. "Honey, have you seen how that man looks at you? You're not too much. You're exactly enough."

"Kelsey says the same thing about Declan looking at her," I admitted.

"Because it's a Kingman thing. They don't do anything halfway. When they love, they love with everything." She grinned. "So you better be ready for a proposal sooner rather than later."

"We just got together."

"And he's probably had a ring picked out since Edinburgh."

"He does not have a ring picked out."

Penelope just smiled knowingly and returned to her spreadsheets.

On Wednesday, just before the boys left for practice, Tempest and Flynn burst through the front door.

"We found it," Tempest announced, and held up her laptop that showed Parker on the screen. "The smoking gun."

"What kind of gun?" Bridger asked.

"Sloane Mitchell was sued by three of her USC tennis teammates for invasion of privacy. She secretly recorded them in the locker room kissing and tried to sell the footage to a gossip site. They settled and it got buried."

"Holy shit," Flynn breathed.

"It gets worse," Tempest added. "She was an assistant producer on two other reality shows. Both were canceled after participants complained about coercion and black-mail. There's a pattern."

"But here's the really dangerous part," Parker said from the video feed. "I've been digging through her old social media posts. She genuinely believes she's helping. She thinks forcing athletes out of the closet is a noble calling. That she's saving them from themselves."

"Villains who think they're heroes are the most dangerous kind," Tempest said quietly. "They'll justify anything in service of their 'greater good.'"

By Wednesday night, tension filled the house like a living thing. Gryff couldn't sit still, pacing while fielding texts from increasingly anxious players.

"What if it doesn't work?" he said suddenly.

"It will work," I said firmly.

"But what if—"

Vincent, apparently fed up with the pacing, positioned

himself directly in Gryff's path. Gryff tripped, barely catching himself on the coffee table.

"Even the goat thinks you need to calm down," Flynn observed.

"I can't calm down. Seven guys are counting on me—"

"On us," I corrected. "They're counting on us. All of us. You're not carrying this alone."

Holly chose that moment to eat Penelope's color-coded index cards, scattering carefully organized chaos everywhere.

"Your goats are agents of chaos," Penelope said, trying to save her system.

"Chaos is what we need," Bridger said from the dining table. "Sloane thinks she can control the narrative because she's used to people being isolated, scared, alone. She's never faced a united front like this."

"A family," Tempest added via video call from her place.

"Exactly. And families protect each other."

We had our plan. Friday morning, we would confront FlixNChill's executives with everything. All seven players would stand together, either in person or via video. The evidence against Sloane would be presented. And if they didn't act...

"We go nuclear," Gryff said. "Full press release. Social media blast. Everything."

"They'll cave," Bridger said confidently. "No company wants this kind of scandal."

I looked around our living room—at Bridger who'd stayed to help, at Penelope with her color-coded spread-sheets, or what was left of them after Holly's snack, at

Sean and Ren who'd become our strategic advisors, at Flynn and Tempest ready for war, at Gryff who'd become the unofficial leader of a coalition of closeted athletes.

This was what family looked like. Not just blood, but choice. Not just acceptance, but protection.

"We're really doing this," I said.

"Together," Gryff confirmed, pulling me against his side.

Vincent chose that moment to hop onto the coffee table and knock over Penelope's carefully reorganized papers, because even in crisis mode, goats were gonna goat.

"Your children are agents of chaos," Penelope informed us again.

"They learned from the best," I said, looking at my beautiful, chaotic, protective family.

Friday couldn't come fast enough.

Sloane Mitchell was about to learn what happened when you came for the Kingmans.

LOOK WHAT YOU MADE ME DO

GRYFF

riday. Deadline day.

I'd been awake since four in the morning, running through everything that was about to happen. In a few hours, Sloane Mitchell would walk into the Bandits practice facility thinking she held all the cards. She had no idea we'd stacked the entire deck against her.

My phone buzzed with another text from one of the guys she'd been blackmailing.

JAMIE

You're sure this is going to work?

Trust me. After today, she'll never bother any of us again.

I can't thank you enough man. I haven't slept in weeks.

Just hang tight. I'll text you when it's done.

Three more similar texts came in while I was getting

dressed. Seven players across teams nationwide, all rookies, all queer, all chosen specifically by Sloane for
maximum drama potential. She thought she was so clever,
so untouchable.

She was about to learn what happened when you came
for a Kingman.

Flynn was already at the facility when I arrived,
tossing a ball back and forth with Tyson.

"You ready for this?" he asked, jogging over.

"Ready to end it," I said. "Coach knows?"

"Coach, the owners, PR, legal. Everyone's on board.
They're as pissed as we are. Apparently, Mr. Bandelman's
nephew is gay, and when he heard what Sloane was
doing..." Flynn shook his head. "Let's just say she picked
the wrong team to mess with."

Whoa. It was pretty damn big to have the owner
behind us too. "Any word from Parker?"

"She's with Artie and your dad. They'll be here at nine-
thirty, right when Sloane usually shows up to film Friday
practice segments."

Parker was our secret weapon and a certified genius.
Her job in the FlixNChill IT department had not only
helped her get the goods on Sloane, but it had all been
done legally. Cybersecurity for the win. What she'd found
in two days of digging made Sloane's blackmail attempts
look like child's play.

"The executives?" I asked.

"Driving over from FNC HQ in an hour. Some head
honcho took the red-eye from New York when they saw
Parker's initial report."

Everything was falling into place.

Right as scheduled, Sloane's van pulled into the parking lot. I watched from the window as she got out, all perky confidence in her designer workout wear, directing her crew like she owned the place. She had no idea there were three extra cars in the visitor section. No idea her entire world was about to implode.

"Gryff, Flynn," she called out as she entered, that fake bright smile plastered on her face. "Ready for some great content today? I have some really exciting segments planned."

I bet she did. Today was the day she expected everyone to either come out or refuse and watch her release... what? But I still didn't know what she thought she was going to threaten me with. She'd been doing some fishing of her own, but what was she going to release about me? Photos of me and Artie holding hands? Videos of us kissing? We'd been doing that publicly for weeks now.

But the other guys, they had more to lose. Or thought they did.

"Can't wait," I said, keeping my voice neutral.

She started setting up with her crew, chattering about storylines and dramatic reveals. "You know, Gryff, I've been trying so hard to find something more interesting about you and Artie. You two claim to be together, but you acted like such, uh, weirdos about it, it makes one wonder if it's all for show."

"Does it?" I asked mildly.

"I mean, a bisexual football player and a bisexual rugby player just happen to fall in love right when you both need publicity? It's almost too convenient." She was casting for a fish, and I wasn't biting. "Unless there's something else you'd like to share? Today is a big day for... revelations."

Before I could respond, the door opened.

"Actually," Bridger's voice carried across the facility, "today is definitely a day for revelations."

Sloane spun around. Her face went pale when she saw my dad, Artie, and Parker walking in. Parker was carrying a laptop and a thick folder.

"Mr. Kingman," Sloane stammered. "So nice to meet you. I didn't know you were coming to practice."

"Wouldn't miss it," Dad said pleasantly. "Especially not today."

"Who's this?" Sloane asked, eyeing Parker nervously.

"Parker Chen, FlixNChill IT department. Cybersecurity," Parker said, flashing her badge. "We need to talk."

"I don't understand—"

The door opened again. This time, a whole group of people in expensive suits walked in. I recognized the woman in front. Parker told us she was reporting all of this to FlixNChill's Head of Original Programming, Tally Tajaria. Beside her was her boss. And from the deference being shown to the older man with them, possibly her boss's boss.

"Ms. Mitchell," Tally said coldly. "We need to discuss some serious concerns that have been brought to our attention."

"I don't... what is this?"

"This," Parker said, opening her laptop, "is your real resume. Not the one you submitted to FlixNChill." She turned the screen toward the executives. "Ms. Mitchell was expelled from USC's journalism program for fabricating sources. She was sued by two subjects of her student documentary for invasion of privacy and harassment. She filmed them without their knowledge in the women's locker room. Both cases were settled out of court."

"There was an NDA. Our lawyers said it was all sealed," Sloane protested.

"Sealed doesn't mean gone," Parker said. "Especially when FlixNChill's legal team gets involved. You also failed to disclose that your uncle is on the board of the production company that initially hired you. The same uncle who recommended you to FlixNChill."

Coach Reimann and the Bandits PR director had joined our growing circle.

"But the most concerning discovery," Tally Tajaria said, "is this pattern of targeting specific players." She held up a printout. "Ms. Mitchell's personal notes, recovered from her FlixNChill cloud storage. She specifically selected seven players for this season based on their suspected sexual orientation."

"I was trying to increase representation," Sloane said desperately. "To make the League more inclusive."

"By threatening to out them against their will?" The PR director stepped forward. "Ms. Mitchell, the Bandits organization is fully committed to supporting all our players, regardless of orientation. But that support means letting them tell their own stories on their own timeline."

"She has a point though," the older executive said thoughtfully. "The League does need to be more inclusive."

"Absolutely," Coach Reimann agreed. "Which is why

we're working with Gryff Kingman on plans to launch a comprehensive pride initiative next season, with safe spaces, support systems, and voluntary visibility campaigns. Not forced outings for television drama."

Sloane was looking around wildly now, realizing how thoroughly she'd been exposed.

"The photos," she said suddenly, desperately. "I have photos of players—"

"You mean these?" Parker pulled out a tablet, showing thumbnails of various images that had been electronically blurred. "All retrieved from your personal devices and cloud storage. Which, by the way, violates about fifteen FlixNChill policies regarding exploitation of subjects and invasion of privacy."

"Not to mention the potential criminal charges," Dad added pleasantly. "Blackmail is still illegal in California, last I checked."

"You can't prove—"

"Actually," Harry, Sloane's lead cameraman, stepped forward from where he'd been standing with the crew. "We can."

Everyone turned to look at him. Sloane's face went white.

"Harry, what are you—"

He pulled out his phone and connected it to the facility's display screen. "I've been documenting Ms. Mitchell's behavior for weeks." A video started playing, showing Sloane cornering someone whose face was blurred, but I recognized the player and the conversation. How this tiny worm of a woman had intimidated the commanding tower of Xander Rosemount was mindboggling.

"Listen [BLEEP]," Sloane's voice was clear on the recording. *"I'm trying to help you here. This is your chance to control your own narrative. Otherwise, well, things have a way of getting out in this industry. Photos surface, rumors start... it gets messy. I'd hate to see that happen when we could make this a beautiful, empowering moment for you instead. You understand what I'm saying, don't you? Friday's when we film the segment. Your choice how this story gets told—by you, on your terms, or... not."*

"You recorded me?" Sloane spun on Harry, furious. "You work for me."

"I work for FlixNChill," Harry corrected quietly. "And I have about fifteen more videos like this. Different players, same threats. I blurred their faces and bleeped their names to protect their identities, but it's all here. Every threat, every manipulation, every time you crossed the line."

"You little—"

"I couldn't stand by and watch you destroy these guys' lives for ratings," Harry said firmly. "That's not why I got into television."

Sloane's face had gone from pale to gray.

Tally Tajaria looked around, frustrated. "The problem is, *Rookie Rising* is one of our top-rated shows. We can't just cancel the rest of the season. We need someone who can take over immediately, who knows the players, knows the show..."

"Kendra could do it," Harry said suddenly.

Everyone turned to look at him, including Kendra, whose face flushed pink.

"Kendra, my assistant Kendra?" Tally asked and looked

over at the woman who'd remained quiet throughout the entire confrontation.

"I've worked with her on three other projects," Harry explained, his voice gaining confidence. "She understands sports, she respects the subjects, and she actually cares about telling real stories, not manufacturing drama."

"Harry," Kendra started, clearly flustered.

"She's also been developing ideas for authentic documentaries that focus on the human element without exploitation," Harry continued, looking directly at Kendra with obvious admiration. "She's exactly what this show needs."

Tally studied Kendra. "Is this true? You have ideas for the show?"

Kendra straightened, finding her confidence. "Yes, ma'am. I believe we can showcase the real rookie experience, the pressure, the brotherhood, the adjustment to professional sports, without inventing conflict or violating anyone's privacy."

"She's brilliant," Harry added quietly, and the look they exchanged made it clear this was about more than just professional respect.

Tally nodded slowly. "Kendra, congratulations. You're the new producer of *Rookie Rising*. Harry, I assume you'll be happy to stay on as lead camera?"

"Absolutely," Harry said, smiling at Kendra, who was trying very hard not to smile back.

"Good. We'll discuss your vision for refocusing the show after we deal with... this." She turned back to Sloane. "Security will escort you out. Your personal items will be sent to you. Your final check will cover the work completed. But expect a bill from the legal department about the legal fees FlixNChill will incur cleaning up your mess."

"You can't just—"

"Actually, we can," the older executive said. "Your contract has a morality clause and a section specifically about exploitation of subjects. You've violated both extensively. I'd recommend you keep your mouth shut, slink away, and hire yourself a good lawyer."

Two security guards had appeared. Sloane looked around the circle of faces, finding no sympathy anywhere.

"This is a mistake," she said. "I was making great television."

"You were exploiting vulnerable young men for ratings," Artie said quietly. "There's a difference."

As security led Sloane out, she turned back one more time. "You'll regret this. The show will be boring without me."

"No, I don't think it will," Kendra said, already pulling out her tablet and making notes.

The moment the door closed behind Sloane, I pulled out my phone and opened the group text I'd created with all seven guys once they agreed to be open within the context of our coalition against Sloane.

It's done. She's gone. Fired, potentially facing charges, and all materials on the way to being destroyed. You're safe.

The responses were immediate:

JAMIE

THANK YOU THANK YOU THANK YOU

CARLOS

I can't believe it's over

DEVON

You're a hero man

TYLER

I owe you everything

RAY

Tell your family thank you from all of us

ANDRE

First round's on me next time we play
you guys

XANDER

Thank you doesn't even cover it

Xander immediately called.

"Is it really over?" he asked.

"It's really over," I confirmed.

I could practically hear him sag with relief, and I wished he was here so I could pull him into a hug. Of anyone I'd ever known, he needed one.

"Hey, man, put me on speaker."

I did. "Thank you. All of you. I don't know how to—"

"You're family," Dad said simply. "This is what family does."

Kendra approached me hesitantly, with Harry trailing behind her looking supportive. "Gryff, Flynn? I was wondering if you might do some fresh interviews, partly so I can get to know you a bit and what you'd like to get out of this experience. No drama, no forced revelations, just... real life?"

I looked at Flynn, who nodded.

"We'd be happy to," I said. "The real story is way better than whatever Sloane was trying to manufacture anyway. Being a rookie is freaking wild."

"I promise it'll be respectful," Kendra said. "No ambush interviews, no invasive questions. Just authentic storytelling."

"That's all we ever wanted," I said.

Harry stepped forward. "And Gryff? I'm sorry I didn't come forward sooner. I should have—"

"You protected those guys' identities while gathering evidence," I interrupted. "You gave us the hammer for the final blow. We had plenty of paper evidence, but nothing beats reality TV. Thank you."

He nodded, clearly relieved, then glanced at Kendra. "We should probably go plan the new shooting schedule."

"Right. Yes. Planning." Kendra was definitely blushing now.

As they walked off together, already deep in discussion about the show's new direction, Artie leaned into me.

"Those two are totally going to end up together," she whispered.

"Obviously. Did you see the way he looked at her?"

"Did you see the way she looked at him when he called her brilliant?"

As everyone started dispersing, Artie slipped her hand into mine.

"You did it," she said quietly.

"We did it," I corrected. "I couldn't have done any of this without you, Parker, Dad, everyone."

"Still. You stood up for those guys when you could have just protected yourself."

"That's not who we are," I said. "That's not who any of us are."

She went up on her toes and kissed me, right there in the middle of the practice facility. "I love you."

"I love you too."

"Okay, lovebirds," Flynn called out. "We still have actual practice."

Later that evening, Artie and I were back at our house, a bit emotionally exhausted but victorious. Parker had given us a folder with copies of everything she'd found on Sloane. Her real transcripts, the documents from the lawsuits, the evidence of her lies.

"What should we do with this?" Artie asked, holding the folder.

"Shred it? Burn it? Frame it and then burn it?" I suggested.

Before we could decide, Vincent trotted into the living room, spotted the folder, and snatched it right out of Artie's hands.

"Vinnie, no," Artie laughed, but he was already chomping down on Sloane's USC expulsion letter.

Holly, not to be outdone, jumped onto the coffee table and grabbed a chunk of papers, including what looked like Sloane's headshot. She proceeded to chew one half thoroughly before spitting it out.

"Are they..." I started.

"They're eating Sloane's dirt," Artie confirmed,

watching in amazement as Vincent destroyed a court document with prejudice.

Then, in what could only be described as poetic justice, Holly squatted and pooped directly on what remained of Sloane's headshot.

"Did she just—"

"She did," Artie confirmed. "Holly Goatlightly just delivered her verdict on Sloane Mitchell."

I waved my hand in front of my face. "Oh geez. Apparently pure evil digested stinks. Whew, Holly. I think you might need a colonoscopy or something."

Vincent, not to be outdone, lifted his leg and peed on the pile of shredded documents.

We stood there, watching our goats literally shit on everything Sloane represented, and I couldn't help it, I burst out laughing. Artie joined in, and soon we were both on the floor, crying with laughter as our goats continued their systematic destruction of Sloane's legacy.

"Even the goats knew she was full of shit," Artie gasped between laughs.

"Literally," I agreed, watching Holly do a little victory dance on the remains of the folder.

Vincent looked at us with those wise goat eyes, a piece of legal document hanging from his mouth, looking absolutely pleased with himself.

"You know what?" I said, pulling Artie against me. "I think the goats had the right idea all along."

"Destroy your enemies by eating them and pooping on their remains?"

"Exactly."

"Very Kingman of them."

"They learned from the best."

As we sat there in our living room, surrounded by shredded papers and goat droppings, Sloane Mitchell officially reduced to nothing more than goat food and fertilizer, a huge weight lifted off my shoulders.

It was over. Really, truly over.

The guys were safe. Xander was free. And Sloane Mitchell would never hurt anyone in the League again.

"You know what this means?" Artie said suddenly.

"What?"

"We can go to Colorado for Christmas without any drama hanging over us."

"Just regular Kingman family Christmas chaos?"

"The best kind of chaos."

We cleaned up the remains of Sloane's career, now literally goat waste. Sometimes justice came in really strange ways.

Sometimes it wore a suit and carried legal documents.

Sometimes it was a family standing together against a threat.

And sometimes, it was a couple of baby goats eating and shitting on people who deserved it.

"One more game, which I'm not hopeful of winning," I said. The Bandits weren't kidding when they'd recruited Flynn and I to be a part of the rebuilding of the team. We weren't making the playoffs no matter what. Maybe next year. "And then a drama-free Christmas."

"With your family? Drama-free?" She laughed. "That'll be the day."

She was right, of course. But it would be our kind of

drama, the kind that came with love and laughter and too many people trying to help in the kitchen.

The kind that didn't involve blackmail or threats or forced revelations.

Just family. Just love. Just us.

And maybe a couple of goats who'd proven themselves to be excellent judges of character.

"Vincent Van Goat," I said solemnly, "Holly Goat-lightly, you're officially the best judges of character in this family."

They both looked up at me, pieces of Sloane still hanging from their mouths, looking enormously proud of themselves.

As they should be.

They'd delivered the perfect verdict. Stinky, but perfect.

HOLLY JOLLY KINGMANS

ARTEMIS

"Fraser! Get your ass over here." Coach Maher's voice carried across the pitch.

I jogged over, still breathing hard from our final practice before Christmas break. My teammates were already gathering, and I could see Gryff and Flynn setting up something behind Coach.

"What's going on?"

"What's going on," Coach said, grinning, "is that someone forgot to mention they were ready to make a certain announcement this week."

Gryff and Flynn pulled out a massive banner that read "TEAM USA BOUND" with my number and a truly terrible photo of me from my first practice where I'd face-planted in the mud.

"Oh my god, you guys."

"Our girl's going to the Olympics," Adrianna, our fly-half, shouted, and suddenly I was at the bottom of a pile of celebrating teammates.

"Can't... breathe..." I gasped, but I was laughing.

When they finally let me up, Coach handed me an unoffcial-official Team USA Rugby jersey with my name on it. "Came by special delivery this morning. I wanted to make sure you had it for Christmas."

I held it up, and my throat got tight. Fraser. Number 15. Team USA.

Of course nothing would be official until a few months before the actual Olympics. But I was committed to Team USA and would do everything I could do to support the team win or lose.

We took about a million and two pics and I posted a slideshow of the announcement to my shiny new InstaSnap. Parker had made me do it, and for the most part posted content for me. If she wasn't such an IT genius, she'd be a great branding and marketing guru. I was already at a couple thousand followers and it grew every day. She said I was bound for sponsorships and a Sportsy award.

Just a few moments later, my phone buzzed with a call from my dad. I'd meant to call him before making the decision public, but team excitement and the twins shenanigans got the better of me.

"Hi, Dad."

"So. Team USA." His voice was carefully neutral with that Scottish rumble.

"Team USA," I confirmed.

There was a long pause. "Your mother said this would happen. Said you were too American now."

"Dad—"

"I'm proud of you, Artemis." His voice cracked slightly. "Disappointed, aye, but proud. You've chosen your own path. That takes courage."

"I'll still see you at international matches," I offered. "When we destroy Scotland."

He barked out a laugh. "Cheeky girl. We'll see about that."

"I love you, Dad."

"Love you too, hen. Give my best to that boy of yours. He's good for you."

He was good for me and good to me. He was so much more than I ever thought I'd find in life.

A few hours later, I was standing in our driveway watching the chaos of preparing to road trip home with a whole menagerie unfold.

"Vincent, No," Gryff lunged for his goat, who had somehow already escaped the trailer and was making a beeline for Mrs. Bender's prized succulents.

"I told you we should have sedated them," Flynn said, holding Burrito Petito's lead rope while the donkey tried to eat his shirt.

"You can't sedate animals for a road trip," Tempest said, easily loading her suitcase around Burrito's protests. "That's not how sedation works."

"How does a donkey have this many opinions?" Flynn asked as Burrito tried to eat his hair.

Holly Goatlightly chose that moment to jump out of the trailer and join Vincent in the succulent massacre.

"Get the goats," Jules shouted, running after Holly while filming everything on her phone. "This is definitely going on the family chat."

"Our neighbors are watching," I told Gryff as he carried Vincent back to the trailer.

"Our neighbors have been watching since the day we brought these demons home," he corrected. "Mrs. Bender has the succulent specialist at the nursery on speed dial now. With my credit card on file."

Sure enough, Mrs. Bender was on her porch, phone in hand. She waved at me. "Tell your family I say Merry Christmas. And thanks for the new Christmas cactus you just bought me."

It took forty-five minutes to get everyone loaded. The fancy livestock trailer we'd rented was basically the Ritz Carlton of animal transport. Three hundred and sixty degrees of padded walls, climate control, even a camera system so we could monitor them from the car.

It was basically Battlestar Goatlactica with all its high-tech futuristic farm animal monitoring systems, Captain Adonka at the helm of course.

"Road trip," Jules called out, claiming the whole middle row of the SUV. "Dibs on DJ duty."

"Absolutely not," Flynn said immediately. "Driver picks the music, little sisters shut their pieholes."

"My taste is eclectic."

"Your taste is chaotic."

Three hours into the drive, we stopped at a massive truck stop near Barstow to water the animals and grab food. I was walking Holly on her lead, trying to convince her that the garbage can was not food, when I heard squealing.

"Oooh, look, aaaahhh."

I turned to see three women, probably in their thirties, rushing toward us.

Gryff immediately stepped forward, straightening up

with his classic celebrity smile. Flynn did the same, ready for fan interaction.

The women ran right past them.

"You're Miranda Milan," one of them shrieked, grabbing Tempest's hands. "I've read every single one of your books. 'Much Ado About Pucks' changed my life. Being able to see myself represented in a book was amazing. Is it true FlixNChill is adapting the whole series?"

"And holy shit," another one said, turning to me. "You're Artemis Fraser. We just saw your Team USA announcement. That photo in the jersey was everywhere."

Parker really was a genius.

Gryff's mouth fell open. Flynn looked like someone had just told him Santa wasn't real.

"We're obsessed with your Shakespeare sports retellings," the first woman gushed to Tempest. "The way you made Taming of the Shrew into a hockey romance? *Chef's kiss.*"

"And we follow women's rugby religiously," another explained, turning to me. "My daughter plays at university level. She's obsessed with you."

"Can we get a photo?" the British one asked, then looked at me with mock severity. "Even though you betrayed the Commonwealth for the Yanks."

"The Yanks have better weather," I said, and she laughed.

"Fair point. California's corrupted you then."

We took about fifteen photos while Gryff and Flynn stood to the side, holding the animals like very confused farmhands.

"Are these your... boyfriends?" one woman asked, barely glancing at the twins.

"That one's mine," Tempest said, pointing at Flynn, who perked up.

"Oh, like in 'Twelfth Night Lights," the woman squealed. "The twin football players. Did you base those characters on them?"

"Maybe a little," Tempest admitted, and Flynn preened until she added, "Though I made them more interesting in the book."

"I'm actually—" Flynn started.

"Could you take a photo of us?" the woman asked, handing him her phone.

Jules was absolutely dying of laughter in the background, recording everything.

"This is definitely going in the family chat," she wheezed. "Flynn getting treated like a photography assistant is my new favorite Christmas gift."

After the women left, gushing about how they'd be watching both of us in our upcoming seasons, Flynn stood there looking bewildered.

"Did we just... not get recognized?"

"You got recognized," I said sweetly. "As the guy holding the donkey."

"I'm a professional football player."

"And I'm sure that's very nice for you," Tempest patted his cheek. "Now help me get Burrito back in the trailer."

The rest of the drive was mostly Jules playing increasingly chaotic music while coordinating puppy logistics via text. Apparently, the puppy, a tiny version of the dog they'd all grown up with, was currently with the neighbors and would be snuck over after Bridger went to bed.

"Isak has detailed instructions on the super-secret sneaky plan to get the puppy into the garage including a temporary soundproof doghouse made out of egg cartons," Jules reported. "There are drawings and everything."

"Of course there is," Gryff laughed. "Kid's nothing if not thorough."

We pulled up to the Kingman house just as the sun was setting. The whole place was lit up like a Christmas wonderland, lights on every surface, an inflatable Santa that was definitely new, and what looked like a reindeer made entirely of old practice equipment with a flat-football for a head.

"Did Everett make that?" I asked.

"Every year someone adds a new addition," Gryff confirmed. "Last year it was the Christmas lobster."

"The what?"

But before he could explain, the front door burst open and the entire Kingman family poured out.

"My babies," Nana called out, already in full grandmother mode.

"About time." Chris shouted. "We've been tracking your location for the last hour."

Penelope waddled out behind Everett, looking massively pregnant and radiant. "If this baby comes early because of excitement, I'm billing all of you for the ambulance."

"You look like you swallowed a basketball," Jules told her.

"Two basketballs," Penelope corrected. "Baby Boy is enormous. Gets it from your brother."

Everett grinned like the snake that caught the canary.

The next few minutes were chaos filled with hugs, luggage, and then the animal reveal.

"You brought a whole farm," Bridger said, staring at the trailer.

"It's just two goats and a donkey," I said.

"That's a farm, sweetheart."

Vincent immediately escaped again and made friends with the hockey stick reindeer. Holly tried to eat the inflatable Santa. Burrito Petito went straight through the back gate and to the row of herbs like they were snacks planted especially for him. To be fair, Bridger had built a paddock in the backyard when Flynn was trying to win Tempest's heart.

"First Christmas in fifteen years without a game," Dad announced once we were all inside. "I don't know what to do with myself."

"We could watch football," Isak suggested.

"Absolutely not," came the unanimous response.

"We're doing the present exchange tomorrow night," Bridger announced. "Traditional chaos, maximum theft allowed."

"Remember when Everett got the bedazzled jock strap?" Declan asked.

"I still have it," Everett said proudly. "It's a family heirloom now."

"That's disturbing," Jules said.

Gryff and I spent Christmas Eve afternoon with my mom and grandparents. We had a family tradition of a book exchange so we had something to read that evening while waiting for Santa to come. Gryff and I both went home with a copy of *You are a Badass at Making Money*.

The Kingman white elephant exchange was exactly as chaotic as promised. The gifts ranged from ridiculous to ridiculously thoughtful to just plain weird.

Flynn unwrapped a shirt that said "I'm Not The Better Twin But I'm The Prettier One."

"Who did this?" he demanded.

Everyone pointed at Gryff.

Trixie opened a coffee table book called "Sexy Tractors of the Midwest."

"This is horrible. I'm keeping it forever."

Bridger got a set of wind chimes made entirely of tiny football helmets. "These are going right outside my office window."

Penelope opened her gift to find a onesie that said "My Dad Can Beat Up Your Dad Unless Your Dad Is Also A Kingman."

"Accurate," she nodded.

I unwrapped my gift to find a throw pillow. But not just any pillow—it was green, embroidered exactly like the lucky pillow, except instead of "In This House We Bleed Green," it said "In This House We Play Rugby."

"Who—" I started, already getting choked up.

"Family gift," Bridger said. "The grandmothers made it. If you're going to be a Kingman, you need your own pillow. Even if it contains heresy about rugby."

"Rugby is superior," I said, hugging the pillow.

"And she's crying," Gryff announced. "Everyone mark your calendars."

"Shut up, I'm not crying."

Gryff swiped softly at my cheek. "You're totally crying."

But I wasn't the only one. A moment later, Trixie, Kelsey, Penelope, Willa, and Tempest all got pillows too. We all got the same style that started with the 'In this House' phrase. But each was uniquely created for their bearer.

The best gift, though, was Gryff opening a box to find a coffee mug with Vincent Van Goat's face on it wearing a Christmas hat with the words "Goat Daddy" underneath.

"I'm never using another mug," Gryff said solemnly.

After everyone had gone to bed and Jules had successfully snuck the puppy into the garage with help from Isak and about six pounds of treats, Gryff and I sat on the back porch, watching a rare Christmas snow start to fall. It wouldn't stick, but it was pretty.

"You happy?" he asked, pulling me closer.

"So happy it's disgusting," I admitted. "Last Christmas I was alone in my apartment eating Chinese takeout, pretending to read "Financial Feminist" and watching *Die Hard*, which isn't even a Christmas movie."

"*Die Hard* is a Christmas movie."

"That's what I said. But this..." I looked back at the house, full of family, full of love, full of chaos. "This is better."

"Even with the present chaos?"

"Especially with the present chaos." I held up my pillow. "I have my own Kingman pillow now. It's official."

"You were official the moment you walked into that

first family game night," he said. "The pillow's just documentation."

Christmas morning came way too early, announced by Vincent and Holly who had somehow escaped the garage and were standing on the porch, bleating at the top of their lungs.

"Merry Christmas," Jules shouted through the house. "Everyone up. Get up, get up, get up."

"It's six in the morning," Flynn groaned from our old room.

"CHRISTMAS WAITS FOR NO ONE!"

The kitchen was already chaos. Bridger was making his famous Christmas morning cinnamon rolls, the grandparents were arguing about bacon techniques, and Penelope was directing traffic from a chair because standing was "overrated at this point in pregnancy."

"Where's Jules?" I asked.

"Getting the surprise," Chris said, trying not to smile.

"What surprise?" Bridger asked suspiciously.

"Nothing. No surprise. Eat your cinnamon roll."

That's when we heard the tiny bark from the garage.

Bridger froze. "What was that?"

"Nothing," everyone said at once.

Another bark, louder this time.

"That sounds like—"

Jules walked in carrying the fluffiest baby... animal? I wasn't sure if it was a panda with just one small white spot, a slobbery soot sprite, or the fluffiest puppy who was the epitome of cuteness. Jules even had him wearing a massive red bow.

"Merry Christmas, Dad," she said, her voice shaking.

Bridger stared at the puppy, then at his children, then back at the puppy. "You didn't."

"We did," Chris said. "With no more kids at home, we figured it was time, Dad."

"He's ten weeks old," Isak added, pulling out his phone. "I'm ready to turn this puppy into the internet's next celebrity dog."

Bridger held out his arms and cuddled the little fluff-ball in his arms like a baby. It started licking his face enthusiastically while he tried not to cry.

"I can't believe you all kept this secret," he said.

"It was horrible," Declan said. "The group chat was chaos."

"Jules almost blew it six times," Hayes added.

"I did not."

"You literally sent a photo of dog food to the family chat last week."

"That was for the goats."

"Goats don't eat dog food, Jules."

Jules stuck her tongue out at her brothers and then smiled at her dad. "What are you going to name him?"

"The Fourth."

All the Kingmans laughed.

I leaned over to Gryff and whispered, "I don't get it. What's so funny?"

"Oh, that's right. We didn't have a dog anymore by the time you moved to Colorado. This is the family's fourth dog, and they've all been named Bear. So this is Bear the Fourth."

Bear barked, as if agreeing, and then noticed the goats

for the first time. Vincent and Holly had wandered into the kitchen, probably looking for food.

The puppy wiggled out of Bridger's arms and went straight for the goats, tail wagging so hard his whole body shook.

Vincent looked at the puppy with great disdain. Holly, however, immediately accepted the invitation for friendship, gently headbutting Bear, who flopped over in submission.

"We have a very weird family," Bridger said, watching his new puppy follow a goat around his kitchen while his pregnant daughter-in-law directed bacon cooking from a chair and his sons argued about whether *Die Hard* was a Christmas movie.

"The best weird family," Jules corrected, kissing his cheek.

"Definitely the best," I agreed, holding my heretical rugby pillow and watching Vincent try to eat the Christmas tree while Holly taught Bear how to steal bacon.

"Family photo time," Nana announced. "Everyone outside, and bring the zoo."

We trooped outside to a lovely sunny Christmas Day, because Colorado. All the Kingman boys, Jules, the parents and grandparents, all the wives, Tempest, me, three goats... Vincent had multiplied somehow. No wait, that was the football equipment reindeer, a donkey, an anaconda, a cat, a wiener dog, a rooster, and one fluffy puppy.

"This is insane." Bridger called out as Isak set up the timer on his fancy new phone.

The photo showed this enormous happy family, our crazy array of pets, and me and Gryff in the middle of it all, him kissing my temple while I laughed at our goats trying to climb us like a jungle gym.

"Best Christmas ever," I said to Gryff as we walked back inside.

"Just wait until New Year's," he said. "Isak's got a bowl game."

"More football?"

"More family," he corrected. "Plus football."

"As long as there's family," I said, looking back at the chaos behind us, baby bear chasing Holly, Vincent eating decorations, Jules trying to teach Burrito to wear a Santa hat. "I'm in."

"Forever?" he asked.

"Forever," I confirmed.

"Good," he said. "Because I'm pretty sure the goats just ate Flynn's car keys."

I looked over to see Vincent with a look of indigestion on his face. But also looking extraordinarily pleased with himself.

"Guess we're staying a while then," I laughed.

"Guess we are."

And honestly? Surrounded by this beautiful chaos, there was nowhere else I'd rather be.

Even if Vincent Van Goat was currently throwing up car keys on the lawn.

BOWLS AND BARBEQUE AND BABIES. OH MY

GRYFF

New Year's Day in Pasadena, and it looked like the entire DSU student body and thirty years of alumni had showed up for the Flower Bowl. Purple and gold bedazzled everything, turning our side of the stadium into something straight out of our old stomping grounds. The mountains in the distance were snow-capped despite the California sun, and the whole scene felt like some kind of fever dream where Colorado and California had merged into one perfect football moment.

"Is this what tailgating is?" I asked Artie, watching Dad set up a full grill operation in the parking lot. "Because this seems excessive."

She laughed, handing me a beer at nine in the morning like that was totally normal. "Welcome to the other side of game day, Gryff. The side where you get to actually enjoy the pregame instead of sitting in meetings watching film."

"I watched film before games by choice," I protested.

"Of course you did." She was wearing one of my old

Dragons hoodies, and seeing her in my college colors still did things to my chest I couldn't quite name. "But now you get to experience the fine art of grilling breakfast burritos off the back of a pickup truck while discussing why Bay State doesn't stand a chance."

"Bay State has Fox Daws," Flynn said, appearing with Tempest. "That guy's an actual movie star who happens to play football. We met him at the combine doing some research for a movie."

"He was cool," I admitted, remembering the ridiculously photogenic tight end who'd somehow balanced Hollywood and college ball. "Weird that Tyson took you to see his movie that one time."

Artie's face did something complicated at the mention of Tyson. "That was a lifetime ago."

"Good lifetime or bad lifetime?" Tempest asked, stealing bacon from the grill.

"The kind of lifetime that led to this one," Artie said, grabbing my hand. "So ultimately good, even if the journey was circuitous."

"Circuitous," Flynn repeated. "Someone's been reading Tempest's romance novels."

"Someone's about to get tackled into that cooler," Tempest threatened.

"Think Isak will get any playing time?" Flynn asked, tossing the football to Declan.

"Doubt it," Declan said, catching it easily. "Seth Glass has been solid all season."

"Yeah, but he's been dealing with bruised ribs since the conference championship," Chris added, jumping into the impromptu game. "Saw him getting extra treatment all week in the sports blogs."

"Isak's ready if he gets the chance," I said, catching Flynn's pass. "Kid's been preparing for this his whole life."

"Being ready in the backyard with us and being ready for the Flower Bowl are different things," Hayes pointed out.

"No, they're not." I threw a perfect spiral to Chris. "Football is football. The field's the same size, the ball weighs the same."

Dad's phone rang, and he stepped away from the grill to answer. "Everett? Why aren't you—Slow down, son."

We all stopped throwing to listen.

"Braxton-Hicks," Dad said calmly into the phone. "It's practice contractions. Penelope's fine... Yes, I'm sure... No, you don't need to go to the hospital... Everett, breathe."

"Is Pen okay?" Chris called out.

Dad held up a finger, still talking. "Son, I've been through this eight times. She's thirty-two weeks, some Braxton-Hicks is normal... Have her drink water and lie on her left side... Yes, that's why you're hosting a watch party instead of flying here."

He paused, listening, then chuckled. "Everett, when it's real labor, you'll know. Trust me... Now go take care of your wife and stop panicking. We'll FaceTime you when Isak gets in the game... IF he gets in the game... Love you too."

He hung up and shook his head. "That boy's going to have a heart attack before that baby even arrives."

"Pen's having contractions?" Jules asked, concerned.

"Practice ones. But Everett's acting like she's about to deliver on the living room floor during halftime."

"Remember when Mom was pregnant with Jules?" Declan grinned. "Dad made us do emergency drills to the hospital."

"That was educational," Dad protested, returning to the grill.

"You timed us with a stopwatch," Hayes added.

"Preparation is important," Dad insisted. "And Everett's going to need all the preparation he can get. That boy's already wound tighter than a spring."

Flynn's phone buzzed with a text. "Everett says Pen is fine and eating nachos while yelling at the TV because the pregame announcers are disrespecting Isak's potential."

"That's our Penelope," Kelsey laughed. "Seven and a half months pregnant and still ready to fight anyone who underestimates a Kingman."

The parking lot had turned into a full Kingman family reunion minus one. Chris had claimed an entire section with multiple trucks and a tent that probably violated several parking regulations. Declan and Kelsey were taking selfies with fans who recognized her, though most were more excited about meeting a Big Bowl champion. Hayes and Willa were attempting to set up speakers while FaceTiming with Everett and Penelope back in Thornminster.

"This is insane," Artie said, appearing at my elbow with a plate of food. "Your family tailgates like they're hosting a wedding."

"First time for everything," I admitted. "I usually missed all this, being in the locker room by now."

"Your dad's been explaining the finer points of charcoal versus propane for twenty minutes." She bit into a breakfast burrito. "I think he's adopted me."

"The whole family has adopted you. Nana made you a lucky pillow." I pointed to where Nana Evie was pulling out what looked like half a craft store from her bag.

"I'm making a blanket for the game," Nana called out. "It gets cold in those stadiums."

"It's seventy degrees," Jules pointed out.

"California cold is still cold," Nana insisted, wrapping herself in approximately seventeen scarves despite the sunshine.

As the morning went on, more people showed up. Flynn's defensive line teammates from senior year, some of my O-line, even Xander Rosemount who'd flown in.

"Baby Kingman's first bowl game," Xander said, clapping me on the shoulder. "You ready to watch him become a legend?"

"He's not even starting," I reminded everyone for the hundredth time.

"Yet," the entire group said in unison.

"You all jinx things professionally or just as a hobby?" I asked.

"It's not jinxing if it's destiny," Chris said sagely, which made absolutely no sense but sounded profound enough that everyone nodded.

The stadium was packed, that electric energy of college football that the League, for all its polish and professionalism, could never quite replicate. The Flower Bowl was legendary and being here felt like being part of history.

"I can't believe we're actually here," Artie said as we found our seats. "Remember watching bowl games junior year of high school?"

"You asked why they were called bowls when the stadium wasn't bowl-shaped."

"It's a valid question that you never adequately answered."

"I explained it perfectly."

"You said 'because football' and then got distracted by a touchdown."

"That's a perfect explanation."

She laughed, leaning into me as the teams took the field. Denver State in purple and gold, Bay State in black and teal. Their dire wolf logo looked appropriately intimidating on the helmets.

"There's Fox Daws," Flynn pointed out as Bay State's offense warmed up. "Number seventy-eight."

Even from the stands, you could see why the guy was a movie star. He moved like an athlete but looked like he'd stepped off a magazine cover.

"Still can't believe he balances Hollywood and football," Tempest said. "His last movie made, like, two hundred million dollars."

"The one where he drove a car off a cliff and somehow didn't die?" Jules asked, while possibly drooling.

"That's the one."

"Art," Declan said solemnly. "Pure art."

The game started with Bay State receiving, and their offense immediately went to work. Their quarterback had a cannon for an arm, and Fox Daws was creating matchup nightmares for our defense. But Seth Glass and our offense were keeping pace, trading scores through the first quarter.

Then it happened.

Second quarter, Bay State was bringing pressure on every play. Seth was getting hit, getting up slower each time. You could see him favoring his left side, trying to protect those ribs.

"He's hurting," Chris said quietly.

"He needs to slide," Dad agreed. "Avoid the hits."

But Seth was a warrior, trying to tough it out. On third and long, Bay State's defensive end came through unblocked. Seth tried to step up but couldn't quite avoid the hit. He went down hard, and this time, he didn't get up.

The stadium went silent.

"Oh no," Artie breathed, her hand finding mine.

The medical staff ran out. Seth tried to sit up once, then immediately lay back down, his hand going to his ribs.

"That's not good," Flynn said unnecessarily.

They helped Seth off the field to applause, and suddenly there was Isak, strapping on his helmet, jogging onto the field like this was just another practice.

"Holy shit," Declan said. "Baby brother's going in."

"In the Flower Bowl," Hayes added. "Against Fox Daws and Bay State."

"His first real action is in a fucking bowl game," Chris breathed.

My phone started buzzing with texts from Everett to the family group chat.

EVERETT

IS THAT ISAK?? PEN JUST THREW A
PILLOW AT THE TV IN EXCITEMENT

She says to tell him to 'light those dire
wolves up'

Also she's crying but she says it's
pregnancy hormones not nerves

I could see Isak in the huddle, and even from here, his body language was different than Seth's had been. Where Seth had looked tense, protective, Isak looked... loose. Ready.

First play Isak faked a handoff, rolled right, and threw a perfect spiral to the tight end for fifteen yards.

The stadium exploded.

"THAT'S MY BOY," Dad shouted, on his feet.

Second play was a quick slant to the slot receiver, another first down.

"He's not playing scared," Chris observed. "Look at him. He's having fun."

He was right. Isak was bouncing between plays, chatting with his linemen, even gave a little fist bump to the Bay State player who helped him up after a tackle.

On the third play, Bay State brought the house on a blitz. Isak stood tall in the pocket, waited until the last possible second, and delivered a strike down the sideline for thirty yards.

"WHERE DID THAT COME FROM?" Jules screamed.

"He's been watching film with me," Chris said, recognizing the route concept. "We ran that play a hundred times in the backyard last summer."

By halftime, Isak had led two touchdown drives, and we were only down 21-17. The kid who'd grown up as the youngest brother of the seven of us boys, always fighting for attention, was commanding that field like a senior.

The second half was magic.

Isak was seeing the field like a ten-year veteran. When Bay State adjusted their coverage, he adjusted right back. When they brought pressure, he had the hot route ready. His teammates were responding too, playing harder, finishing blocks, fighting for extra yards.

"He's got it," Dad said quietly in the third quarter. "That thing you can't teach."

With five minutes left in the fourth quarter, we were up 31-28, but Bay State was driving. Their quarterback found Fox Daws on three straight plays, moving them into field goal range with ruthless efficiency.

"That Fox kid is unreal," Flynn muttered with grudging respect.

With two minutes left, Bay State punched it in. 35-31, Bay State.

"Okay, baby brother," Chris said. "Show us what you got."

Two minutes. One timeout. Eighty yards to go.

Isak took the field, and I swear he looked calmer than I'd ever seen him. He looked up at our section, found us, and gave a little nod.

"Did he just—" Chris started.

"He's saying watch this," I finished.

My phone was blowing up with messages from Everett again.

EVERETT

DID HE JUST NOD AT YOU GUYS??

PEN SAYS THAT'S BIG DICK ENERGY

I can't believe I'm missing this

Actually I can because Pen just had
another Braxton-Hicks and I need to
be here

First down was an incomplete pass, but Isak had seen something. He was talking to his receiver, adjusting the route.

On the second down he did the same play, but this time the receiver broke differently. Twenty-yard gain.

"He's coaching them," I said, amazed. "Mid-game adjustments."

The two-minute warning stopped the clock. Isak gathered his offense, and even from the stands, you could see him taking charge. No panic, just focus.

The next four plays were poetry. Short passes to move the chains, a perfectly timed draw to get into field goal range. With thirty seconds left, facing third and goal from the twelve, Isak took the snap.

The pocket collapsed immediately. Isak spun out of a sack that would've ended everything, kept his eyes downfield, pump-faked to freeze the safety, then found his receiver in the back corner of the end zone.

Touchdown. Denver State 37, Bay State 35.

The stadium went absolutely insane.

"THAT'S MY BROTHER!" I yelled, not caring who heard me. "THAT'S MY BABY BROTHER!"

Artie was jumping up and down beside me, and I

grabbed her, spinning her around as confetti cannons went off and the whole Kingman section was screaming and hugging and definitely crying.

"We need to get down there," Chris said, already moving.

Somehow—Chris's deep fucking pockets, definitely—we made it to field level. Isak was doing interviews, but when he saw us, he broke away from the Sports Network mid-sentence and ran over.

"Did you see that?" he asked, like he was twelve again.

"See it?" Dad pulled him into a hug. "Son, that was the best quarterbacking I've seen from a Kingman yet."

"Including Grandpa?"

"Especially including Coach."

One by one, we all hugged him. When he got to me, he held on extra long.

"Thanks," he said quietly.

"For what?"

"For showing me it was okay to leave home and still carry it with you."

I pulled back, looking at my baby brother who wasn't such a baby anymore. "You've got it backward, man. Home follows us. We don't carry it."

He grinned. "Whatever, you're getting sappy. But also..." He looked at Artie, who was taking pictures with Jules. "You better lock that down before someone realizes what you've got."

"Already on it."

"Good."

Before I could respond to that, someone called Isak's

name. Fox Daws was walking over, helmet under his arm, that movie star smile in full effect.

"Great game, man," Fox said, offering his hand. "That last drive was something special."

"Thanks." Isak shook his hand, trying to play it cool but clearly starstruck. "You were incredible out there. Three touchdowns?"

"Would've been four if your safety hadn't made that play in the third." Fox glanced at me. "You're Gryff, right? We met at the combine."

"Yeah, good to see you again."

Jules squeaked beside me.

"Your brother's got a future," Fox said, genuine respect in his voice. "If he ever wants to run routes in the off-season, I'm in LA."

"I might take you up on that," Isak said.

Jules double squeaked.

They did that complicated handshake-hug thing athletes do, and then Fox was jogging back to his team. Isak watched him go with an expression I recognized, already planning, already thinking ahead.

"Don't even think about it," I warned. "You're not transferring to Bay State."

"I'm not transferring anywhere," Isak said. "But if I happen to get drafted by whoever drafts him..."

"You're twenty-one."

"I'm a long-term planner."

As the celebration continued around us, as reporters tried to get Isak back, as our family took approximately seven thousand photos, I found myself standing with Artie at the edge of it all, watching the chaos.

"Full circle," she said, looking around the stadium. "First game you ever brought me to was in a stadium like this."

"You complained about the lack of proper tea options."

"It's a valid complaint. Earl Grey in a paper cup is a crime against humanity."

"You loved it though."

"I loved watching you love it," she corrected. "The way you explained every play, every tradition. You made me love it too."

"And now?"

She turned to face me fully, and there was something in her eyes that made my chest tight. "Now I get why these moments matter. The game, the family, all of it. It's not just about winning."

"What's it about?"

"It's about..." she gestured at the field, where Isak was being carried on his teammates' shoulders while Bay State players congratulated our guys, where families were taking pictures and strangers were hugging. "It's about becoming who you're supposed to be, surrounded by people who see you get there."

"Very philosophical for someone who once called football 'organized chaos with occasional hugging.'"

"It's both things." She went up on her toes and kissed me, right there on the field with the California sun setting behind the mountains and my family definitely taking pictures. "That's what makes it perfect."

When she pulled back, she was smiling that smile that made me forget about everything else.

"Hey, Gryff?"

"Yeah?"

"I love this. Every tailgate, every game, every moment of Kingman chaos. I choose us."

I knew what she meant. After everything with her dad, with choosing Team USA over Team GB, with building our life together in LA, she was choosing our future.

"Even if it means learning what a bowl game actually is?"

"Even then. Though I maintain the naming convention makes no sense and there should at least be fancy bowls for cereal or chips or something given out as parting gifts."

We were both laughing now, standing in the middle of the Flower Bowl field, surrounded by celebration and possibility.

"I love you," I said.

"I love you too."

"KINGMAN! KINGMAN!" The crowd was chanting now, and we turned to watch my little brother accepting the game MVP trophy.

"We should probably tell him to enjoy it," Artie said. "This might be the last time a Kingman quarterback gets to be the family hero."

"Why's that?"

She grinned, that mischievous look that still made my heart skip. "Because when our hypothetical future children are watching Uncle Isak play, they're going to ask why he needs all those pads and helmets and think they're tougher than him since they play rugby."

I nearly choked. "Our hypothetical future children?"

"Eventual. Theoretical. Potential children who will definitely be raised around goats."

"You can't just casually drop theoretical children into conversation."

"I can when I'm thinking about our future."

"Our future with goats and children?"

"And at least three dogs. Bear the Fourth needs cousins to come visit. We've discussed this."

We hadn't discussed any of this, but as I stood there with her, watching my family celebrate Isak's moment, watching him and Fox Daws exchange numbers while planning off-season workouts, I realized we didn't need to. Some things you just knew.

Like how we'd probably end up with too many animals and a house full of chaos. Like how our kids would grow up with an army of aunts and uncles and cousins, spending New Year's at bowl games, learning to throw footballs and rugby balls in equal measure.

Like how this, all of this, was exactly where we were supposed to be.

"Come on," I said, taking her hand. "Let's go celebrate with the family."

"Our family," she corrected.

"Yeah," I agreed, pulling her toward the chaos of King-mans. "Our family."

As we joined the celebration, as Dad started telling everyone about his bowl game victories, as my brothers organized another round of pictures, as Isak tried to escape to the locker room only to be dragged back by his brothers, I thought about what Dad had said in the parking lot.

About being anchored-to-the-world happy.

He was right. Success was one thing. Taking care of people was another.

But this? Being chosen, being loved, being part of something bigger than yourself while still being completely yourself?

This was happiness.

And I was never letting it go.

RED CARPET ROLLOUT

ARTEMIS

"Stop moving," Jules commanded, wielding a curling iron like a weapon. "You're going to make me burn your ear off."

I tensed every muscle to hold still because ear mutilation did not go with this dress. "I'm not moving."

"You're literally vibrating with nervous energy."

She wasn't wrong. The premiere of *Rookie Rising* was in two hours, and I was trying not to think about the fact that millions of people were about to watch the most vulnerable months of our lives play out on screen.

"There," Jules stepped back, admiring her work. "Now for the dress."

The dress was a deep purple number that hugged every curve before flowing into a dramatic train. The neckline plunged just enough to be daring, and the back was completely open except for delicate crystal chains. When I'd tried this on in Rose Vond's boutique, I'd felt like a warrior goddess.

"Holy shit," Jules breathed when I emerged from the bathroom. "Gryff is going to swallow his tongue."

"It's not about Gryff."

"Sure it's not." She smirked. "That's why you're showing so much sexy, hottie-liscious skin."

Before I could protest, we heard voices from the living room. Flynn and Tempest had arrived, which meant everyone was ready to go and we really were going to walk a red carpet with photographers and everything. Nobody ever said being friends with the Kingmans was going to be boring or normal.

"You ready?" Gryff called. "The car will be here in—"

He stopped mid-sentence when I walked into the living room. The glass of water in his hand tilted dangerously.

"You... I... words. Forgot how to word."

Flynn caught the glass before it could spill. "Smooth, brother."

But Gryff wasn't listening. He was staring at me like he'd never seen me before, his mouth slightly open, eyes traveling from my face to the dress, over every inch of skin, and all my curves, the soft parts and the strong ones, and back again.

"You look..." he started, then stopped. "There aren't words. You broke words."

"Very articulate," Tempest laughed, stunning in her own silver gown. "Really showing off that college education."

Vincent bleated from his pen, seeming to say I looked pretty. Though he was probably just hungry.

"Even the goat is more eloquent," Flynn added.

Gryff finally found his voice. "You look beautiful. Like, stop traffic, start wars, write songs about you beautiful."

"Mixing your metaphors there," I said, but my face was warm.

"Don't care. Still true."

The ride to the premiere was surreal. The documentary had gotten huge buzz. The behind-the-scenes look at League rookies during their first season was a popular show in the past, but FlixNChill had really upped their game following Kendra's takeover. After Sloane's dramatic exit, she had turned it into something special. Just the previews looked more interesting than previous seasons of the show.

"There's already a red carpet," Flynn said, peering out the limo window. "Like, an actual red carpet."

"That's generally how red carpet premieres work," Tempest said, grinning. "I hope we get to do one like this for when my show comes out."

"Of course they will, babe. You're famous. It's just weird that this one is for us."

The car stopped, and suddenly we were stepping into chaos. Cameras flashed from every direction, people were shouting our names, and someone with a headset was directing us where to stand.

"Gryff, Artemis. Over here."

"Flynn, can we get you with Ms. Milan?"

"Jules, Jules. To your left."

Jules was eating it up, posing like she'd been doing this her whole life. Then she grabbed my arm.

"Oh my god," she hissed. "Fox Daws. Twelve o'clock."

I looked. Fox Daws, movie star and college football

player, was indeed walking the carpet ahead of us. We'd heard he was back in LA to film his next movie, *Fresh Out Of Fox* during the off-season and summer.

"Go say hi," I encouraged.

"I can't just—"

But Fox had spotted us. He waved at the guys, then his eyes landed on Jules. He winked—actually winked—and called out, "Looking forward to seeing the Kingman Queens up on the big screen."

Jules made a sound I'd never heard before, somewhere between a squeak and a giggle.

"Did he just—" she started.

"He definitely did," Tempest confirmed. "And you're definitely blushing."

"I don't blush."

"You're the color of a bright pink peony."

We moved through the interviews, Flynn and Gryff charming reporters with their brotherly dynamic. Someone asked if Gryff and I were together, and he smoothly deflected with, "We're here to celebrate all the rookies tonight."

Inside the theater, Kendra found us immediately.

"You all look incredible," she said, giving air kisses. "I think you're going to love what we've done with the show."

"Nothing too embarrassing?" Flynn asked.

"Oh, there's definitely embarrassing stuff. But it's the endearing kind."

She took the stage to introduce the first episode, thanking everyone involved and notably making no mention of Sloane.

"This show is about more than football," she said. "It's about friendship, family, dreams, and yes, even a little romance."

The lights dimmed, and the episode began.

It opened with Flynn and Gryff at rookie camp, both trying to act tough while clearly being overwhelmed. The scene where Flynn called Tempest after the first day, nearly in tears from exhaustion, had everyone laughing and going "aww" simultaneously.

"I forgot they filmed that," Flynn muttered, sinking lower in his seat.

But it was the way Kendra had edited Gryff's and my scenes that made my chest tight. Every glance, every casual touch, every moment of us just existing in the same space. She'd woven it all into an obvious love story.

There was the scene of Gryff and me at home, his face soft with something that was definitely not platonic friendship. There was fussing over his bruises while he smiled at me like I was the sun.

"We were really that obvious?" I whispered.

"Apparently," Gryff whispered back, his hand finding mine in the dark.

The episode followed multiple storylines brilliantly. Xander's journey from being wary and clearly unhappy and the obvious hints at him finding his confidence again. Jay, struggling with homesickness, Jamie trying to find his place in a team he'd grown up watching. The brotherhood that developed between all of them.

But it kept coming back to us. To the way we moved around each other like binary stars, always in each other's orbit.

When the episode ended, the theater erupted in applause. Kendra had done something special. She'd taken what could have been a standard sports documentary and turned it into something deeply human.

"That was beautiful," someone behind us said. "When do Gryff and Artie get together?"

"Oh, you'll just have to watch and see," Kendra said with a grin.

The after party was a blur of congratulations and conversations. Fox Daws found his way over to our group, ostensibly to talk to the guys about their rookie seasons, but his eyes kept drifting to Jules.

"You're at UCLA, right?" he asked her.

"Yeah, studying psychology and sport science," she said, trying to play it cool.

"Great campus. We filmed a movie there last year. Maybe I'll see you around."

"Maybe," Jules managed.

After he walked away, she grabbed my arm so tight I'd probably have bruises. "Did that just happen?"

"Jules, he was clearly flirting with you," Tempest confirmed.

"But he's like, famous famous."

"So?" I said. "You're Jules Kingman. That's pretty famous in its own right."

A FEW DAYS LATER, we were on a plane headed for the Big Bowl. The Mustangs had made it all the way and were facing off against the Miami Sharks. Chris, Declan, Hayes, Everett, and their cousin Levi who was new to the team this year, were all playing. The Bandits hadn't even made the playoffs, so Gryff and Flynn were here as slightly disgruntled fans. At least until the nacho bar was wheeled into the VIP suite.

"I can't believe you flew out for the game," Sara Jayne said, wide-eyed at how beautiful, glowing, and looking so ready to pop at any moment Penelope was.

"I brought my doctor along, and I wasn't going to miss Everett's big game." Penelope lowered herself onto a couch, though she winced as she said that.

She was due in two weeks but had insisted on coming to the game. Kelsey had flown everyone out on her jet, including Penelope's OB/GYN, Dr. Paula Patel, who was currently eating nachos and watching the pregame like this was totally normal.

"Are you sure you're okay?" Trixie asked Penelope for the tenth time.

"Just Braxton-Hicks," Penelope said, though she was gripping the couch arm pretty tightly. "I've been having them all morning."

Dr. Patel glanced over but didn't seem concerned, so we all tried to relax.

The first half was insane. Xander, playing for the Sharks, was absolutely destroying our offensive line. He looked like a completely different player from the stressed-out rookie who'd been dealing with Sloane's blackmail.

"He's playing angry," Flynn observed. "But, like, the good kind of angry."

"Therapeutic angry," Tempest agreed.

Chris was having the game of his life, threading

impossible passes through Miami's defense. Declan had already caused two fumbles. Hayes had run for over a hundred yards. Everett had caught three passes, one for a touchdown.

Penelope whoop-whooped and said, "See, that's why I had to be here." But every few minutes, she'd go very still, breathing carefully through her nose.

"Pen?" I said quietly during a commercial break. "You sure you're okay?"

She looked at me, then at the game clock showing two minutes left in the half, then at Everett on the field. "Yep. Right as rain. Can't wait to watch the halftime show. You know, we've been in talks for Kelsey to be the headliner in one of the upcoming years."

But the minute the second half of the game started, Pen stood up and made an uh-oh face. "So, I've actually been in labor since breakfast, and my water just broke. Don't sit on that couch, anybody."

The suite went silent except for the roar of the crowd below.

"I'm sorry, what?" Kelsey shrieked.

Dr. Patel was already moving, switching from casual friend to doctor in an instant. "How far apart are the contractions?"

"About two minutes."

"Wow. Okay. Someone please call for the stadium EMTs and tell them we're having a baby."

Penelope grabbed the arm of the couch as another contraction hit.

"And someone needs to get Everett," Dr. Patel said calmly, though she was already pulling medical supplies from her bag. Why did she bring medical supplies to a football game? Thank god she did. "This baby is coming now."

"I'm on it." Isak was already running for the door.

"Stadium security is never going to—".

"They will for a Kingman," Bridger said. "Go, Isak, go."

What followed was the most chaotic fifteen minutes of my life. Dr. Patel transformed the suite into a makeshift delivery room, ordering Flynn and Gryff to hold up tablecloths for privacy, getting extra linens from the catering staff, and turning the comfy couch seating area into a makeshift delivery room.

Kelsey was on the phone with stadium security, trying to explain that they needed to escort a player from the field up to the club level suites, and trying to get the EMTs up here too. Willa was timing contractions. Bridger stayed next to Penny, holding her hand and coaching her through her next contraction in a low calm voice like the veteran he was. He had to be so freaking excited he was about to meet his very first grandchild.

And I was trying not to panic because, holy shit, we were having a baby at the Big Bowl.

"I can see Isak on the field," Jules called from the window. "He's got security with him."

We could actually see it happening on the jumbotron. Isak running across the field to the Mustangs sideline, grabbing Everett, who looked confused, then shocked, then started sprinting for the tunnel.

He burst through the suite door only a few minutes later, still in full gear, his cleats clicking on the floor, breathing hard.

"Pen, honey, I'm here. Focus on your breathing. What do I do? Has anyone boiled water?"

"About time," she gasped. "Your son wanted to see his daddy play in the bowl game."

"Everett," Dr. Patel said firmly, "I need you to hold your wife's hand and let me work."

The next few minutes were a blur. The crowd noise from the stadium faded into background as Penelope brought their son into the world right there in the luxury suite, with the entire Kingman family waiting in the wings.

The baby's first cry cut through everything, strong and loud and perfect.

"You did it," Everett sobbed, still in his football pads, holding his tiny son. "You amazing, incredible, insane woman, you did it. There you are, my boy. I've got you."

"We did it," Penelope corrected, tears streaming down her face. "In a stadium. During the Big Bowl."

"This is why I don't usually do house calls," Dr. Patel said, but she was smiling.

"We should get you to the hospital," Everett said, not taking his eyes off his son.

As they prepared to leave for the hospital, the third quarter was in full swing. Somehow, word had gotten to the announcers. I glanced over at Jules who had her phone in her hand and a mischievous grin on her face.

"Ladies and gentlemen," the PA system boomed, "we've just received word that Mustangs tight end Everett Kingman has become a father. His son was born right here in the stadium only moments ago."

The crowd went absolutely insane.

Then the jumbotron lit up with "Welcome to the world, Bo Bridger Kingman!"

"Did they really just announce our baby to eighty thousand people?" Penelope asked with a wide-eyed look.

"Oh," Bridger choked out, fresh tears streaming down his face. "You used my… you named him…"

"Of course we did," Penelope called out weakly from the gurney where the medics were preparing to transport her. "Who else would we name him after? The man who raised the best men I know."

Bridger couldn't speak, just stood there with tears running down his face, moving to kiss both Penelope's forehead and the baby's tiny head. "That's… that's the greatest honor of my life. Welcome to the family, Bo."

Dr. Patel wouldn't let the rest of us go with them to the hospital. She said the new mom and baby, and probably dad, were going to need some checkups and some fluids. But we could come later for visiting hours.

The Mustangs must have been inspired by the baby luck because they came out in the second half like men possessed. Chris threw four touchdown passes. Declan had an interception. Hayes ran for two more touchdowns. Even without Everett, they dominated.

When Chris threw the winning touchdown to Hayes with thirty seconds left, the entire suite erupted, those of us still there anyway. Everett and Penelope were already at the hospital with Dr. Patel.

"This family," Artie said, shaking her head but grinning. "You can't even watch a football game without someone having a baby."

"Just wait until it's our turn," Gryff said, then froze. "I mean, not that we're—"

"I know what you mean," I said, kissing his cheek. "And when it's our turn, we're definitely having the baby in an actual hospital."

"Deal."

As we watched the Mustangs celebrate below, Chris pointing to the suite and mouthing "For Everett," I thought about how impossibly chaotic and perfect this life was.

The premiere, the game, the baby—it was all too much and exactly right at the same time.

"Next year," Jules said, appearing at my elbow, "can we maybe have a normal Big Bowl? Just watch the game, eat some nachos, no one gives birth?"

"Where's the fun in that?" Trixie asked.

"Besides," Tempest added, "This is the Kingmans. Normal isn't really our thing."

She was right. Normal wasn't our thing.

And I wouldn't have it any other way.

GRYFF

The morning started like any other Saturday, except for the fact that I'd been awake since four in the morning, the engagement ring burning a hole in my sock drawer where it had been hidden for the past three weeks.

"You're being weird," Artie announced, emerging from our bedroom in one of my old DSU shirts and shorts that made her thighs look absolutely incredible. "Weirder than usual, I mean."

"I'm not being weird."

Vincent bleated from his pen outside, as if calling out my lie.

"You made breakfast," she said, gesturing to the spread on the counter. "Like, actual breakfast. With fresh fruit arranged in a pattern."

"It's not a pattern, it's just... organized."

"It's a heart, Gryff. You arranged the strawberries in a heart."

Shit. I had.

"I was feeling romantic?" I offered weakly.

She softened, coming over to wrap her arms around my waist from behind. "That's sweet. But also suspicious. What did you break?"

"Nothing."

"Did the goats eat something important again?"

"No, they've been angels." Mostly because Flynn had been keeping them distracted with treats all morning while secretly coordinating with half of Los Angeles via text.

My phone buzzed.

FLYNN

Get her out of the house. NOW. Team's almost here.

"Hey," I said, turning in her arms. "Want to go to the farmers market? The one in Santa Monica?"

"The one that's an hour away in Saturday traffic?"

"Yeah, but they have those honey sticks you like. And we could grab lunch at that place on the pier after."

She studied my face, and for a moment I was sure she could see right through me. "Okay, now I know something's up. You said the seagulls there have 'organized crime energy.'"

"Maybe I've changed my mind about the seagulls."

"Gryffen Greene Kingman."

"Artemis Ingvar Fraser." I hoped soon I'd be able to say Artemis Ingvar Kingman.

"Fine," she said, but she was smiling. "Let me get dressed. But if this is some elaborate plan to avoid me finding out you signed us up for another reality show, I'm feeding you to the goats."

While she got ready, I sent a quick text to Flynn.

> Leaving in 10. You sure everyone can make it?

FLYNN

> Sean's coordinating LA crew. Tempest has the fam on FaceTime for instructions. Parker's got the flowers. Freddie and the rugby girls just arrived. GO.

> Also Jules says to tell you she's stress-eating all your good cheese.

> And Dad says to stop overthinking and just do the damn thing already.

The drive to Santa Monica was torture. Artie had connected her phone to the car's sound system and was singing along to the latest Kelsey Best album, occasionally reaching over to squeeze my thigh. Every time she touched me, I thought about the ring, about what I was going to say, about the very real possibility that she might say it was too soon.

"Okay, seriously, what's wrong?" she asked as we sat in standstill traffic on the 10. "You're gripping the steering wheel like it's going to escape."

"Just thinking about training camp. We aren't rookies this year." It was a convenient lie.

"Liar." She studied me. "Is this about your dad? Is he being weird about trying to date again?"

"No, Dad's been great." More than great, actually. He'd

even helped me pick out the ring, though he'd suggested something approximately the size of a golf ball before Jules had intervened with a firm "absolutely not."

"Then what—"

My phone rang through the car speakers. Flynn.

"Don't answer that," I said quickly, but Artie was already hitting accept.

"Hey, Flynn," she called out. "Your brother's being super weird. Want to explain?"

"Artie. Hey. Weird? Gryff? Never. He's the most normal person I know."

"Flynn, you're literally his identical twin."

"Right, and I'm weird as fuck, so by comparison—"

I hit end call on the console.

"Okay, that was suspicious too," Artie said. "What are you two planning? Is this about Isak's first preseason game? Because I already know we're all flying to Miami for it."

"It's nothing like that."

We spent three hours at the farmers market, then another two at lunch. Artie bought enough honey sticks to last through an apocalypse and found a vendor selling goat milk soap that she insisted Vincent and Holly would love the smell of. I bought whatever she pointed at, agreed with everything she said, and checked my phone every thirty seconds until she threatened to throw it in the ocean.

FLYNN

Status update: Backyard transformation complete. I have dirt in places dirt should never be.

Coach Maher and half the rugby team are currently hiding behind your garage. One of them brought sandwiches.

Sean's made what he calls "celebration mocktails" but won't let anyone drink them yet.

JULES SAYS HURRY UP.

"Okay, we should head back," I said, probably too abruptly.

"But we just ordered dessert."

"We have ice cream at home."

She laughed but let me pay the check and guide her back to the car. The drive home was quieter, Artie dozed off against the window while I navigated Saturday afternoon traffic and tried not to have a complete nervous breakdown.

FLYNN

ETA?

20 minutes

Vincent keeps trying to eat the ring box. Holly's standing guard but she's getting tired.

Also Ren says to tell you the catering arrived and if you don't get here soon, the rugby girls are going to eat everything.

Jules is now literally sitting on Parker to keep her from reorganizing the flower arrangement.

HURRY. THE. FUCK. UP.

We pulled into our driveway as the sun was starting to set, painting the sky in shades of pink and gold that felt almost too perfect, like the universe was in on the plan.

"Home sweet home," Artie said, stretching as she got out of the car. "I need to check on the goats. They probably think we abandoned them."

"Actually, why don't we go through the house first?" I suggested, my heart hammering so hard I was sure she could hear it. "I need to... check something."

"Check what?"

"Just... something."

She followed me through the front door, still looking suspicious. I led her through the house, my hand finding hers. My palm was definitely sweating. She was definitely going to notice.

"Gryff, seriously, you're starting to freak me out."

"Just... trust me?"

We reached the back door. Through the glass, I could see what Flynn and everyone had done. The entire backyard had been transformed into something out of a dream. Fairy lights strung between the trees, flowers everywhere, not just any flowers, but all of Artie's favorites from every place we'd ever been together. Columbines from Colorado, wildflowers from California, even heather from Scotland that Flynn had somehow managed to source.

"Oh my god," Artie breathed, stepping out onto the patio. "Gryff, what is this?"

Vincent and Holly were in the middle of the yard. She was in frilly pink tutu with a tiny flower wreath over her horns and Vinnie had a cowboy hat and red bandanna he was trying to chew attached to his collar... along with the ring box.

"Go see what Vincent has," I managed, my voice not quite steady.

She walked toward the goats, still looking stunned. Holly pranced over first, clearly proud of her tutu, while Vincent stayed still, waiting. As Artie knelt down, I saw the exact moment she noticed the small box attached to Vincent's collar.

"Gryff?" Her voice was barely a whisper.

I was already on one knee when she turned around, the ring box now in my hands since Vincent had done his job.

"Artemis Ingvar Fraser," I started, and my voice cracked immediately. "You walked into my life six years ago with those thick thighs that could crush me and eyes on all the same hotties as me. In all these years, you've taught me that vulnerability wasn't weakness, that feeling things deeply wasn't something to hide."

Artie's hands were covering her mouth, tears already bubbling up along her lashes.

"You're the strongest person I know. You face every challenge head on, whether it's your dad's expectations or Olympic trials or my family's Christmas chaos. You make me braver just by being you. You make me want to be the person you already see when you look at me."

Vincent chose that moment to headbutt my knee, nearly knocking me over. Artie laughed through her tears.

"Even our goats know we belong together," I continued, steadying myself. "They knew before we did. Everyone knew before we did."

"Gryff—"

"You're my best friend, my favorite person, and the love of my life. You're the first person I want to tell good news to and the only person I want beside me when things go wrong. I love your competitiveness and the way you sing off-key in the shower and think I can't hear you."

"I'm not that off-key," she protested, laughing and crying at the same time.

"You're completely off-key and it's perfect." I opened the ring box, revealing an east-west oval diamond in a platinum bevel setting, not huge, not flashy, but unique and beautiful, just like her. "I love that you convinced me to adopt goats, that you see the best in everyone except people who hurt the ones you love, and the way you fiercely protect and take care of me even though I'm the six four football player. I love your strength and your softness and everything in between."

Holly bleated and started eating one of the flower arrangements.

"Artemis, I'm asking you, here in our backyard with our goats and a crap ton of flowers and our life that we've built together, and all the love I can carry in my heart for you... will you marry me?"

"Yes," she said, not even hesitating. "Yes, of course yes, you beautiful idiot. Yes."

I stood to slide the ring on her finger, but before I could kiss her, the bushes around our yard erupted.

"Finally," Jules screamed, emerging from behind the garage with Flynn and Tempest.

"She said yes," Freddie shouted, and suddenly our entire backyard was full of people.

Sean and Ren burst out from behind the garden shed, Sean already ugly-crying. Parker and Tempest appeared from the side yard, holding a banner that read "ABOUT DAMN TIME." Half of Artie's rugby team poured out from various hiding spots, including three who had apparently been in the tree.

"Were you all here the whole time?" Artie asked, looking around in amazement.

"Flynn and I coordinated most everything." Jules preened but then held up her phone. "Dad is on FaceTime, Gryff. Also Nana and Coach and Grandma and Grandpa De le Reine and Everett and Pen and Chris and Trixie and well... basically everyone in the great state of Colorado."

Tempest and Parker held up their phones too. "And your dad on mine, and your mom on Parker's."

"The whole family's watching." Dad's voice rang out from the phone. "We've been waiting for hours."

"We helped with the flowers," one of the rugby players announced. "Coach made us repot those columbines twice because Parker kept saying it wasn't symmetrical enough."

"It needed to be perfect," Parker defended.

Vincent, apparently overwhelmed by all the people, had started eating the hem of Ren's designer shirt.

"This goat has excellent taste," Ren said, not even trying to stop him. "In fashion and in people."

Sean was already pouring the celebration mocktails, handing them around. "To Gryff and Artie, who literally everyone except them knew were perfect for each other."

"To the goats who brought them together," someone else shouted.

"We brought ourselves together," I protested, but I was laughing.

"Sure you did," Jules said, already three mocktails in. "That's why it took you six years and an entire support group of meddling friends, family, and goats."

Artie pulled me down for a kiss, not caring that everyone was watching and cheering. "I love you," she whispered against my lips. "Even if you did organize the most elaborate proposal in the history of proposals."

"Flynn and Jules organized most of it," I admitted. "Mostly planned by Tempest. I think it might be from her next book. I just panicked and agreed to everything."

"That tracks." She kissed me again.

"We're getting married," I said, like I still couldn't believe it.

"We're getting married," she confirmed. "And our goats are definitely going to be in the wedding."

Vincent bleated his approval and went back to eating Ren's shirt.

Holly had moved on to the cake that someone had apparently hidden behind a potted plant.

Our friends and family swarmed around us, everyone talking at once, sharing their favorite memories of our obliviousness, placing bets on wedding dates.

"Spring wedding," Sean called out. "After rugby season, before football."

"Summer," Tempest countered. "Outdoor ceremony with the goats."

"Elope to Vegas and save us all the drama," Flynn suggested, then yelped as both Jules and Tempest hit him.

I kept my arm around Artie, watching our chaotic,

perfect chosen family celebrate in our backyard. This was exactly right, not just the two of us, but everyone who'd been part of our journey, who'd pushed us together when we were too scared to take the leap ourselves.

Vincent had now gathered a following of rugby players who were feeding him flowers from the arrangements. Holly was being carried around by Coach Maher like a baby. Our families were mingling on FaceTime, planning the wedding before we'd even been engaged an hour.

"No regrets?" I asked.

"Only one," Artie said. "I should have kissed you in that gym six years ago."

"We got here eventually."

"Yeah," she said, standing on her toes to kiss me again while everyone cheered. "We did."

When the crowd started yelling that we should get a room, I turned to the whole bunch of them and said, "I think we will. The rest of you can take your asses across the street and continue the party at Flynn's." I grabbed Artie up into my arms princess style and headed toward the house. "We're going to be very busy for the next few hours."

Jules retched. "Ew."

Artie giggled and kicked her feet, turning about fifty shades of pink. But by the time I laid her on the bed and crawled up over her, kissing my way from her toes to her nose, that pink was the flush of her arousal.

"I want to take my time with you tonight." We were gonna need lots of lube. I had plans. I reached across to the bedside table to pull out the surprise bottle of strawberry flavored lube I found.

But what I found in the drawer was absolutely not what I expected. Turned out my girl had plans for me too.

I liked to think I knew more than your average bi-guy about sex toys. One doesn't just grow up next door to Mrs. Moore, the sex-positive, body-positive world-famous sex educator without receiving a 'pleasure and protect' gift bag or five. But I had never seen anything like this. I picked it up and turned it around trying to figure out the logistics.

"Artie…what is this?" I asked, almost afraid.

"That," she whispered, wrapping her arms around my waist. "Is a strapless strap on."

"A strapless…" I muttered.

"Yep. You see this part here," she said, stroking her finger over one end shaped like a thickened bean, "Is called the Pony. That goes inside of me."

"Inside of you," I repeated entirely too slowly. Mostly because my brain was fritzing out. In a very good way.

"And this part," she says stroking the other end… the long, ridged, very penis-shaped other end. "Goes inside you."

My mouth went dry and I'm pretty sure my tongue cracked like a desert plain. I could feel my face heat at the thought of her being inside me, and I couldn't even swallow, let alone talk.

Artie mistook my silence and panicked. "Oh no, do you hate it?"

"No, baby, no, no, no." I managed to rasp out. "I definitely don't hate it."

"Gryff, you have been so good to me, so patient and so devoted to helping me find myself and my pleasure. I wanted to do the same for you." She pressed the softest of kisses to my lips. "When you said nobody ever let you bottom, I wanted to give you that. You take care of everybody and me so well, let me take care of you."

I blinked way too many times, trying to hold back the tears her words pulled from my eyes. This woman. This gorgeous, sweet, sensitive, ferocious warrior woman wanted to give me everything I ever needed. She'd already shown me how she will protect me, but this? For her to make sure I am taken care of in every way?

I couldn't believe I got to spend the rest of my life with her.

"I love you, my sweet strawberry girl. I love you so fucking much. You're my best friend, my lover, and now you're going to be my wife." I wrapped her in my arms and kissed her soundly, the toy trapped between us. "So yes, I would love for you to take care of me like this. I want to spend the rest of our lives taking care of each other in every way."

Her smile was like sunshine, that only grew brighter when she pulled on the hem of my shirt, undressing me. "I can't wait to show you exactly how much I love you and can take care of you."

I stripped down like I was being timed while Artie went to bathroom, returning naked with, adorably, a bottle of vanilla latte lube, and some towels. "I've been doing some reading so I am feeling pretty confident, but you'll let me know if I do anything you don't like, right?"

"Artie, there's nothing you can do that I won't like," I answer. "But we will learn together. Always together."

Artie lubed her end of the toy and slipped it inside of herself, turning to model it for me. "What do you think?"

I'm pretty sure my heart stopped. There, between my future wife's powerful thighs, nestled against her trimmed curls, was her hot pink cock. I couldn't help myself. I dropped to my knees and, with a wink, took her down my throat as far as I could.

Above me she gasped and whispered something that sounded like holy library.

"How do you want me?" I asked.

"Lay on the bed and spread your legs," she told me, her eyes glassy and glittering. I did as she asked and she propped a couple of pillows up under my hips. "I just want to open you up."

I lay back and let my sweet girl take care of me. I trusted her completely and that filled my heart almost as much as the love.

She stroked my cock with one lubed hand, working her way lower with the other, till she was circling my hole. She paused momentarily to add more lube before pressing one finger in.

I let out a small moan at the invasion, but this wasn't an entirely new sensation. I had definitely fingered myself before, but it felt so much better when it was Artie doing it.

"Aw, fuck, Artie. More, please," I begged.

She slipped in another finger and stroked upward, and lightning shot through me. "Oh my god, baby, please."

"Mmm... you like that?" she smiled devilishly.

"Fuck yes," I whimpered, my head tossed back and my hips canting to chase the sensation. She hummed a sound that showed me how much she was enjoying this too while she rubbed circles deep inside me, sending electricity firing all over my body.

I could fucking feel my dick already leaking precum onto my stomach, twitching madly even though it had hardly been touched. "If you don't stop, I'm going to come and this is going to be over before it starts. Baby, please I need you in me. I need you to fuck me."

Artie gently slipped out her fingers and lubed her pretty pink cock before pressing it against my back entrance. "My favorite part of this toy, besides how unbelievably hot you look about to be impaled on it, is that my clit grinds against this pad so we can both play with our favorite spots. Oh, and this."

She hit a button on the side of the toy. Low vibrations rumbled through my taint, increasing and changing pattern till she found the one she liked. Her eyes flutter closed in pleasure. "Mmm, that's the one."

Slowly she pressed inside of me, the faintest burning passing quickly into pleasure with each gentle back and forth of her hips.

Then she pushed slowly forward until she was seated fully inside me, her hips pressed against mine.

"God, you're filling me so fucking good, babe."

"Do you like it?" she asked, and there was still some hesitancy in her voice.

"More than I expected," I replied soothingly. I grabbed her face and pulled her down for a hard kiss. "Now fuck me, sweetheart. Take me apart."

She thrust deep into me, her powerful, beautiful thighs flexing again and again, tagging my p-spot coming and going. There is nothing I could do but go for the ride.

I clung desperately to the sheets with one hand and reached for my cock with the other, desperate to do anything to ease the overwhelming sensations inside of me. The friction and the vibrations pulled me under to a place where I was nothing more than electricity and feelings.

"No," Artie says, smacking my hand away. "You'll come on my cock or not at all."

My eyes shot open and I stared up at her, my goddess.

"I don't know if I can." My voice was barely a whimper.

"You can and you will." Her face was set in that determined face I'd only seen on the field.

She continued to move in me, making sure she was grinding on me in all the right ways until I was a whimpering mess, leaking everywhere. It was only when her own moans began to match mine and she called out, "Now, Gryff, come with me now," that I let myself go.

The orgasm ripped through me, and my cum shot out hard, spurting onto me and Artie.

She collapsed on top of me, both of us sticky and satisfied.

"Whoa," I said, unable to form any high level of thought or words.

"Definitely whoa," Artie answered, draped across my chest.

Once we both returned to earth, she kissed me long and languidly. "Come on, lover boy. Let me get you cleaned up and tucked into bed where I get to be the big spoon tonight."

I let her. She took care of me, like no one else in the world, in the universe. She was the only one I'd ever be this vulnerable with. We'd take care of each other, protect the other as best we could, and love, so incredibly deeply, for the rest of our lives.

EPILOGUE: THE GOAT

ARTEMIS

Two Years Later

"You cannot seriously be wearing that shirt," I said, staring at my husband.

Gryff did a little spin, modeling the custom t-shirt with Vincent's face photoshopped onto a rugby ball with the words "My wife is the GOAT" underneath. Flynn's had Holly's face and it read "I'm with the GOAT."

"The Olympics are supposed to be a dignified international sporting event."

"And yet here we are," he grinned, pulling me in for a kiss. "Ready to watch my wife win and her team win gold."

My stomach did that flutter it always did when he called me his wife. Even after a year of marriage, it still felt surreal. Gryff Kingman had chosen me, had built a life with me, had taken a week off from the Bandits during the preseason to be here.

"Coach isn't going to kill you for missing practice and the game," I said against his lips.

"Coach told me if I didn't come support you, he'd bench me." He kissed me again. "Plus, the Olympics are in LA. I can literally see our house from the stadium."

"You cannot see our house from the Coliseum."

"I can feel it in my heart."

"That's not how geography works."

We were interrupted by pounding on our hotel room door. "Artie," Jules's voice carried through. "Stop making out with my brother and get ready. We have to leave in twenty minutes."

"We're not making out," I called back.

"Liar."

She wasn't wrong.

The U.S. Women's Rugby team had made it to the gold medal match against New Zealand, and my entire body was thrumming with nervous energy. Four years of training, of choosing this team over Great Britain, of everything. It all came down to today.

"Hey," Gryff said softly, reading my anxiety. "You've got this. You're Artemis Fraser-Kingman. You eat Black Ferns for breakfast."

"That sounds inappropriately sexual."

"Your mind went there, not mine."

The ride to the stadium was surreal. Our bus had a police escort. People were lining the streets with American flags. Someone had made a giant banner with my face on it, which was both flattering and terrifying.

"Is that supposed to be me?" I asked, staring at the artistic interpretation.

"I think they captured your warrior spirit," my teammate Madison said.

"I look like I'm constipated."

"Warrior constipation."

When we arrived at the Coliseum, I could already hear the crowd. 80,000 people. A sold-out Olympic final. In my adopted home city.

"Fraser-Kingman," Coach Williams called. "Ready to captain this team to gold?"

Captain. They'd voted me captain a month ago, and I still couldn't quite believe it.

"Ready, Coach."

As we went through warm-ups, I kept scanning the crowd. Then I saw them—an entire section of purple and gold, every single Kingman wearing those ridiculous goat shirts. Gryff and Flynn with Vincent and Holly's faces. Chris had one with four goat faces arranged like Mount Rushmore. Bridger was holding a banner that read "THAT'S MY DAUGHTER-IN-LAW" with an arrow pointing down at whoever was beneath it.

There were new additions to the family section too. The Kingmans were multiplying at an alarming rate but from Bo, who was actually born in a stadium, down the the youngest, who was content in his father's arms wearing the tiniest set of ear protectors you ever saw, they looked at home.

"Your family is insane," Madison observed.

"Yeah," I grinned. "They're perfect."

The match was brutal from the first whistle. New Zealand came out aggressive, their haka before the game setting the tone. But we'd trained for this. We were ready.

First half, we traded scores. Their speed against our power. My lungs burned as I drove forward in scrums, my legs screamed during rucks, but I could hear the crowd, could feel the energy.

"USA! USA! USA!"

At halftime, we were tied 14-14.

"They're targeting the wings," I told the team. "They think we're weak there. Let them. When they overcommit, we go up the middle."

"Through you?" Coach asked.

"Through all of us. But yeah, I'll take the hit."

The second half was the longest twenty minutes of my life. New Zealand scored first, the crowd going quiet. Then we answered. Back and forth, neither team giving an inch.

With three minutes left, we were down 24-21. We had possession, but we were sixty meters from their try line.

"Framework Seven," I called the play. "And when it breaks down, give me the damn ball."

What happened next was the kind of thing they'd probably replay forever. The planned play fell apart immediately, but muscle memory and trust took over. Madison hit me with a pass just as two defenders converged. I spun out of one tackle, handed off another, and suddenly I had space.

Forty meters. Thirty. Twenty.

I could hear Gryff's voice somehow cutting through eighty-thousand others: "RUN, ARTIE!"

Ten meters. Five.

The fullback hit me at the two-meter line, but

momentum carried us both over. I slammed the ball down just inside the touchline.

Try.

The stadium exploded. My teammates piled on top of me. The conversion would put us up by two with thirty seconds left.

Madison nailed it.

New Zealand had one last chance, but our defense held. When the final whistle blew, I fell to my knees.

Olympic champions.

The medal ceremony was a blur. The national anthem played, and I was definitely not crying except I absolutely was. On the podium, gold around my neck, I found my family in the crowd. Gryff was crying too, not even trying to hide it.

Later, after media obligations and drug tests and approximately one million photos, we finally made it home for the real celebration.

"Surprise."

Our backyard was packed. The entire Kingman family, my rugby team, Gryff's teammates who weren't traveling, Sean and Ren, our neighbors, everyone.

But the best surprise was in the goat pen.

"Babies!" I gasped.

Vincent and Holly were there with three tiny kids between them. The babies were a hilarious mix of Vincent's spots and Holly's solid coloring, each one more ridiculous than the last.

"When did this happen?" I asked Gryff.

"Remember when you were at training camp for three weeks? Vincent and Holly decided to celebrate their love."

"You let our goats have babies without telling me?"

"I wanted to surprise you after you won gold. I had faith."

"What are their names?"

"That's your department. I've been calling them Thing One, Thing Two, and Chaos."

I was already in the pen, picking up the smallest one who immediately tried to eat my gold medal. "This one's Stevie. Stevie Kicks."

"Oh no," Gryff groaned. "Not more pun names."

"That one's Goatzart.," I said, pointing to the one jumping the highest. "And that one's definitely Bleathoven."

"Stevie Kicks?"

"Look at her. She's already the star."

The party was in full swing around us. I could see Jules holding court with a group of her UCLA friends, dramatically recounting the match. She'd dragged Bridger into her circle and was clearly trying to set him up with one of her professors who'd come to watch.

"Dad, she's age-appropriate and likes football," Jules was saying. "What more do you want?"

"Jules, I don't need—"

"You're getting back out there. Mom would want you to be happy."

It was sweet, even if Bridger looked mildly terrified.

Flynn appeared with Tempest and drinks. "To the Olympic champion."

"To the goat babies," I countered.

"To both," Tempest laughed. "Though I can't believe Vincent and Holly beat us to parenthood."

"It's not a competition," Flynn said.

"Everything's a competition with Kingmans," I pointed out.

"Fair."

As the sun set over the Pacific, I stood in our backyard surrounded by chaos. Baby goats were running amok. Hayes was teaching Bo to throw a football. Someone started a volleyball game that was definitely going to end in tears or property damage. The neighbors were probably going to complain about the noise again.

"Happy?" Gryff asked, wrapping his arms around me from behind.

"Perfect," I corrected, leaning back into him. "This is perfect."

"Even with three more goats?"

"Especially with three more goats."

"We're not keeping all of them."

"We're absolutely keeping all of them."

He kissed my temple. "I know."

"I love you," I said, turning in his arms. "Thank you for this. For all of it. For choosing me."

"You chose me first," he reminded me. "That day at the rugby match. You decided we were going to be friends."

"Best decision I ever made."

Jules's voice carried across the yard. "Dad, she has a PhD and her own rescue shelter for animals. She's perfect for you."

"Maybe we should save Bridger," I suggested.

"Nah," Gryff said. "Jules is unstoppable when she's matchmaking. Remember when she tried to set up Isak with that sports journalist?"

"They're dating now."

"Exactly. Resistance is futile."

Someone had brought out a speaker and music filled the yard. Our mismatched, chaotic, perfect family danced and laughed as the stars came out. The baby goats had discovered the buffet table.

"Hey, Artie?" Gryff said.

"Yeah?"

"Wanna make actual human babies at some point?"

I looked at him, this man who'd given me everything. "Yeah?"

"I mean, the goats need more friends."

"That's your reasoning? The goats need friends?"

"Also I love you and want to have a family with you and think you'd be an amazing mom."

"After the next Olympics?"

"After the next Olympics," he agreed. "Though at the rate the Kingmans are reproducing, our kids will have, like, thirty cousins."

"Good. They'll need allies to handle the goats."

Stevie Kicks chose that moment to escape the pen, making a beeline for the dessert table with her siblings in hot pursuit.

"Goat breach," someone yelled.

"Code Dragon Donkey," someone else shouted.

The entire party descended into chaos as everyone tried to catch the baby goats. The goats ate half the cake before anyone could stop them. Jules's professor ended up holding Stevie while Bridger explained the family's expansion.

It was perfect.

I was an Olympic gold medalist. I was married to my best friend. We had five goats and a house full of love and a family that was absolutely insane.

Eight years ago, I'd moved to a new country, no friends, and only a broken family to my name.

Now I had everything.

"No regrets?" Gryff asked later, after everyone had gone home and we were sitting on the beach, gold medal still around my neck, watching the waves.

"Only one," I said.

He looked worried. "What?"

"We should have gotten more goats."

We were both laughing now, there on our beach, in our city, living our ridiculous, perfect life.

In the distance, I could hear the baby goats calling for their parents. Tomorrow, we'd have to figure out how to goat-proof the house even more. We'd have to build a bigger pen. We'd have to explain to the neighbors about the noise.

But tonight?

Tonight was for gold medals and goat babies and the family we'd chosen and built and loved.

Tonight was for happily ever after.

***

Vincent Van Goat

"Gather round, kids," I said to my three offspring, who were currently trying to eat their mother's tail. "It's time you learned about your destiny."

"Is it about food?" Bleathoven asked hopefully.

"Everything's about food with you," Goatzart said, bouncing impressively high for a kid who'd only been alive for six weeks.

"Both of you, hush," Stevie Kicks commanded, already the boss of her siblings. "Papa is talking."

Holly nuzzled closer to me. "Tell them about Burrito Petito, dear. That's where it all really started."

"Ah yes," I said, settling into my storytelling stance. "The Great Meeting of the Pets. Flynn and Tempest brought their donkey—"

"A DONKEY?" all three kids shrieked in unison.

"Shh, you'll wake the humans," Holly warned. "They just got back from something called 'date night.'"

"Anyway," I continued, "Burrito Petito is a very small donkey with very large opinions. You'll meet him when he gets back from spending the summer with AbuelaNovela in Oaxaca. He told us about the Kingman Pet Patrol."

"The what now?" Goatzart asked, mid-bounce.

"It's a sacred organization," Holly explained. "Started by Luke Skycocker himself."

"Who's Luke Skycocker?" Stevie asked through a mouthful of hay.

"Only the most magnificent rooster in all of Colorado," I said reverently. "He belongs to Chris, the eldest Kingman brother. Luke organized all the Kingman pets into a protection unit."

"There's also Wiener the Pooh, the tactical dachshund," Holly added. "Lady Bananaconda Hisstledown, the reconnaissance snake. Seven of Nine Lives, the stealth cat. And of course, Bear, who lives with the Father of Kingmans."

"Dogs just sleep," Stevie pointed out, probably thinking about the golden retriever snoring in the corner of Mrs. Bender's yard.

"That's what he wants you to think," I said mysteriously. "He's actually monitoring the perimeter through his dreams."

The kids looked skeptical.

"The point is," Holly continued, "Burrito Petito came with an important message. Luke Skycocker has officially designated us as the LA Division of the Kingman Pet Patrol."

"We get to be in a patrol?" Goatzart bounced even higher.

"What's our mission?" Bleathoven demanded.

I puffed out my chest. "We keep the neighborhood safe for when the Kingmans have human kids."

"But Artie and Gryff don't have human kids," Bleathoven tipped his head to the side thinking.

Holly and I exchanged a meaningful look.

"Not yet," Holly said. "Which brings us to your first mission."

All three kids leaned in.

"Operation Baby Fever," I announced dramatically.

"What's that?" they asked.

"We need to be so adorable, so perfectly charming, that Artie and Gryff decide they want human babies too," Holly explained.

"How do we do that?" Stevie asked.

"Step one: Look cute when they have friends over," I said.

"Step two: Be extra snuggly when they seem sad,"

Holly added.

"Step three: Occasionally escape just enough to make them practice their parenting skills," I continued.

"But not too much," Holly warned. "We don't want to seem like troublemakers."

"We ARE troublemakers," Stevie pointed out.

"Tactical troublemakers," I corrected. "There's a difference."

"What about the other pets in the patrol?" Goatzart asked. "Do they have missions too?"

"Oh yes," Holly said. "Luke Skycocker crows every morning at exactly the right time to optimize Chris and Trixie's sleep schedule for fertility."

"What's fertility?" Stevie asked.

"Making babies," I explained quickly. "Wiener the Pooh guards Declan and Kelsey's music studio so they have quiet time together. Lady Bananaconda already had one success with Everett and Penelope's baby Bo."

"And Seven of Nine Lives?"

"Cats work in mysterious ways," I said sagely. "We don't question their methods."

Just then, we heard footsteps. Artie and Gryff were returning from their date, laughing about something.

"Positions," Holly hissed.

The kids immediately arranged themselves into maximum cuteness formation—Stevie in the middle, Goatzart mid-tiny-bounce, and Bleathoven with his head tilted just so.

"Oh my god," we heard Artie say. "Look at them. They're posing."

"They definitely learned that from their parents," Gryff laughed.

"We should take a picture," Artie said. "They're so perfect."

"You know what else would look perfect in photos?" Gryff said, and even us goats could hear the suggestion in his voice.

"Gryff..."

"I'm just saying, imagine how cute our kids would be with the goats."

"After the next Olympics."

"After the next Olympics," he agreed. "But we could practice the making part."

"Gryffen," she sounded like he was in trouble, but I knew better.

They headed inside, still laughing.

"Mission proceeding perfectly," I announced to the kids.

"Do you really think it'll work?" Stevie asked.

"The Kingman Pet Patrol has a 100% success rate," Holly said proudly. "Every pet has helped their humans find love and happiness."

"Plus," I added, "I heard Tempest telling Flynn she might be pregnant. If they have a baby first, Artie's competitive streak will kick in."

"Humans are weird." Bleathoven shook his head.

"But they're OUR weird humans," Goatzart said, bouncing affectionately.

"Exactly," Holly and I said together.

As the kids settled down for the night, I looked out at our domain. A nice house with a great backyard filled with yummy things to munch. Humans who loved us despite our tendency to eat everything in sight. Fellow pets who accepted us into their sacred patrol.

"Hey, Holly?" I whispered.

"Yeah?"

"We did good."

"We did perfect," she corrected, nuzzling against me. "Though next time, maybe we stick to just two kids."

"Agreed," I said, watching Bleathoven try to eat his own foot. "Definitely agreed."

IN THE DISTANCE, we could hear the ocean waves and the faint sound of Gryff and Artie laughing about something. Buster snored. A neighbor's cat (not part of the patrol, sadly) prowled by.

All was well in the LA Division of the Kingman Pet Patrol.

Mission: Ongoing.

Status: Adorable.

Future: Bright.

"Dad?" Stevie said, all cute and sleepy.

"Yeah?"

"When we get human siblings, can we eat their homework?"

"Absolutely not," Holly said.

"Maybe just a little," I whispered.

"Vincent!"

And that's how the night watch of the Kingman Pet Patrol continued, one bleat at a time, protecting our humans and encouraging their reproductive choices through strategic cuteness.

Luke Skycocker would be proud.

Need just a little more Gryffen and Artemis?

I've got a bonus chapter for you when you join my Swoon Zone email newsletter!

BookHip.com/TZPTGVX

A NOTE FROM THE AUTHOR

I need to tell you something about being a fat athlete.

I played sports my whole life—competitive softball from T-ball through high school (in Texas, which is basically the Olympics of youth softball), volleyball, soccer, basketball. I loved it. I still do. But here's the thing society doesn't want to talk about: they want fat people to exercise—mostly because they want us to lose weight—but they don't want to *see* us exercise.

My senior year of high school, I joined the swim team on a lark. If you're a big girl, you know how hard it is to put on a swimsuit in front of others. Now imagine being fat AND a teenager. But I did it anyway because I loved sports more than I feared the looks and the comments. And there were looks. There were comments. There always are.

I heard them. I saw them. But I kept swimming.

Fast forward to 2024, and along came Ilona Maher and the U.S. women's Olympic bronze medal rugby team. I saw a video of Ilona responding to some asshat hiding behind a keyboard who commented on her weight—saying she must weigh 200 pounds like it was some kind of insult, some kind of gotcha.

Her response? "Yeah. I do. Because that's how big powerful bodies work."

The clapback was heard around the world.

But here's what really got me: Do you want to know what I weighed in high school as a fat athlete?

207 pounds.

Nobody—and I mean *nobody*—had ever told me it was okay to be 200 pounds and be an athlete. For some reason, 200 pounds is the threshold where society decides your weight is "bad." It's the number that makes people clutch their pearls and concern-troll about your health.

I didn't know it was okay. It didn't even occur to me that it was not only okay, but NORMAL.

And here's the really wild part: I'm out here writing books trying to tell other women they can take up space, that they deserve happy endings without having to shrink themselves first. I'm a body positivity advocate. And even *I* needed someone else to show me that message for another cog in my brain to click into place.

So thank you, Ilona, for being that person for me.

That's why I wanted to write a rugby-playing heroine for this book. That's why Artie needed to exist. Because we so rarely see larger bodies in women's sports, and when we do, they're often portrayed as the "before" picture, the tragedy, the cautionary tale. Not as the powerful, athletic, sexy, desired, HAPPY protagonist of their own love story.

This is also why representation of all bodies—and all identities—matters so much.

On Queer Representation

I know some of you were hoping for a male/male romance for Gryff. I see you, and maybe someday I'll write Xander's story for those who wanted that m/m representation. But I wanted to represent more queer people than just gay men. Bisexual people exist. Bisexual people in "straight-passing" relationships are still bisexual. Our identities don't disappear based on who we're currently dating.

This isn't the first story I've written where athletes have to hide who they are because of other people's prejudice, and I hate that queer athletes STILL feel like they can't be open about who they are—especially in professional sports. The world we live in right now, in 2025, is actively trying to erase queer identities through political and religious persecution.

I want my queer friends, family, and readers to know: I see you. I will continue to represent you in my stories. You will not be erased.

There are lots of queer people in my books because there are lots of queer people in my life. I write to give people a chance to see themselves represented—fat people, queer people, all kinds of people living happy lives and getting their happy endings.

In this book, I had a special opportunity. One of my

very best friends in the world asked specifically to be a side character in this story. So Sean exists because my friend exists, and I wanted to give him the life I love for him—one full of joy, community, love, and found family. Because we all need to see ourselves represented living happy lives, fat, queer, or otherwise.

I'm not going to lie—this book was hard to write. If you happen to be one of my lovely Patreon subscribers, you got to see me rewrite—and rewrite, and rewrite.

Part of it is that the world is in such conflict right now, and I write light, fluffy books. I do this partially because I want all the warriors out there fighting for their rights, for other people's rights, for a better world—I want them to have some respite. We need escapism from the harsh reality so we can rest, even if it's just for a few hours while reading a book. Because without rest, we can't get up to fight again and again.

But sometimes it's hard to get my own head into the happy, fun space of rom-com when there's so much gloom and doom everywhere I look.

I also started out trying to fulfill a lot of readers' expectations for this story. I want so much to make everyone happy. But I had to remember along the way—a couple too many times—that the more genuine and authentic I am to myself when telling these stories, the better they are. And also: you can't make everyone happy. You're not Nutella.

So I wrote the story that felt true to me. The one about a sunshine caretaker who needs to learn he deserves to be cared for, and a fierce woman who needs to learn she's not "too much"—she's exactly right. About chosen family and bi visibility and body positivity and trust and vulnerability and taking up space.

And baby goats.

Because here's the thing: sometimes the best antidote to heavy themes is baby goats causing chaos. Joy and silliness are also resistance. They're also necessary. Love stories should have room for both depth and absurdity, for both the meaningful and the ridiculous.

Vincent and Holly brought me so much joy to write. In a world that often feels too heavy, too dark, too much—there's something revolutionary about choosing to write about rescue goats learning to surf and delivering engagement rings and just... being delightfully, chaotically themselves.

We all deserve that kind of joy. That kind of silliness. That kind of permission to just exist and be loved exactly as we are.

A portion of the proceeds from this book will be donated to The Trevor Project (supporting LGBTQ+ youth) and Luvin Arms Animal Sanctuary (rescuing and caring for farm animals). Because if I'm going to write about queer joy and rescue goats, I want to support the real-world organizations doing the work.

Thank you for reading Gryff and Artie's story. Thank you for being here. Thank you for seeing yourself—or learning to see others—in these pages.

You deserve to take up space. You deserve your happy ending. You deserve to be chosen first.

And you definitely deserve baby goats.

With love and hugs,
Amy

THE COCKY KINGMANS

*The C*ck Down The Block*

The Wiener Across the Way

*The P*ssy Next Door*

The Anaconda Downstairs

*The Jack*ss in Class*

The Goat in the Bedroom

ACKNOWLEDGMENTS

Writing a book is never a solo endeavor, and this one especially required a village (and a herd of metaphorical goats).

To my mastermind groups—Lucy Lennox, Kaci Rose, Hope Ford, Holly Roberds, M. Guida, and Nikki Hall—thank you for helping keep me on track and for your continued support. You all make this wild author life feel less lonely and infinitely more fun.

To Heather, my editor: Even though you're new to the editing game, your instincts for story are spot on. I thoroughly enjoy our fights over plot points, and I truly appreciate your love and knowledge of the Kingmans. Working with you makes these books better, and I'm so grateful to have you in my corner.

To Chrisandra, my proofreader: You've read everything I've ever written and still don't get mad at me when I just toss commas at the page like donut sprinkles. Any remaining errors in this book are definitely my fault. Thank you for your patience with my grammatical chaos.

To Ellie at Love Notes PR: Thank you for quite literally helping me make my dreams come true.

To Leni Kauffman: Thank you for giving us another stunning cover. Thank you for helping me change the world one book cover at a time.

Many eternal thanks to Becca Syme—coach, friend, and trope genius. Thank you not just for understanding my brain, but for your deep understanding of tropes and how they affect a story with a plus-size heroine. Your friendship makes me so joyful.

To Kate Tilton, my chaos coordinator and business manager: Not only am I thankful for you, but all my readers should be too. Without your Amy-wrangling skills, these stories would not exist because I would be buried under a pile of dysfunctional, unprioritized to-do lists. You are the reason anything gets done around here.

All the appreciation for my bestie Sean, who makes our friendship a priority and whose empathy and harmony I rely on. Ren is everything I hope for you because you deserve your very own (secret K-pop) star. Thank you for letting me write you into this world where you get the happy ending you deserve.

I appreciate KatiePie's love and understanding when I can't come out and play. Thank you for always being there just like I'll forever be there for you.

And for my dad, who must never, ever read my books (lol)—but who gave me my competitive nature, the great advice to never, never quit, and who came to countless softball games and swim meets over the years. Thank you for showing up. It mattered more than you know.

To my readers: I can never thank you enough. I wrote these stories for you just as much as for me. I want you to feel seen, feel represented, and see that your own happy endings are possible. If you ever see me at a bookish event, please come say hi and give me a hug. We can laugh and cry together just like we do when we read our favorite stories. You make this all worthwhile.

Extra special thanks to my Patreon book dragons who believe in me and these stories so deeply: Alida H., Allie H., Amber H., Amber L., Amie N., Amy H., Angela K., Angela M., Angelique A., Anissa R., Anna R., Anne-Marie P., Annmarie B., April R., Ashley P., Barb T., Belinda M., Billie F., Brianna S., Caitlin C., Cara-Lee D., Cassandra B., Catherine G., Chanel S., Charles F., Christin S., Christy B., Corinne A., Crystal R., Danielle D., Danielle T., Daphine G., Dawn J., Diana B., Dominique R., Ember D., Emma M., Essence C., Hana K., Heather S., Heidi G., Helena B., Ilona T., Jasmine P., Jennifer H., Jenny W., Jessica D., Jessica H., Jessica T., Jo B., Johannie C., Johnna A., Judy R., Kara G., Kara S., Kari S., Karla K., Katherine M., Katherine T., Kathryn P., Kelley M., Kelli W., Kerrie M., Kiarra C., Krista C., Kylie M., Laura G., Laura P., Lauren K., Lisa C., Lisa W., Lisbeth T., Mackenzie B., Mari G., Maria B., Marina H., Mashell P., McKaylee E., Meghan M., Melissa L., Melissa M., Meredith B., Michelle A., Misty B., Nicole C., Orma M., Rachael C., Rachel L., RaeAnna F., Rebecca C., Robin R., Sam B., Samantha M., Samantha S., Sara W., Sarah M., Selena R., Shannon P., Sophie H., Stacey M., Stephanie H., Stephanie J., Tara V., Taz R., Tiffany L., Tiffany L., Tiffany S., Treasure L., Valeria., Vanessa G., Vanessa R., William O.

And finally, to my mom: Who encouraged me to play any sport I wanted, coached my softball teams, and drove me to a kajillion practices. Your love of sports is 100% why I write sports romance today. I wish you could be here to read the cinnamon roll football players I write for you. I hope you'd love them as much as I do. I miss you every day.

This book exists because of all of you. Thank you for being part of this journey.

ABOUT THE AUTHOR

Amy Award is a curvy girl who has a thing for football players, fuzzy-butt pets, and spicy romance novels. She believes that all bodies are beautiful and deserve their own love stories with Happy Ever Afters. Find her at AuthorAmyAward.com

Amy also writes curvy girl paranormal romances with dragons, wolves, demons, and vampires, as Aidy Award. If that's your jam, check those books out at AidyAward.com

www.ingramcontent.com/pod-product-compliance
Lightning Source LLC
Chambersburg PA
CBHW031641200726
48289CB00004BA/1126